Addled

Addled

a novel

JoeAnn
Hart

LITTLE, BROWN AND COMPANY

New York Boston London

Little, Brown and Company
Hachette Book Group USA
237 Park Avenue, New York, NY 10169
Visit our Web site at www.HachetteBookGroupUSA.com

First Edition: May 2007

The characters and events in this book are fictitious.
Any similarity to real persons, living or dead, is
coincidental and not intended by the author.

Library of Congress Cataloging-in-Publication Data

Hart, JoeAnn.
Addled : a novel / JoeAnn Hart.—1st ed.
p. cm.
ISBN 978-0-316-01500-4
1. Country clubs—Fiction. 2. New England—
Fiction. 3. Upper class—Fiction. I. Title.
PS3608. A78573A33 2007
813'.6—dc22 2006021292

10 9 8 7 6 5 4 3 2 1

Q-FF

Book design by JoAnne Metsch

Printed in the United States of America

For Gordon

And the wind shall say: "Here were decent godless people:

Their only monument the asphalt road

And a thousand lost golf balls."

—T.S. ELIOT, *The Rock*

Addled

The Stance

Pearls clicked on knotted strands as a tidy cluster of women gathered outside the library, nodding to the one with the ebony cane. Then they dispersed, off on their assigned tasks. After a brief interval, two of them returned, cooing to an inebriated young man in a dinner jacket hanging between them; then they continued on to a third-floor guest room to put him to bed. Another, with the practiced mannerisms of a museum guide, led a leather-skirted lady up the back way. The sound of stilettos echoed down the marbled halls, then stopped abruptly as the professional closed the door firmly behind her. The other women smoothed the wrinkles from their silk outfits and stood back, waiting.

The one with the cane removed a stethoscope from her clutch and placed the business end of the instrument on an exposed water pipe in the hall, listening for signs of life in Room #13. She smiled grimly and gave the nod. The women swept smoothly into action, the rapid clacking of their heels fading away down the stairs, then rising again. This time, they had a fresh young thing in their midst, excited about the game the women seemed to be playing. Where were they going? She laughed in anticipation, until one of the women put her finger to her lips.

Chapter One

The Angle of Approach

IT WAS a perfect lie. Charles Lambert handled his 3-iron as reverently as a divining rod, its finely calibrated balance sending a golden hum to his brain. The fairway lay open at his feet, presenting no obstacles between him and Plateau, the elevated green of Hole #14—200 yards away, still well within his capabilities. Still. Up at the clubhouse, he heard fabric slap and cables clank as Old Glory fought the morning breeze, and he made a mental calculation to correct for the wind. If only he could freeze it all, these precious moments before the club made contact with the ball, when anything was possible.

He could even win. He was playing a decent game in spite of not getting out on the course nearly enough that spring. Freedom at the office had been sorely curtailed, what with one corporate scandal and SEC investigation after another. Here it was, the Fourth of July weekend, and he wasn't even tan yet—not naturally so, at any rate. He'd had to borrow bronzing gel from Madeline's bag of tricks for these ambered arms, making him feel like the vigorous youth he was not so long ago. Indeed, his muscles were still firm, his wrists supple and pronated, his hands—properly

V-clasped firmly around the staff—as strong as ever. In a nod to authenticity, he'd even kept the bronzer off his left hand where a golf glove would have blocked the sun.

He looked down at the dimpled ball, then back up at the broad fairway. To the right, the wall of vegetation that straddled his backyard threw a purple shadow on the course. When he was a boy, he used to play over there, knocking acorns around with a stick—looking over the gate. How proud he was the first time his father brought him along for a game. He was no taller than a golf bag and yet he'd felt like one of the men, a hunter of balls, a conquering hero. But hunters and heroes did not, as a rule, wear bronzing gel, did they? When had vanity replaced his old self-assurance, his self-mastery—his self? Why was it that when his father turned silver at the temples he'd been called distinguished, but when his own chestnut hair lost its depth he was simply growing old? It wasn't fair to change the rules like that. Slings of flesh—*jowls*—had begun to round off his chin, once so pointed and cleft. His entire infrastructure was aging. After the game, he had to go see his dentist about a cracked tooth.

He tried to focus, reaching back to a lifetime of lessons: straight arm, bent knee, head down, eye on the ball. Or *inner* eye on the ball, as Steeve from the Buddha Ball Clinic would say—the double *e*'s in his name like hooded eyes—enigmatically adding that "the hole and the ball have been one throughout eternity." If that were the case, Charles sniffed, then what was the point of going through the motions? And "be the ball" was nothing more than what Chevy Chase said in *Caddyshack,* a movie Steeve claimed never to have seen. What sort of golf pro was that?

But the three days and twelve hundred dollars were not entirely wasted. He did grasp the concept about forging a connection between hand, mind, and club, and the importance of keeping the head still—mentally, not just physically—to make room for abundance in his shot. But stillness eluded him. Steeve told him that it could not be sought, and the best he could do was prepare himself to receive it.

"How do I do that?" Charles had asked.

"You must find your own path," Steeve had said, with what Charles felt was a spiritual smirk. "No one can tell you. Be natural. Let it go to let it in."

"Of what?" Charles had been exasperated. "What do I let go of?"

"Striving. Trying so hard." Steeve had stroked his severely clipped beard and studied Charles. "And if you can't let go, try loosening your grip."

Finally, some decent golf advice.

Charles waggled his club and breathed in deeply as he relaxed his hands, but then a chunk of air lodged at the base of his throat. How had a moment of peace degenerated so quickly into another opportunity for anxiety? He shifted his weight to his left foot and rotated his shoulders. At least he was tall—not shrinking yet!—and that gave him an edge. Even an inch or two made a difference in being able to assess the lay of the land. He could see, off in the distance, that old duffer Howie Amory disappear into the dogleg of #16, and over there, a stately parade of Canada geese was marching up from Oxbow Lake. The birds acted like they owned the place, posing in their formal attitudes, luxuriously plucking at the green turf. If they could hold a club with those feathered limbs, they'd be better than he was by the end of the summer. It used to be his fortunes that were on the rise; now it was his handicap. But a man's game only improved in proportion to the time available to work on it, and since his fiftieth birthday he'd felt he had no time at all.

He readjusted his grip and felt the scorecard in his pocket dig into his groin. He could sense his partners shifting uneasily as they ran out of small talk, waiting for him to take his shot. Gregg, Neddy, and Andrew, all friends and colleagues, had only a two-minute reserve of conversation, even among themselves. That is, unless they were involved in some sport so they wouldn't have to look at one another, but only look at the ball, and discuss the ball, what the ball did, why it did it, and what could be done to either encourage it or keep it from doing it again. It could be a golf ball on Saturday morning, or it could be a baseball tuned in to the radio in an air-conditioned Land Rover. It could be a football on a home-theater screen as they fended off another sleety New England winter on tufted-leather sofas. They could even be entertained by a Day-Glo tennis ball soaring over the heads of their wives in mixed doubles. The ball made them happy, but it had to keep moving. It made them nervous when it stopped for too long, foreshadowing the inevitable day when it—and they—would stop moving altogether.

Charles wrapped himself in a tight cocoon of concentration as he raised his club high, determined not to hesitate at the apex, hesitated anyway, and swung. The contact reverberated through his body as if he were sending a piece of himself into the universe, soaring. Up and up—the small white voyager sailed through the blue sky as through a heavenly sea, and his mind's eye followed along, looking at the course from high above, down at the giant amoebas of putting greens, the luxurious tops of trees, the reflective gaze of water hazards, all fitting together like pieces of a master puzzle. Then the ball—and the vision—began to fall from flight, plunging down, and down again, until the pieces broke apart. Neddy gasped in an asthmatic wheeze, simultaneous with the distant *squa-a-ak*. A grazing Canada goose fell over in a violent gesture, then went still.

The golfers, too shocked to laugh, stared at the inert body in the distance and waited to see if maybe it wouldn't decide to get up and shake off the whole affair. When they realized that such was not going to be the case, they walked over in trepidation, stepping over the divot.

Charles got there first and squatted by the goose spread in supplication on the flawless grass. He was about to touch it, until Andrew, slight and sandy, put his hand over his mouth and shook his head. Holding his 3-iron like a harpoon, Charles prodded the feathered body until it rolled over, causing the head to settle at an unnatural angle. Blood appeared at its nostrils.

"How disgusting," said Andrew, scrunching up his face, an act that made his Adam's apple protrude even more.

"Well done, Charles," said Neddy, laughing. He lowered his fireplug of a body and tugged at a wing feather. "What a pity hunting season doesn't open for another six months."

Gregg, a massive hulk of a human, bald and bubble-gum pink, got his best club out of his bag: *The USGA's Rules of Golf.* "You can't play the game without knowing the rules," he always said. He began to pace, digging his cleats into the turf with every lumbering step as he turned the pages, searching for an answer. Andrew, abnormally upright by orders of his doctor and chiropractor, who catered to his tight, flinching spine, stepped away from the body and pulled a cell phone out of his pants pocket. Phones were forbidden on the course, but then again, as he often pointed out, so was foul language. And besides, he kept the phone on vibrate and only made outgoing calls when he had to. He dialed the grounds crew to clear away the mess.

Charles collapsed to a one-legged kneel, using his club as a staff to balance himself. He pressed his lips together and tasted blood where his cracked tooth had rubbed at his inner flesh, and he stared at the bird. The feathers of one wing were spread open like a fan, the tip pointing up, beckoning him. The bleakness and terrible reality of existence seeped into his very being, all on this fine blue day, played upon this smooth green grass. He'd been aiming for the other side of the fairway altogether. How was one to go on with the game?

"Is there a penalty?" asked Gregg, stabbing a finger in his book. "What do I look under?"

"Augury," croaked Charles.

"There's nothing here about that." Gregg paced in wider and wider circles with every rotation, not looking up from the *Rules*. "Is a goose a natural obstruction or an outside agent?"

"Augury?" Neddy snorted, then stood with a groan, straightening the crease of his butter-yellow pants. "Charles, we should never have let you go to that wacky clinic this winter. Soon you'll be playing golf and buying bonds by examining the entrails of birds."

"Entrails!" Andrew turned his back to the men and shouted into the phone, his hand over one ear. "You'd better hurry."

Charles stood up with great effort, trembling at the joints. "I can't say we wouldn't all do any better if we did." He wiped his forehead with his arm, smudging his skin-deep glow, and looked up in time to see a lone crow sweep over them to inspect the carnage.

Chapter Two

The Lay of the Land

GERARD WILTON traced the grain of his polished mahogany desk with the tip of his finger as he gazed out his picture window at the golf course, as plush and curvaceous as a green velvet pillow. Since 1882, Eden Rock managers had overseen the smooth running of the Club from this very desk, and he was proud to be part of that noble line, heir to this exceptional view. It was a land of no extremes, just how he—and he felt he could speak for the members in this regard—preferred life in general: the present constant and content, with the future leisurely coasting ahead from one tee to the next.

The in-house phone trilled and the kitchen indicator light flashed red. That would be his chef, Vita, short-tempered, self-assured, and so indecently sensual that if the kitchen weren't already in the basement, he would have to put it there, such were the sounds she made when she tasted her own cooking. But she would not be in the throes of ecstasy now. He'd left a memo on her desk last night about iceberg lettuce. Food at the Club was as recreational as the golf, so it had to be both interesting and fashionable. It was unfortunate for Vita that her boyfriend / produce supplier had just dumped her for another chef, but the members could not go to their outside worlds with head lettuce on their breath because of it. No, indeed.

He picked up the receiver with resolve, then quickly held it away from his ear. Vita was threatening some perverse violence with canned fruit cocktail. But he knew she was just letting off steam. She would never keep such an abomination in her kitchen, and she was, underneath it all, self-controlled in the way that people who work with knives generally are.

When the screaming died down, Gerard spoke to her with excessive, professional calm. "Vita, listen to reason. You don't have to buy mesclun from your old boyfriend"—and he correctly put the emphasis on the *-clun*—"but you do have to find someone else, soon. The membership can't eat fast-food filler just because the chef is no longer bedding the greengrocer."

"I don't know what you're talking about," she said, with a cracked voice and a sniffle.

"You know exactly what I'm saying," Gerard said. "Don't rattle the members."

One of the reasons Gerard had hired Vita when he arrived on the scene three years ago—aside from the fact that the previous cook had specialized in warm gray meat—was that despite her Colombian heritage, Vita had a great unpretentious American style. She favored neither the chilies and spices of her people nor the experimental puddles of yellow and purple sauces of her peers. She made halibut poached with fennel, roast lamb with rosemary polenta, and skewers of shrimp and mango. Food that was different but not unfamiliar. The members, conservative in all things, were suspicious of strange ingredients, but once they were conditioned to something, like mesclun, they could not be turned back easily. They could, in fact, be quite rigid.

"There's nothing low-life about head lettuce, Gerard." As Vita spoke into the kitchen phone, she absently fondled a bowl of fuzzy kiwis on the stainless-steel counter in front of her. "Those old Wasps prefer it. With a little Thousand Island dressing, it brings them right back to Mother's dear old cook. As for the others, it's retro. A crescent of iceberg juxtaposed with a few truffle shavings puts both truffles and iceberg in a whole new context."

"The members don't think food, Vita—they eat food. Don't cook over their heads."

"*And* as far as the greengrocer goes, my private life is my business. It's a wonder I can still have one with the hours I put into this gastro hell. I just happen to think that Utah Riley is unreliable, that's all." Her voice cracked again as she crushed two kiwis in her fist until juice ran green on the counter. "Everything he has is wilted and he can't deliver."

"I have a few suggestions of whom to call," Gerard said, rifling through some papers on his desk. "I think, for efficiency's sake, instead of using a dozen specialty suppliers, it's time to go to one of the big restaurant companies where we can get everything from toilet paper to tomatoes in one neat order."

"Gerard!" Vita flung the mangled kiwis into the trash. "How can you say such a thing? Good food is more about shopping than cooking. Not everyone knows where to find the perfect radish or the plumpest chicken—*some* people wouldn't know a ripe avocado if they stepped in it. The only food you're an expert on is the pickle you keep up . . ."

"Listen, Vita, we'll talk about this later. But in the meantime, if a farmer comes to the back door and wants to show you his zucchini, just say no. No, *thank you.* Do something other than iceberg for tonight, and you'd better hurry before Mr. Quilpe gets wind of this. He'll have us paying for air shipments of baby weeds from the South of France."

"The Food Committee is full of beans," she muttered, using her apron to wipe the pulp off her hands.

Gerard made some comforting murmur of "there, there" and got off the phone. Romance always came to this. His own love life, such as it was, was played far from the home field. He never brought girlfriends to the Club. It was important that the female members believed he was available, even though he had never acted on a single come-on. Seductive behavior made everyone happy. Always feeling wanted, never being had.

He returned to contemplating the landscape, which never failed to provide him with a pleasant perspective, much as it surely had for Jonathan M. Curtis, of Curtis Mills, who in 1881 had acquired a taste for pastoral scenes on a tour of the English countryside. In what was then a rural area west of Boston, he had a manor house built of stucco and timber, with seven thatched cottages out back for staff, and a dozen imported Devonshire sheep to keep the lawns trim. Curtis died soon thereafter in a hunting accident, when his own gamekeeper, also imported, mistook him for a poacher. His wife sold the estate to the original Club corporation with the black bunting still on the door.

Ever since then, members had been enjoying Curtis's expansive view from the pillared porch or flagged terrace, but Gerard preferred his own. It was more select. The world was easier to swallow when contemplated through a single window. It cut out the periphery; it cut out the oversized homes that had sprung up in the woods on either side of the course, with their fanlights and columned entries all painfully out of scale, revealing the imperfections that come with enlargements. The only structure marring his line of vision was the pool house down the hill, fetchingly converted from the old slate-roofed stable, thatch being considered unsafe for horses. According to *The History of the Eden Rock Country Club* (privately printed on the occasion of the Club's centennial, available in the gift shop for $29.95), the pool was part of the overhaul of 1924, the year the original six-hole golf course was redesigned by the legendary Alister MacKenzie to its current glory. The change had involved a major reordering of the natural elements, but to Gerard, the course looked like Earth on the Day of Creation, give or take a few hole markers. Two miles off in the wooded distance, a white church steeple rose up from the trees as if God had put His very signature on the landscape.

Of course, there was another view. There was always another view. Gerard reflected sourly on the mess behind the clubhouse, with its kitchen Dumpster, employee parking lot, and mismatched tangle of aluminum utility sheds. A macadam drive led unceremoniously to the service entrance on the frontage road, and there, on the other side of the ivy-covered walls, lay the cheap housing and storage facilities where the city's workers and materials were incubated. He was loathe to admit it, but he lived out there—if it could be said that he lived anywhere outside his office—in a complex that was more penal colony than apartment. Every day, on waking up in that grim outpost, he felt a wild rush of yearning for the Club.

Just as he was beginning to relax in his swivel chair, his head groundskeeper appeared at his door, filling it. Gerard automatically glanced at Barry's shoes to see if they were clean before motioning him to come in. But Barry, wearing a pained expression on his freckled face, shook his head. "Best come outside, boss."

Now what? Gerard thought. He turned to take a quick look in the Chippendale mirror behind him, straightening the collar of the black ERCC polo shirt under his plum linen jacket. Not bad. At twenty-nine he was considered young for his position, but he felt his studied manner and professional calm gave him the authority needed to do the job. He reached in his top drawer for a comb, which he swept through his dark hair, simultaneously examining his bleached teeth and admiring the balanced architecture of his features. His skin was so finely shaven as to make facial hair seem a crude throwback of the species.

Barry was not so natty. He was well scrubbed and firmly packed but, like the rest of the staff, wore a beige T-shirt and khaki pants. Gerard deplored that franchised look, but it was a comfort to the members not to have to wonder whom to order about.

The two men slipped out the side door to the employee parking lot, the only area staff was allowed to smoke. The crow parking lot, the members' children called it, because a pack of crows, big as chickens, sat crouched along the Dumpster's rim all day, waiting for workers to bring them their meals. The lid was always left open, in spite of the House & Grounds Committee's tirades on keeping it closed, but who among the kitchen staff was tall enough or strong enough to close that panel of welded metal up and down? It was as though the birds had designed the thing themselves.

"Won't believe this," said Barry, lighting both their cigarettes with an ERCC lighter that was no bigger than his pinky. "Charles Lambert killed a goose."

"Killed? On purpose?" Gerard tried to think if he'd ever seen Lambert in a rage. Members' tyrannical frenzies were as common as lost balls, but outright violence? Not since Freddy McWhorter attacked Deacon Swanson with a putter last summer had there been a physical attack at the Club, but that was only after Mrs. McWhorter declared her intention to become the third Mrs. Swanson. And such incidents were quickly excused.

"Freak accident at Plateau." Barry squinted his pale blue eyes against the smoke as he placed his finger on his temple. "Smack in the head with a Pro V1. Andrew Sortwell called to say entrails were all over the grass, but Pole said it was a fairly bloodless shot."

"Was there a penalty?" Gerard looked out at the goose-studded course. Some birds had their necks straight up in a gargle, others had them bowed to the ground, but all of them, who numbered in the hundreds some days, were hell-bent on ripping out his expensive sod and fouling the water hazards.

"Going to the Rules Committee." Barry adjusted the tip of his ERCC duck-billed cap. "Mr. Lambert played the ball near the carcass, but there were bad feelings. Guess he felt he should have been given a chance to start over."

"We should pay him a bounty."

The two men looked up at the sound of honking, and three more geese landed in a *plumpf* and trotted with their wings spread in exaggerated breadth to slow them down. On the ground they were somewhat elegant in their Prince Albert coats, but they were buffoons in getting borne aloft, honked in continual panic while flying, and could barely land without falling on their necks.

"Where should we bury it, boss?" Barry studied the ash on the end of his cigarette.

Gerard exhaled smoke. "Just toss it in there." He pointed to the Dumpster, just in time to watch a rat emerge from the top of the pile, sleek and sated. The Club's vermin ignored the exterminator's weekly bait, as they could well afford to. "What about getting some of that new UV turf treatment? It's supposed to make geese sick as dogs."

Gerard had by necessity become an expert on ornithological control. He had tried addling, oiling, laser beams, and electronic black boxes, but the geese still went about their business unperturbed. The summer before, he thought he had the problem licked with three Border collies trained to patrol the course and scare off the geese, but that ended in disaster. If the working dogs were allowed to run free, the members claimed, so could theirs. The experiment lasted one week, although the Club had to pay for the whole season, as contracted, plus all the vet bills.

Barry whistled through his teeth as he crushed his cigarette underfoot, then ran his fingers through his rusty upright hair. "Don't know. Pretty expensive stuff. Balloon eyes worked okay a couple of years ago until the birds got used to them. We can try them on this generation."

Gerard looked around and shrugged. "Okay." He sighed. "And while you've got the catalog out, let's see if there's anything short of bazookas we haven't tried yet. For now, send Pole out in a cart and have him scare the geese off the fairways. At cocktail hour, I want the members to see we've taken decisive action." He tossed his butt into the Dumpster and gave Barry a thumbs-up.

Barry stood where he was, pretending to watch two crows descend on the garbage, but when Gerard was out of sight, he hurried to his office in one of the utility buildings. He didn't like all that talk about making geese sick. It made his stomach turn. Fact of the matter was, ever since Gerard sent him to addle eggs out on the island in May, he was a changed man. He'd only found one active nest so late in the season, but he'd done his job, luring the mating pair away with cornmeal in order to shake their eggs to sterility. But the first egg he shook broke in his hand, and instead of a runny yolk, a wet chartreuse gosling fell to the bottom of the nest.

"Knock me down with a feather," he'd said. "How cute is that?" He'd touched the little bird, awed by the newness of life.

He'd heard its parents coming through the brush, and although they had no teeth, the business edge of a gander's wing was a powerful weapon. He ran his hand over the gosling and blew hot breath on him to keep him warm until they arrived. There was no fear in the little fellow's glassy gaze, only openness. Even adoration. Barry had never felt anything but ill will toward the creatures that ate and dug their way through his greens—the deer, rabbits, voles, and who knows what else, but the worst were the geese. So many of them, so aloof and superior. But they must not start out that way, because look, a few seconds old and the little thing seemed to recognize him as an equal—or a god.

The approaching sound of snapping twigs and rustling feathers grew loud and frantic. Frogs plopped into the water for safety. With a lump in his throat, Barry waved good-bye to the gosling, who raised himself up on his teeny webbed feet and shook his prickly stub of a tail. Barry escaped through the underbrush, but so did the gosling, still groggy and damp, with its naked wings in the air, leaping and jumping to catch up. Barry stopped, intending to bring the baby back to its nest, but when he held it in his hands, he just couldn't. Fate had thrown them together, man and beast, and who was he to question such a force?

Barry unlocked his office door and looked over his bulky shoulder before closing it. "Forbes," he whispered.

"Beep!" And the six-week-old foot-high gosling came running to his open arms.

Chapter Three

The Rules of the Game

ARIETTA WINGATE had skin the color of egg whites, with hands as smooth and veined as a good Stilton. Her eyes were a striking Nordic blue, fringed with lashes thick with mascara. She touched her downy hair to check for loose strands but found it perfect, as always. With the help of her cane, she inched her chair next to the library's fireplace, whose *verde antico* marble mantel was carved with Roman divinities. The fire she'd requested seemed token in its cavernous maw, which was large enough to roast a heretic. Yet the small flame was necessary because even in July the paneled room was raw, receiving only the weakest sun through the casement windows framed in heavy velvet. The fire also served, as Arietta well knew, as a heavy-handed symbol of the hearth.

She sat with care, adjusting herself on the relic beneath her, then arranged her burgundy linen skirt around her legs. The furniture was positively punitive, but she would not have it changed. Gerard Wilton, that wheedler, once broached the subject with her, explaining that if he put cushions on the rush seats, the committees might actually want to meet in there, the room for which such events were intended, instead of in the lounge. Only the Board of Governors met in the library, and then only on rare occasions for the privacy of formal vote taking. That the others held their meetings elsewhere was fine with Arietta. She'd just as soon have the place to herself and her teas, and even now, waiting for Madeline Lambert, she enjoyed the library as her own. The stained-glass lamp over the table glowed, darkening the recessed shadows of the wooden ceiling, as coffered as a honeycomb. The ambient light washed over the smoke-stained portraits of past Club presidents along the walls, casting them deep in thought.

The door creaked. "Hello, Arietta." Madeline waved away a dark puff that rose from the hearth when she opened the door. Then she locked it behind her, slapping the heavy deadbolt in place with the edge of her hand. Madeline, dressed in straight gray slacks and tan blouse with a pink cameo at the collar, was a handsome woman, thought Arietta, with her good posture and elegant profile. A smile would make her beautiful, but composure was much the better. It was odd, now, to think of what a shock it had been, back in the late seventies, when Charles brought her home to the Club, an unnaturally blond and outgoing California girl whose own mother had never even married. Good Lord. Who knew how the daughter would behave? But Charles had chosen wisely, because after only a few blunders—casual touching, singing to herself, a preference for revealing clothes—Madeline had fit right in. Even her blond hair had mellowed into light brown with professional highlights.

Madeline kissed Arietta on her suede cheek. "You're looking well today."

"Traffic?" Arietta asked in a corrective tone, pretending as always that she'd been kept waiting.

But Madeline was punctual to a fault. Even as they spoke, they heard four bells from the church in town, and they both glanced instinctively at the imposing grandfather clock, which could neither confirm nor deny. It had come with the house, complete with steeples and brass fittings, inlaid with bits of ivory and Roman numerals. It had everything but time. The clock had stopped at six thirty during World War II, when there was no one on the home front to fix it. Afterward, in the postwar years of high suburban living, the Furnishings Committee, an elite subcommittee of House & Grounds, decided it was more charming to let the clock be so they would not be pestered at parties by its insistent chimes, reminding them of the ephemeral nature of their fun.

"You know I'm exactly on time." Madeline sat down in a peaked chair, which was so Gothic it might have been stolen from a parsonage.

"Let's move on now, dear. We don't want to be caught short before Ellen Bruner arrives." She peered closely at Madeline's shirt pocket. "What is that?"

"Oh." Madeline pulled out a prickly sprig of tight white rosebuds, the heads already limp. "I forgot all about them. I pinched them from the garden this morning."

"Toss them in the fire before they look any worse." Arietta unscrewed the brass pistol handle of her cane and pulled out an exquisitely ornate key.

Madeline looked at her sprig. It was too late to revive the blooms, wasn't it? She placed it on the little flame, where it hissed rather than burned.

Arietta held the key out to Madeline by its red silk ribbon like a hypnotist, then pulled it back. "Did you lock the door?" she asked.

"You watched me do it." Madeline was slightly exasperated that after all these years Arietta still questioned her capability. She took the key from her and walked to the distant corner of the library, near where the papier-mâché globe stood on its intricate iron base, another original artifact. Arietta followed, tapping the Oriental carpet with her cane, severing the indigo fibers from their warp. She pulled a chair right behind Madeline, who knelt before a cabinet.

"Well?" Arietta leaned forward, both hands on her cane.

Madeline was letting a moment of nausea pass, having lingered awhile at the Club the night before drinking cake-batter martinis. That Beryl Hall. The woman kept close tabs on Boston's cocktail culture and passed her lethal information on to Enrico, the Club's head bartender, whose dark face was as impassive as an executioner's. Beryl then forced these concoctions on innocent winesippers like herself, who knew better than to accept, but she had succumbed out of politeness, as always. Looking back, it was just as well that Charles had made them leave early, or she would have gotten a good deal drunker. He'd been so antsy since that silly goose incident last week, and there'd been no arguing with him. But as she was leaving in her tipsy fog, she'd noticed Ellen Bruner conspicuously drinking sparkling water with lemon and patting her still-flat stomach, making a case for pregnancy. It gave Madeline pause. She wondered if a lawyer might balk at recording the intimate details of her impregnation in the book, the Club's biological genealogy as opposed to the merely legal. Maybe an attorney wouldn't see the law as being secondary to nature. "I'm a little worried about today. I hope Ellen won't give us trouble."

"Nonsense. She's in family practice, isn't she? She'll see the reason for the book more than most."

That reason was not to be found anywhere in *The History of the Eden Rock Country Club.* According to Arietta, there'd been stiff competition when the Club was being formed, with two men, Enoch Winship and Oliver Stallybrass, duking it out for president. Clethera Winship, a proper Victorian matron with an industrial age temperament, extended certain courtesies to one of the incorporators, Granville Barker, who repaid her many kindnesses by voting for her husband. The upshot was that her family enjoyed the benefits of such a position in terms of social and business contacts. They were invited into all the right homes, which meant access to potential investors for Enoch's fledgling securities business, which meant more money, which meant more access, and on and on, a felicitous intersection of wealth and friendship.

The only glitch had been the baby girl born the following season, who had the pointed little ears of a fruit bat, just like Barker's. When the girl was ten, Clethera got sick and, in her fever, feared that her daughter, in her absence and in the closed world of the Club, might marry one of Barker's children. Who could warn her that such a marriage could not take place?

Clethera called for her childhood friend and comember, Pauline, and confessed the matter without naming names, at which point Pauline admitted that one of her own was not her husband's, without naming names. So they each wrote the identity of the biological sires in a book and hid it well. From then on, the two of them kept their eyes open, drawing out young wives for questioning, and in time a system developed of inviting the newly pregnant to tea in the library. There, a discussion would ensue about the need to protect the future in which the young women were about to be delivered. They were asked to search their souls, for the sake of their children, and if there was any question about paternity, it needed to be scribbled on the blank space. And when, years hence, that child was shopping for cuff links for the ushers, a steward of the book would check the background of both parties to make sure the coast was clear. Sadly, this spring it had not been clear for Eliot Farnsworth and Nina Rundlett.

Arietta watched as Madeline emptied the cabinet of moldering stacks of *National Geographic*s and then struggled with the false back. The metal releases were rusting. It would fall on Madeline to install new ones.

"Hit it hard, with the palm of your hand," said Arietta. "It always worked for me."

"It's coming."

"I won't always be here to help you with these things, Madeline. You've got to start thinking of your own apprentice. Soon."

"There." Madeline pulled the back out and leaned it against the magazines. She retrieved a small flashlight from her pants pocket and aimed the beam at the minuscule keyhole of the hidden compartment. The key turned easily and the door popped open. She reached for the leathery book with both hands to lift it from its dark space, as if she were delivering a baby. Arietta took it in her lap while Madeline put everything back to rights.

"Did you hear what I said?" Arietta watched Madeline close the cabinet. "I'll be eighty next year."

"I heard." Madeline stood up and brushed loose crumbs of leather from her pants. "You don't look likely to drop off your perch today. I'll pick someone in due time."

"What time is it?" Arietta knew the answer to her question, but she wanted to distract Madeline while she tested the cabinet door.

Madeline looked at her watch. "Ellen should be here soon. I'll call the kitchen for the tray to be sent up."

"Think carefully whom you pick," said Arietta. "There's no going back." Arietta had passed over her own two daughters, either of whom might have served, being docile enough, but neither, to her great disappointment, had ever become mothers themselves. They'd married too late, willfully so it seemed to her, to produce issue. Not that this fact in itself disqualified them as caretakers of the book—it just seemed too much to have them in charge of the Club's reproductive history. It would be as affected as having eunuchs for caddies.

Arietta had also passed over the next logical choice, Linzee Gibbons, a Club baby herself. But Linzee was too quick to speculate how even the most casual acquaintance might be brought into her purposes, so she would have too much leverage with the information to be had in the book. Not that she would use it in outright blackmail, but Linzee was keen on organizing events, charitable and uncharitable alike, and was always soliciting help or money. What, shuddered Arietta, would those requests mean to the women who had revealed indiscretions in her presence? They might feel an unspoken pressure to do what Linzee asked. And that would not do. Arietta would not have mistrust of any kind tarnish the hallowedness of the book's purity. The women had to believe that no one would read the entries until it was absolutely necessary, and then only for the highest of purposes. She had never regretted choosing Madeline, even though she had only married into a Club family. Madeline was easy and went about her duty without a manipulative bone in her body.

"Have you thought of Phoebe?" asked Arietta as she tapped back to her seat by the fire. "It's in her blood, after all."

Madeline almost laughed, except she knew it would make her head hurt. Her daughter. Last year, while Phoebe was home for a few weeks after college graduation, Madeline had to listen to a constant harangue about vegetables, cars, and cleaning fluids. Madeline couldn't make a right choice about anything. Then Phoebe started in on the Club, launching a crusade in the name of organic food and turf. Not that anything she proposed was wrong; it could even be called noble, if unrealistic—it was her stridency that was such a bother. Where had that insistence of hers come from? It had seemed sort of cute when she was a teenager, but now, at twenty-three, excuses could no longer be made for youthful exuberance. Madeline realized with a start that when she was Phoebe's age she was already a mother.

She shook the thought out of her head. "For one thing, Arietta, she's determined to stay in Seattle. And two, if she even suspected what went on here, she'd organize a class action suit against us."

Madeline picked up the phone and sharply clicked the kitchen button. While she talked with Vita, reminding her to include herbal tea packets on the tray, Arietta leafed through the book's brittle pages with care. She looked up and mouthed the words "lemon squares" to Madeline, who repeated them to Vita, who assured her they were already on the tray. After Madeline hung up, she turned and leaned against the Puritan oak library table.

"I saw Nina at the pool the other day." Madeline gazed out the diamond panes of the casement window. She'd watched Nina grow up at the Club and was fond of her, even though you could have fit her brain in a teacup. She was fairly pretty too, but her one flaw, an elongated chin, was now exaggerated by her sadness. What a shame her engagement had to end the way it did. "I hope we did the right thing. . . ."

Arietta pulled a handkerchief from her sleeve and dabbed at her face, causing a few flakes of foundation to flutter to her blouse. "Don't be silly. The dust is settling nicely. Eliot's been hustled off to an archaeological dig in Ghana for the summer, where he will surely forget about everything. As for Nina, she goes on a restorative trip to Europe next week with her aunt Tessa. That will put the color back in her cheeks." She inspected the yellowed pages. "Now, what do we know about Ellen's family? What sort of stock do they come from?"

"New people," said Madeline, thinking that Nina needed more than just a bit of color. "They moved here a while ago to set up practice and did Jim Hudson's first divorce. He was so impressed, he put them up for membership. They're from New York."

Arietta's shoulders gave an automatic shudder. "Fine, so we only have to get her to register, for the future. There's no possibility that either of them have ever had relatives in the Club that we'd have to cross-check."

"It doesn't matter," said Madeline. "Even if they were related, it would be too late now."

"Never say never," said Arietta. "Better to have the facts."

There was a knock on the door. Arietta, with some difficulty due to a hip that she refused to have replaced ("I'm going out with all the parts God gave me"), went to answer it and, as she had done for more than half a century, pushed aside the deadbolt and opened the door to the most recently pregnant Club member.

Ellen Bruner stood there and looked at the two women. She was forty-three years old, but she looked younger than Madeline remembered, and less severe. She was dressed like a Catholic schoolgirl: blue cotton cardigan, red plaid skirt, cabled kneesocks, penny loafers, white shirt with Peter Pan collar, and a face that showed a history of battling acne. The tip of her nose glowed pink, and then she smiled. Arietta kissed her on the cheek, and Madeline breathed with relief. Ellen didn't look like she was going to be difficult at all. In fact, she looked as if she welcomed the occasion.

Chapter Four

The Easy Birdie

A COUPLE of hours later, the disheveled tea tray was back in the kitchen, where Vita stood attached to the wall by a long, umbilical phone cord. She wore no-nonsense kitchen whites but still managed to look as lush as a harem girl in a painting. She had fat, but was not fat. Her black hair was pulled back, but the unruly ends were poorly restrained by her toque and hung in her face, whose color was that of crème brûlée. Her mouth, normally red and expansive, was drawn tight. "Don't wait up for me, Momma."

"Evita," her mother pleaded, "I scrub floors so you go to good schools, have future, never to slave in the Anglo's kitchen. Now look! Almost thirty-five and working fourteen-hour shifts like you never got degree!" She choked back a sob.

Vita sullenly picked at a crumb of lemon square on the tray in front of her. She had nothing to say. She used to tell her mother that working at the Club was only practice for a bistro she was going to open someday with Utah. Third generation and she still had an immigrant's dream of owning her own restaurant. But she had dreamed too much too fast and had made the critical mistake of moving back home to save money for a down payment. She had risked it all because she was stupid enough to think he'd loved her. But why wouldn't she, the way he had lavished praise on her body in their own little language of food? Butternut squash for the soft curve of her back. Parsley for the short, curly hairs. Ripe figs for her . . . Now she had no man and no dream, and was living with her mother on the top floor of a Roxbury triple-decker.

"Get job where you wear smart suit, have briefcase, meet nice businessman, not some potato peddler," her mother continued to wail. "What was education for?"

Her mother was still not over the fact that after graduating from Wellesley, Vita had chosen the Culinary Institute instead of an office, which was, in her mother's eyes, the pinnacle of American success. And yet, for all her mother's scorn of the food industry, she was taking the breakup with Utah hard, for there went another possibility of grandchildren. The woman wanted everything.

Vita licked confectioners' sugar off her fingers. "Leave the hall light on for me, okay, Momma?"

Her mother sniffed good-bye, and Vita stood for a moment listening to the dial tone and contemplating her lie. She didn't have to work that night—they'd had a late brunch buffet at the Club instead of Sunday dinner—but she just couldn't bear the thought of sitting in that apartment with her mother armed with a fresh batch of photos from the cousins. All those babies, and none of them hers. How could Vita tell her that it was okay, that this was where she wanted to be, in the kitchen, where she could begin again, day after day, with every new meal? How could a baby ever compare with that? She wanted to stay in her kitchen alone, in peace, and play with some oxheart tomatoes, perfecting her chutney. It was Utah who'd introduced her to oxhearts. He'd taught her so much. She remembered the first time they met, him kneeling on the floor of her kitchen, lifting two eggplants from the crate, one in each hand to show her the difference between the sexes. The heavier ones were female, full of seed. "Go ahead," he'd said. "Touch one."

She wiped a tear from her eye, then wheeled the tea cart over to Pedrosa so he could clear it and go home.

"Pedrosa, tomar este pasteleria a casa, por su esposa."

Pedrosa put the lemon squares aside to be wrapped up. *"Gracias, Vita."*

Then again, maybe she shouldn't send the pastry home to his wife. Every time Jordan, her pastry chef, baked them for Mrs. Wingate's teas, a baby shower always seemed to follow on its heels. Pedrosa could hardly afford to feed another mouth.

She reached behind him and washed her hands thoroughly, removing all traces of the pastry, just in case, and wishing everyone would finish up work and leave her to her tomatoes. Scott, who worked the snack bar, was taking his sweet time with the receipts, lingering while he waited for a ride from Merle, one of the caddies. Luisa, her all-around helper, slumped at the stainless-steel counter, exhausted. No longer a teenager but still not much bigger than a twelve-year-old, Luisa had tended the steam tables all afternoon, a physically demanding job since the heavy pans had to be lugged up the narrow steps to the dining room. There was a dumbwaiter, but there never seemed to be enough time to wait for its ancient gears to turn. Luisa flipped her single long braid behind her back and unwrapped the foil package she'd brought from home. Vita was a little miffed. Luisa had worked for her for two years now and still would not eat her food. *Blando,* was all Luisa had to say about it. She pulled out a poultry leg and chomped.

Vita sniffed the air. "What is that?"

Luisa hesitated. *"El ganso,"* she said, and took another bite.

Vita pulled up a stool and sat very near. "Goose?"

"Those nasty fairway birds?" Scott's voice was so nasal that his words seemed to come out of his nose rather than his mouth. He scratched his stomach, tipping the balance of wrinkled khakis on his hips, revealing the elastic band of his boxers. He might have stepped out of an Abercrombie & Fitch ad, except that his long elfin locks were tucked up in a blue sanitary cap.

"Scott," said Vita. "Pull those up. You're obscene."

He absently yanked at his pants but could not take his eyes off Luisa's drumstick. "Dude, how can you eat that?"

Vita was wondering the same thing. After Charles Lambert had accidentally killed a goose, Pole had ridden out to the fairway to scare away the flock. But there were so many geese and they were so unafraid of humans and their little carts that he had backed over one, killing it, much to the alarm of the players. One of those was Humphrey Clendenning, president of the Board of Governors, who was, for all intents and purposes, the boss. Poor Gerard had been dining on humble pie ever since. The two dead geese should have been tossed in the Dumpster, but Luisa found Barry in the employee lot, unable to complete the act. Understandably. Vita knew all about Barry's secret gosling. After examining the birds, Luisa had pried them from his grasp and stuffed them into waxy Chiquita banana boxes, storing them in the walk-in until it was time to go home. Vita thought she was crazy for thinking her mother could make them edible, but said nothing. She'd only warned her not to let the members see her leave with the boxes, or else they'd think she was stealing food.

Luisa took another bite and sighed with pleasure. "Momma, she work magic. Special recipe."

Vita snorted and adjusted her toque. "I have a recipe for Canada goose too," she said. "Put a stone in a pot of water, add the goose, and boil for three hours. Then throw the goose away and eat the stone. Even rat tastes better than those greasy, stringy beasts."

Merle, who bore a strong resemblance to Tiger Woods, arrived to pick up Scott. The Club kept a squadron of caddies for those members who wanted to walk the four miles of a game with someone who cared passionately about their stroke, and Merle's education at UMass was being financed by the profit to be gained in this walk. "Sounds like you, Scott," Merle said as they watched Luisa eat. "Greasy and stringy."

The two young men play-punched each other until Vita raised her hand and stopped them cold.

"This food scene is getting way too weird, dude," said Scott, taking off his blue cap and tossing it in the trash. "Can't wait to get my certification next week so I can work at the pool. Then all I have to do is wear a bathing suit and look hot."

"For that rich girl of yours, eh?" said Merle, holding the door open to the outside steps. "Scotty's moving up in the world. Maybe Mr. Quilpe'll give you a job at his bank, huh?"

Merle laughed, but Scott put his finger to his mouth. He didn't want Vita to know he'd been hooking up with Sarah Quilpe, daughter of the Food Committee chairman. Fraternizing with members was strictly taboo.

But Vita was too fascinated by the bird in Luisa's hand to care about who Scott was diddling with this week. "Which goose is this?" Vita asked her. "The one that got run over or the one that got hit in the head?"

"Run over, hit, what matter?" said Luisa. "You see bruises? No. Momma an artist." Luisa held out the meat in a tantalizing gesture. "Bite?"

Vita snatched it from her and gave the flesh a professional squeeze. It was firm and not at all slick. The skin was an excellent bronze color and not too puckered for having been refrigerated. She held it under her nose like a fine brandy, and oh, the smell! Woodsy and dark, with unidentifiable herbal undertones. She took a small bite, moving the piece around her tongue so she would not miss a single sensation. As she chewed, she felt herself filling with primal images, misty landscapes of smoldering volcanoes and giant ferns where small mammalian creatures scavenged and pawed on the floor of a neolithic jungle. A waterfall released a sweet subterranean scent, and from her own core rose an elemental gasp of pleasure. To taste this meat was to begin again at Genesis.

She opened her eyes and looked at Luisa, who was smiling but, all the same, watching the leg. "How did your mother do this?"

Luisa tapped her wrist. "Time. Birds hang all week on our back porch, they mature. Then special rub under the skin." She leaned in close. "Releases fat. We should sell in gift shop."

Vita used the leg to point at Luisa. "Bring me to your mother."

Luisa removed it from Vita's hand. Her long lashes closed softly on her high cheeks as she took a slow, deliberate bite. "Momma won't talk to you," she said with a full mouth. "She not think it right I lose my chance at big money because you must oil the food. She says food must stand on its own. No cheating."

Vita darkened with guilt. Earlier that summer, Luisa had finally gotten a chance to wait tables, but a plate of halibut had slipped from her grasp and onto Mr. Clendenning's lap. He was, of course, gracious about it. Insufferably so. But Gerard took Luisa off the floor, permanently, in spite of Vita's pleading on her behalf. Of course, Vita knew full well that Gerard had never wanted Luisa waiting tables to begin with because of her accent, but it was Vita's fault for supplying him with an excuse: a slippery plate. The halibut had lost its first youth from sitting under the heat lamp, so she had sprayed a little oil on it. A small cheat that made food attractive again, since appetite was as much in the eyes as in the tongue.

She knew better, but sometimes it was just so much easier to embellish on real life, just a little, especially if it was getting dry. But from now on, if the food started looking tired before it went out, she would do the dish over. "Tell her I'm sorry, Luisa," said Vita, reaching unsuccessfully for the leg. "Tell her I'll make sure you get another chance at waitressing."

"No oil?"

Vita raised her right hand. "No more oil. But I want to know everything, do you understand? I want to see how it's done. Step by step."

"See what? See golfers kill another goose?"

"Call your momma and tell her we're coming over for a lesson. I know where I can score a nice fat goose in Chinatown on the way."

Luisa shook her head. "You need wild animal, not overweight, spoiled thing."

"Farm-raised will be fine," said Vita, winning the leg back again. "After all, we can't go around killing the fairway geese on purpose."

Luisa shrugged and wiped her hands. She didn't see why not.

Chapter Five

The Long Drive

THE FOLLOWING evening, Gerard turned out of the Club's gates and gunned his little black convertible down Eden Road, flying too fast over the speed bump and coming down hard with a lurch. It had been a difficult day, but then again, Mondays always were. Over the weekends, members were thrown together with too much alcohol and time, and by Saturday night the topics of money, goods, and one another had been picked to the bone. By Sunday they would start sniffing around at the Club itself, and the staff in particular, until they puffed a mild grievance into a crisis, muttering their birdcall, "something must be *done,* something must be *done,*" and would not rest until they had their goat. Gerard could always count on someone storming into his office every Monday to bite his head off. This afternoon, it had been Linzee Gibbons, the chair of the House & Grounds Committee.

"The balls have got to go." She absently slashed her tennis racket through the air. "All week, golfers have been returning from the back nine talking about the new blight on the landscape. And now they're *here,* even on the terrace. Haven't you any aesthetic sensibilities, Mr. Wilton?"

Gerard had nodded thoughtfully and squinted his eyes, as if giving his aesthetics serious consideration. "You're right, Mrs. Gibbons." He smiled his self-deprecating best and opened his palms like a flower. "I was so determined to fix this goose infestation, I just wasn't thinking about how the balls would look on your lovely grounds."

In truth, he knew exactly how they would look. Obvious. He wanted them to stand out and be seen, the physical evidence that he was on top of the problem. If only the wind hadn't acted up, rolling a few inflatable eyeballs close to the clubhouse, making his plan seem messy and slipshod. As it was, the geese, with their usual insouciance, had quickly become habituated to them, not even bothering to look up when one rolled by.

If only humans were as adaptable. After the two bird fatalities during the Fourth of July weekend, the members had become fixated on the subject of goose control. The board organized a Goose Committee, divided into two subcommittees: Prevention, which was the information-gathering arm, and Eradication, which aimed to take action. As usual, however, as soon as they were in a group they were incapable of rendering an intelligent verdict. They had one joint committee meeting to select a steering committee, and then got drunk in the course of discussing the comparable worth of Canada geese and spotted owls. The Rules Committee, sitting in on the joint committee meeting, had located a golf course in the Pacific Northwest where there was a two-shot penalty for hitting a spotted owl. Then there was the recent incident in Maryland, where a golfer, his shot ruined by a honking goose, had bludgeoned it to death with his 7-iron. That was a criminal matter, they all agreed, and not a regulatory one, and so beyond the ken of any committee's concerns.

But meetings had meaning in spite of their disjointed results, as Gerard had written in his thesis at the Cornell School of Hotel Administration, "A Guide for Selective Clubs Operations" [Chap. 2, Sec. 3]: *Members are to be encouraged in their committee labors and praised for bearing the brunt of the work.* Arnold Quilpe must be sustained in his illusion that he ran the food service, Linzee Gibbons in hers that she maintained the house and grounds, unaware that Gerard spent most of his days undoing their pigheaded attempts at management. While the committees argued about spotted owls, he and Barry had just gone ahead and ordered the yellow vinyl eyeballs.

"They're tossing about behind the service sheds like fleas," chomped Linzee Gibbons. Her skin, feathered with lines, was deeply tanned, which made her tennis outfit seem aggressively white and brought attention to the teeth crowded to the front of her mouth, making her look very Windsorish. "What is the point of all my work if the course is to be made into a circus?"

Gerard stood next to her looking out the window, his hand on his chin, shaking his head. "I'll have Barry round them up and stake them again around Oxbow. They weren't meant to scare the members, after all, just the geese." He swallowed his weak attempt at a laugh when she glared at him from under her pink plastic visor, which cast her eyes in red shadow.

"My father would have known what to do." She lowered her voice. "A shotgun. *That* would take care of your geese."

His geese. It was *their* Club, *their* grounds, even *their* manager, but the geese were all his. He clasped his hands and looked at the ceiling, imploring the ghost of Mrs. Gibbons's father. "The trouble is, of course, the state," he said, appealing to her staunch Republicanism and forcing her to flick her head in agreement. "The hunting season is short and in the fall, at any rate. Maybe we can make a dent then, but for now . . ."

"But for *now*." She grasped her racket handle with both hands. "You're to gather those balls and dispose of them. When my father was president . . ." She tightened her pink mouth.

Oh, no. Gerard glanced around for the tissue box. What was it about fathers around here, that they produced such overpowering sentiment? So much mythmaking with so little material. But maybe that was it. Maybe the fathers were such an unknown quantity that anything could be projected on them. "I'll have Barry right on it, Mrs. Gibbons," he said softly. "Thank you for getting the ball rolling on this."

She lifted her head and seemed confused for a moment, then straightened her posture. "Good." She gave the tennis racket a quick, decisive movement, narrowly missing Gerard's diploma on the wall behind her.

After she left, he adjusted the frame and, while he was at it, rubbed a spot off the glass with the sleeve of his linen jacket. At school, he'd taken Spanish so he could communicate directly with housekeeping, but the cleaning industry in the Boston area had since changed to Brazilian immigrants, and he knew no Portuguese. The head of the service spoke English, sort of, and translated the instructions to the Brazilian crew, but Gerard wished he could talk to them personally, and in detail.

After he'd finished writing a memo to the head of the service, he buzzed Barry's office but got no answer. It was Monday, after all. Barry would still be out patching the turf as meticulously as a surgeon grafting skin, while his crew roamed the course like a pack of hunting dogs, retrieving broken tees, pencil stubs, cigarette butts, beer cans, torn pieces of scorecards, and whatever else the members had tossed aside over the weekend. Gerard didn't want to bother him, so he didn't page. Instead, he left a message about the balls on Barry's voice mail, to make sure they were taken care of first thing in the morning.

All part of a day's work, he reflected as he stopped at the light. And he was very good at his work, if he had to say so himself. Not just in the handling of the forty-five employees under his wing, but the way he worked the two hundred bond-holding members as well, like Mrs. Gibbons. Some days he felt he held them in the palm of his hand. And for this they showered him with gifts. Ski weekends, bottles of wine, envelopes at Christmas, all for what they considered extra attention but which Gerard bestowed to every one of them.

But he would have to get rid of the geese or the members would start looking around for someone who could, since their loyalty extended only to their immediate level of comfort. Staring at the red light, he considered Mrs. Gibbons's father. Gerard had always assumed they couldn't shoot any geese until hunting season, but the animals were interfering with the Club's livelihood. A farmer had the right to kill a predator. What about the rights of a country club? The geese were spoiling the grass, his grass, the very surface the game was played on, without which there could be no Club. There used to be skeet facilities over by the curling rink. Maybe some members could take up shooting clay pigeons again, and then who could blame them if a goose wandered into the line of fire?

By habit, Gerard glanced to his left and groaned. On the rare day when geese were not an active thorn in his side, the billboard at the intersection was, looming offensively across from the warm brick walls of the Club. Two previous Club managers—one, old Desmond, who had been there for thirty-eight years (and awarded a full page in the *History*), and the Australian woman with an ersatz-uppers accent who'd lasted mere months—had been fighting both the zoning board and the owner of the property to have the billboard dismantled since its erection ten years before. Now it was up to him.

This winter, though, it had been unpatriotic to complain, bearing as it did the image of firefighters raising a flag on burning remains. Gerard was relieved to finally have the public service ad gone, giving everyone permission to return to normal, and he could begin lobbying again for the board's removal. This new ad was a promotion for corrective laser surgery at the ophthalmologist clinic in the next town, showing a man giddily throwing away his glasses.

When the signal changed, he turned right onto the frontage road and immediately braked in traffic. Maybe he should have left by the service road, which would have cut off a few hundred yards of this rush hour mess. But then he shook his head. No. The service road was too abrupt a change from beauty to squalor. Better a soft transition on bucolic Eden Road before the assault of drive-through Polynesians and mattress discounters. Besides, it was important he experience the Club with the perspective of a member, from the first moment of turning into the gated and urned entrance in the morning, with the clubhouse in the curvy distance crowning the roundabout like a tiara, to the final salute from the security guard at the gatehouse at the end of the day. He'd hated to leave the Club on such a fine evening, but he had to go to his apartment to shower and dress so he could return for an events consultation after dinner. When the Rundlett-Farnsworth wedding was abruptly canceled in June, the Webers and Cranes jumped on the October date for their children, Bonnie and Duncan, whose engagement had not even been announced. But good dates were hard to come by, so sometimes the cart had to be put before the horse.

Gerard stretched his neck and saw a mangle of cars ahead. He wished people were more attentive so that these things wouldn't happen in the first place. He looked at his watch. This traffic had better start moving or he wouldn't have time to stop at the dry cleaners. He settled back down into the leather seat of his Mercedes, an older model he bought from Jay Freylinghuysen, a member who sold semivintage cars from the parking lot of his insurance agency. A Samaritan hobby, like Poodle Rescue, he called it, as if he'd found them abandoned by the side of the road. Smiling at the thought, Gerard automatically looked at the side of the road and caught the sight of a ball bouncing along the divider.

No. Not one of the vinyl eyeballs. It must have blown out of the service entrance. He signaled to pull over and retrieve it, before it caused an . . . ! Or was *that* what this traffic was all about? He sank deeper into the cracked leather, almost below the level of the wooden steering wheel, and watched in horror as a burst of wind lifted the ball and dropped it solidly in the middle of the oncoming lane. An animal cry escaped his lips. He closed his eyes, but he could not shut out the metal cacophony of screeches and honks that sounded on and on, ringing, beeping, and shouting his name.

The plump gosling pecked furiously at a red-veined yellow ball that had washed up on the distant, deserted shore of Oxbow Lake.

"Forbes." Stripped down to his boxers, Barry stood ankle-deep in the water, trying to entice his gosling to go for a swim. "Leave that alone. Come here."

Forbes would not be deterred from his hatred for the eye until Barry whistled a series of maternal calls, which made the gosling pause, then come waddling. Barry had kept him in the back of his office these past few weeks while he worked, supplying him with a bowl of mash and keeping him quiet as best he could, but now he was feathered out and eager to take his place in the world. It was time to train him to stay near but at a distance, so Gerard wouldn't suspect they were together. A metallic beetle ran across Forbes's path, so he stopped to examine it. Barry waited patiently, as always. He liked the whole deal, feeding the gosling, cleaning up after it, protecting it from predators, i.e., Gerard. And because he didn't want to leave the little feller home alone at night, he stayed in, cooking dinner and watching TV instead of going out and causing trouble like he used to. In a funny way, he was the one being domesticated, not the other way around.

Forbes maneuvered the beetle onto its back and poked at its stomach with his little beak. Barry never tired of watching Forbes. It let him see the world through those bright little eyes, and that world was big and mysterious and full of surprises.

The beetle having escaped, Forbes stopped to taste a bit of interesting vegetation. The leaves were white from insecticide, and Barry took a quick step out of the water, waving his arms. Forbes cocked his head in wonder but let the leaf fall from his beak and continued his trek to the water.

Note to self, Barry thought: Check the ingredients on the can of insecticide to make sure there was nothing that could hurt his baby. Barry had been taught that the chemicals used on the course were as safe as mother's milk, to one degree or another, and that the hazmat suits were more to protect the workers' clothes than anything else. And it was true, he'd never seen a goose lying around dead from poisoning, but maybe they changed in other ways. Maybe the flock didn't migrate anymore because the birds were depressed and couldn't drag their feathered butts in the air.

Maybe they had shorter life expectancies. Or panic attacks. He'd better check that label.

"Let's go, Forbes." Barry whistled again, and Forbes ran toward him, his neck lowered for balance, beeping in joy when his feet touched the water. It had taken years for Barry to learn to swim, awkwardly at best, but Forbes just did it, simple as breathing. Humans were pretty helpless creatures in comparison. No wings, no webbed feet. All they had were smarts to survive, and sometimes it seemed not too much of them.

They both looked up at the sound of the pager, hidden in the folds of Barry's khakis on the shore. It buzzed and buzzed. He was tempted to answer it in case it was one of his crew with a problem, but it couldn't be. He'd sent them home early. It could only be Gerard, and he always had problems. Everything was an emergency to him.

"Man." Barry leaned back into the water, with the sun wheeling westward overhead, experiencing the simplicity of being an animal on earth. "Gerard's got to learn to relax. He's wound tight as a golf ball."

Barry submerged his head, to the great delight of Forbes, who dunked his as well. After shaking water from their ears, the two of them paddled away from shore while the pager continued to sound its alarm.

Chapter Six

The Backswing

AS SHE rubbed Lancôme sunblock on her neck, Madeline Lambert wondered just what was going on with her husband. Charles had left for the office that morning so reluctantly, so sad, seemingly dissatisfied not just with work but with life itself. He used to bounce out the door, chipper and alive, ready to embrace each day. Now it had been weeks since he'd even embraced her. When she saw him sitting on the back porch steps, fully dressed in his three-piece suit, staring at the golf course like he'd never seen it before—the same exact view he'd known from childhood—she wanted to throw her arms around him and coax him back to bed. She was still in her gauzy nightgown, enticingly so, she thought, and it wouldn't have been the first time Charles had to get dressed twice for work. But his sadness had seemed so untouchable, she hesitated, unsure of herself. Then he started up about the goose again, pointing to the distant spot where it fell and putting a quick end to her plans.

And yet she couldn't blame it all on the goose, as much as she wanted to. Charles hadn't really been the same since he went to that Buddha Ball Clinic in New Mexico last winter. It sounded like something her mother would do, if her mother played golf. Would Charles become like her, always searching for a miracle cure? When Madeline was growing up in Santa Cruz, psychoanalysis had been the great drama of her mother's life, but later she abandoned Freud for high colonics, isolation tanks, and est seminars. She lived in Sedona now, and the last time they talked it was harmonic hot stone massage, with crystal bowls and suede mallets. Over the years, each new therapy enhanced her mother's belief that there was something wrong with her, which propelled her into the next nutty treatment. Her pursuit of sanity had become a madness of its own. What cure was Charles looking to find? And what would happen to them both if he found it?

She dropped the sunblock back in her quilted tote, and her hand instinctively adjusted her bathing suit under her left arm, letting her finger trace her scar. It wasn't so nice of Charles to leave for the clinic so soon after her scare either. Granted, the lump turned out to be nothing, but still, there had been a few anxious weeks. For her. For him, apparently nothing. He seemed far more moved by two dead geese.

"Madeline Lambert. How I love saying that name. Gives the tongue a workout. How are you this afternoon, my pet?"

She sighed inwardly. It was Thursday, the day Dr. Nicastro closed up his office at noon and came to the Club—not to golf with his colleagues but to sunbathe. He didn't even play tennis, but he liked the pool and he liked the food. His size was proof of that. He was a urologist, a "colorectal man" he liked to say as he extended his hand during introductions. He was put up for membership the year before by one of his prostate patients and was generally considered a hero among the middle-aged men at the Club. Because of that, the men ignored his occasional bouts of bathroom humor. The women tried to play polite keep-away.

"I don't want to intrude," he said, with the confidence of a man who'd been doing just that for years.

Madeline was miffed. There were empty lounges at a more mannerly distance, but she feigned a smile, remarkably like a real smile, and silently opened her palm to the one next to hers. Frank fluffed a magenta towel and laid it down, then spread his ample self on it, sunny-side up. Sweat immediately began to pour off his skin in glistening sheets as the sun rendered it from his body.

"I'm glad for the company." She inched herself up to a halfway-seated position, keenly aware that Frank was watching her readjust her legs. She'd had looks once, but now she didn't know what she had, except that lately she was being ogled by the caddies, and now by the likes of Frank. Was she exuding a subliminal message from her pores?

"I just came from the snack bar." Frank ran his fingers through his black mane of hair. "No meatless burgers on the menu this summer. That must mean your daughter's not around."

Madeline nodded and looked away. Phoebe had a "job" with some oddball nonprofit group in Seattle and claimed her work was too important to come home even for a couple of weeks. Although Madeline suspected it was Eric, her boyfriend, who was too important to leave. "It'll be a quiet summer, just me and Charles."

"I'll miss her," said Frank. "And the Boca burgers. They weren't half bad with bacon."

"Phoebe's in charge of organizing hatchery demonstrations. She says the chickens are abused because they're forced to lay eggs." Madeline laughed lightly, pretending to find Phoebe's radicalism endearing.

"If a vegetarian eats vegetables," said Frank, "then what does a humanitarian eat?"

Madeline groaned and Frank snorted. He took the edge of his towel and dabbed at the sweat on his forehead. "Speaking of eating, did you try Vita's new salad yet?"

"New?" Madeline didn't consider the menu in terms of new or old offerings; it just was what it was—food. But for Frank, whose conversations revolved around what he'd eaten at his last meal and what he'd be eating at his next, menus were holy scriptures, open to endless interpretation by the faithful.

"Pale endive, with pomegranate seeds like drops of blood. A very emotional presentation." He ran his tongue around his mouth, shaped to receive.

"I had the shrimp cocktail the other night," Madeline murmured. "It was lovely."

"The shrimp! Grilled, chilled, and served with tomato chutney. Vita makes the chutney herself." He propped himself up on his elbows, ready to lunge for the kitchen at any moment. He knew that as a chef Vita was not fully ripe, but he sensed she was going to break open soon, about to carve her signature on the food. And he'd be there, all tucked in at the table. "She's a tease, that woman. Won't give me the recipe. And she says I'm her favorite."

Madeline nodded. "It's a trick mothers say to their children, to keep the peace. I even said it to Phoebe, and she was my only one." To her surprise, she felt a pang of grief at the sound of her own words. When the time came to start thinking about a second baby, she'd gotten a puppy instead. Ben was just like a member of the family, and yet, when he died a few years ago, she'd decided not to complicate her life with another. Had she been so afraid of complicating her life the first time around?

"Speaking of mothers," he said, reluctantly putting the subject of food aside. "I hear Ellen Bruner is knocked up."

"Yes, so I've heard." It was official now, written in the book. At the tea on Sunday, Ellen had listened attentively to Arietta's customary speech about the necessity of being honest, about how a bit of privacy had to be sacrificed for the greater good. Not to mention for the good of one's own personal bloodline. Ellen had absolutely agreed. She had seemed a little nervous, but got the job done quickly in the end. "We're all very happy for her."

"She's getting a little long in the tooth for such shenanigans," Frank said. "I'm surprised old Alex could still crank it up. Notice how she didn't get pregnant until Viagra came on the market."

Madeline blushed. "The Bruners have worked hard at their law practice. She's finally just finding the time."

"I'm in the wrong specialty. I should have gone into geriatric obstetrics." When he laughed, sweat sprayed off his body. "But I suppose there'll never be a shortage of assholes either. Not here, at any rate."

Madeline's face stiffened with the effort of pretending she hadn't heard what he'd said, and she gazed purposefully at the horizon.

"Pet, you're too young to have such tightly pursed lips. If I told you what they looked like right now, you'd never make that face again."

"Ellen will make a wise mother." She turned to look at him, smiling excessively. "Age has its advantages. It wouldn't have hurt me to wait." A comment that came out of nowhere, which she immediately regretted. Frank certainly had a way of opening people up.

It was his turn to smile. "No, you were the wise one. Motherhood's a young woman's sport. Now you can enjoy yourself, let go a little, instead of limping around with a cane, both you and your kid wearing diapers."

"Ellen will get help. She's got to get back to work, after all. Law offices don't run themselves."

"You know what's brown and black and looks good on a lawyer?"

Madeline shook her head, afraid to hear the answer.

"A Rottweiler."

"Frank, that's terrible." Although, deep inside, Madeline had to admit that Ellen's profession seemed to strip her of any appeal as a human being. Madeline had made no effort to get to know her since she'd joined the Club, and even at the tea, no intimacy was gained when their business was over.

With a great effort, Frank rolled over on his stomach and looked up at her with his black eyes, his chins resting on his knuckles. "How is Charles doing?"

"Fine." She closed her eyes, pretending to doze.

"Good. I was a little worried. I heard he missed his game Saturday morning. His partners were so desperate they even called me." Frank laughed through his nose. "There was a time I thought I might take up golf. It's like bowling, one of the few sports where you can eat and drink while doing it. But then I found I could do all those things without leaving the table. Besides, I don't wake up that early unless it's to urinate."

"I'm sure they found someone," said Madeline, yawning. "Charles had an emergency at work."

"Yes, one of those bond emergencies I've heard so much about." Frank sounded serious, which made Madeline open one eye to look at him. He smirked. "That first Saturday tee is a hereditary position, from what I can make out," he continued. "Neddy Fenwick told me a long-winded saga about how in 1983, when the Club finally succumbed to the women's demands to play on weekend mornings, Charles had successfully fought to keep his place in line. But, as Neddy said, you've got to use it or lose it."

"Charles is not losing anything." Madeline tightened her mouth. The truth was, he hadn't gone to work Saturday morning; he'd been in bed, smothering himself with blankets and refusing her offer of a back rub. Refusing her, period.

Frank let a pointed silence build before he spoke again. "If you don't mind my saying so, pet, he's been looking like the last man out lately."

Madeline stared straight ahead. It was Frank's usual proctological prying, always wanting to get inside of things. She returned the minimum. "Thank you for your concern," she said, with as much ice as she could deliver. She'd heard those words a few times herself when she first arrived at the Club. It was time for Frank to learn what the limits were.

He smiled. "You're right," he said. "Talking about our personal problems is such a bore. Let's talk about other members instead. Did you see the paper Tuesday?" The hair on his shoulders bristled in glee. "Clendenning sounded like a complete ass."

The *Boston Globe* had reported, in detail, about a multicar pileup near the Club's service gate. The wind had blown the inflated eyeballs across the back nine, where they bounced off trees like giant pinballs until a couple rolled out onto the frontage road and into the traffic. The reporter made great sport of the incident: CLUB ROLLS EYES AT REST OF WORLD. The opening paragraph contained a comment that was even more damning: " 'It certainly does matter whether it's a Mercedes or a Mercury,' said Mr. Humphrey Clendenning, president of the Eden Rock Country Club."

"He was quoted out of context," said Madeline, happy to be on another subject, and happier still to have inside information. "Brenda says that the reporter called him at his office, and it was the first he'd heard about it. He only wanted to know what kind of cars had been involved, thinking of the Club's level of liability."

"Madeline, open your eyes," said Frank. "It was a cold, elitist statement, and he deserves the flack."

Madeline readjusted herself on the lounge, unable to get comfortable. "That's not fair, Frank. Humpy's not like that at all. He supports all sorts of charities. Brenda sits on the Scholarship Committee at Nobles. They're nice people."

Frank pushed a loose strand of dark hair from his face and smiled. "Did you know that the Latin base of *nice* means *ignorant?*"

Madeline looked away, hoping that if she didn't engage in the conversation the man might go away and leave her alone. But no, he went on, unabated.

"Besides," he said, "it's Gerard Wilton whose ass is in a sling right now. I guess the balls had been his idea and he'd been told to remove them by that clawed wonder Linzee Gibbons. But he didn't, and the balls became a *li-a-bility*."

Madeline adjusted her sunglasses. Was he making fun of her? And for what? Liability was a serious issue, but before she could respond to his attack, she was rescued by her cell phone.

She peeked in her tote to see who was calling. "That's funny, it's from home." What was Charles doing home so early? That couldn't be good. She clicked on the phone, expecting the worst.

"Hello? *Phoebe?*"

It was her daughter, come home to roost after all. After first jumping down Madeline's throat about the ham in the refrigerator ("How can you eat an animal that's smarter than a dog?"), she launched into a teary recital of her breakup with Eric. "Can I, you know, hole up here for a while, Mom?"

"Of course," said Madeline, with a slight tremor in her voice. Of course she wanted her daughter home. Hadn't she just been wistful about her being gone? She sensed Frank pulling himself up with interest. "I'll be right there, honey. Don't worry." She kissed the air, then clicked the phone shut. "I've got to run."

Frank struggled onto his back again, and his belly swayed slightly before settling, like a waterbed. "Rub some lotion on me before you go?"

"Some other time, perhaps." She stood up and shook out her towel. Frank pointed to the copy of *Martha Stewart Living* under her lounge. "Don't forget that. Way under there."

Madeline contemplated her situation. The issue had an article on flower arranging she wanted to save. But now that Phoebe was back, would she put an end to the brutal cutting of flowers? Be that as it may, to retrieve the magazine would mean bending over and giving Frank quite a show. To walk around the lounge to retrieve it would look prissy. Doing nothing seemed the only way out.

"I'm finished with it," she lied. "It's all yours."

She waved two fingers, heaved her bag to her shoulder, and left, bracing herself to face her daughter, who, even while heartbroken, was probably already tossing out everything in their cabinets, trying to change their life.

Frank chuckled to himself as he warmly caressed his stomach with oil.

Chapter Seven

In the Deep Rough

CHARLES, wake up," said Gregg. "Choose your club already."

Charles smiled weakly. He'd been staring down Hoodoo, the sixth fairway—a chute to oblivion, ready to suck him in. He could hear the crows impatiently flapping their wings in the trees. A mere hour on the course and he was exhausted, mentally and physically—tired of hacking his way from one black hole to the next—rattled from the stress of being in the game at all, what with its unpredictable turns of fortune pressing down on him from all sides. He was unable to control his emotions, and because of that, he, who used to be a hitter of the long ball, could now barely get it up.

It was the first time he'd been out on the course in two weeks—since "the day of the goose." He'd been telling the guys that he couldn't play because of work, but the truth was, he didn't know what the truth was.

"Sorry," he said, with a wan smile. "I was up late talking to Phoebe last night."

He wished he could talk to her now. They could go back to the museum. It had been the most amazing thing—yesterday she'd come to the office to drag him out, saying he looked terrible, and asked, "How long has this been going on?"

"What? How long has what been going on?"

She'd given him a strange look, and they drove off to the Isabella Stewart Gardner—he went reluctantly, thinking of museums only as a social duty. He had not visited there since he was showing Madeline his city, before they got married, but those visits had been a means and not an end, and the art was new to him, as if he'd never been. Unfortunately, he and Phoebe had started bickering about what to see, and he was sorry to get off on the wrong foot with her after being home only a day—but really, their tastes were very different. Or so he thought. He lingered too long in front of European landscapes, dotted with ruins and sheep, and she yanked him away, telling him enough of pretty views, then sat them both on the bench in front of Sargent's Spanish dancers. Phoebe sat cross-legged, playing with her knotted blond hair as she explained that the title, *El Jaleo,* meant the spontaneous cheering that comes like an *olé* at the apex of a performance. Then she refused all conversation and would not look at him until, finally, he turned his attention to the painting to placate her—and then he could not extricate himself from its grasp.

He was stunned. How had he not seen before the wildness, the animality—but also the humanity—of the dancers? He thought of the back-bending image of the one woman with her arm up and heart open, and it cleared his mind. He hadn't had such focus and concentration in months—that must be what Phoebe meant. How long had he looked so lost and bewildered? The time at the museum made his spirit buoyant; when he got back to the office, glowing with vitality, he'd had to bear the golf jokes of his colleagues. He let them think it—for, unlike art, golf was good for business. A quick nine holes could win a brokerage deal or bring in a new institutional client. If they knew he'd spent half the day at a museum, there would be talk. It seemed—sensitive. It smacked of—vulnerability. That was not the Charles Lambert they knew, a solid family man, a tough but fair executive in the office not afraid to put in the extra hours, a competent and well-respected bond analyst in the industry. He had always played ball—let them think he still was.

For now, he would simply have to make the best of being out on the course. He pawed through his clubs of titanium and graphite, searching—and still didn't find what he wanted. What club could remove the despair from his shots? He could tell by the silence behind him that his partners were giving one another the eye. Gregg had pulled him over after the third hole, where he had completely butchered his shot, and placed a hand on his shoulder.

"Better book some time with the pro, Charles. You're just pecking at the ball out there. He'll straighten you and your drive right out." Then he patted him on the back and winked kindly. If Gregg was getting that intimate with him, he must really be in trouble.

Then, there it was. He grasped the Hawk Eye 3-iron he'd last held when the goose died at his hands. When he pulled off the cover, the sun glinted off the silver head, blinding him.

"Charles," snapped Andrew with rigid irritation. "It's under twenty feet. Use your seven-iron."

Charles looked around in wonder. He spotted one of the white-suited groundskeepers, poking around with a sprayer under the pine trees, and thought that maybe if he'd lived a simple life, not cluttered with the weight of possessions and responsibilities but communing with nature, like that man over there, then maybe he'd be feeling more fulfilled with life at that moment instead of drained by it. He heard honking in the heavens above and felt the vibration of it in his sternum. His heart was bursting.

"Fucking birds," muttered Neddy.

The geese had become a matter of much concern to the entire Club after the *Boston Globe* article. The members felt they'd been pulled into some tawdry affair over the whole thing—not to mention the liability. The geese splatted down in their awkward postures only a short distance from the men.

"Or try your putter, Charles," said Gregg, wiping his lumpy face, looking behind them at Windy, the short fifth. "There's Thornton's group waiting for us to get on with it."

"Thornton wants to talk to me about a new realty investment trust of his," said Neddy, scraping grit and grass out of his club's grooves with the tip of a tee. "What do you think, Gregg?"

Gregg waved at Thornton Clay to let him know they were moving soon. "Humpy's been pretty satisfied with the one he bought into."

"A-hm," Andrew said. "While you two have been buying real estate, we have lost Charles."

Sure enough, Charles, Hawk Eye under his arm, had wandered over to a water hazard no bigger than a puddle, where the geese strutted and plucked. He sat on a granite outcropping, hugging the club and settling in to watch the birds go about their day. He wasn't completely oblivious to the fact that his partners were now irritated with him. Things did not seem particularly well between him and Madeline either. His people skills were falling apart—but maybe he could get on better with the beasts. Phoebe had often said that animals could remember things that human beings had forgotten. Maybe they accepted him because they remembered a common ancient history, before a random division of cells sent protohumans out on one limb and protobirds on another.

"Should we do something?" Andrew asked, with a shoulder spasm.

"You'd have thought it was Charles who got hit in the head a couple of weeks ago, and not the goose," said Neddy, taking a few practice swings.

Gregg wiped his forehead again and put away his handkerchief. "This is insane. Can't we make him play?" He took out the *Rules* from his bag.

Andrew rubbed his lower back in contemplation, then took out his cell phone. "Madeline? Andrew here. Look, there seems to be a problem with Charles."

Chapter Eight

The Sweet Spot

GERARD, acting as maître d' for the evening, stood by the lectern at the entrance to the chandeliered dining room and surveyed his territory. Originally the ballroom, where Jonathan Curtis had once expected to bring his daughters out to a society of merchant princes, the dining room now sported burgundy damask hanging from gilt-grooved rods and mauve walls encrusted in plaster detail. The chairs were upholstered in the Club's baby blue tartan, which was featured in the gift shop on everything from bridge books ($12.99) to hair scrunchies ($3.99). Gerard sighed with pleasure as the music of tongues rose around him and the air blossomed with perfume. It was a fine crowd indeed, with the bright, polished looks of indulged people in the summer. That *Boston Globe* thing would blow over. How could anything so mundane as vinyl eyes and a few fender benders upset these charmed lives for very long?

He looked outside to reassure himself that all was well and free of balls. The three sets of French doors opened onto a wide terrace, where junior members—adult children of members still covered under their parents' dues—often lingered on the fieldstone wall until late at night.

Last summer, the couple most likely to linger had been Eliot Farnsworth and Nina Rundlett. So much for them. Now he had to worry about the seating of the older Farnsworths and Rundletts, who could not even be in sight of one another. Worse, Roger and Gwen Rundlett were dining with Ellen and Alex Bruner, and seating a foursome that included a pair of lawyers was an exercise in tolerance itself. It took a good long while to negotiate the demands of where they were to be seated, with Ellen Bruner having the gall to suggest that he move people to accommodate their party. Move people already seated! If it was true what the rumor mill said about that woman being pregnant, it was horrific to think of her genes being duplicated.

He flicked something—a little feather?—off his new Armani suit as he watched Luisa approach the Titewater table nearby, then busied himself with picking up an imaginary speck of dirt off the parquet to listen. He hoped to catch her at some substandard delivery of service so he could send her back downstairs. He heard her ask Mrs. Titewater whether she wanted more water. When Luisa returned to the workstation, he was waiting for her.

"Don't say, 'Do you want,'" he said. "Say, 'Would you like.'"

As it was written, so it shall be done. In his Cornell thesis, and later in the *ERCC Employee Manual,* he codified rigorous standards of etiquette because in this day and age the workers might very well be the only ones who knew what they were. So many people had become afflicted with sudden wealth syndrome in the nineties that correctness had become a cult. There has to be a class that sets the tone, and that responsibility now fell to him and his staff. He dreamed of a Club where everyone, from the youngest caddy to the oldest member, had the manners of a country house butler. The members easily went along, always showing one another to their table. The newer members, especially, looked to him for cues on how to behave, reflecting his every gesture. If only his staff were so compliant.

"Would you like," Luisa repeated slowly. "Okay. Mr. Farnsworth wants to talk to you about the wine list again."

"He *would like* to talk to me," he corrected.

"He would like to talk to you," she repeated. "He *wants* wine."

Then she turned back to her duties, mumbling something in Spanish that defied translation. Gerard was miffed. He would leave a memo for Vita about this, but he doubted it would do any good. Vita, for some reason, had dug in her heels about Luisa.

He picked up a tasseled wine list from the lectern and arranged his face. As he passed Palmer Stillington, he heard him growl to his wife that one of his shots had skidded on goose grease out on Burningbush, ruining his game. Gerard was sure to hear about this on Monday.

He nodded to the Lamberts as he maneuvered between the tables. The couple was picking listlessly at their food, obviously not wanting to be there. But Gerard knew they had to make an appearance in order to avoid being the sole topic of conversation. What Mr. Lambert had done that morning, dropping out of a game to sit with the geese, sounded ominously like a breakdown. That sort of thing was happening more and more at the Club these days. But Lambert would get over it soon enough. That's what the Club was for, so men like him could retreat into its warm embrace and find solace among their friends and games, becoming fully restored to go back out into the cold world to grab a buck. He'd be just fine.

At a large round table in the center of the room, the Clays were entertaining a substantial party, all nonmembers. Realtors, most likely, a few of whom were visibly uncomfortable, knowing that in one way or another they were being fattened up for something. Thornton Clay, enormous and easygoing, was smiling broadly and kept the bottles coming. Helen Clay, whose faculty of enjoyment was as large as her husband's, saluted Gerard and winked one of her big horsey eyes.

Gerard bowed from the waist before veering past the Henry Harcourt and Peter Gibb table. The two men and their wives were leaning across the table toward one another as if concluding some shady business, so he did not intrude. At the next table sat the skinny dowager Arietta Wingate with her two daughters, who seemed even older than their mother, and their two invisible husbands, one of whom had recently taken up the art of English bell-ringing, and that was the subject of conversation. He'd heard that Mrs. Wingate's husband had died of drink back in the eighties, and who could blame him?

Gerard forced himself to stop at the Clendenning table. They were with the Hollowells, the vice president and his wife, discussing the imperfections of the other members. Brenda Clendenning gestured with arms so thin that the meat appeared to be sucked out of her body, nodding but not smiling at Gerard. It was whispered that her husband's statement to the reporter had compromised her position on the Scholarship Committee at Nobles, where there could be no whiff of prejudice toward an applicant's family car.

Clendenning made a small noise from his throat by way of a greeting. His upper lip extended down and beyond his lower lip, like a cod. His blue-green eyes were steady, almost staring because he didn't blink much, and he had a studied, laconic manner, as if for generations his family had been bored from the effects of wealth. But Gerard knew, as he made it his business to know, that Clendenning was one of those millionaires who made all his money in one day—by marrying it. But the slight rasp in Clendenning's voice, along with his excessively polite manner, made what he was about to say seem important, and so when he finally uttered, "Hope all is going as it should, Wilton," Gerard took it to mean he was halfway out the door.

Gerard passed the rest of the tables in a grinning funk but, out of habit, kept his ear on every word. Mostly the talk was about which houses sold for what. The members tended to talk obsessively about real estate, an informal way of talking obsessively about money. But Gerard's radar was tuned in to the ordering of complicated meals, with their many vetoes and provisos. It was his job to foresee problems. If a husband whispered to his wife that there was a smudge on his fork, Gerard would have the waitstaff place a new service in front of him, anticipating the needs of the members before they themselves knew what they wanted. Or what they would *like,* he corrected himself. Why, oh why, hadn't he anticipated the problems with the inflatable eyes?

He greeted Mr. Farnsworth with a flourish of the list. Their guests were from outside the Club that evening and seemed as eager as the waiters to serve their hosts. This attention inspired Farnsworth to display his wine knowledge more than usual. Gerard had learned wine at Cornell, had been tested extensively on grapes, vintages, methods, buying, and food pairings. He knew trends. He knew values. He could, without fail, pick the perfect wine. But he wore his knowledge lightly. He could not appear to know more than the members, many of whom prided themselves on their private cellars. It was best not to lock horns. Farnsworth's question: "What dessert wine do you suggest with the zabaglione, Wilton?" was actually just a springboard for Farnsworth to expound upon muscats.

Only Dr. Nicastro, sitting in the corner, getting ready to eat a meal fit for a boa constrictor, truly appreciated Gerard's expertise, so when Gerard finished steering Farnsworth toward the proper Sauterne, and commended him by saying, "Excellent choice," he went to say hello. Dr. Nicastro was not married and did not even have a date that evening, but he was with the Fishers. They were new members, not from the area at all, and yet they seemed to be doing remarkably well for themselves in making friends. The Club was hard to penetrate to begin with, and the walls inside could be even higher than the ones out. But Hilary Fisher, with a cheerful, oversized head and the spindly limbs of a marionette, often broke grim silences with a scream of exaggerated amusement, which raised the happiness level in the whole room and reminded them they were all having a good time. Her husband, Carl Fisher, was less lively. Some people even thought him a little simple, and it did sometimes seem that she led him like a tame bear from one event to another, but he was a damn good listener. He sat, trim in his blue blazer and Club tie, hands folded on the table and looking intently at Dr. Nicastro while he spoke, alternately squinting and raising his eyebrows to indicate unwavering attention, smiling and nodding, smiling and nodding. Gerard paused. A flush of recognition swept through him like the avian flu, as if he were looking in a funhouse mirror.

Vita stood with her back to the stove, a line of computer-generated papers waving in front of her face like Buddhist prayer flags. She was simultaneously reading orders and giving orders in an atmosphere of pure rush and panic, but she exuded calm, like the duck who seems to glide without effort on the surface while its feet are madly churning below. It was the life of a cook, her life: the crazy hours, the intensity of the work, the beauty of the product. She thought of her crew—her sous-chef, two prep helpers, dessert woman, five waitstaff, three runners, and busboy—as a single organism fighting for food. The kitchen was a room of hunger and desire, and Vita loved it because she, by and large, was the one person who could satisfy everyone. If only she could make her mother understand with what passion she embraced her job—her mother, who she knew was obediently sitting by the phone at that very moment, waiting until the rush was over so she could call her daughter.

"You do the shrimps," Vita said to Sloane, her competent but silent sous-chef. "I'll take care of this."

Sloane mechanically spooned tomato chutney into two large martini glasses, executing her duty like she was changing a tire for all the food touched her soul. She did her job perfectly, and bloodlessly.

Vita reverently placed a hot squab on a plate, and arranged sage and grapes around it. Ordinarily she didn't handle appetizers, but this was for Dr. Nicastro, and he noticed every detail. She sent the dish up to the dining room as proudly as if she had hatched the pigeon herself.

Two waitresses argued over whose salmon plates were whose, and a waiter dropped a glass and cursed, and another asked where his veal was. Oops. Now that Vita had sworn off oil spray to freshen up food, she was cooking closer to the bone. She turned her attention to the pan of floured veal medallions on the counter, as scrumptious as powdered baby bottoms. She peeled a latex glove off her hand and gave the cutlets a loving pat, then chose two to throw in the hot pan in front of her. As she added a handful of shallots, she wondered, along with her mother, if she would ever pat the real thing. Children could be a mixed blessing. Phoebe Lambert, for instance. When Vita heard she was back in town, she put Boca burgers back in the snack bar to avoid another scene like last summer, when Phoebe lay covered in ketchup at the pick-up window, lobbying for a beef alternative. Vita flipped the medallions and gave the shallots a stir. And as soon as word got out that veal had been on tonight's menu, Phoebe was sure to charge, but Vita was ready with a counterattack. This rosy meat had a pedigree even a vegetarian might approve. She turned the meat out on a plate and, with a spattering of hot fat, used Madeira to deglaze the pan. A warm, loving woman in upstate New York raised free-range calves, bringing them up like her own children. The animals lived bucolic, natural lives right up until nine months of age, when the woman, calmly and with compassion, slaughtered them. It was flesh of the highest quality and could be consumed with a clear conscience.

She poured the glaze over the veal and placed a scoop of morel whipped potatoes on the side, not underneath, not being a fan of Viagra towers of food presentation. She wanted her food to be easily seen, and admired, and not to make the members hunt for their starch. The waiter snatched the plate from her hand. Her bare hand. Oops again. Reluctantly, she flipped another latex glove from a box on the counter. Gerard was a bear when it came to Department of Health regulations. It tore her apart to have this artificial barrier between her and her food, but she wore them when Gerard was on duty and to set a good example for the staff, some of whom she wouldn't want touching her food with naked hands either.

She gave the mussel soup with saffron a quick stir to keep it from settling, then prepared a plate of duck, arranging loganberries at the cut where the leg had joined the body so the member would not be reminded that the bird once walked the earth as he did now, and sent it up. She ripped tendons from an uncooked leg with a flick of her knife to prepare it for the next order. Luisa came down the steps from the dining room holding a glass.

"Spots! Mr. Stillington says spots. He raise it at me!"

Vita motioned to Pedrosa to lift the steaming tray of glasses from the dishwasher. Poor Luisa, to get Mr. Stillington her first night back. Everyone hated to wait on him, since every request came with a storm of abuse. The only comfort was that as hard as he was on the staff, he was even worse to his comembers. He treated everyone badly, as if that were the mark of being well bred. But she'd been around long enough to know that talking about everyone badly while treating them like long-lost siblings was the gold standard of the Club. And yet Gerard had assigned this monster to Luisa, setting her up to get her off the dining floor. Gerard would have to do better than that. She instructed Luisa to grab a spotless glass by its hot stem and place it on a linen-covered tray. Then she selected a split of Bordeaux and placed it next to the crystal.

"We should throw him a couple of Christians, but this might do." Vita was liberal with wine splits because they smoothed any dining disaster. The richer the customer, the more he liked free things. You just had to know how to tickle the stomach.

Luisa thanked her in a rolling Spanish, and Vita corrected her. "If the members hear you talk like that, they'll think you're plotting something. Learn to say thank you in English, and learn to say it often. Like Gerard."

Luisa muttered, "*El sapo,*" and laughed her way up the stairs with her offering.

Toad? Vita shrugged and went back to her stove, turning the heat up on the duck. The duck, the squab, and the guinea hen with baby turnips and artichoke puree on the menu that night were all a pitiful excuse for the special game dinner, featuring goose, that she had hoped for. But last Sunday, Luisa's mother, Mrs. Suarez, had scoffed when Vita showed up with a domestic goose that had already been plucked and gutted so that it was no longer a candidate for hanging. Mrs. Suarez slapped the bird on its pimpled rump. "Goose must live, must love." And with this she patted her heart. "Taste is from life. Go make friends with your birds. Make them fat and happy, and a week before you want to eat, I bring my boys and we kill them. Yes?"

Kill them? Vita had gotten an uneasy feeling. Every ounce of meat and fish she had ever prepared and served had been killed by someone, somewhere, but not at her command.

Or had it? When she ordered the veal through her supplier, was she not asking for the knife to be put to the calf's throat? How different was this? And it wasn't like she was going to see it happen. She would have no blood on her hands. The more she thought, the more intense her memory of Mrs. Suarez's goose became.

She lowered her voice. "How do I fatten them up?"

Mrs. Suarez had smiled and tucked her hands in the sleeves of her black cardigan. "*Maiz.* Not pale yellow flour you people eat. Dark cornmeal, full of the sun."

You people. Mrs. Suarez had meant her as well, her Hispanic heritage notwithstanding. Her mother would love to hear those words, her dream of putting distance between her precious daughter and an impoverished Colombia fulfilled. Her parents had never even spoken Spanish at home, for fear little Evita would not learn proper English. She'd had to pick it up from her cousins, like profanity.

Vita flipped the duck leg, splashed in some wine, and covered it. She thought of the wildness she had felt along with her grief over Utah, when the two geese spent the day in the kitchen with her, so primitively dead. Even now, when she entered the walk-in, her eyes went to the space where the Chiquita boxes had been. She wanted the fairway geese. She needed them. She would start tonight, with her bag of coarse cornmeal and her eyes on the Fothergill Cup banquet at the end of the summer.

She heard Luisa pant down the stairs again, going, "Ah, ah, ah," and wondered what Mr. Stillington found fault with now.

"*El cabra,*" Luisa shouted, half laughing, not able to catch her breath.

Goat? thought Vita. Had Stillington pinched her? Before she could sort out her thoughts, Gerard came running down after

Luisa, grabbed the phone, and stabbed in three digits. Vita moved closer, but he didn't even look at her. He rested his forehead on the wall.

"Police?" Gerard struggled to manage his emotions, deepening his voice, but it still came out like a squeak. "Eden Rock here. We have . . . *goats.* Out on the terrace. No, *real* animals. I don't know. Hurry."

Chapter Nine

The Follow-Through

GERARD KNEW Gwen Rundlett to be a fair woman. Fair of skin, fair of temperament, fair of hair. Even now, as she patiently explained to Officer Dyer, an unmoving block of a man, how it happened that her husband had gouged Mr. Farnsworth in the thigh with a fork, she was fair to a fault. Alex Bruner sat on the other side of her, taking notes as directed by his wife. Ellen Bruner had performed the same service for Roger Rundlett and was now sitting with him outside on the low fieldstone wall, where the goats had so recently frolicked. Officer Dyer had had no success with Mr. Rundlett, who'd kept his arms folded and his mouth shut. All he would say was that if they wanted to arrest him, then they should get on with it.

Gerard, a rictus smile frozen on his face, wiped his forehead with a mauve linen napkin left in a crumple, like a rose. The dining room was littered with such fallen blooms—on the tables, on the chairs, on the floor, maybe even in the chandelier. The staff hurried around like hummingbirds, collecting untouched dinners and full bottles of wine from abandoned tables.

"Tell your staff not to disturb the crime scene, sir," Officer

Dyer said, his mouth seeming to creak as he spoke. "We still haven't recovered the weapon."

Crime scene! Weapon! Gerard prayed that Mrs. Rundlett stop being so determinedly fair and start lying like a rug. He and everyone at the Club knew bad blood existed between the Rundletts and Farnsworths over the broken engagement, but the outside world had to see the forking as an accident. His job would not survive another bout of bad press.

"It seems to me that he merely neglected to release the fork when we got up from the table," Mrs. Rundlett said, turning the simple gold bracelet on her wrist around and around, trying to unscrew her hand. "We *had* to go see the goats, after all. Goats out on the terrace! There they were, right out of a picture book, two of the sweetest things, not smelling at all, if you can believe that, standing on the wall and eating the geraniums. My favorite-color flower, that salmony pink, and I was so afraid they might tip the urns over and break them. They're original to the house, and I just don't see how the House and Grounds Committee would ever be able to replace them."

"If he forgot to release the fork, then where is it?" Officer Dyer leaned toward her from his ankles.

"Maybe the goats ate it!" said Gwen, finally letting go of her bracelet. "I understand they eat anything."

Alex Bruner smiled broadly at the officer.

"Can you tell me what happened, ma'am?" said Officer Dyer. "After you went out to the patio."

"Terrace," she corrected him.

"I object." Alex Bruner scrunched up his nose, causing a red wave of wrinkles to form on his forehead. "Mrs. Rundlett doesn't have to testify against her husband."

"This isn't a trial, sir." Officer Dyer refused to look at him. "We're just taking witness statements."

Witness statements. Gerard shuddered at the words. They should be going after Phoebe Lambert. She was responsible for all of this. Her goats were the reason he'd called the police, who arrived to find not animals but a bleeding Farnsworth. In the meantime, the real criminal had escaped. Phoebe had pulled the goats by their horns to her parents' house, whose backyard abutted the golf course near Plateau. An ancient privet hedge kept golfers out, but failed, apparently, to keep goats in. Or maybe Phoebe had left the gate open just to cause trouble. And he thought she was safe in Seattle, harassing someone else this summer.

"Now," Officer Dyer said patiently to Gwen, tipping ever more in her direction. "Why don't you just tell me what you saw out on the terrace."

"As I was saying, when we heard what was going on, we hurried to see the animals. Roger was having the duck, which is so tender you could eat it with a feather the way Vita prepares it. Maybe there's some left." She looked around.

Officer Dyer grunted without inflection. "Go on."

"You see those drapes, how they go right to the floor? They are not original to the house of course—fabric is not nearly so stable as marble. But I think the committee did a good job at keeping them in the same 'tone' as what would have been here." She looked at Gerard for confirmation, but he was too numb to nod.

Officer Dyer made a stiff motion with his hand, and she continued. "The way I see it, Roger must have tripped on the damask while holding the fork, and the next thing I know Willard is screaming some nonsense about being attacked."

Alex Bruner frowned in agreement.

Officer Dyer closed his pad. "Mr. Farnsworth says it was on purpose, you say it was an accident, and your husband won't say a thing. I think it's time we all talked down at the station."

Gwen clasped her hands together and let them fall in her lap in exasperation. "But there's no *need*."

"Don't worry, Gwen." Alex Bruner put his liver-spotted hand on hers. "Ellen and I will be right there with you."

"Or," said Officer Dyer, "we can finish this up right here. Just tell me: Do you know of any reason your husband may have had to injure Mr. Farnsworth?"

Gwen pinked up, mirroring the color of the walls. "I'd have to think," she said, not wanting to think at all about the many reasons why Roger would want to do harm to Willard. It was a mess, all of it. Two families about to be united until Arietta Wingate spoke up: The marriage could not be because of some distant diddling between Karen and Willard. Poor Karen had died of breast cancer before Nina even started dating, and so she was not there to stop the relationship before it had gone so far as caterer deposits. The women, including mortified Anne, Willard's wife, had to take matters into their own hands, intoxicating innocent Eliot and bringing in the working girl. But what else could be done? It was unthinkable, the consequences. Half-siblings, marrying. If only Roger, assuming it had just been an unfortunately timed last fling by Eliot, hadn't tried to bring the couple back to the table—he was just that sort of man, she thought warmly, a real mediator—well, if he hadn't started that process, she wouldn't have had to tell him the truth. And what a mistake that had been. Roger had been sick for weeks, thinking his Nina might not be his, not to mention that his departed wife had been unfaithful.

Oh, she was such an idiot sometimes! Gwen twisted her rings around her fingers. She knew, absolutely, the purposefulness with which Roger fell into Willard, business end of the fork first, even though she believed Willard provoked it with that look he gave Roger. Truly, anything could have been read into that smile.

Alex whispered in her ear, and she automatically repeated his words. "It's hard to say," she murmured to Officer Dyer, who had just accepted a cup of cappuccino and a pastry from Vita. He parted the drapes to check on Roger, then took a seat.

For the briefest of moments, with the officer more focused on his pastry rather than a fork, Gerard felt that this too might pass, that life would one day return to normal.

"Our children were once engaged," Gwen suddenly blurted out, bringing the conversation back to the abnormal.

Officer Dyer put his coffee cup down and sat up straight with his pencil and pad. Gerard wondered if he should simply start screaming as a distraction. Alex whispered sharply into Gwen's ear, his jowls brushing up against her neck. Just then, Anne Farnsworth entered the dining room, delicately coifed, her pink lipstick fresh, her silk dress impeccable in blue and purple. Her pearls glistened against her neck, as if from her own inner fire.

"Officer, may I interrupt for a moment?" Anne glanced ever so briefly at Gwen, with a flicker of a nod. She held herself very erect, and when she made a gesture with her hands, she kept her elbows close to her waist. "My husband is fine. Dr. Nicastro bandaged the wound, and he believes it will heal quite nicely. Willard was upset earlier when he told you that Mr. Rundlett attacked him. Perhaps, and I can trust you not to let this go any further, he shouldn't have had that salsa martini before dinner. We have a friend, and Mrs. Rundlett knows who she is, who is incorrigible when it comes to these silly drinks. She wants everyone to join her in her fun, and Willard, well, he has a hard time saying no to a woman. The fork, the stab . . . it was obviously an accident. He is not going to press charges. At least not against Roger. Maybe against the goats?"

She laughed without moving her mouth, and they all, Vita, Gerard, and Mrs. Rundlett, joined in with a forced hilarity. Even Officer Dyer lightened his face for a moment. Only Alex Bruner remained unamused.

"The Club, however, will definitely seek charges against the animals." Gerard stood and adjusted his tie. "This isn't going to happen again."

"We must be more generous, Mr. Wilton," said Anne Farnsworth. "We must be forgiving of the animal nature."

"No, they can't help themselves," said Gwen, looking up at her old friend and almost in-law. "Can they?"

Anne gave Gwen a wry smile, then kissed her on the cheek. "Good night. I should get Willard home now."

"We're so sorry, Anne. We'll pay for the suit, of course."

"I think it can be repaired. There's no need for a whole new one." As she left the dining room, she passed Arietta Wingate at the door without looking at her.

Officer Dyer put his pad back in his pocket; then he and his partner—who had failed to collect any witness statements from the small pool of members hiding in the lounge—left the Club with a paper plate of cookies.

"This is some bouillabaisse," Vita said to a listless Gerard as she peered out the window, watching the red taillights disappear down the driveway. "What do we do about charging the members for ordered-but-not-served food? I have forty plates lined up for takeoff downstairs."

Gerard put his head into his hands. He'd have to talk to Clendenning about the charges. "That Lambert girl," he said, moaning. "If there was any justice in the world, she'd be paying."

"It wasn't the goats, it was the screaming and blood that drove everyone out of here," said Vita. "Away from my food." Then she sent Luisa to the lounge to see if anyone was left and if they would still like their dinners now that the police were gone.

"Vita, may I give my compliments and condolences?" Dr. Nicastro called from across the empty room, recently returned from attending to Farnsworth's leg. He picked up a paper-thin bone from his squab and sucked the marrow from it. Two tiny skeletons were arranged with paleontological care on his plate, as he had to finish off the Fishers' appetizers as well. In the moment of shocked silence after Farnsworth screamed, Hilary Fisher had coolly downed her drink, thanked Frank excessively for a dinner they had not yet been served, pulled her pliable husband to his feet, and ran. "All the rats have left the ship, Vita, but I'm still game if you are. Why not put your trotters in the trough with me?"

Vita beamed. Her savior. Dr. Nicastro, whose skin was the color of her best pan gravy, appreciated the enormity of her loss in something other than economic terms. She felt incomplete having been unable to serve what she had created. She felt hungry. She went down to the kitchen and brought up his entrée, lamb kabobs with spicy celery-root puree and mint vinaigrette, and one for herself.

"They're suffering a bit from heat-lamp wilt," she said, spreading a napkin on her lap.

"You're an honest woman." He lifted a skewer from the plate. "Some chefs would have sprayed the plates with oil."

Vita smiled and toasted him with her skewered meat.

Gerard noticed this breach of the *Employee Manual* (Ch. 6—*Member-Staff Relations: At no time may an employee sit with a member on Club premises and disturb the impenetrable veil that must separate the server and the served*), but he was too weak to make a fuss. Besides, who would see them? As he wandered the empty room, half-heartedly straightening chairs, he recalled with cold clarity the stare Clendenning had given him as he and his party smoothly rolled out of the dining room. But why pick on him? None of this was his doing and it had nothing to do with geese. It had to do with goats. If they hadn't been on the terrace, the two men wouldn't have been thrown together with Mr. Rundlett clutching a fork. It must have been an irresistible temptation to take one little poke. And now, praise God, it was officially an accident. An accident with purpose, but an accident nonetheless.

And for this he might very well lose his job.

Chapter Ten

The Bunker

ON MONDAY MORNING, Gerard met with Clendenning, who in as few words as humanly possible told him that, regrettably, the members were to be charged for the uneaten dinners. The Club could not sustain a loss of that magnitude. The economic times were uncertain at best. Some members were behind in dues; others had requested leaves of absence. A few had to resign altogether, as they needed their $25,000 bond to pay for tuitions or mortgages or lawyers. Clendenning had to admit, early on in the recession he'd looked on it as a time when the Club could "sift out." But now it was going on too long, and if there weren't going to be job cuts—and he said this slowly and significantly—then care had to be taken in matters of billing. And, after all, no one had made the diners leave. He and his party, of course, had to leave so abruptly because Mrs. Clendenning had taken ill—he hoped it was not from something she ate—and he'd had the foresight to cancel the remaining part of his order before leaving. Those who had not canceled would have to pay. And that was most of all the rest.

On Thursday, the monthly bills went out, never a happy day

for the membership but an even worse one for Gerard. When money got tight, members felt more strongly than ever the need to appear careless about it, so instead of complaining about bills, they freely, and repeatedly, complained about the Club and the geese. And, by association, Gerard.

Ralph Bellows, for instance. Gerard could guess he was smarting about being charged several hundred dollars for what amounted to a round of cocktails and nibbles for a party of four. But instead of arguing about that, Bellows arrived at the office holding his tartan golf bag out in front of him as evidence of Gerard's incompetence and mismanagement. It was fouled by a single splat of goose dropping, which had unfortunately landed on a baby blue square and not a green one, where it might have just blended in. The splat on the bag, however, was inconsequential compared to the mess on the Oriental rug carried in on Bellows's tasseled cleats.

"Mr. Bellows, do have a seat. Let me buzz Barry and have him hose this off. I'm glad you came in because I've been meaning to talk to you, man to man, about this goose situation, if I may. Coffee?"

Bellows, tan as a tobacco leaf, hair white as swansdown, sat in a huff, as if he had a great many other things to do, even though he had not much to do at all except to cater to his many sporting affections, such as golf, sailing, and shooting. His was a life of almost senseless ease, and yet he wore a look of constant aggravation. His white eyebrows were angled sharply in a V, pressing his eyes into black slits from which he viewed the world with marked disdain. Even his nose cast a shadow on his face, and nothing cheered him so much as a thoroughly good grumble. "No."

Gerard buzzed Barry, then closed his venetian blinds. He never used to shut himself off from his glorious view, but now it was ruined by the silhouettes of hawks applied to the glass by the House & Grounds Committee after a kamikaze sparrow had crashed into it that week. The death was not an uncommon occurrence, the difference being that this time Gerard had not run out fast enough to scoop up the body for a quick Dumpster burial. Not fast enough at all. One of Palmer Stillington's princess terrors had watched the accident from the lawn and shrieked so loudly you'd think her own plump white neck had twisted and broke. Stillington accused him—him! Not the bird! Him!—of traumatizing his daughter, and the incident moved on wings to the committee. The upshot was the silhouettes, and Gerard was reduced to dwelling in a dark, viewless cell, a prisoner of the birds.

Gerard poured himself a splash of the Club's exclusive blend of kona and Peruvian beans (available in the gift shop, $11.95 a pound) from a stainless-steel thermos. He contemplated the Eden Rock emblem printed on the paper cup. It was the Curtis family crest, commissioned in England before the old man died, a shield surmounted by a peacock, his mate, and what seemed to be a gopher. Below, the words *occupo et porto.* "I seize and carry."

Yes. He must seize the situation and carry the day. Here sat Ralph Bellows, a member of the Fox Run Hunt Club, known for warm blinds where members played poker until the staff alerted them to birds coming in. Maybe Bellows knew what the rules were.

"Barry will be right up to take care of the bag, a real beauty I might add. A Simmons from Scotland, isn't it? Understated, elegant, rugged . . ." Gerard trailed on, then, failing to elicit any sort of response from Bellows, who was picking at a loose cuticle, got to the point. "I wonder, Mr. Bellows, if you knew, or if you could find out, what the law might be about the shooting of Canada geese?"

Bellows made a guttural sound, like that of a large hibernating animal being awakened, but did not look up. Gerard poured a packet of sugar slowly into his cup, as so much sand through an hourglass, watching Bellows. Then, out of the corner of his ever-observant eye, he saw Barry standing at the door, and behind Barry—*a young goose?*

"Here to collect that bag, Mr. Bellows, sir," said Barry.

Bellows grunted and continued to pick at his cuticle. Gerard could not get a word out of his mouth, and what word would he use if he could? Should he cry "Goose!" in the same way one might yell "Fire!"?

When Barry turned to leave with the golf bag slung over his shoulder, he tripped over his baby bird and almost dropped the bag. Forbes must have jumped out of the open window of his office. Did the little guy take his first flying steps without him being there? Barry felt the twinge of guilt familiar to working mothers everywhere as he swept up the wiggling bundle in his arms before running out the door. Bellows, being Bellows, had never even turned his head to acknowledge Barry's presence, and so never saw his feathered friend.

"Excuse me for just a moment," said Gerard, standing with shaking knees. "I want to tell Barry where the Citra-Solv is."

Gerard caught up with Barry outside the back door, and they looked at each other in disbelief. Forbes, just beginning to exhibit the black markings of his adult coloring, beeped.

"Don't look at him like that, boss."

"What are you doing consorting with the enemy, Barry?"

Barry took a breath, inflating himself to his full height. "Maybe it's time to open our hearts to our enemy. We must embrace them, get to know them. There's too much hate in the world as it is." He stroked Forbes's head. "Besides, it's your fault. You're the one who made me addle those eggs in May. He thought I was his mom, so I had to take him. Was hoping to keep him a secret, but this is for the best. No more lies."

Gerard steadied himself by holding on to the cold metal banister and stared out at the Dumpster, where crows lethargically picked at the morning's offering from the kitchen.

"I've got to go back inside," Gerard said slowly. "When I'm done, you and I are going to have a very long talk about your bird."

"Forbes." Barry stroked the top of the gosling's head and gave it a little peck with his nose. "His name is Forbes. He took a fancy to the magazine I used to line his box." Barry and the gosling both looked up at Gerard, their eyes bright with moisture.

"I'm sure if you check the *Manual,*" said Gerard, turning away, "you will find that employee pets are disallowed on Club premises."

"He was born here," said Barry defiantly. "The Club is more his than ours."

Gerard paused but did not answer.

"Boss, please. When there's not too many of them, they can trim the grass and fertilize it at the same time. Maybe we should think about ducks too, because they'll eat the bugs. Did you know that a dozen ducks can pick a small orchard clean of plum curculio in an hour? You shake the branches, and the bugs fall. . . ."

"We don't have plums." Gerard was tempted to add "you idiot" to the sentence but restrained himself. "We have a golf course. The best golf course in New England. And I intend for it to stay that way."

"I never meant for him to follow me into your office. Little devil musta flew out the window. *Flew.* Isn't that something?"

Gerard tapped the banister. Would he be forced to fire a valued employee over a goose? Or would that be playing into the birds' hands? He closed his eyes tight. "Just don't let me see him in this clubhouse again." He opened the door slowly, poised at the gates of hell, then entered, letting the door sweep closed behind him.

When Gerard skulked back into his office, Bellows raised his head stiffly and blinked. "Somethin' wrong?" he asked.

"No, no, he's getting right on it." Gerard put his smile back on a second too late.

"Now wha' about the geese?" Bellows looked at him with one eye.

Gerard checked himself in the mirror before speaking and calmed his features. "I was wondering, Mr. Bellows, if maybe, do we have the right to, if you understand what I'm saying, dispose of the geese?"

Bellows snorted. "There's a short season in the beginning of September, longer one in the winter." He sat up straight. "Not sure what the bag is, though. But we could get a few of the boys from the Hunt Club and have a go at them."

"What about now?" asked Gerard. "We're allowed to kill all the rats we want, year-round. The geese are just as dirty and spread disease. They interfere with our livelihood. They alter game results and create stress for our members. Tell me, Mr. Bellows, do you think some sort of permit might be had for a special reduction in the numbers?"

Bellows thought, or at least looked as though he thought. "You've got a point. Let me ask around. Could be quite a bit of fun, eh?"

He stood up, his eyebrows lightening their heavy load for a moment, and shook Gerard's clammy hand.

Chapter Eleven

The Unplayable Lie

"HEY, MRS. LAMBERT." Scott Volpe hung the NO LIFEGUARD ON DUTY sign on the gate. "Got to go tidy the locker rooms now that the kids have split, but I can stay if you'd feel, um, safer."

"I'll try to keep from drowning." Madeline suppressed a smile. Earlier in the summer he was asking how she wanted her burger, and now he wanted to know how much protection she needed. According to Frank—who, after being here a little more than a year, seemed to know more about the staff than she ever had—Scott had gotten his Red Cross certificate to win a girl: Holly Quilpe's daughter, Sarah, who was apparently game for a lifeguard but not a kitchen worker. Holly would make quite a scene if she found them out, but Scott, while definitely not son-in-law material, was sweet, really. And cute in a way, especially now that his hair was shorter. Black swimming trunks were a great improvement over his old khaki uniform. He had the torso of a grown man but was not quite cooked through yet, so his body was as hairless as a Ken doll. She peered at his chest. There were two small indentations near his left nipple, like a snakebite.

"That's weird, huh?" Scott touched the spot. "But Gerard, he said I had to remove all body jewelry on duty. I said that's not in the *Manual,* and he says he doesn't care what it says, no nipple rings."

"Ah," said Madeline, beginning to move away. "I suppose he has his reasons."

Scott stepped closer. "But I don't, um, take off the ones he can't see." He grazed his crotch with his fingertips so quickly she thought she'd imagined it; then he unfurled his tongue, where a small golden stud glinted on its tip. He smiled and put his finger to his mouth. "Our secret," he said, and left.

Madeline was stunned. It looked so uncomfortable. It could chip his tooth enamel. And what was the point? Phoebe would know, but Madeline was afraid if she asked she'd only be inviting a lecture on the rights of body parts to be mutilated. She shook out her white towel as she shook her head. She didn't want to think about Phoebe right then, or about much of anything. It's why she preferred the pool later in the afternoon, after the children were gone but before the adults started arriving for post-work swim and sunset cocktails. At this time of day she didn't have to talk to anyone if she didn't want to. As if anyone would. Between Phoebe and her livestock, and Charles and his breakdown, her life had become too untidy for polite conversation. Members cracked sympathetic smiles, but there were no kind words, not even any unsolicited advice. She was apparently beyond redemption.

As she smoothed out her towel on the lounge, someone splashed her, and she gasped. She liked the pool, but the older she got, the more she hated getting wet. To think her adolescence was spent surfing the waves.

It was Frank Nicastro. He was panting as he leaned his arms on the tiled edge of the pool, water pouring down his face.

"Afternoon, pet," he said, still trying to catch his breath.

"Look at you, swimming." She tugged at the skirt of her bathing suit before sitting down. "Next thing we know you'll be playing golf."

"I couldn't hit a beach ball with a two-by-four." He dog-paddled to the ladder, where he rested before climbing the steps. "I'm not a natural like Charles. What a pity he's given it up."

Madeline sighed as she arranged herself on the lounge. For all the chilly berth she'd been given lately, ignoring her problems was still better than having to talk about them. It wasn't just that Charles had left the game Saturday. That was bad enough, but she'd made matters worse by insisting they keep their dinner reservations, desperate to make their lives appear normal. But he'd barely touched his food and just played with his cutlery until all the commotion started. Then, of all things, he'd wanted to help Gerard pull Roger off Willard, to throw himself right in the middle of it. She'd never dug in her nails so deeply, getting him out the door.

Frank lugged his carcass out of the water and with a weary posture walked to the picket fence for his towel, leaving a watery trail. He straightened his spine as he rubbed his face, then pulled a piece of something from his nostril. "A little wet feather," he said, and wiped it on his teal bathing trunks. Then he shook his whole body like a dog, starting at his head and ending with his toes, propelling drops in a twenty-foot radius. Madeline received the brunt of this lather and, with an exaggerated motion, wiped herself dry.

"Mind if I sit here?" Frank had already laid his towel down on the lounge next to hers, which creaked as he dropped his full weight upon it. The olive-green skin under his eyes turned black. "My doctor tells me I have to exercise. I have to change my 'eating habits,' as he calls my life."

Madeline's eyes went to his waistless stomach, where beads of water dimpled and pooled. He would be a handsome man if only he hadn't been such a hungry one. "It's not good for the heart to carry around extra weight, Frank."

"There are worse things for the heart to carry around."

She blinked. She could never be quite sure if he was pulling her leg, so she turned the subject back on him. "You have the choice, Frank. You can lose weight and live longer, or not."

"Psh," he said, picking his flawless teeth. "Why live longer if I can't have my food? I'm only going to try because Vita's offered to help. She's going to make special low-fat and salt-free meals for me. She says we can do this thing together. But I don't know."

The church bell in town rang a few cheerless dongs. Frank and Madeline were contemplative for a few minutes, both looking out on the golf course as the sun ratcheted a peg lower in the sky, he mourning his excellent digestion, she a normal family. The stored heat of the day rose up from the cobblestones beneath them, and a formation of eight crows flew silently above, then swooped over the baby pool, looking to see what had been left behind.

"Tell me about your goats," said Frank, turning over with a grunt. "I didn't run out to see them the other night because I was in the middle of the most delectable little pigeon on my plate."

Madeline deflected the conversation. "I saw you with the Fishers. Such nice people."

"Yes, I give them dinner now and again because I've found that if I keep their mouths full they can't talk about me."

Madeline smiled. It was too true. Hilary used to call her every few days to retail the Club's gossip, but now Madeline was the gossip, and so Hilary had nothing to say. Madeline understood how that went. "Stop that. You know you ask them because they're fun."

"I laugh, they laugh; I have more wine, they have more wine. They draw the line at belching, though. They have their limits, I'm glad to see. And Hilary confided that I'm the only one she really likes here. It would be quite the compliment, except I happen to know she tells it to everyone. Even to Stillington. Especially to Stillington, because he controls the guest list to some museum function." Frank chuckled. "Such is the cleansing effect of art and money on a shitty personality."

Madeline flushed. Hilary had told her she was the only one she really liked here too. But unlike Frank, Madeline had believed her. Her silence went on long enough for Frank to come to her rescue and change the subject. Resting his fleshy cheek on one hand, he leaned in closer. "How is Charles? I heard he went AWOL from a game last week."

Madeline put on her sunglasses. Didn't Frank ever just want to talk about the weather? She cringed at the memory of the call from Andrew on Saturday telling her that Charles had cracked and where to collect the pieces.

"Do they forgive me, do you think, Madeline?" Charles asked when she showed up.

"Andrew seemed pretty peeved on the phone—you know how he gets. I didn't talk to Gregg or Ned."

"Not them," Charles said, pointing his club at the birds around him. "The geese. For killing one of their own."

"Charles, it was an accident," she said. "Forget it. Let's go home."

He stood up, and she took him by the arm. "Look at the light through the pines," he said. "It makes the trees translucent, transparent even. We can see through a great deal more than we give ourselves credit for."

"Charles, please. Start walking."

"I have an idea," he said, turning back to look at the birds. "Let's go to the Museum School. We can stop at the Gardner afterward."

Madeline agreed just to get him off the course, and so they walked home past the sand traps and through the calculated bits of wildness, and got in the Land Rover. She drove, since he was unable to, what with the Hawk Eye clasped to his chest. At the Museum School, where she'd thought they were going to an exhibit, Charles signed up for a sculpture class.

"I want to make something," he said when she stared at him.

"Oh." And in her head she thought she heard the distant ping of suede on crystal.

Madeline took off her sunglasses and turned to Frank. "Charles didn't go AWOL. His partners must not have understood he had an appointment to keep."

"A doctor's?"

"The Museum School, actually. He's taking a course." She choked on the words and put her glasses back on. All week, he'd been going to his metal sculpture class during long lunch hours.

God knows what the office must think of that. Then, when he came home at night, he patted the goats before locking himself in the garage to do his homework. What ever happened to their lovely little routine of a glass of wine and a rundown of their day? She should just go to the garage and invite herself in to have a look at what he was up to, but she dared not. Talking to him these days was like walking on eggs.

"Excellent." Frank hit her chaise with his hand, giving her a start. "We need more art and fewer doctors. Just today, I saw Nina Rundlett at the professional building, going to see some quack, and for nothing as far as I'm concerned. She'd just gotten back from Italy, and her father sent her to the medical group to get her throat swabbed." Frank idly pulled Madeline's beach bag toward him, tipping it to see if there wasn't any food squirreled away.

"For what?" Madeline asked. Any mention of Nina made her fidget. She pulled her bag from Frank and busied herself looking for something—she had not yet decided what.

"Anthrax, smallpox, SARS," he said, with a wave of a hand. "They've got it ass backward. Why put a healthy person through the anxiety of testing? If she was exposed to something, she'll find out soon enough."

Nina had been exposed to more than Frank would ever know. Poor girl. Poor Eliot. Him half-naked, draped in the arms of the call girl in her merry widow. It was like one of those faded Club photos hanging in the powder room. *Tableaux vivants,* a Gilded Age form of fun for which the female members would spend weeks supervising the construction of elaborate sets and costumes to create a historical scene, usually some Helen of Troy fantasy or another. They would wear diaphanous gowns and pose in frozen attitudes, glorying in their self-designed perfection.

Here they were, more than a century later, and she and Arietta had set a scene just as contrived. Wasn't there some other way to keep people from making a mistake?

She pulled out a lip balm and dabbed her lips as she talked. "Roger might just be keeping her busy to keep her mind off 'the incident.' "

Frank rolled on his back and put his hands beneath his head, exposing his furry pits to the sun. "If he wants to distract her from 'the incident,' as you so delicately call finding a hooker with your fiancé, then maybe he shouldn't go around knifing her almost in-laws."

"Frank, don't joke about something like that. The knifing was an accident. Besides, it was a forking."

"Forking, fucking, there's no such thing as an accident either way. Took Rundlett long enough to defend his daughter's honor."

Or his dead wife's honor, thought Madeline, capping the balm. Or simply his own. Arietta confirmed that batty Gwen Rundlett had spilled the paternity beans to Roger to keep him from reuniting the couple. They had to be very careful now. He might tear the Club apart looking for the truth. "People don't go around doing that sort of thing on purpose."

"You live such a sheltered existence, pet. In these treacherous times anyone could be hiding a weapon in the folds of his robe."

Madeline looked out at the hazy landscape. She didn't feel that sheltered. She felt exposed and abandoned. If she'd made more of an effort to reach beyond the narrowly defined limits of friendships here, maybe she wouldn't be left with just Frank to talk to. "It's all Phoebe's fault, with those goats." She heard her voice break up, and she swallowed. "They created so much chaos, anything could have happened."

"Don't blame the innocent creatures."

"I can blame them. They live in my backyard. They've eaten my shade garden."

"I've had goat," he said. "Delicious. A Moroccan curry, served on enamelware as delicate as stained glass. Tiny hot peppers, sweet preserved fruits, an ancient vinegar pressed from figs. Yum." He flipped himself over on the chaise like a heavy pancake, bottoms-up. "I don't suppose we'd be so lucky to have Phoebe raising those goats for our culinary pleasure?"

"Hardly." Frank's teal trunks had twisted when he flipped, pulling them down an inch and allowing her to see into the crack, an open advertisement for his profession. "She and her friends 'liberated' them from an agricultural station where they were going to be butchered. They're rescue animals; no one can eat them."

"Too bad," said Frank. "Think how plump they'll get on the golf course grass."

"That won't happen again. The fence company came this week to make a pen. Not only did Humpy insist, but so did Phoebe. She said she didn't want the goats eating the golf course grass with all its poisons."

"She's right," he said. "What they put in their bodies we put in ours."

"We're not eating these."

"Don't remind me of what I'm missing. I can't believe I have to watch what I eat from now on. Just the other day I had the most spectacular dish at the new pan-Asian place out on Mass. Ave. Short ribs braised in a Khmer broth with ginger, garlic, young coconut juice, mushrooms, tamarind, and chilies. I was just telling Vita."

"Mmmm," said Madeline. And she was not just trying to encourage him to talk about food rather than other less digestible subjects. She was starving now that Phoebe was home. Brown rice, cooked celery. Brown rice, lentils. Brown rice, yams. Phoebe was never such a picky eater as a child. Until she went off to college, she was always so obedient. Wasn't she? Or had something been hidden there all along, just waiting to get out? "Where on Mass. Ave.?"

Frank smiled. "Already a war of attrition at the house?"

"You know Phoebe," she said, trying to sound light. "It's hard to eat anything without her looking at us like the condemned."

"She's got that food disorder," he said, flipping back again and raising his lounge to a sitting position. When he was fully upright, he burped, like someone who could burp the alphabet. "*Orthorexia nervosa*. People who are so obsessed with health food that they develop phobias about regular food. They think that purer food will make them purer people."

Was everyone in her family doomed to one insanity or another? "It's just a phase," she said. "All young people go through some crazy thing or other, it seems. Like the lifeguard." She pointed her chin toward the pool house, where Scott stood stretching in the doorway. "He has a piece of metal stuck in his tongue. What do you think could be the point of that? You can't even see it."

"It's not how it's seen," said Frank. "It's how it feels that counts."

"I don't understand."

"Oh, that cloistered world of yours, pet. That stud in his mouth, it's like peacock feathers. The females of the species love it."

"What?"

"The tongue stud is to attract sexual partners."

"Don't be ridiculous," she said, laughing. "It's not a Porsche."

"Don't confuse a sex symbol with sex. Not every male can afford to attract mates with the power of his possessions, so he has to come up with an alternative strategy. Scotty's tongue stud has to do with enhancing the sexual pleasure of a woman."

"You mean, when they kiss?"

"Yes and no," said Frank, with a wet smile. "Let me explain. Some people are uncomfortable talking about labial folds and clitoral response, but not me. I'm a medical professional. Now stop me if I get too explicit . . ."

"Stop." Madeline looked over at Scott, who was walking back to his chair, staring at her, and when he smiled, she thought she saw the sparkle of metal between his parted lips. She bent her head to hide her face as she gathered her things, dropping and picking up her sunglasses twice in the process. "I've got to run, Frank. I'm late for a flower-arranging class down at the Community Center." Which was true, she'd signed up last week, but she hadn't planned to go after she'd heard that the instructor was sort of "out there." But the excuse came in handy now, so she might as well just do it. What else did she have to fill up her time, after all?

"I need to attract a mate," said Frank, still smiling to bursting. "If I'm going to give up fat, I'll need a replacement to keep me warm at night. But I'm afraid a metal tongue stud will throw off the taste of wine."

She threw a beach shift over her bathing suit, not even bothering to go inside to change. She gave Frank a lame smile as a good-bye, then left. He threw her a kiss she did not see, then cradled his stomach warmly in his arms, like a baby.

Chapter Twelve

The Divots

HOLD ON, hold on." Ralph Bellows shushed his three buddies from the Hunt Club, Anthony Paxton, Goody Cooke, and Malloch Smith. They were all drunk, it was almost dawn, and they were uncomfortably squeezed into a single golf cart with gun cases rattling in the back. The gentle curves of the course rose and fell like heavy tides to their inebriated senses.

"Stop," said Cooke. "For God's sake. I'm going to spew."

"Almos' there," said Bellows. "Quiet. Ssh. There's houses along here."

"Houses?" said Paxton, swaying gently left and right in the backseat with Cooke, excitement and alcohol competing for his posture. "What are the geese doing in houses?"

"That's not even sporting," said Smith. "I'm going to shoot one out of the air, like a man." He was ordinarily sullen, but tonight he was buoyed up by the adventure and was now almost annoyingly cheerful. He, like Paxton and Cooke, was still dressed in the tailored suit he'd begun the evening in, minus jacket and tie.

"The geese aren't in the houses, you idiots," said Bellows, who, without any self-consciousness, had taken time to put on his sandy tweeds, a Norfolk jacket, and a pith helmet before leaving his apartment, where the men had made their plan. Earlier in the day, their wives had announced preemptive headaches, so it had been stag night from the start, beginning with the Somerset Club. The four men had attended a banquet hosted by an old school chum who was whiling away time until his indictments were handed down. The many-coursed dinner had displayed his power and desirability, no mean trick in the face of certain financial ruin. There was a game fellow, Bellows and his friends agreed, and they made heartfelt toasts to his past business achievements, back in the days when avarice was no crime at all.

Then the foursome went for nightcaps at Bellows's place on Louisburg Square, where he lived alone after the recent dissolution of his second marriage. They sipped a venerable liquor bottled the year before the Depression began, because Bellows liked to provide the best to people who knew what they were drinking. They got deliberately drunk, and the closer they got to the bottom of the bottle, the closer they came to being the boys they were at Andover. They munched on the apples of their youth into the wee hours, wandering in the land of golden shadows. Goalposts and the Lower Field. The sound of Coach irritably shouting their names. From the amber spirits, they conjured up the day when they had skipped English composition to shoot squirrels with the BB gun smuggled from Paxton's home. Bellows suddenly remembered the geese at the Club.

"Wouldn't it be a bit of fun, eh?" he'd said, and after one *pour la route,* they were off. It was four in the morning.

Before they left, Bellows had brewed a thermos full of strong coffee and filled a flask with brandy for warmth, even though, being late July, you could have fried an egg on the sidewalk. But it was brisk September in their heads, the fresh start of an Andover semester: the smell of rain on fallen leaves, wood smoke twirling in thermals, the stiffness of new clothes. It had been a time of hope. They loaded Bellows's collection of shotguns into the back of his Lexus SUV and took back roads so as not to draw notice from the police. They had expected to scale the brick wall of the Club but had found the service entrance unlocked.

"That jackass, Wilton," Bellows had said. "Can't even lock the door behind him anymore. No wonder the place is falling apart."

"Can't we scale the wall anyway?" wondered Paxton, and no one answered him.

After they'd found a golf cart, they spent a good long time traveling in circles in the dark looking for their prey and threatening to be ill. Bellows drove haltingly because he was driving blind as well as drunk, since, for security reasons, he didn't turn on the headlights. Suddenly he was spitting with excitement. "The geese are down there, by the water, sleepin'. See 'em?" The sky was a sickly grayish color, which made it impossible to see anything with great certainty, but he sped toward them, the electric cart silently gliding like a sled over the turf.

"'By the dawn's early light . . . '," Smith, a sentimental drunk, began to sing mournfully.

"Isn't that a tree up ahead?" asked Cooke.

"Possibly," said Bellows, not slowing down or redirecting the cart. "It's crisis, after all, that tests the basic soundness of a man. I wonder if I packed the goose call?"

"I've always welcomed obstacles myself," said Paxton.

As the obstacle hove rapidly into view, it announced itself as definitely being a tree, and they all lurched forward when Bellows braked hard. Smith's fine voice was abruptly cut off at "the land of the free."

They decided to set up camp. "Distribute the firearms," ordered Bellows, and they organized the guns, which had tumbled out of the back of the cart. The men crawled for their weapons in the dim light.

"Shouldn't we build some sort of blind?" said Paxton, unlatching the leather gun case.

"No need," said Bellows. "It's too dark for them to see us."

"'It's always darkest before the dawn,'" said Cooke, leaning against the tree to steady his stomach.

"If we can see *them* . . . ," said Paxton.

"Wish I had my old hunting dog, Beau," said Smith, his voice cracking in grief. "He could retrieve an egg without cracking it."

"We're not going to retrieve the damn things," said Bellows, looking at the other three for signs of intelligence. "Are we? Those Canada geese are foul."

"Ha!" said Cooke. "Foul? *F-o-u-l.* Fowl? *F-o-w-l.* See what I mean?"

"Sssh," said Bellows. "Everyone sees what you mean, it's just that everyone sees it as stupid. Get your gun and don't drop the box of shells. And be quiet. We don't want to wake them yet."

"Who's going to flush them out?" said Smith, sinking into alcoholic gloom. "We don't have a dog with us. Beau was a tremendous flusher. God, I miss him."

"Please," said Paxton. "It's been twenty years. He was just a dog."

"What would you know about dogs if you've never had anything but pit bulls?"

"But I've never had a pit bull," said Paxton indignantly. "I've only ever had goldens and you know it. Claire wouldn't have anything else in the house."

"Oh, you get my point," Smith said, wiping his eyes. "Hand me that gun."

"Where's *my* gun?" asked Cooke, sinking now to the base of the tree in a squat.

"It'd be a whole lot easier to shoot them in their sleep," said Paxton, squinting in the crosshairs, pointing his gun up at the sky, then lowering it down to the sleeping geese. "Seems like a lot of trouble to scare them up."

"We're hunters," said Bellows disagreeably. "We're going to shoot a quick round, bag as many as we can, then speed away before the neighbors wake up or security swings by. Ready? Prepare for engagement."

"*Primus, maximus, optimus,*" said Smith as he cocked his shotgun. The first, the greatest, the best.

"Where's my gun?" Cooke whispered, curled up at the base of the tree, his eyes closed tight.

Paxton cocked. Smith knelt. "Shoot quickly when they take off," Bellows said. "And if you can't see, shoot at the sound." He threw a small rock near the settlement of sleeping geese, but their heads remained tucked neatly under their wings.

"The spirit of a lion cannot be roused by the teasing of an insect," announced Smith, his voice thick with emotion. "Someone said that, and it's true. Beau was no tease, and neither should we be," he said, bending to pick up a stick and swaying slightly on becoming upright again.

"I've shot a lion," said Bellows, leaning on his shotgun. "From a helicopter, but then the hide was confiscated at the border. I paid a fortune in fines. They're all in on it. It's a racket, it's all a racket."

Once Smith steadied himself, he threw the stick at the geese as if playing fetch. The startled birds squawked and honked, waking one another up. They stood on their webbed toes and raised their long necks in alarm, but it took another rock from Bellows to encourage a couple of them airborne.

"Fore!" shouted Paxton, and fired.

Chapter Thirteen

The Wayward Shot

"HERE, GOOSEY, goosey, gander," Vita whispered, tiptoeing across the small sandy shoal to where the geese slept in the watery underbrush. It was five thirty in the morning, time for the Early Bird Special. "*El ganso,* come eat." She sometimes spoke to them in Spanish because it made her feel closer to what she imagined were her family's agrarian roots back in Colombia, even though the geese didn't care whether words or stones fell from her mouth. Their common language was food. Her kind of relationship.

The thirty or so geese who slept on the island were developing healthy profiles thanks to the bird buffet that Vita had been hostessing morning and night for two weeks. It was worth the extra effort to row to the island geese because it was cheaper than feeding the huge mainland flock. She did not want the common hordes to get in on the cornmeal action. Ever the efficient kitchen statistician, she only wanted to fatten up as many as she could use. She should have just enough for a hundred plates, since she guessed that at most only half of the members would care for goose. But Dr. Nicastro would. He would roll around in the grass with one if he could, and butter himself with foie gras! Hers wouldn't be the traditional bloated liver of the Toulouse geese either, whose webbed feet were hammered to barn floors so that cornmeal could be funneled down their throats. Her livers would be smaller, but they'd have much better Karma. She wouldn't have enough to go around, but there was plenty for those who could appreciate its subtleties.

She heard her birds shaking themselves awake. She cooed softly, "Here, honey. Eat, eat." She made kissing noises, and they ran to her, the young and the old, the sleepy and the alert. The male and female? Gender was a mystery, but it didn't matter. Females were tastier as a rule, but with enough hanging, she was going to tame the vile hormones out of the male. She thought ruefully of the female's thicker layer of subcutaneous fat and pinched her waist. The geese spread out their wings and thrust their humped necks forward, but Vita calmed them with food. They lowered their heads and vacuumed up the grain, arguing quietly among themselves. She did not want them to honk, or else they'd attract the geese from the mainland, and after them, the opportunistic crows would arrive, dive-bombing her for food and creating a scene, as they do.

Here, as in the dining room, Vita demanded a calm atmosphere for proper digestion. She knew that much of what tastes like good food was really just a peaceful setting, and that's why she made the effort to arrive on the island so early, cutting into what little sleep any one chef was allotted in a lifetime. She had also learned, after an unintended drenching, to finish up before the automatic sprinkler system went on. Then there was Gerard. With his canine devotion to the Club, he arrived at the crack of dawn some days, and she did not want to alarm him with her new venture in goose husbandry. She was so early at the Club that she often bumped into the cleaning service, all those Brazilian girls dusting and emptying trash and chattering away in Portuguese. It was strange to meet people who looked Latina like her but who spoke another language. Same people, different conquerors. Vita would have liked to offer them a little pastry, but by the time she got the kitchen up and going, the crew was always long gone.

While she waited for the geese to clean up the feed, she poked around in the leaf litter for mushrooms. To think she had once completely relied on that swinish Utah for her raw ingredients! No more. How elemental she felt now, so in tune with food and its origins. What a fool she had been to think that a domestic bird could do the job! An animal that had not lived had no tale to tell on the table. If a bird could not fly, could not pluck grass, could not engage in relationships and saunter freely through the world, such a bird was just so much dead meat. A heavyset bullfrog leaped out from behind a rock, and she watched him slip into the water, creating silent circles where he'd disappeared. Most people said they didn't like frog, but what they didn't like was frozen frog. She knew that fresh frog, skinned right over the pan, was heavenly. Next time she would bring a net. She wondered how many calories were in a frog.

One of the geese jabbed at her leg with his beak, treating her like a mechanical dispenser of feed, and it worked. She shook out the last of the cornmeal, all the while wishing she had a bird to practice on. She felt so ineffectual next to Luisa's mother, the talented Mrs. Suarez, able to take a bird as ornery as a Canada goose and hang it by its scaly ankles until its flesh was made not just palatable but divine. It was a process that took more than a week, but it was going to be worth it. The memory of that first bite still lingered on Vita's tongue.

A goose rubbed against her leg as it passed, and she inhaled deeply to capture its acrid essence, as elemental as warm mud. She wished she could do the night feedings as well, but she could not be spared from the kitchen. Before dark, Luisa rowed out with their dinner, the only one of her workers who knew what the banquet plans were. She'd had to confide in Barry too, who was horrified, and for a moment Vita was afraid he might even turn her in to Gerard, but it had to be done. She needed a favor: There could be no herbicides or pesticides, no fungicides or fertilizers, nothing whatsoever, applied to the turf until after the butchering. The chemicals would poison the flesh.

She had picked up fluffy Forbes and kissed him on the head.

"That toxic grass isn't good for this little guy either, you know. It could give him tumors."

Barry took his bird back from Vita and hugged it to him. "Tumors?"

"There are courses you can take to learn other ways, Barry."

"I spent four years in college to learn how to superintend greens and you tell me I have to go back?"

"Sometimes we have to go back before we can go forward," she said, and stroked the top of Forbes's feathery head.

"Tumors, huh?"

And so the greens went green, cold turkey, and none the wiser. Barry, whose career depended upon the perfection of his fairways, hunted down organic alternatives to chemicals on the Internet and signed up for a course on integrated pest management at the Aggie. He spent his days in his office shed with Forbes, pulverizing insects and hot peppers in a blender, making his own natural pesticides. He praised the earthworm with a lover's passion.

Vita stood guard over her feathered friends and watched them finish the main course; then she pulled out a black garbage bag from the skiff filled with all the kitchen leftovers from the night before and tossed them on the ground as a dessert. The birds were vegans, so Vita did not save meat or dairy or eggs, but there were vegetable parings, outer leaves of lettuce from the salad station, and all the rolls that had been left untouched on the bread plates, the sacrificial lamb of many a diet. Onion skins and carrot ends she kept for her stockpots, which she needed more than ever now that she was cooking special dishes for Dr. Nicastro, making exquisite fatless, low-salt stock to use as a base for sauces instead of cream. She still wanted to tantalize his taste buds, even though she must no longer contribute to his flesh.

As the sun began to glimmer on the horizon, she threw the empty bag into the plastic skiff and launched it back into the water for the short row back to the mainland. She fixed the oars in the locks, leaned forward, and pulled back in a stroke, propelling the boat across the surface. Some mornings she took the skiff for a quick spin around the lake before heading back to the Club just because she enjoyed it, not to mention the need to control that subcutaneous layer of fat. But she had lingered too long and had to hurry now in order to miss the sprinklers.

"Damnation," she whispered to herself just as she was getting ashore. She saw the silhouettes of four men in the distance, across the water. Was it the rat exterminators, who conducted their nefarious business in the off hours? Or impatient golfers? She wondered if one of them might not be that nice Mr. Amory, who'd been so cute all summer, always first at tee, so eager to start chasing his little white ball around the course. But no. This was a rowdy bunch, crouching and stumbling over by Trough with their clubs raised, playacting. She would have to start locking the service gate behind her.

"Just like little boys," she muttered as she got out and pulled the boat up to its regular spot. She turned and peered again, trying to identify them at this distance and in the dim light, but couldn't. Two geese were flying toward her, soaring flashes against a colorless sky.

"Too late," she called to them. "Go find your own breakfast."

A storm of blasts broke the morning air, shaking thousands of feathered beasts out of the branches and up off the ground in a single roar of wings. *Snipers?* Hunters? The blasts came again and she screamed. An airborne goose seemed to pause to reconsider its flight path, then dropped, hurtling toward the earth. The bird splashed, half in, half out of the water. If it had landed on her it could have killed her, and she hunkered down. Just then the sprinkler system came on, forming a series of watery V's on the course. Some spray hit her in the face, and so she screamed again but stopped when she heard the men curse and yelp, quickly gathering themselves up and scooting away in the cart.

When all was quiet, Vita stood and stared at the rolling fairways spouting water in the pink glow of dawn. The mainland geese were scattered and distressed. She hoped her own flock was not too upset, for anxiety at this stage might cause weight loss, or a flush of enzymes that would taint the meat. She bent to attend to the fallen goose. Its head hung limply at the end of its neck, and blood oozed from the cavity of shot that had entered its chest.

The goose had landed in such a way as to snap a wing back violently, almost severing it from its body. How odd to have poachers, she thought; it was practically feudal.

She looked around. Homeowners would report the blasts, if they hadn't done so already. She stared at the bird. The police would want it for evidence. But she had just prayed for a bird to practice on, and look, one had fallen from the sky. It was a goose from God. She stuffed the still-limber carcass under the skiff seat, casually arranging the garbage and feed bags over it. She'd send Merle to get it later. He owed her for letting him have access to the kitchen and its ice machine even after Gerard forbade the caddies such freedom. Merle could sneak the bird back to the kitchen later, in a golf bag.

She rinsed her hands of blood in the lake water, then stood, facing the long rise to the clubhouse. If the police wanted to know what all the noise had been, she would tell them, within limits, what she knew. As she ducked and darted through the forest of sprinklers, nine crows circled above in the fresh morning air.

Chapter Fourteen

The Greens Committee

PHOEBE STOPPED at the bottom of her lawn to adjust her rubber sandals, really wishing she'd worn the soft leather ones instead. But she'd sworn off wearing the skin of other species, and this time she meant it. Still, it would be nice not to have to cope with stupid blisters right now. After all, she didn't want to miss seeing the police bring Mr. Bellows and his merry band of killers to justice. She couldn't wait! And it was all because of her. *She* was the one who dialed 911, standing naked at her third-floor window, her heart still pounding from being woken by blasts; *she* was the one who witnessed their overloaded golf cart retreating through the sprinklers like some crazy windup toy.

"You'd better block the exits of the Club," she told the police dispatcher, kicking the pile of clothes on the floor until her denim shorts rose to the surface. "I'll meet you guys over there."

She hung up the phone, found her PETA T-shirt in the rubble, and, as she tied her dreads back, examined the course again from her bird's-eye view. It was from that very spot, after her first violent jolt from her futon, that she'd seen the goose fall through the purple sky. But all was quiet now. Was it dead for sure? She hadn't seen them retrieve a body, so maybe there was hope.

She hurried, not even putting on her beads, and headed out of the house to the course she'd known her whole life, since before her family moved in after her grandfather died and her grandmother moved to Florida. It was a kids' paradise, even if she did have to play by herself most of the time. She didn't have sibs and not much going on in the way of chums either. There weren't many other houses in the neighborhood back then, and even though her mom arranged all these playdates for her, it was harder to arrange for friends. She must have been born into some demographic black hole because there were hardly any kids her age at the Club either. And most of *them* were prissy things anyway, even the boys, none wanting to build elf-houses with her or help her construct stone-lined mazes. But it was just as well if they were all destined to grow up to be like Mr. Bellows in his silly helmet, playing British imperialist. Anyway, she always had Ben, half black Lab, half standard poodle, the result of some wild escape at the breeder's but just the greatest dog. He died of old age and heartbreak during her first semester away at college. Home still seemed empty without him.

She shushed the goats and clicked the back gate behind her quietly, not wanting to wake her parents, who would try to keep her from her mission, the way they were so tight with the other members. Or used to be. Something was going on with them now, though, something *totally* weird. Dad hammering away in the garage nights and weekends like some deranged gremlin, and Mom sitting on the screened porch with her wine watching the garage, no one saying boo.

But when did the two of them ever say boo about anything? They were so dormant they'd barely commented on her new dreadlocks, which were sort of a pain, cool as they were, so people had better notice. But all Mom could say was "Oh." And they wouldn't even fight for their food. Where was the reward in converting them to vegan when there was no philosophical battle? She felt her whole education at Evergreen College was going to waste, all her books and papers and statistics on the fragility of the planet—how would her parents *really* understand if they never got to hear what she'd learned? Mom still brought home ice cream, like it was exempt. If only! Not a word about flavor either, the one argument she would have lost. She was only human, after all. Right? But not Eric. No-o-o. When he found a Dove Bar wrapper in the backseat of her VW he accused her of being more interested in her own desires than in stopping the suffering of animals.

She had to pause for a minute on the course and wipe her eyes on her shirt. He'd told her . . . he'd told her she was just one of those rich white kids who joined movements so they could feel good about themselves.

Well, when was it, exactly, that this good feeling was supposed to start? She sniffed and continued walking, keeping her distance from the sprinklers and thinking back to her rebuttal, which was maybe a bit more truthful than she'd intended. "A-and *you* are such a dry, sanctimonious stick sometimes," she'd stammered. "It's *your* fault I have to take my pleasure in ice cream because I'm certainly not getting it in *bed*."

He left that afternoon to join a raw-foods collective in the Willamette Valley. After a week of lonely nights, when it was clear that he was gone for good, she moved back east to lick her wounds and regroup.

"Ahh!" Phoebe looked up and saw a shocking white heron with legs dangling, flapping overhead. It must have flown off when the guns sounded, and now, somehow, in that magical way that animals had, it figured it was safe to come back home again. As much as the Club tried, it could not kill all beauty. The grounds crew in their white hazmat suits were always tormenting the land with power equipment, spray-gunning poison, saturating the air and the earth until the birds began to teeter on shaky legs, then die. She'd seen the butterflies become still, then disappear; she'd listened to the peeping of the frogs grow weak, then silent. The Club's chemicals seemed to kill everything except for the geese, somehow immune, so now Mr. Bellows was sent to finish the job. If only there were an emergency number to report the crime of total ecological annihilation.

She walked beside a manicured hedge and ran her hand along its flat top. Like this place was some real environment! It was sort of crazy, the way she loved the course and wanted to help it, for all its artificiality. It wasn't exactly like saving the redwood forest. Most of the tree species weren't even native, and even those that were were kept at some ideal, unchanging size with saws. There was a Norway spruce up by the clubhouse that was pruned so unnaturally it looked like a cell phone tree. The gullies were fake, the creek beds phony, and the falling off at the end of the course beyond Hole #2, where once it had seemed to her that the earth's crust had truly ended, was as much a Victorian folly as the little stone bridges that spanned nothing at all. And the lake . . . oh God, the lake! . . . *it* was lined with clay and as tidy as a kidney-shaped bathtub, kept sterile and blue with Aquashade. She couldn't imagine what the geese even saw in it, except that maybe they had nowhere else to go.

And that was really it, wasn't it? Where were they all to go now that their old habitat surrounding the course had been stripped away? What that rat-bastard Eric would have called a "Northeastern mixed-woods ecosystem," and what she simply called her old woods, full of birch and maples and scrub, had been totally replaced by mansions built so close together they cast one another in shadow. They had lifeless lawns, and on these sterile green carpets sprouted not trees, not even gnomes, but warning signs of ARMED RESPONSE. *Armed response.* She came back from college one day and she felt like she was surrounded by the military.

Because of this, the golf course had become the last refuge for the little creatures. Not just the birds, but fox, deer, raccoons, fishers, squirrels, chipmunks, all feeding on the tainted turf, messing up their DNA for the next generation of wildlife, the next generation of *us*. Didn't they *get it?* Poison a single amoeba with herbicides and the next thing you know, wham, another case of breast cancer in the world, and the researchers still shaking their heads about where it all starts as they play another round of *golf.*

A few geese had returned to the scene of the crime, tentatively plucking at the turf. One hissed at her as she passed, carefully making her way down the slope, where she found golf cart marks but no dead or dying goose. A squirrel chattered at her from a tree branch, and she looked up. Hmmm. If the Club balked at going organic on the basis of reason, well then, maybe she would just chain herself to this handsome oak until they saw the light. Of course, she'd have to work out the logistics of food and facilities, and she wasn't real sure about using a bucket, but there were some things that had to be endured for a greater good, and that might be one of them.

She widened her circle, hoping against hope to find the goose still alive, but nothing. It must have fallen in the lake. But . . . What was *that?*

A gun. One of those dodoes must have dropped it. The barrel was cold, so it hadn't been fired. She knew she shouldn't, but she picked it up, ran her hand along the polished wood, and, after checking to make sure it wasn't loaded, rested the butt against her right shoulder. Her grandfather had brought her out to the range once and showed her how to shoot skeets. It was her best memory of the old guy. She looked down the length of the barrel, aimed it in the direction of the clubhouse, and laughed at herself.

She lowered the gun. She and her buddies at ALF, the Animal Liberation Frontier, had been kicking around the idea of freeing some turkeys from what Eric used to call a CAFO—a Confined Animal Feeding Operation—and what she still called a farm. Bentham's Farm over on Route 2, where her mom used to bring her to see the turkeys, some of them Bronze Beauties, with their bright feathers and purple wattles, just like out of her picture books. The birds scratched and mingled in the fields together. But those fields were gone now, sucked up by development, the poor turkeys imprisoned in long corrugated buildings with no room to lift their wings. Didn't anyone understand that the suffering of animals was the suffering of us *all?*

But how was she going to end this suffering if she was too afraid to go on missions? When she helped liberate the goats a few weeks ago she'd almost got them all caught because she froze. But what if she had the gun with her, to give her confidence? Not even to point, just to have hanging around, like she meant business. She couldn't *really* get in trouble if it wasn't loaded, could she? After all, unlike some ALF members, she prided herself on drawing the line at sabotage and arson. Keeping an unloaded gun seemed pretty tame compared to that.

She heard a siren out on Eden Road. She had to hurry. Clutching the gun, practically scrambling up the slope on all fours, she ran back to her yard. When the goats saw her they propped their hooves on the top of the wire fence and cocked their heads, thinking of breakfast. Instead, Phoebe entered their pen and hid the gun in the eaves of their shed.

"I'll be right back," she whispered, and kissed the black one on his musky forehead. "I've got to go save the Earth from idiots." The white one baaed, and so she kissed him too. "If only idiots knew they were idiots," she whispered into his silky ear. Then she headed back to the Club to tell the police, within limits, what she knew. She thought maybe she'd better not say she'd seen Mr. Bellows and his friends shooting, because now that she'd taken the gun, she didn't want to get in trouble herself. The police would catch the offenders without her testimony. She hoped. As she tromped through the course, her feet rubbed raw from the stupid rubber sandals, a band of crows swept through the air in formation above her, flying to the lake.

Chapter Fifteen

A Few Practice Swings

GERARD WAS FEELING very smug as he stood in the early morning air near the sheltering presence of his clubhouse. The world seemed green, luxuriantly green. And to think it had been so recently bleak. When he'd arrived at the Club, the adrenaline froze in his marrow at the sight of Phoebe Lambert talking to the police. Then an asphyxiating constriction seized his throat when he saw a photographer from the *Boston Globe,* who told Gerard—when Gerard informed him he would have to leave the premises—that he had picked up the news of gunshots at the Club over the police radio.

Bellows. Gerard had almost said the name out loud, and looked around in a panic. If it was Bellows, he'd better have gone far and fast. If he was caught, Gerard was sure to be implicated. He was the one, after all, who had, in a moment of desperation, brought up the subject of goose hunting. And yet, in spite of the legal and professional circles of hell that were opening before him, he could not help wondering if Bellows had made any dent in the goose population.

Gerard had taken immediate control of the situation, successfully insinuating himself in between Phoebe and the police, talking over her. He jabbered his name, his occupation, and his deep regret that the police had been called out on what could only be a false, incredibly false, alarm. He jostled Phoebe, trying to push her away from the authorities, and as he did he could feel, through the fine mesh of his pink ERCC polo shirt at his shoulder blades, her nipples. She was not wearing a bra. This realization stunned him, so that it took a second before he understood that she was telling the police she wasn't sure if she'd heard guns or backfire.

Gerard moved out of her orbit to give her space, carrying with him a whiff of incense, and he looked at her. Her skin, smooth as milk, still showed the imprints of rumpled sheets, and as his eyes slid down to her toes, he caught the sight of a tattoo on her calf: a teeny Earth, splitting open like an egg. "You know those SUVs," she continued. "Anything they do, even backfiring, impacts the environment in a negative way. Some noise woke me up, and when I saw those dudes out on the course, I freaked and assumed it was them. But they might have just been playing golf or something. You'd better track them down and ask them yourself."

Vita, who'd been standing outside this circle waiting to be pulled in, stared at Phoebe too, wondering. There was no reason on earth why she'd want to protect goose hunters. Unless, of course, she knew one of them. Vita had heard rumors that Mr. Lambert had been losing it ever since he killed that goose. Maybe he was one of those poor souls who was compelled to repeat a trauma over and over again.

Her old snack bar help, Scott, arrived, stripped down to his black swimming trunks and Birkenstocks for working at the pool, but she still felt a proprietary right to his time. "Scotty, go fetch some coffee," said Vita, pointing toward the police officers. "And take last night's ladyfingers out of the walk-in."

One of the officers went inside to talk to the cleaning crew, and the other one turned and nodded to Vita in recognition. It was Officer Dyer, the same one who'd come round for the stabbing incident. "You were here, Ms. Pasto, when the blast occurred?"

"I was." Vita smiled, playing with the neck of her sweatshirt. "I sometimes come early to take a walk, and I heard a loud blast just as the sun came up. It was probably nothing. A backfire or two from beyond the wall."

"Did it sound like a gun?" he asked

"I'm not familiar with the sound."

"Okay then." Officer Dyer's eyebrow hairs bristled like antennae. "Maybe you could tell me why your clothes are soaked."

Vita looked down at herself, spattered with water. "Right after the shooting the sprinklers came on, and I had to walk back through the spray."

"Shooting?"

"The backfire. The noise. Whatever it was."

Phoebe looked at Vita, wondering who or what she was protecting. If Vita really was on the course, then she would have *known* it was a shooting. Why didn't she just say so and get this over with so Phoebe could have her gun *and* get the goose murderers busted? And what was Vita doing at the Club then anyway? Eric used to bring all sorts of shit home from the café where he'd worked, and he did it by going to work early and hiding stuff, coming back for it later. Maybe that's what Vita was up to. Phoebe wouldn't put anything past someone whose job it was to chop up pieces of animals and make people eat them.

But this was no time to bring all that up, not if she wanted to protect her gun. The police should just go looking for clues and leave her alone. "It could have been either," Phoebe mused as she scratched her exposed stomach. "A backfire from a pig car could sound like an army." Officer Dyer looked up from his pad.

"Horrid things, those SUVs," said Gerard, hoping to get them all to agree that that's what the sound was and leave him and his Club alone. He wished Phoebe would leave her stomach alone too. With great willpower, he forced his gaze from her abdomen to her hair, which was twisted into ropey things, but it had its own charm, as did the hoops that lined the crescent of her left ear. He especially liked her crisp little mouth, her upper lip a wedge of pink that moved quickly and mechanically when she talked.

Phoebe regarded Gerard in return. He'd always reminded her of *someone,* but she could never put her finger on who. And what was up with this environmental awareness? He was so mulish last summer when she'd tried to make some changes around here, but maybe he was ready to listen to reason. She was thinking of how she might work on him, when her thoughts were interrupted by the sound of tires crunching into the turnaround. Ugh. Mr. Clendenning. Look at him, parking his Stinking Unforgivable Violator so Mr. Amory in his little sedan couldn't even squeeze by.

Gerard, on seeing Clendenning, didn't feel quite so smug anymore. But it was still okay. It was probably just a backfire. A backfire and an impetuous, braless young woman.

"It's nothing," he shouted, two octaves too high, to Clendenning, who sat in his car with the window rolled down, looking at the group with suspicion and at Gerard with offense. Even his Grand Cherokee seemed threatening, its vertical grille reflecting the red morning light like fangs. "Everyone was just leaving," Gerard continued, exaggerating a calm he did not feel.

No, they can't leave, thought Phoebe. The police had to stay and figure it out on their own. She looked around, wondering what she could do to lead them to Mr. Bellows, when her eyes met Vita's. Their exchange was dark and appraising.

Clendenning, as segmented as a wooden snake, unfolded his body from the driver's side, while Gerard opened the passenger door for his granddaughter. The girl, Leila, with her overshot lip and unblinking eyes, was clearly from the same Clendenning batter. She jumped down and landed purposely close to his feet, making him leap back. She made an elaborate show of adjusting her golf skirt while he chuckled at her little joke.

Clendenning, like most of his peers, viewed the police as a service agency, and so only gave the officer a brisk nod before turning his attention to Phoebe. "Miss Lambert," he said, putting a great deal of spin on the greeting.

"*Ms.* Lambert," she corrected him. "We were just talking about your car. You know, the way you SUV dudes are burning up the future of our doomed planet."

Gerard braced himself, but Clendenning only nodded at her, then turned his eyes upon Gerard. His face was expressionless, but Gerard could read it well.

"Everything's fine," Gerard chirped. "There was a sharp noise in the street, and I guess *Ms.* Lambert got jumpy and called the police. Everyone's just getting ready to leave."

"And him?" Clendenning said, pointing his stately nose in the direction of the photographer, who was slumped against the hood of his car, disappointed in the morning's catch. "Can't the police arrest him for trespassing?"

Then Clendenning turned on his heels, back to his car to get his clubs, letting Gerard do the dirty work of making his whim a reality. Before Gerard could say, "Yes, sir," Scott arrived with a tray of coffee and pastry, which attracted not just the police officer but the photographer, and while they were all together, Gerard moved toward them with open arms, trying to shepherd them to their cars. There was a loud commotion of crows over by the lake, and everyone glanced up.

Barry came out of the side door of the clubhouse. "Vita," he called. "Your mom phoned. Wants you to call her."

Vita saw Scott smile as he passed the coffee tray around. Her mother's calls had become a running joke. "Thank you, Barry," she said, in that way that really means *fuck you*. "I'll call her later."

He smiled and turned to go back inside, but then put his hands on his waist and whistled softly at the sight of all the crows in the sky. Forbes stood at attention by his khakied leg. Gerard mouthed, "Hide that bird," and Barry tried to hustle Forbes along. It was at that moment Leila saw him and screamed out, "Forbes, my baby boy," running up the steps and collecting the gosling in her arms. All the children at the Club knew him and had joined with Barry in an unspoken conspiracy to keep Forbes safe from the adults, who as a rule rarely saw what they weren't supposed to see anyway. But Leila seemed to have no such code of honor and fondled the gosling with impunity, even though it might mean his removal from the Club.

"Put that creature down, Leila," said Clendenning. "Wilton, what is that animal doing here?"

"Keep your friends close and your enemies closer?" Gerard said, with a squeak.

The other officer emerged from the clubhouse and told Dyer that the cleaning crew's van had been sideswiped by a car leaving the Club when they were coming to work. He'd already called in the license number to the station.

Gerard and Clendenning reluctantly joined the police to deliberate about this mystery car while Phoebe glowed with satisfaction, happy to have the killing unfold naturally in front of them all. A crow flew low over her head, carrying a tidbit in its beak. Then came another.

"Barry, go down there." Gerard turned to him, not needing the distraction of birds right then. "Take away whatever it is they're fighting over."

Vita was worried. Maybe the crows were having a go at the scraps she left for her flock, although it sounded like the cries were on the shore, not the island.

The skiff! She put her hand to her mouth. Her goose! She'd seen crows eviscerate a roadkill rabbit in minutes. It was too late to make a run down there and save her hide by saving the goose, so she slipped away from the group and headed for her sanctuary, the kitchen.

"One of those birds dropped something," said Clendenning. "Barry, go clean that up."

Gerard felt this as a rebuke to his own authority. "Yes, Barry, take that with you when you go."

But when Barry bent to pick it up, he let out a whimper. In his hands was a piece of goose flesh, the black feathers wet with blood. Just then, another crow flew overhead, lugging a bloody string of intestine behind him. But he'd been too greedy and had to let it go. A third crow dove for it but missed, so that the length of gut splatted on the hood of the gold Grand Cherokee.

"Ewwww!" said Leila, screwing up her face. "Gross!"

Forbes squeaked in her arms and raised his stubby wings to Barry, who hurried to protect his gosling from the ghoulish sight of feathered flesh falling from the sky. As the anxious bird was transferred from arm to arm, it pooped on Leila, and she released a wail that raised the white hairs on her grandfather's neck.

Phoebe walked over to the SUV and stared at the goose gut. "Poor dead thing," she whispered. She would avenge its death, even if she could not testify on its behalf. She couldn't wait to contact her ALF people and hatch a plan of action.

Gerard continued talking to the officers about what the cleaning crew may or may not have seen, making believe nothing was happening, but the police nodded at each other and headed down to the lake. Dozens of crows were clustered at the skiff, grabbing shreds of Bellows's goose from one another in midair, making one another release pieces, swooping in greed and retaliation. The crows that had grabbed the most had the most to lose, dropping strips of goose along the fairway, almost hitting the officers.

The *Boston Globe* photographer ran two steps behind them, as was his habit.

Chapter Sixteen

Pulling the Stroke

ARIETTA WINGATE drew the ruby-colored drapes tightly across the diamond panes and blocked out the world. As she retreated to her chair by the sputtering hearth, she ran her fingers along the undisturbed leather-bound volumes that lent the library an intellectual calm. Bedlam might take the day outside, but here, all was order and civilization. She noticed a trace of dust on her puckered skin, like ash. She tched, then tched again. Taking a lace handkerchief from her sleeve, she wiped her hands clean. Gerard Wilton had certainly gone soft on standards this summer, what with geese falling dead left and right. On the other hand, the Club might fall apart altogether if old Humpy meant what he said and fired the man.

"Such a lot of fuss," she said to Madeline. "Police. Wildlife agencies. All for a silly goose. And those animal rights people dressed up as poultry. What a bunch of loonies." Arietta looked up, forgetting to whom she was talking. "Oh. Sorry, Madeline."

Madeline feigned deep concentration in the open book on her lap, trying to block out the image of her daughter, Phoebe, wearing wings and a beak, locked in arms with the other vegetarians at the gates and singing endless rounds of "All We Are Asking Is Give Geese a Chance." Safer to focus on Bonnie Weber and Duncan Crane, whose engagement had been announced over the weekend. Madeline ran her finger down the index for their mothers' entries, then gingerly turned the pages back in time, careful not to let her eyes fall on other names. She hated being so cozy with the underbelly of the Club. She'd only agreed to the job years ago for Arietta, to whom she owed so much. When Madeline was a young bride, fresh from a turbulent childhood and with no guidance from her own mother, it was Arietta who had taken her by the hand and taught her the value of domestic ritual: how to pass a tray without servility, mix a dry martini, choose a lawn service, and bolster chicken salad with grapes. Arietta showed her that out of attention to detail came order.

A police siren wailed in the distance. "Phoebe waved as I drove by," said Arietta. "You must have a talk with her about support garments. Even in the shade of her wings I could see everything, if you understand my meaning."

"You're a brave one to come through the main gates." Madeline ignored the braless comment, since she'd ceded that battle long ago. "I walked. I'd rather get hit in the head with a golf ball than be yelled at by those kids. They make me feel so, I don't know. Guilty, I guess."

"Nonsense. For what?" Arietta arranged herself closer to the small fire, as if it were the dead of winter and not a hot summer day.

Madeline closed the book with care and waved her hand around at the richly paneled room. "For this. For belonging to a place that would produce a Ralph Bellows."

"Fowl Play at Club" the headline had read, the eviscerated goose splayed out in the photo like a poorly executed autopsy. Bellows, who believed in the law when there was no alternative, eventually owned up to the shooting itself but denied any knowledge of how the dead goose found its way under the skiff seat. He was, however, quite pleased to hear that he'd bagged it, since further investigation matched the number 6 shot found in the chest cavity to Bellows's gun. "An unbelievable feat considering how schnonkered I was," he'd told the police. And so now he was faced with a DUI along with all the other charges: leaving the scene of an accident, hunting out of season, and illegal discharge of a firearm. He told Arietta he'd hired Bruner & Bruner. It would take time and money, but Attorney Ellen Bruner, who seemed to be enjoying a robust first trimester, had assured Bellows that in the end it should just be a matter of a few fines, as most of the charges could not be made to stick, especially the more serious DUI. After all, the police had arrested Bellows at home, not at the scene of the crime; plus, the only witnesses to the car accident were immigrants. She hoped, for her purposes, illegal ones. Her assistant was following up on that. In the meantime she'd told Bellows to just shut up.

"Him?" Arietta adjusted her ivory skirt around her calves. "Every institution has its share of idiots. It's nothing to be embarrassed about. Listen to me. What you need is a vacation, a few weeks in Bar Harbor. I'll give Reggie Witherspoon a call, see if he's using the cottage this year. You'll come back with a whole new outlook." After a moment's pause, Arietta leaned closer to Madeline. "Tell me. How's Charles doing with all this?"

Madeline continued to gaze intently at the book in her lap, unable to focus. Charles had almost joined Phoebe that morning, even going so far as canceling a bond presentation.

"What do you mean, you're going to the gates?" Madeline had asked.

"Bellows was wrong to shoot the goose," Charles had said. "We have to show the world that the rest of us don't believe in taking matters into our own hands. Yes, the geese need to be controlled, but we must arrive at a consensus, and not become vigilantes."

"You forget," said Madeline, moving closer. "You, of all people, can't throw stones."

"Absolutely not," said Charles, rubbing SPF-15 on his face. "Phoebe promised me, none of that. A little red paint, maybe, but that's all. How do you think I strap these on?" He held up a four-foot-long pair of cardboard wings.

Madeline grabbed him by his arm and made him look at her. She leaned in so close she could feel the heat from his body on her cheek, and her voice dropped to a whisper. "You've killed a goose, Charles. Even though it was an accident, if they find out they'll turn on you too. That's how crowds are."

Charles played with one of the wide elastics meant to hold the stiff oval wings to his wrists, and snapped it. "I thought I could atone for that by doing this," he said. He pulled away from Madeline, and her hand dropped to her side. "Is there no hope?" he said to no one, gently laying the wings on the pickled-pine kitchen table. An ironstone pitcher of purple dahlias and pink Sweet Williams sat nearby. Madeline had arranged them days before, and they filled the room with a sour smell.

Then Charles left for the garage, slamming the screen door behind him. The sound of wood and wire had more passion in it than he'd expressed all year. She knew she should follow, but deep down, she didn't really want to find out what was eating at him, because it might very well be her.

"Charles is fine," Madeline said to Arietta, closing the book. "Everything is fine with Bonnie and Duncan too, as you suspected."

Arietta looked at her significantly. "Yes, but it's a good thing he was attracted to Bonnie and not her cousin Courtney."

Madeline ignored her. She didn't want to know why not Courtney.

Arietta went on. "Linzee told me she saw Charles walking into the Goodwill downtown this week. She looked through the window and there he was, rummaging around in a box. Trust her not to miss any awkward situation. She asked if you were under economic strain and I laughed it off, but it made me think. Far be it from me to intrude, but some professional advice might be in order for Charles. At the very least, he needs a trip to the barber."

Madeline stared at the closed curtains. He needed a great deal more than that. When she'd organized the dry cleaning that week, she found an entire set of Club cutlery in his jacket pocket. What was he amassing an arsenal against?

"I'm sure she was mistaken," she said. "Charles wouldn't know what a Goodwill store was. But you and I have got to talk about the engagement that wasn't so fine." She stood up to put the book away. "I'm worried. If Roger's angry enough to attack Willard, he could be angry enough to do anything."

Arietta adjusted the tortoiseshell band on her head and sighed. "What was Gwen thinking, telling Roger the truth? She's put the book at risk."

"I'm not worried about the book." As Madeline walked over to the cabinet, her Bermuda shorts dryly chafed her thighs. "I'm worried about feelings. What must Roger be going through, finding out his dead wife had been unfaithful?"

"Karen was always a bit of a strumpet," mused Arietta. "You know, she wasn't from around here. New York State, as I recall. Near Albany."

Madeline knelt on the bare wood and wrestled the book back into its hiding place. "It doesn't matter where she came from, Arietta, she's dead now."

Arietta brushed a silver hair from her face. "Yes. A striking urn. Limoges. She bought it herself after her diagnosis, and it still has pride of place on the Rundlett mantel. She was a brave woman, in her own way. Looked at the facts head-on."

Madeline locked the secret compartment but did not move. Karen had been a friend, or at least it had seemed that way since they played tennis in summer and lunched in winter. And yet, where was Madeline when Karen was in her decline? She'd stopped calling, thinking that was how Karen wanted it, to be left alone. Or had Madeline just been sparing herself? And how inappropriate her response had been when the end mercifully came. No running over to the house with a warm casserole for the family. Instead, she'd called a caterer and had a seafood lasagna sent over, not even touching the food meant to ease the grief. She'd done everything expected of her, and yet it seemed to fall short of being human. After repositioning the false back of the cabinet, stacking the *National Geographics*, and shutting the door, she stood up and rubbed her knees. "Poor Roger."

Arietta gave the fire a prod. "At least we can be certain he's keeping the matter to himself. Men don't crow about being cuckolded. Give me the key."

"So much pain." Madeline squinted against the smoke as she dropped the key into Arietta's yellow palm. "And for what? With better birth control and abortion, old families dying out and new ones coming in, there are far fewer complicated engagements at the Club these days. Eliot and Nina were rare, and it wouldn't have hurt anyone to let them slip through the net. Horse breeders cross siblings all the time."

Arietta stood up so abruptly she hit a brass andiron with her cane, causing a smoldering log to spark. "Madeline, don't be a ninny," she said. "Breeders can keep more detailed records than we possibly could. They have complete control, while we must make do with the information at hand."

To hide her agitation, Arietta turned to the marble mantel and gazed up at the life-sized portrait of the Club's second president, Henry Fothergill, with a mustache the size of a beaver, dressed in hunting tweeds and leaning on a shotgun with a brace of pheasants at his booted feet. A bachelor to the end, he'd never once bred in captivity, but his name appeared in the book with impressive frequency in the years before and after 1900. Pale green eyes still popped up once in a while in a Club baby, but only Madeline and Arietta were in on the joke. Not that it was funny. He was, in fact, Arietta's real grandfather. Her own mother knew this and more besides; if only she had access to this sort of information on Binkie when Arietta had become engaged. It was easy enough to gather Binkie's social credentials, but impossible to detect his biological ones since Arietta had foolishly chosen from outside the Club. Not far enough outside, though. Ironically, for all the ways she and Binkie were incompatible, they must have had a rogue gene in common that caused bad blood. After a series of miscarriages, Mother quietly suggested she might have the wrong gander.

So she reached outside the marriage bed (but within the Club this time, where Mother could give the all clear) to get her robust baby girls, and she was grateful for them. It was just monstrous bad luck that she'd had to sabotage their first romantic entanglements due to her own philandering. By the time they finally married it was too late. She had no grandchildren, and she never would.

Binkie had them, however, not that he ever knew. In spite of their own bad chemistry, he was apparently more simpatico elsewhere. She remembered the heat of her humiliation each time his mistress of the moment entered the library looking like she'd swallowed a canary, and then proceeded to write down Binkie's name as the father. He was so flagrantly indiscreet that his only good quality was that he made her look like a saint. In her generous moments, Arietta felt these children and their families to be her heirs. On bad days, she had nothing but the book. She turned to face Madeline. "We are a service to the community. If it weren't for us, the Club would be swarming with imbeciles and lunatics."

They both flinched at the distant roar of a bullhorn, the police ordering protesters to move back and keep the road clear. Was Phoebe so sane? thought Madeline. Or Charles? She could think of more than a few members who looked as if their family tree never branched, but she was easily cowed in the face of fervor and so said nothing. Arietta took her role as lifeguard of the Club's gene pool with great seriousness, but Madeline had no firm beliefs to lean on. She had nothing.

Arietta settled herself back down in her chair like a ruffled hen and unscrewed the pistol handle of her cane. "There are things that must be done for the sake of future generations," she said, dropping the key in the hollow compartment. "And they must be done without question. We must maintain the ancient vigor."

Madeline sat down at the window seat but dared not peek outside the velvet. "So what do we do?"

"Don't worry about Nina," said Arietta. "Gwen tells me the girl knows nothing. Roger has at least that much sense."

"Maybe there's nothing to know," said Madeline. "Karen was not definite. She had only written *possible* in the book."

"She was being coy. Women know by whom they are impregnated, believe me."

"I wouldn't know about such things," murmured Madeline. Her words came out as a reproach.

Arietta sniffed. "Madeline, don't be such a prude. Look at the geese." She reattached the handle and pointed her cane in the general direction of the lake. "For years they were thought to be faithful, but scientists have found that their eggs are fertilized by many different fathers. The geese might mate for life, but it has precious little to do with whom they carry on with. Nature does not intend for us to put all our eggs in one genetic basket."

"You can't compare us to birds," said Madeline. "Humans are complex. We have morals, not instincts."

"If that were true, then there'd be no need for divorce court, or the entire judicial system for that matter. Our instincts are geared toward survival, and monkeying around, if I may call it that, pays off in practical advantages for one's issue. School admissions. Jobs. Summer rentals. You think these connections just happen? A certain amount of social glue must be squeezed out of the tube first."

Madeline stared at the dying fire. She should talk. She barely knew the tall, bearded man her mother claimed was her father. He'd offered marriage, but her mother refused, calling it a patriarchal plot to imprison women; then he died in a surfing accident when Madeline was still quite young. And she'd hardly been lily white herself. In her Santa Cruz days, casual sex was just that, as enjoyable and fleeting as going out to eat. It wasn't until she met Charles at a concert that she realized there existed a stable universe to her disordered one. There he was, dragged along by a cousin from the university, so sweetly out of place in his clean khakis and polo shirt among the colorful rags and ripped jeans of her peers. While everyone else was swaying, dancing, and carrying on, he stood apart, unto himself, attentive and smiling. She loved him the first time she laid eyes on him. To her, with his even temper, self-assured air, and regard for tradition, Charles was security personified. She remembered the intensity of their desire and thought of Nina and Eliot. "Maybe this was the one great love of their lives and we've ruined it."

Arietta stood up and caressed the wrinkles from her skirt. "At their age, there is nothing easier than doing what nature intends. Biology will send them another grand passion soon enough. Come along. It's time for drinks."

Madeline got up uneasily. It was time for something. She followed Arietta, as always, who hurried down the hall toward her gin martini. Madeline opened her mouth to tell her about the dark smudge of fingerprints on her skirt, and then decided, no.

Chapter Seventeen

Bogey

OKAY, FOLKS, listen up," said Gerard. "As of today, and until further notice, employees must park out by the service entrance."

A groan rose up from the group of twenty or so workers gathered in the kitchen on Sunday afternoon. Some of them sat on the counters, others on thrones of produce crates, and the rest just stood, ready to run. Many had to punch in just for this meeting, as it was supposed to be their day off. Barry was taking care of the grounds crew and caddies out in the parking lot, since Gerard didn't want them in the clubhouse with their muddy shoes, dirty clothes, and gosling.

"You're kidding, right, Gerard?" asked Vita. "That's got to be a quarter mile away. What's wrong with our parking lot?"

Gerard cleared his throat and fumbled with the clipboard in his hands. A couple of sheets of paper floated to the floor. He could barely hold on to anything these days, not paperwork, not his job, not even his sanity. Luisa, beat from running the steam table, handed him his lost notes, and he nodded without looking at her. "Many of the members prefer not to use the front drive and parking area anymore, and there's not enough room for all of us out back." Neither did they care to drive past the billboard at the intersection, which had turned into some sort of guest book for the protesters, thickly scrawled with eco-graffiti. "If we forget about the environment, maybe it will go away"; "The trouble with man is man"; and "Remember, we all live downstream."

"Not enough room for us in our own space?" asked Sloane, who held her arms tightly around her torso. "I don't want to walk that far late at night. It's not safe."

"Are the members afraid of a few kids at the gate with signs and strap-on wings?" asked Vita. "After that first day, there's not been more than a handful of them at any one time. You know that. I've seen you down there."

"While we're on the subject, Vita," he said, pointing a finger at her, "do not feed the vegetarians. No more cookies."

Vita, with perverse pleasure, had been riding out to the gates in a golf cart every afternoon to bring the kids a plate of vegan cookies, baked without dairy or eggs, because one of them had piously informed her that no species drinks the milk or eats the reproductive products of another species. She liked to watch them try to swallow.

"A few dry cookies aren't going to hurt anyone," she said.

"We don't want to encourage them." The police had told him the demonstrators had a right to be on the street as long as they didn't block the entrance, and the best thing to do was to ignore them, it would all peter out on its own. But here it was, a week later, and no petering in sight. "The bottom line is, the protests disturb the members, so they want to come in by the frontage road, which has no sidewalk and, therefore, no public space for the crazies to do their dirty work. End of story."

To avoid the probing snouts of cameras on Monday morning, it was Clendenning who had first parked out back. He then slithered into Gerard's darkened office with the *Boston Globe* rolled up in his fist, looking like he was about to housebreak a puppy.

"I only asked Bellows about the hunting season," Gerard had

pleaded. "The *legal* hunting season. How could I know this would happen?"

"The man's as suggestible as a child when it comes to sport," said Clendenning. "As the manager, you're the one ultimately responsible. As to whether or not you will continue to be the manager, I've called a board meeting for next week. We'll decide what to do then."

A soldier in the war of self-preservation, Gerard then called today's meeting to reinforce his own authority. He might not be able to control the geese, Clendenning, or the press, but he could still control the staff.

"That's not fair," said Ping, one of the waitresses and a BU pre-law student. "The check-in clock should be down there too. Otherwise, we'll have been at the Club for twenty minutes before we even start getting paid."

"It's not forever, people." Gerard turned away from her, still annoyed that Vita hadn't asked what Ping's major was before she hired her. "We all have to make some sacrifice. For instance, to create space, the Dumpster will be moved behind the utility buildings. Unfortunately, it will then be visible from the fifth green. Because of this, there's no more smoking by the Dumpster. Don't think this doesn't hurt me too."

The employees growled.

"Wait," said Josh, one of the kitchen help. "Does this mean we have to lug the garbage all the way out there now?"

Luisa whispered to Pedrosa, who looked at Josh in comprehension. Pedrosa's job was just about to get that much harder.

"That's right, but as I said, these measures are only until the fur stops flying. Any questions?"

The group stared in silence.

"Good," he said. "While I've got you all here, let's go over some other issues. Standards have been pretty shoddy lately."

Vita could barely suppress a smirk. It was Gerard who'd fallen below the mark, in both mood and hygiene. Not that he was a mess, but compared to his old exemplary self, he was positively ragged. One collar tip of his yellow ERCC polo shirt was up, the other down. His dark hair was spiked in the back from careless combing, and one of his pleated loafers had a smudge of green goose grease along the heel.

"First and foremost," he said, reading from his clipboard, "there's the matter of cutlery. Vita tells me some pieces were missing at the last inventory." He looked up sternly and folded his arms, dropping his pen to the floor. After he retrieved it, he eyed each one of his suspects. "Well?" he said at last. "What's going on? Is someone assembling a hope chest, or is it just carelessness?" At this he glared at Luisa, who looked to Vita for help.

"Gerard," Vita said, "the waitstaff and backs have been extremely careful with the garbage all summer." She knew that for a fact because she'd been having them paw through it for goose goodies. "If I thought it was my staff, I would have taken care of it myself."

"What about the caddies? Are you still letting them just walk right through here?"

Vita knew that by "them" he meant Merle. She smoothed out her apron. "What about the members?" she asked. "Ask them if they've been helping themselves."

Gerard snorted. "They hardly need our silver plate."

"Kleptomania is about sexual thrills, not need," she said, and the group giggled.

"Vita, please," he said. "I just want everyone to be on high alert on this matter. This is no time to protect your coworkers. Theft hurts us all. Next item." He puffed out his chest as if declaiming Shakespeare. "As it says in the *Employee Manual: Members and guests will be acknowledged within thirty seconds by host or hostess.* People, be on your toes. If you see someone at the door, quickly alert the host or hostess on duty. Mr. Stillington says he was kept waiting at the lectern for ten minutes the other night before someone noticed him."

"The man lies," said Audrey, who worked as hostess most weeknights. "He and his party were greeted and seated as soon as he arrived."

"Well, he must have *felt* ignored somehow. Let's move on."

Gerard looked down at his list. "Next item. Don't let the members think you're stupid." He looked up at his lifeless audience. "Even if you are." Gerard laughed, alone, then continued. "As it says in the *Manual,* if a member asks a question, never say, 'I do not know.' Say, 'I will find out.' Got that?"

There was a stony moment, during which Vita passed around a tray of cranberry-nut muffins. As she moved through the group, pressing food on them, she gave each a look that begged for pity and patience.

"And remember," Gerard said. "Make it a game to anticipate the members' needs."

"What about their wants?" said Ping. "How do we tell their wants from their needs?"

A couple of people giggled, but not Gerard. "This," he said, slamming his clipboard on the counter, "is the Eden Rock Country Club, where the members' wants *are* their needs. And we forget it at our peril."

And on this confusing, dismal note, the group scattered for the day, taking their muffins with them.

"Vita," said Gerard, when everyone was gone, "may I have a word with you?"

She stiffened. She'd been on edge ever since her goose from God was discovered in the skiff. Fortunately, the police had not pointed a finger at her, presuming that Mr. Bellows had hidden it there. But Gerard was sometimes smarter than he looked.

"I don't like the food invoices I'm seeing on my desk," he said. "Let's not forget that we're here to buy food, fix it up, and sell it at a profit." He waved a frenzied hand at the many stacks of boxes in the kitchen. "Cases of this, cases of that. And most of it organic, at almost twice the price. Here, I want you to take this." He released a glossy catalog from his clipboard and handed it to her.

"Ugh," said Vita. "Should I serve frozen peas in the middle of August?" She had Dr. Nicastro's diet to think of, after all, which heavily relied on fresh vegetables. And she had to consider her geese, who ate the scraps. Quality mattered, and organically grown produce was not just healthier, it was denser and more flavorful, not engorged with chemically induced water weight.

"I don't think you're giving enough consideration to prepared foods," said Gerard. "The thing about fresh ingredients is that you never know what you're going to get. Say, for instance, you use this instant zabaglione." He pointed to a pale pudding on the cover. "It will behave the same way every time. Consistency is crucial. If someone returns for a great dish, it must be exactly as they had it before. Eggs can be very unpredictable."

"Oh, Gerard," she said, shaking her head and holding the catalog away from her. "Talk about falling standards."

"I'm not saying for everything," he said. "But take today's brunch. You were scrambling eggs for hours." He paged through the catalog, still in Vita's hands. "Look at this. All you have to do is add water, seal the bag, and lower it into a simmering pot until solid. Done! Just pour it into the warming pan. And all without anyone having to crack a single shell!"

"That's appalling."

"What's the problem? It says right here, 'one hundred percent dried egg.' No chemicals, no added anything."

"You can't remove the soul of food and expect to put it back in the same way. Something is lost."

"Not taste. The salesman fixed me a sample and I couldn't tell the difference. I'm just asking you to try. It's safer too. We won't have to worry about anything being undercooked this way. No salmonella."

Vita ground her molars. When had people become so afraid of food? The chances of getting salmonella or E. coli were exceedingly slim, and yet, by law, she had to put that paranoid statement at the bottom of her menu about undercooked food being a health hazard. How silly. She believed that animals should never be abused *or* overcooked. Grilled tuna had to be pink, lamb blue, beef bloody, otherwise what was the point? All pleasure involved some risk.

"I won't," she said. "First, you come in here and accuse my staff of stealing your tawdry silver, then you give me this." She threw the catalog into the open trash can.

"Why did you tell me pieces were missing if you didn't want me to find the culprit?"

"Open your eyes, Gerard. Have you taken a good look at Mr. Lambert lately? Or do you just have eyes for his daughter?"

Gerard stepped back as if slapped, but he could not keep himself from blushing. "Don't be ridiculous. If I keep an eye on her at all it's to make sure she doesn't lead an attack on your meat-filled kitchen. And what *about* Mr. Lambert?"

"Luisa says that more than once she couldn't find all the pieces at his table, or the tables around him."

"She made that up to cover her own carelessness. Or theft."

"Gerard, even from down here, I can tell members are giving him a wide berth. My bet is that he was even in on the goose hunt. I think Phoebe realized it only after she called the police, so she had to lie to protect him."

"*You* were on the fairway, and yet you claim you didn't see the goose hunt. What about *that?* What were you even doing out there so early? I'd understand if you were in the kitchen," he said, waving his clipboard around the room, "because you chefs are crazy that way, but you were out on the course. Are you hiding something?"

Vita ripped her toque off her head and threw it on the counter. "What would I be hiding, Gerard? A life? Because I seem to be missing one around here!"

"Simmer down," he said, and pinched the bridge of his nose to stop a searing pain in his head. "I'm just trying to get the overhead under control here. To get something, anything, under control. I'm already afraid to ask what you're going to order for the Fothergill Cup banquet."

"I'm going to be very thrifty, as a matter of fact," said Vita, turning her back on him to hide her smile. She busied her hands arranging a plate of muffins. "We'll talk about the menu later, when I have it laid out. Here, I made these for you."

Chocolate-cherry, Gerard's favorite. "Let's not you and I start getting short with one another," he said, accepting the plate. "There's enough going on as it is." He picked at a crumb and turned to leave, but as he did, something in the outside stairwell caught his attention. "What's that?"

Vita held her breath. There, on the stone steps, stacked like a World War I entrenchment, sat ten twenty-five-pound bags of cornmeal. "Misdelivery," she said in a pitched voice. "They're coming back to pick it up tomorrow."

Gerard bent down for a closer look. At Cornell he'd been taught all the many ways that employees could rob a restaurant. Over-ordering, then reselling the stock was common. But that was usually shrimp and steak, not cornmeal. Cornmeal was chicken feed. But what if it wasn't cornmeal? Wasn't she Colombian? Her family may have left cartel country before she was born, but it could still be in her blood. Could this have something to do with why she was out on the course before dawn? A drug pickup?

"Wait a minute." Gerard stood up, startled, as a memory unfolded before him. "I know this logo. An empty bag was in the skiff with the dead goose." He turned and looked at his chef, who held her forehead in her hand, mentally wringing the necks of the chickens that had come home to roost. "What's going on, Vita?"

"I think you're right. It's time we had a talk about the Fothergill banquet," she said, looking up and smiling. "Take a seat, Gerard. Let me pour you some coffee."

"Don't coffee me, Vita. Have you been feeding the geese? Have you lost your senses, like Barry, and let yourself become attached to those dirty creatures?"

"No," she said gravely as she poured a cup. "I haven't let myself become attached. Not too attached, anyway." She looked up at him. "You shouldn't get to know your food."

Gerard reached out for support and felt the stainless-steel counter alive and shaking beneath his hand. Even the inanimate objects in the room seemed afraid of what was coming. "This is a joke, right?"

Vita placed the ERCC mug near him and shook her head sadly. The truth would either set her free or get her fired. "I'm raising geese out on the island to butcher for the banquet."

The response was immediate and electric. "No! No, no, no,"

he screamed, putting his hands on both sides of his head, fearful that his own pale neck was about to be put on the chopping block. So little oxygen reached his brain he nearly fainted, and he had to marvel at the elegant mechanism of the autonomic reflex system, which kept his heart and lungs operating even now.

"There's no going back." Vita calmly pointed to the bags of cornmeal on the steps. "I've invested so much, Gerard, not just feed, but time. I have to get my business done with the geese before they wander off for the day. That's why I was on the course so early. I saw it all. The bird fell practically in my arms." She held out her open arms to Gerard, as imploring as any medieval saint. "I wanted to try the recipe before the banquet. That's why I hid the goose and lied about what I saw. Not for Bellows, but for you and me, for all of us here at the Club. We're in this together."

"N-no," Gerard sputtered. "You're in this alone and out on the street if you feed one more beak."

"Other investments are at stake." She attached her hand to one of his shoulders. "I asked Barry to use biological controls on the turf. He's gone to seminars, bought supplies. The geese can't eat grass full of herbicides, can they? Otherwise, that's what we'd be serving to the members. Poisoned meat."

Gerard pushed her away. "Impossible. Barry would never change turf protocol without consulting me. This is a golf course. The greens are our glory, and the only way to maintain that glory is through constant applications of chemicals."

"Barry has seen the light," she said, thinking how his love for Forbes had led the way to the green revolution on the Eden Rock links. "But if you're going to force him back to his evil ways, wait. I only need two more weeks of grazing before the geese have to hang."

"Hang?" said Gerard, his mind still tumbling around the words *biological controls.*

Vita did not, at that moment, care to explain what hanging entailed and so skipped to what she thought would be her closing argument. "The best part is, my plan will deplete the geese and feed the members. We'll kill two birds with one stone."

Her poorly chosen metaphor set Gerard on a run around the counter for the exit. But for a woman of voluptuous dimensions, Vita was not just fast, but agile. She leaped over the counter and beat him to the swinging door, latching it shut.

"The answer is no, Vita." He ducked and swayed, trying to get around her. "Absolutely not. Start planning another menu."

No, she was in too deep now. She had to preserve her culinary vision, her chance at excellence. It was no longer about doing it for the Club—she had to do it for herself. "Let's make a deal, Gerard." She straightened her chef's double-breasted jacket, preparing for battle. "You let me do this, and I'll make sure you come out alive from the Board meeting."

"How?" he croaked, weak with frustration. Was there no way out? What Vita was doing was illegal—albeit, as she said, highly practical—and as he was ultimately responsible, he would be the one to hang for the crime. But if he did not give her permission, he might lose her or force her deeper underground with her birds, where he would not be able to monitor the situation. He was tired of surprises. He might as well hear her out. "You don't have that kind of power."

Vita picked up a chocolate-cherry muffin from the tray, took a bite, and sighed with contentment. "Oh, yes. I do."

Chapter Eighteen

Fading the Ball

FRANK NICASTRO broke the polished surface of the pool as he wearily executed his strokes, shattering the golden glow of the water. So engrossed was he in getting from one end to the other, he didn't see Madeline arrive. But she did not pass by unnoticed from above, in the lifeguard's chair.

"Hey, Mrs. Lambert," Scott called in his nasal, slow-motion speech.

Madeline shielded her eyes from the sun behind him. She felt the heat of it on her face and tried not to look directly at his legs, splayed at the hips and draped over the white armrests. His position made her curious about body jewelry. Where, exactly, on genitals did an earring hang?

"Hi, Scott." She put her things on a teak table and shook out her towel with undue enthusiasm. "How are you?"

"Whipped. Spent the day with this bad boy in my mouth." He fondled the silver whistle that hung around his neck, cradled in his hairless sternum. "There was some screaming and whining around here today, I'll tell you. I'm blowed out."

Madeline understood. Just picturing the pool at prime time

made her anxious. Kids crying over nothing and everything until mothers or sitters pressed goodies on them, and so they learned to cry even more, until everyone was locked in a cycle of outbreak and appeasement. After a few seasons by the pool with Phoebe, a puppy started making a lot more sense than another baby.

She smiled at Scott in sympathy, then turned her attention to rubbing Clinique SPF 8 on her arms, watching the white lotion soak into her flesh, then disappear.

"Want me to get your back?" Scott asked, untangling his legs to climb down.

She shook her head with such force that wisps of streaked hair fell across her eyes. "That's okay. My husband did it before I left." Which he most certainly hadn't, but she could not allow a lifeguard to do what Charles had long ago stopped doing, even if it meant burned skin. It would feel like cheating. Then she smiled at her own silliness. Perhaps Arietta was right, maybe she was a prude.

She settled herself on a chaise longue out of Scott's conversational range, tugging at her bathing suit where it bunched and clung. Women's voices rose from the tennis court. Her old partners. They'd told her they were disbanding their group since no one's schedule seemed to mesh this summer. Apparently, only Madeline did not mesh. Anne Farnsworth, Beryl Hall, and Ariel Weber talked simultaneously, while Hilary Fisher, Madeline's replacement, rhythmically nodded as they strolled single file along the ridge toward the clubhouse in silhouette, like a string of paper dolls. Madeline could tell by their overly determined postures that they were actively not looking at her, except for Hilary, who was not quite so talented as all that yet. She glanced in Madeline's direction and her hand began to rise in a friendly reflex, but then she caught herself, rubbing her nose instead. She disappeared from sight over the hill, and they could both make believe she hadn't seen Madeline after all.

Madeline told herself they were just being polite, not wanting to place social demands on her right now, what with her life so embarrassingly in disarray. Perhaps they had gotten tired of hearing her say Charles was fine, when he was so clearly not.

They had eyes. She would have thought they'd be glad she'd taken the trouble to lie, but maybe even they had a limit to pretense. What safe subjects were there to talk about, after all, in Madeline's world? How's Charles? How are the goats? How are you?

Pain spread from her temples, forcing her eyes shut. It was not, as she first thought, a headache coming on, but the pressure of unshed tears. She could never bear to cry, and what good would that do anyway?

She put her sunglasses on and pulled *Elle Interior* out of her bag, through which she hoped to find a solution to her life, a very large distraction by way of a home renovation. Flower arranging was not going to be enough. Her compositions were positively rigid and gave her no pleasure. At last week's class, she was given a Japanese ink print of flowers and told to "capture its essence." Lucy, the overall-wearing instructor, said it was all about *looking.* Madeline copied hers perfectly, she thought, but when Lucy came around, she pointed out that in the print, a beetle clung to a partially devoured rose leaf, which spoke of beauty surpassing flaws and imperfection being part of life. She must train her eyes not to pass over these important details.

Madeline didn't get it. Was she really supposed to include damaged material in her arrangements? Maybe what she needed instead was a new bedroom, like the one on the page in front of her, something romantic, with faded chintz at the windows, petit-point pillows on the settee, an antique frame next to the bed. The article said that one's husband should be made to feel like a guest in the bedroom. Unfortunately, that's just how Charles behaved, like a guest, slipping into bed after an evening spent clanging around in the garage, then sneaking out early to get to the rubbish bins before the bums sobered up. What she needed was a husband, not a guest.

Drops of water fell on the page. She touched her face. It wasn't her; it was Frank dripping from his swim.

"Madeline, my pet," he said, wiping his face with his towel. "Why so glum?"

She smiled, and it hurt. "Too much thinking, I guess." She closed the magazine.

"Do your husband and child figure into all this thinking?" He cleaned out an ear with the corner of the towel.

She nodded, barely moving her head. There was not much left to hide.

"Excellent." He bent in a crescent to shake his head clear. "Thinking about them will take your mind off of what other people think about them for a minute."

She did not even attempt to disguise her irritation and loudly reopened her magazine.

Frank raised a hand above his head and dried his hairy underarm, giving it a sniff before spreading his towel on the lounge next to Madeline's. His flesh, while still substantial, no longer quivered when he sat down. "Is that some shelter porn you have there?"

She looked at him without comprehension; then he leaned over with a grunt and lifted the magazine from her hands. As he paged through it, a withered fuchsia bloom being used to mark a page fell in his lap. He stuck it behind his ear. "I've been invited to many a home since I've joined the Club," he said, examining a layout of a bathroom. "All beautiful, but as impersonal as a luxury hotel."

Madeline thought living in a hotel wouldn't be so bad. When she and Charles were first married, they lived in the Back Bay, renting a sweet apartment that looked out over the river. There was no outside maintenance to worry about because its public face was the superintendent's problem, not hers. Things got a little crowded when Phoebe was born, but it didn't matter. She could just pop her into the stroller and the whole city would be at their feet. Parks, playgrounds, outdoor cafés, children's museums. They were never lonely or bored. That didn't happen until they took Charles's parents' house over when his father died and his mother hightailed it south. In the suburbs, there was nothing to do and nowhere to go except for the Club, which became her lifeline.

Frank continued talking as he paged through the magazine. "The members seemed stiff too, but with a few drinks, most of them loosened up. Sometimes too much so. The first month I was here, people bought me drinks and confided the most intimate details of their lives. Maybe they thought in my line of work I couldn't be shocked by anything. It's unbelievable the pain some of these people live with. Families riddled with suicides, addictions, bankruptcies. Relatives with extended hospitalizations or jail terms. DUIs, restraining orders, involuntary manslaughter. Debilitating disease, rampant cancer. Public lewdness. My whole life, I've wanted to join a place like this, only to find it barely functions." He closed the magazine with a slap of thick, glossy paper.

They went silent, as Madeline refused to encourage him to tell more. She knew too much as it was. A group of teenage girls entered the pool area, giggling and touching one another. Sarah Quilpe, flat-chested and leggy, wiggled a few fingers at Scott. She should be more discreet, thought Madeline. There had been a golf pro at the Club in the eighties whose name appeared so often in the book that Arietta felt it necessary to arrange for his dismissal, and she'd hate to see that happen to Scott.

"But what's to be done?" Frank yawned then let his chin sink into the cushion of his throat. "All we can do is let the sensual pleasures to be had here give us strength to face the ugly world out there." He threw the magazine back on her lap. "So you're looking for a change?"

Madeline's mind was far away, and it took her a moment to realize that Frank was talking to her. "Charles has been after me for a while to renovate. The kitchen is basically the same as when we moved in." She hadn't intended for that to happen. In fact, she'd wanted to make the house hers right away with new everything. Before she'd dropped out of school to marry Charles, she'd been an art history major and had all sorts of ideas about design and architecture. She'd had opinions. Where did they go? She'd told herself that Charles was happier the way things were, but to be honest, she was the one who had stalled. She'd been afraid.

The rooms, with their mellow carpets and invisible antiques, spoke of generations of stability, a look she dared not tamper with, for fear her home would start saying something about herself she hadn't intended. "At the very least, I need some new appliances."

Frank's eyes were closed as he soaked up the day's enduring heat. "Just make sure you get a stove you know how to turn on. The Viking is the sacred altar of my religion, but for most of these bozos, it's just another surface for the delivery boy to lay down the ham and pineapple pizza." He shook his head, deeply grieved.

"What's your kitchen like, Frank?" she said, turning too quickly toward him. "Do you have a stove you know what to do with?"

Frank opened his black eyes in delight. "I know where all the buttons are, if that's what you mean. But it's lonely to turn it on by myself. It's why I eat out. But if I were married, I'd never leave home."

"So why aren't you married, then, if you think it's so wonderful?" She was surprised by the agitation in her voice.

So was Frank. It tickled him so much he flipped himself over on his stomach so he could look at her directly. "I haven't found the right one. I date. But most of the women who are ambitious enough to hunt down a doctor are too thin for me. Deprived. I don't want someone who deprives herself. She might end up depriving me."

Madeline caught him glancing at her legs. "You're dieting, Frank. Depriving yourself, as you call it."

"Not with Vita cooking." He nuzzled his chin on his hairy arm. "I went to the kitchen last night for a to-go package. Poached catfish rémoulade with caviar and smoked tomatoes." His gaze was distant, transfixed in memory. Then he shook himself to the present. "Anyway, we got to talking about the Bellows goose. We were laughing about it, and I said at least Charles Lambert hadn't killed it, and she said don't be too sure."

Madeline automatically looked up to see if Scott could have

heard, but he was chatting with the girls clustered in the corner. "What do you mean, 'don't be too sure'?"

"It's so absurd, I shouldn't even tell you. Vita thinks Charles was with Bellows and that's why Phoebe changed her story from a gun to a backfire once she suspected her father was in on it. Just goes to show—blood is still thicker than goose."

"That's insane." Madeline sat up straight, pressing her fingernails into the teak armrests as she considered the possibility. Charles hadn't been next to her when she woke up the day of the shooting. Then she settled back in her lounge and composed her face. But he rarely was these days, was he? He usually fell asleep in the garage, wrapped in his hammock like a giant larva.

"I wouldn't put too much trust in what Vita has to say," she said. "After all, why was *she* at the Club so early that morning? Phoebe thinks she was trying to hide something."

"What do you mean?" Frank's face turned heavy.

Madeline shrugged. She didn't necessarily want to repeat Phoebe's theory, knowing her general attitude toward chefs, "those dead-animal handlers," as she called them. She worried about her intentions. Phoebe had recently asked about Gerard Wilton, of all people, and Madeline professed ignorance about his life outside of the Club, which was only the truth. To what extremes might her daughter go to save the world? To what nefarious ends might she employ personal information? On the other hand, Madeline needed to discredit Vita so no one would believe what she had to say about Charles. "I don't know exactly," she said, picking up the magazine and paging through it. "Stealing, I suppose."

"Oh," said Frank.

Madeline pretended to read about heated towel racks, while Frank stared over at the clubhouse, its Tudor facade deep in shadow with the sun lowering behind it. Then he stood up with an effort. "Last one in is a rotten egg," he said flatly. He trundled to the pool, as graceless as a Neanderthal. Before Madeline could tell him it was probably all just a bunch of nonsense, he dove into the water. The fuchsia floated to the surface.

She felt like a complete jerk. She shouldn't have suggested that

Vita was up to no good. That was mean. Besides, trying to cover up Charles's behavior was not going to make him any saner. While she was mulling over how to repair the damage, Scott left the girls under the umbrellaed table where they sipped Diet Coke through straws.

"Anything I can do for you, Mrs. Lambert?" he said, massaging the side of his neck. "Get you a towel or a drink or something?"

His crotch was at eye level, and all she could think of was genital jewelry, and genitals in general. "No," she said, blushing. She looked at the watch clipped to her beach bag, as if someone were expecting her at home. "I've got to go. Thank you." She would smooth things out with Frank later.

As she packed, ten crows landed one by one on the slate roofline of the pool house, waiting to clean up the day's mess.

Chapter Nineteen

The Grip

CHARLES STOOD in the open door of the garage, his welder's mask flipped up on his forehead like a duck's bill, and decided that while Madeline was still at the pool, a visit to the geese was in order. Fresh air was the universal salve, as his father used to say—and maybe it would unblock his art as well as his tongue. When Madeline came to the garage door to let him know she was going, he had no words to share what was inside him. But did anyone? People made noises and thought they were talking—saw facial expressions and thought they knew what they meant—but how close did anyone come to communicating the pain of living or the ecstasy of life? His own language had been cultivated for commerce, to assist in the trafficking of financial bonds. But where were the words for the bonds of love? He couldn't even say good-bye. It must be something about the way she stared at him—uncertain, questioning, confused—with eyes that once held only love and adoration. She used to call him her rock, and it made him glow to think of himself as such an adult. But last fall, when she had that lump, he realized he might not always be able to see himself through her eyes—he had to see himself through his own. And he saw nothing.

He put his torch down on his workbench and took off his mask, brushing his hair back with his fingers. He knew now he had been too reassuring about the lump, too glib, and then when the biopsy came back negative, he'd had nowhere to go with his happiness, since he had never admitted how terrified he'd been. He had to reach her somehow, even if he had to forge a whole new language with his hands. But something was as wrong with his sculpture as it was with his marriage, and he felt that if he got one right, the other would follow. And he was so close now—he could feel it. His head was still swimming from his meeting with his instructor last week. Charles—as always—had been too tentative in class, standing at his workstation, welding together small bits and scraps, trying to find his way, politely agreeing with everything Vincent had to say—and not understanding a thing.

When Vincent passed his work area again, he stopped and held up the minuscule creature Charles had been working on. "Cute," Vincent had said. "But is that what you want to say? Cute? You've got to get braver, Lambert."

Charles had just nodded and smiled. "Okay, I'll do that."

Then suddenly Vincent was shaking him by the shoulders. "Wake up, Chuck! Wake up!" he'd shouted. "Fuck cute! Let's see what's inside."

Charles was afraid to even blink. The heat, the flames, the smoke, and now Vincent—it was all so overwhelming. "I don't understand. Inside what?"

Vincent closed his eyes and shook his head, letting his long, singed hair fall across his face. He pushed it back with both hands, squeezing exasperation from his skull. "Let's go somewhere after class. Okay, Lambert?"

Charles kept his head down for the rest of the day, pretending to work, sure he was getting the axe. Every once in a while a student would brush a hand across his shoulders while passing, or rumple his hair. Nod, the kid with the jawline beard and iguana on his shoulder, put his face close to his so that Charles was eye to prehistoric eye with the reptile. Nod patted Charles's face. "See you next week, right, man?"

Charles nodded weakly, thinking how much he'd miss Nod, who had taken him—an outsider—under his wing. His very first week, he'd brought him to an Army & Navy to exchange his khakis for Carhartts, his tasseled loafers for steel-toed boots. That would never have happened at the Club. He reflected with shame that he had never been all that welcoming to newcomers himself.

When class ended, he and Vincent were tucked side by side in a dark booth at the bar around the corner, and he braced himself for the fatal blow.

"Chuck," Vincent said, wiping suds off his mustache. "It's time you stopped confusing emotional expression with feeling."

"Okay."

"Did you understand what I was saying?"

"No."

Vincent threw a sweaty arm around his shoulders. "Let's take Italian men. We hug one another. Men are allowed to do that in our culture. You people aren't, not even your women from what I can tell, but that doesn't mean we don't all have the same emotions. Do you understand what I'm saying? What's on the surface doesn't necessarily reflect what's going on in the mind and soul. Let's take you." Vincent pulled him even closer. "I wish I had a mirror so you could see your face. It's as expressionless as an egg. But is that how you feel inside right now?"

Inside? Charles pondered. Inside, a large mechanical device was tightening every cord in his body from his thumbs to his chest, churning and twisting his thoughts and emotions. His skin was taut, his skull creaked with unbearable pressure. He shook his head. "No."

Vincent picked up his glass. "I knew it. I can see something trying to escape in those little pieces you've been doing in class. Don't try to hold it in any longer. Let it out in your work. I give you permission. How's that?"

"I don't think they'd much appreciate 'letting out' at the office," Charles said, and Vincent spritzed a little beer across the table.

"Okay, let me put it another way: Art can say things that a person can't. You might have all these things inside, but they're locked in. But the intense heat of a torch can cut through anything. Even your tough hide. I want you to do something big for your final project. Bigger than you."

Charles reflected on the enormity of what he was being asked to do, and it frightened him. "I don't know about that." He looked up at the TV screen over the bar, on which some new hotshot golfer played to a hushed crowd. The scene looked so calm and controlled. He wished he could crawl inside and join that safe little world. "I could get hurt."

Vincent took both of Charles's hands in his scarred ones. "Look at these smooth palms. You don't even know what there is to be afraid of yet." He ordered another round, then sat back. "Besides, scar tissue is stronger than the surrounding tissue. Just like a weld."

That had been a week ago, seven days of internal changes. He picked up a sketchbook, put a pencil in the back pocket of his jeans, and closed the garage door behind him, heading off to work. Vincent was right. His "work" was no longer in the office. His work was on a whole different plane now. He was also right about what he said about his own kind. Yes, his friends and family might stiffen with a touch, but they still had their feelings—it didn't mean his father had been a cold fish inside, even if he acted like one. And who knew? Maybe even fish had feelings, only we don't have any way of finding out what they are because they don't know how to tell us.

He headed to the wooden gate in the privet hedge that separated their backyard from the course. On his way, he stopped to pat the goats and wished he could take them with him—they were such good company, and he was sure they'd get along famously with the geese. He wondered why it was he'd rather be with animals these days, instead of his friends. Maybe it was because he never heard from his friends anymore—not even Andrew, who used to be a compulsive phoner. What had happened? What was happening?

Charles strolled toward the lake, an area he had once viewed as treacherous because a slice at an adjacent hole could mean a ball in deep water. Now he drew comfort from the spot, often coming to sit on the bench under the oak to contemplate the beauty of the geese and to chew on that old acorn, *What is life?* As he crossed the fairway, he noticed how few golfers were around. There was Howie Amory, of course, probably on his second obsessive round of the day, trying to break 100, but other than him and a foursome, that was it. Phoebe's daily demonstrations were having quite an effect, and he was proud of her for such tenacity—just look at how many others she was able to talk into joining her. It was a real movement, and he hoped the geese appreciated all the effort. Oddly enough, they seemed to be in hiding, staying clear of the fairways and congregating at the far side of the lake. Then he saw what they saw—Ralph Bellows, huffing about on the slope.

Charles was going to turn back to the house, but then he thought, no, he had to face the man sometime, let him know that he didn't appreciate the discharging of firearms so near his family.

"Lambert," called Bellows, out of breath. "Come help me. Goody Cooke dropped one of my guns somewhere around here a couple of weeks ago and I still can't find it. The police stole it, that's what I think. I know how these operations work."

"Goody was with you?"

"Well, you don't think I came out here alone?" Bellows lifted up the branch of a pine tree and peeked underneath, almost knocking off his fore-and-aft deerstalker hat. "I had Anthony Paxton and Malloch Smith too. Hunt Club men. We prepped at Andover together, did you know? We had some wild evening, Charles, you should have been here."

"The newspaper said you were alone."

"I told them I was alone," said Bellows, scratching around in the deep rough with his feet, looking for the gun. "The others aren't members, so why drag them into it? Good eggs, those men, smart enough to hunker down as we drove past the cleaning van coming in. If only I hadn't swerved into it. Foreigners. Can't speak a word of English, but they know how to read a license plate? What's this, eh?"

He reached under a bush and pulled out a hunk of goose feathers, the blood dried to black, then threw it back where he found it.

"The crows couldn't leave well enough alone, could they?" he said. "Wish I'd been there when they dropped a gut on Humpy's car." Bellows rubbed his lower back, exposed where his pink Lacoste shirt rode up his flesh, and chuckled through his nose. "That shook him up some, eh?"

"Romans used to cut open birds and read the future by the intestines," said Charles, looking at the sky. "I wonder what that goose gut said about ours."

Bellows glanced at Charles suspiciously. "The guts predicted my goose was cooked." He snorfled at his own joke. "I guess everyone agreed it was a backfire until then."

"Phoebe had thought it was a gunshot at first," said Charles. "That's why she called the police."

"She's the one?" Bellows straightened up. He squinted at Charles. "Did she see all of us?"

Charles turned and looked at the back of his white Colonial off in the distance. There was Phoebe's third-floor window. If she had looked out when she heard the blasts, how could she have missed seeing four men with guns, even in poor dawn light? "I don't know."

"Well, she was right to call the authorities," said Bellows, scratching his inner thigh in deep thought. "You can never be too careful these days. Tell her she's forgiven."

"She doesn't need to be forgiven," said Charles, chafing at the suggestion that Phoebe had done anything wrong. "You might have killed someone."

Bellows lifted his hat and wiped his forehead with the back of his hand. "Warrants. Court dates. Such a bore. As soon as it's over, I'm going to Penobscot for the rest of the summer." He looked around him. "If the police didn't steal the gun, I'll bet the grounds crew did. I should check the pawnshops."

Charles reached under the bush for the piece of goose Bellows had thrown back. Two joints of a wing. A fox must have dragged it this far and then abandoned the meatless appendage. He stood up and weighed it in his hand—it was like air, as he supposed a wing should be—all hollow bone and feather. He opened it up like a fan, then closed it. Opened it, closed it. The feathers spread and then condensed—folding in on themselves.

"Remarkable," said Charles as he turned away from Bellows to wander back to his garage.

"Hey," called Bellows. "Give me a hand here."

Charles kept on walking, with his sketchbook under one arm and a wing in his hand, marveling at nature's miracle of engineering. Open and close, open and close. And from this simple movement, access to the heavens.

"Lambert!" called Bellows. "This isn't sporting!"

Chapter Twenty

The Dress Code

VITA SAID GOOD-BYE to her mother and hung up the phone, and in the same motion let her head come to rest on the counter, knocking off her toque. Her mother wanted her to take Saturday night off to go to a Wellesley alumni event, which was going to include MIT as well.

"Evita, honey, what better pool to draw from?"

Had her mother flipped like a crepe? Didn't she know by now that Saturday was her showcase night at the Club, and the busiest?

"Don't you remember the T-shirt I used to wear, Ma? 'MIT Men: The odds are good, but the goods are odd.' Besides, I don't want a man. I want a skillet. A family doesn't mix with my professional life right now."

There had been muffled silence at the other end, and the good-bye was distant and sad. Now Vita would have to carry that sorrow with her for the rest of the day. Usually only cooking could cure her of the mother blues, but today she had to tend to a different pot, making sure that all the board members were thoroughly buttered by Monday night. She'd already dazzled them with servitude. Her staff had been spreading it on thick all week, bowing and scraping, but she only had the weekend left to cement the board's loyalty to Gerard with food.

It was Friday morning, just three more days until the board meeting. She turned her attention to the computer screen in front of her, scrolling down a year's worth of orders, sifting through to see what the board members had eaten. Did they like seafood? Red meat? Were they wine drinkers? Or drunks? It was a form of archaeology, discovering what sort of people they were by examining past evidence, but instead of religious artifacts, dinners. Stillington was no surprise. His meals burned as hot as his temper. She could serve him red coals on the tip of a trident and he'd still ask for Tabasco, which he used so liberally as to kill all other sensations. This weekend, no matter what he ordered, she would add a side of her habanero chutney, and at the end of the night, she would present him with a jar to take home.

By the looks of it, Mrs. Gibbons and Mrs. Wolfe, like many women, began their dining experiences with great intentions, starting with salad greens with dressing on the side, fish and rice for an entrée, sauce on the side. But they would begin to lose their inhibitions as whiskey and wine worked their magic, and they let their desires override their waistlines so that their meals ended with outrageous chocolate desserts and multiple coffee drinks with whipped cream. If they didn't starve themselves so early in the game, they wouldn't turn excessive later, for which they probably hated themselves, and might even blame her—and by extension, Gerard. Hunger had to be assuaged early so that the meal could be appreciated on other levels. She'd been experimenting with a grilled scallop and seaweed salad for Dr. Nicastro that was low in fat but had a soul-satisfying crunchy sweetness. She would ask them, as her salad experts, to try it for her and then steer their appetites down an even, low-calorie, and enjoyable path. They could end the evening with a fruit ice in a frozen lemon rind, decorated with a single, intense candied raspberry, instead of falling facefirst on a pile of mousse that would make them feel like pigs.

Mr. Quilpe was the head of the Food Committee and considered himself a gourmet—even though as far as she was concerned, he had no tongue, only a devotion to foodie mags. She would cater to his pretensions. She picked up a *Saveur* from a pile on her desk and paged through it. What would have caught his eye? Something expensive and complicated, and completely out of reach for the rest of humanity. Maybe this Maine lobster tail appetizer with creamy corn and goat cheese tamales? Peeky toe crab napoleon with wasabi crème fraîche? So precious but so Quilpe. She would call her seafood supplier. And as much as she avoided food fads, she would feature some entrée or another covered with mushroom foam, and it would delight him no end.

Hollowell had a digestion so irritable that he seemed to subsist entirely on hothouse grapes, and there was little she could do about him, but Clendenning was a piece of cake. He would order beef, and she would make sure it was fit for royalty. She'd better go check what other cuts she'd need for the weekend before she called the meat man to have him kill the fatted calf.

She swiveled on her stool, and her foot hit a large cardboard box on the floor. "What's this?"

"A tip!" said Ping. She knelt next to the box and, with elaborate ceremony, presented Vita with a starched white shirt. "That Mrs. Clay carried the box down this morning, huffing and puffing. She said she was moving and that these shirts were too good for Goodwill. Maybe the staff would like them? Ha!"

Vita examined the stiff square of shirt, then opened the box wider to reveal three dozen of them, folded, strapped, and wrapped in plastic from the cleaners. "What are we supposed to do with a bunch of men's button-downs?" she asked. "And since when are we a charity?"

"They make a good Frisbee," said Ping, tossing a tight square of shirt up in the air and catching it.

"Size eighteen," said Vita, looking at the collar. She ran her fingers along the stitching, then over the white-on-white monogram on the sleeve—*TIC*—Thornton I. Clay. "This shirt must've cost a couple of hundred dollars."

"Let me see," said Luisa.

Vita flipped the shirt across the counter to Luisa, but she had a bowl of tuna salad cradled in her arms, so she let the shirt skid past her and onto the floor. "Stiff as toast!"

"True," agreed Vita. "But you wear a shirt like that, people think you know what you're doing."

Luisa put the bowl aside and bent to pick up the shirt out of curiosity. "My brothers, they know nothing, but my sister, she works at the day care. Shirts make good smocks."

"Take them away then." Vita set off to do a meat inventory but was distracted by the sight of the morning's produce delivery. Through the slats of the crate she spied a mango the color of sunset and bent to sniff it. She closed her eyes and felt tropical sands sift through her toes. Her new supplier, a young woman just starting out in the business, was more forager than buyer, and brilliant at that.

When she opened her eyes, she caught sight of a shirt sailing through the air. Ping had thrown a shirt to Pedrosa at the sink, who caught it with two wet hands. "*Gracias,*" he said, his broad face lighting up from this unexpected gift.

Luisa grabbed an armful from the box and, like an Olympic discus thrower, began to fling the shirts around the kitchen, one after another, first to Pedrosa, then to Vita, then Ping, then back to Pedrosa, but in this second round they were laughing too hard to catch them, so the packets piled up on the floor. Ping gave one a kick, and it skidded across the rubber tile like a hockey puck, landing at Dr. Nicastro's feet, who stood at the door, looking confused and uncomfortable.

Luisa, stifling a laugh, gathered up all the shirts and threw them back in the box, which she lugged to the outside steps.

"Hi, Dr. Nicastro," said Vita, putting her toque back on and tucking in her hair. She gave his body an approving look and was tempted to squeeze his thigh to test for leanness. "Here to talk about tonight's dinner?"

Nicastro smiled but felt unsure. "Do I ever want to talk about anything else?"

They both laughed, and the staff made themselves scarce, busying themselves with their designated duties. "I hoped you would stop by today," said Vita. "I have a scallop and seaweed dish for you to try." She turned to the walk-in, pushing a crate ahead of her.

"What's this?" Nicastro, with difficulty, bent to pick up a shirt overlooked by Luisa.

"I bet that would fit you like a sausage casing," said Vita as the metal door closed behind her. From inside, her words continued to echo. "Take it, we've got plenty."

Nicastro examined the custom label from Hong Kong, the careful hand stitching around the collar. It wasn't new, but it had hardly been worn, still in its pristine packaging from a good hand-laundry in Chinatown. He looked at Ping and tried to erase the terrible thought that passed through his mind. Maybe Phoebe was right about Vita fencing goods.

Even as he tiptoed out, he wondered about the salad and was never so miserable in his life. When Vita came out of the walk-in, he was gone.

"That's strange." As she stood there, looking at the kitchen door continue to swing, she stuck her hand under the plastic wrap and chose a succulent scallop to chew on.

Chapter Twenty-one

Taking a Mulligan

THE BOARD of Governors met in the library, with moonlight reflecting off the open casement windows. The varnished globe, sitting in its filigreed iron stand in the corner, seemed to visibly swell with the heat and humidity, expanding its crack. No one, save Clendenning, wanted to be there. The temperature was too hot, the subject of giving Gerard the boot too uncomfortable, and the day's news about the Clays just too juicy.

"Please." Using a wooden mallet, Clendenning rapped the table once, with meaning. "May we get started?"

"It's unbelievable," hissed Regina Wolfe as she pulled herself to the table. "Marshall told me the FBI found the Clays' Porsche at a private airstrip in New Hampshire."

"You think you know people, huh?" whispered Arnold Quilpe, whose profile was so patrician it could have been struck on a Roman coin.

"There's no knowing anyone, apparently," she said, and shook her head in wonder. "On Saturday night, they bought a round at the bar as if all were rosy with the world."

"I heard they played *golf* yesterday," said Linzee Gibbons, leaning in. "Knowing the whole while that the court was going to hand down indictments this morning."

"You've got to give them credit," Regina said. "I mean, it was considerate not to upset others with their bad news."

"*Bad news?*" snapped Palmer Stillington. He leaned back in his Jacobean chair, then let it fall forward again, like a stomping beast. "You don't call what they did bad news, you call it theft. Once this is all out in the open, the Admissions Committee will have something to answer for."

Clendenning rapped the table again to keep Stillington from lathering and get the talk off the Clays. "Let's get started." It was he who had rashly put them up for membership five years before, being an initial investor in Clay Realty Trust. But according to the indictments, they'd been selling more trust than realty. This put not only Clendenning's own investments into question, but also the Club's. Before the meeting, Gerard had nervously revealed the Clays' outstanding receipts, upwards of $18,000. They had even charged new clothes at the gift shop on their way out the door.

The group of six finally settled down, rearranging their drinks in front of them. The roll call was taken. Present were Regina Wolfe, Arnold Quilpe, Palmer Stillington, Linzee Gibbons, Eugene Hollowell, and their leader, Humphrey Clendenning. Absent were Peter Weber, bareboating on the St. Lawrence Seaway; John Payson, at his summer place in Blue Hill, Maine; Maggie Fenwick, home babysitting a new grandson; and Helen Clay, whereabouts unknown.

Clendenning cleared a dry throat. "At issue this evening is the question of Gerard Wilton's suitability as manager of the Club." He began to read from the papers in front of him, which listed the blunders he believed Gerard responsible for, from the plate of halibut on his lap ("inability to properly train waitstaff") to the eyeballs in the road ("inability to properly implement plans") to the present horror of demonstrations at the gate ("inability to contain controversy in a proper manner"). While he rasped on, the board members could not sit still, twisting and turning in their stiff chairs. None of them minded voting when it came to authorizing funds or some other mindless procedure, but when it came to matters of consequence, they could be reluctant to act.

Clendenning finished, then looked up and eyed each person at the table before asking Vice President Hollowell to make a formal motion.

But before Hollowell could open his mouth, Linzee Gibbons spoke. "Surely the Bellows shooting wasn't Gerard's fault," she said, fluffing up her blond bangs. "And look what a fantastic job he does otherwise. God knows I've had my misgivings about the man, but I think he's just coming into his own. The service lately has been stellar."

"He's exposed us to ridicule and censure," said Clendenning. "I want him out."

"I agree with Linzee on this," said Arnold Quilpe. "We can't switch horses midstream. If you're still all het up about him in a few weeks, we can revisit it later, after Labor Day."

"I won't have my family's summer disrupted by a change in management." Palmer Stillington stood up, his round face puffed and mottled. He leaned on the edge of the table with both soft hands, his fingers white, and through his small teeth, dyed yellow from tobacco, he spat his warning. "I'll sue the entire board if you vote for his removal. And you in particular, Clendenning."

Clendenning, understanding full well that suing was just another form of violence, half stood and leaned toward Stillington, and on his thin lips were the words *screw you*. But he paused. Once he crossed that line there would be no going back. Everyone at that table would spread the news around the Club like an airborne virus, and they would tear out his liver for what they would see as a vulgar loss of control. They put up with Stillington because they were used to putting up with Stillington and because they all wanted to stay on the Museum Ball guest list, but they expected their president to have the restrained, laconic temperament of a golf pro. More to the point, a crude attack would cause people to talk, which would lead to more talk, possibly unearthing the nefarious business dealings of his early years, which had led to his association with the Clays. Clendenning settled back in his seat. Besides, Stillington was so repulsive an individual, Clendenning didn't care to engage in the intimacy of battle with him. "That's enough, Palmer," he said softly.

Stillington went rigid with rage, and his doughy hands clenched and unclenched. Before he stomped out, he turned to the group, all of whom were looking elsewhere. "Remember, I'll sue all of you, for everything, if you do something stupid in here tonight."

When the slammed door stopped reverberating, Quilpe spoke up. "I guess that's what board insurance is for."

"It's so *hot* in here," said Regina, who ran her ringed hand through her pixie haircut, a style she had worn since the day she got married in 1966. "Let's just table the matter until September, when Gerard's due for his annual review anyway."

Everyone mumbled agreement, looking at Clendenning to put a merciful end to their trials. Hollowell made a noise, indicating that he might speak, but because he was so conflicted—whether to come to the aid of his friend Clendenning or to go along with the majority—no words formed. Like a !Kung bushman, he seemed capable of communicating only in clicks and clacks of his tongue.

"No, this is not acceptable." Clendenning barely moved his mouth. "I want him gone, today."

"I'm not even sure we have a quorum now that Palmer's gone." Quilpe used the corner of a cocktail napkin to clean his nails while he spoke. "I don't think we should make a decision like this with so few of us."

"Humpy, we fired the last manager on your recommendation," said Linzee, doodling on the blank notebook in front of her. She was the acting secretary in Helen Clay's absence, but Helen had never taken minutes either. Custom dictated they wait until after the fact, then agree on what should be included for general consumption. "We can't keep doing this. We'll get a reputation as a black widow employer and no one decent will ever want to work here. I say we put a warning in Gerard's file and give him another chance."

"No," said Clendenning, turning from white to blue. "I have never sat on a board that didn't vote in full agreement. We will vote as one on this."

The room went very still. The only sound was that of the deathwatch beetles clicking in the coffered wood ceiling.

"Speaking of managers," said Regina brightly, shifting focus. "I saw our old one at the mall the other day. She's just moved back to the area, and she had a little boy with her."

"Some fool actually married that dried-up fruit?" Quilpe laughed at his own question, even though nothing was funny.

"Well, no," said Regina, smirking. "When I said, oh, who's the lucky man? she said there was no man. She was a single mother."

Clendenning tried to say the words *Let's move on,* but they would not form in the dry, sticky cavity that had become his mouth. When he heard Eugene Hollowell mumble something about age, he started coughing.

"He's over three," said Regina, politely ignoring Humpy's seizure. "She must have gotten knocked up . . ."

They all counted on their fingers and looked at one another, not sure of their results.

Clendenning slammed the mallet on the table and they flinched. "Enough," he said, straightening in his chair. "Maybe it's too hot to make an intelligent decision tonight. In the meantime, I'm going to talk to our legal counsel and get our ducks in a row so that when we do fire Wilton, there's no suing for wrongful dismissal."

A nocturnal insect beat against the screen, distracting Clendenning as he stood to leave, and he knocked his glass over. The bourbon poured out on the table in sheets, soaking Gerard's employment folder.

"Ducks, smucks," said Quilpe, standing up and stretching. "The staff seems to love him. And a happy staff makes for happy members, no matter what way you look at it. As head of the Food Committee, I'm going to blow my own horn and say that the food here is the best it's ever been. When I told Vita as much this morning, she said she owed it all to the board's leadership, not to mention Gerard's relentless dedication to exacting service."

After Clendenning left, general amiability broke out in the room. Conversations were picked up where they were left off as if there had been no meeting at all, and they hurried to get to the porch or air-conditioned lounge, eager to find out if anything more had been dug up about the Clays. It was so much fun to have a scandal!

Chapter Twenty-two

The Slice

A FEW DAYS after the board meeting, Vita sat on the cold stone bench in the garden contemplating the abyss of darkness around her. She clicked the illumination on her watch, then turned it off. It was almost four o'clock in the morning, which meant that Mrs. Suarez and her sons would arrive soon. Vita felt another rush of anxiety come over her, and she clasped her stomach. A bird trilled sharply, then all was silent again.

Greek gods, cloaked in ivy and set into niches along the brick walls, kept watch with her. They must be lonely, she thought. When she first started working at the Club and saw the enclosed garden tucked away at the back of the building, she'd asked Gerard why the members ignored it. True, it was a bit frayed around the edges with overgrowth, and the bronze sundial with the inscription *I Count Only Sunny Hours* had fallen off its pedestal long ago, but the overall atmosphere was darkly romantic. And after all, even bloodless Wasps needed a decent place to propose. Gerard had rolled his eyes and pointed to the adjacent employee parking lot. The garden was in an unfashionable neighborhood.

It must have been au courant at one time, though, because in the Club's kitchen files she'd unearthed yellowed menus for Teas in the Garden, Cocktails by the Sundial, and even one for a White Food Party in Moonlight: White Grapes, Cold Chicken with White Glaze, Poached Sole with White Sauce, Endive Salad, and Meringues with White Crystallized Violets. As revolting as the food sounded, it was not nearly as repulsive as the penciled note on the menu reminding the manager to hire coal-black musicians to make the white seem whiter.

But the world, even the Club's world, changed after World War II, when the workers, who had always lived on premises (Vita imagined the cook curled up on a rug in front of the stove) began to live independent lives and commuted to work. They parked their jalopies by the kitchen door, and over the years this parking area expanded until one day it was just too close to the garden for comfort. It wasn't long before it was abandoned; until now it was hardly remembered.

And here we are full circle, Vita mused, with the employee cars exiled to the frontage road and the back parking area reclaimed by the members. She ran her fingers along the carved egg-and-dart trim of the bench seat. Would the members come back to the garden now?

No, they wouldn't. They liked the sweeping vistas from the porch, big scenes that made them feel expansive. Brick walls only turned them back on themselves, and that was far too close for comfort. But that's just what she liked about the place, the enclosure of it, the safety, its sense of being untouched by man. Until recently, that is, when Gerard banned smoking by the Dumpster, scattering employees to every hedge and boulder. She stood up, the seat of her jeans cold from the stone, and walked over to the marble urn in the corner. Even in the dark, she could see a pile of white-and-tan cigarette butts snubbed out in the mossy dirt. Ashes to ashes.

She felt weak, on top of being sick to her stomach, so she went back to the bench. This time she lay down, crossing her hands to her shoulders like a saint on a sarcophagus. As much as she tried to distract herself, there was no escaping what lay ahead of her.

She shut her eyes, but there it was: By dawn the geese would be dead. "*No dolor,*" Mrs. Suarez had promised. No pain.

Vita's eyes flashed open. A painless death. Did that make it right? The geese had led happy, hand-fed lives, but still, was it okay to kill and eat them just because they'd been treated well?

She could only stare at the mute night sky. The stars were already gone, the half-moon fading away as its black backdrop changed to a deep lavender. Her eyes were burning from lack of sleep this past week as she wrestled with the business of taking a life. Something else bothered her too. Night after night, she stewed over the sudden absence of Dr. Nicastro. The one she loved to feed, who loved to be fed. Now, gone. In her sleepless haze, the two—killing and feeding—had become all mixed up.

At first she thought he'd been offended that she'd offered him that shirt, that she was out of line. But then, as she lay awake pondering the goose question, she realized it was more serious than that. Dr. Nicastro, with his exquisitely attuned sensory organs, must have detected the scent of murderous intent upon her. She'd seen how the members had avoided Mr. Lambert after he hit the goose with the golf ball, as if the act of killing had set him apart, turning him into something sacred, or simply insane. Would she too be changed to the core by the carnage that lay ahead of her this morning?

As she massaged the tightness from her shoulders, she wished she was still as innocent as she had been earlier in the summer, when she'd negotiated the butchering arrangements with Mrs. Suarez (who was to receive a set amount of cash and two of the geese). Vita had assumed that she herself would have nothing to do with the grisly act. She imagined she'd take delivery of the animals at the kitchen door as nonchalantly as if accepting a crate of mangoes. But through her daily interaction with the geese, she began to see them as more than just raw material for her art. They became, against her will, individuals, and even though she knew better than to name them, she could not help herself. The largest one was Wilbur, the smallest, Penny. When she started calling a particularly annoying goose Gerard, she knew that what she had on her hands was a moral struggle with the very nature of food and life itself.

She closed her eyes again, and Dr. Nicastro's face appeared to her, with his dark, amused eyes, his rumpled hair, and his cheeks shapely from a lifetime of contented meals. If only she could feed him again! Her job was to nourish life, not snuff it out.

But maybe the one could not be separated from the other.

She sat up with the chill of sweat on her forehead. Must food preparation begin with a death? She had, with deep regret, come to the conclusion that the answer was yes. Life came from life, and in the end even humans were just meat for worms. The battle raged inside until she thought her head might burst. Vegetation was life too, wasn't it? It had to be killed, if that was the word, in the name of dinner. Was a head of lettuce so different from a goose? What separated the goose from man? The goose, the grass, the gorilla in the trees—all manifestations of the same living cell. Where did it end? And where did it begin?

She swam in these questions, drowning in her misgivings, and still had no answers. But she had come to one conclusion: Instead of merely accepting delivery of the geese, she was going to accept responsibility for them. She had fattened them with dignity and respect, and now she must likewise kill them with her own hands.

She would kill that very morning. If she could not, she would give up meat entirely and renounce her world. Her delectable world, full of Maui-onion-and-garlic-stuffed lamb, lobster ravioli with oyster cream, and, not the least, maple-glazed duck breasts with duck-fat hash browns. Dr. Nicastro's favorite.

She gulped back a sob. Yes, there were vegetarian avenues open to her, but staying at the Club was not one of them. She would have to work in some back-alley organic café, serving wet tofu to customers with carotenemia, orange-palmed picky eaters who had replaced their taste buds with ethics. How could she possibly live that way? She was devoted to the rapture of the senses. It was her religion.

Why, oh why, hadn't they taught her at the Institute that to be a chef was to feed by murder? Her instructors had brought in prepared carcasses and taught her how to negotiate with suppliers, how to jolly them up to get choice picks, pretending they were the very source of food and not just an intermediary. No one ever made her look into the eyes of an animal and see for herself what life meant. But now that she had looked, she knew: Redemption for the meal's blood could only be won by reverence of the sacrifice itself. There was no going back. In order to continue her vocation she must master the primal act of food prep. She must kill the geese with her own hands.

She stood up with a start, impatient now to begin. *No dolor.* She tugged at her sweatshirt and paced, making a full circle around the crumbling brick walks. Last fall's leaves were still piled in the corners. She should get Barry to clean it up a bit, get the fountain working again so that water would once more pour from the mouth of Green Man, with his hair of wavy lettuce.

She stopped and looked around her. Lettuce. Rising up in her mind were the elegant parterres she had visited during her semester in France, with orderly triangles of sea-blue kale and rusty nasturtiums and lettuces so creamy they bruised when touched. She could do that here, in this space. An herb and salad garden. A steady supply of fresh organic greens in season. She thought of that rat bastard Utah, and her eyes narrowed. Never again would she let herself be at the mercy of some two-timing greengrocer. But Dr. Nicastro, surely he would come to visit her raised beds, pinching the basil and sniffing the thyme.

She heard a car. The muffler was coughing, so it had to be Luisa's ancient Toyota, a luxury she could finally afford now that she was a waitress. Vita ran to the gate and clutched her hands on the wrought iron. They had come for her. She watched the headlights switch off as the car pulled up behind a utility shed. Mrs. Suarez, who was dressed, as always, like a nun, in a dark dress and sweater, black stockings, and sensible shoes, came out of the darkness and into the circle of the security light. Her teenage boys, Anselmo and Paolo, both a head taller than their mother, were dressed like Vita, in hooded sweatshirts and jeans. They were armed with buckets, boards, and burlap bags, which they loaded into the two golf carts left ready by Barry. Luisa waved good-bye to her family, then, even though she could not see Vita in the dark, gave a thumbs-up to the garden as she passed to the kitchen, where she would wait for the call making sure all was safe to smuggle the dead geese back to the Club.

Vita, for whom all occasions, even this one, called for food, picked up a basket packed with croissants stuffed with scrambled eggs and chives, fresh orange juice in one thermos, hot coffee in another, and, in case her strength failed her, a flask of cognac, as sweet and heavy as sacrificial wine. In the other hand, wrapped in suede, she carried her knives.

"*El puerco,*" Mrs. Suarez whispered, folding her hands tightly on her lap. On the drive across the golf course, she sat in the back of a cart with Vita while Anselmo drove. Paolo followed closely in the other cart with the equipment. They did not turn on their headlights, and so the turf was black beneath their wheels. Vita turned her palms up, indicating that there was nothing she could do about the waste Mrs. Suarez had just seen in the Dumpster.

Mrs. Suarez was indignant. The Club should get a pig, *el puerco,* not a Dumpster. They could fatten a dozen pigs with a steady supply of garbage such as she had seen. Vita turned away to smile and looked out at the course. Pigs at the Club. She could make some unkind comment about that, but even as she smiled to herself, she could not help envisioning succulent roast pork, the fat scored and crisp, surrounded by aromatic vegetables and served with a dried cherry sauce. They drove past a thickly wooded copse, and she imagined a pig pen tucked away in the trees. What a golf hazard that would be. Then she shook her head back to her senses as the carts rolled up to the water's edge.

In complete silence, the two women and the sleepy teenagers moved the butchering equipment to the two small skiffs. Paolo rowed his mother and Anselmo took Vita, too antsy to row the boat herself. She put her hood up, leaned back against the stern and closed her eyes, listening to the gentle splash of water against the oars and she felt herself drift into a different realm. All her misgivings fell away, one by one, with every stroke. When the boat's bottom scraped the sand of the island, she was as ready as she was ever going to be.

The boys mumbled as they emptied the skiffs but were shushed by their mother. Vita led the group, single file, through the narrow paths of the underbrush. With hoods up and burlap sacks over their shoulders, they looked like monks to matins. What few words they exchanged were whispered in Spanish, simple commands, *"Cuidadase"* and *"Silencio."* Take care and be quiet.

This was not the boys' first time on the island. They had come at dawn the day before to hammer in three open-ended metal killing cones into the trunk of a swamp maple at the edge of the clearing, and they had brought with them mesh cages to round up the sleeping geese. The birds had to fast. No food for twenty-four hours, just water. The intestines would be cleaner that way. Vita had not questioned—she was coping with enough questions—but now, as she stepped into the sandy center of the island where little would grow, she was unprepared for the sight. The utilitarian arrangement of cages stacked on one another was a stark reminder of the cold-blooded truth of her task. The geese slept with their long black necks curled elegantly under their wings. So beautiful. So alive, even in sleep. Vita worried that she might not be able to go through with it after all. And yet, there was no turning back. Was there?

She put down her basket and knelt to unwrap the suede knife carrier, unrolling it on the damp ground. Her knives, with their metal rivets, honed edges, and wooden handles made dark by the oil from her palms, were extensions of her own hands. They beckoned to her. She picked one up. The familiar, balanced heft gave her strength. This was her calling. It was her life.

"*Vamos a seguir el andando,*" she whispered. It was time to get on with it. She stood up. They had close to thirty geese to stick and gut, which was not in itself time-consuming—the more labor-intensive job of plucking would take place next week—but they had to be finished before any obsessive golfers—or Gerard—showed up.

Her conscience twitched ever so slightly. She'd never quite got around to explaining about the hanging to Gerard. The dead, feathered geese would need a cool room for a few days to get "high," so the tendons and muscles could relax. Rather than bother Gerard with these details, Vita had made the necessary arrangements directly with Fergus, the maintenance man, who missed his mum's cooking. So, with one of Vita's haggis in his backpack, Fergus told Gerard that the air conditioner in Room #13 was out being repaired, so not to rent it out. Later, after the deposit of a box of fresh shortbread in his supply closet, he gave Vita the only key to the recently changed lock on the door.

The plan was to hang the geese by their feet on a rope stretched across the room, and when they were ripe, Mrs. Suarez and her boys would return in the middle of the night, and, using the barbecue grill outside to boil water, they would scald the birds and strip them of feathers. Then the fun would begin. First, the geese would get washed with warm water and bran to whiten the skin. Mrs. Suarez's seasoned salt rub would be massaged into the birds, and they would sit that way for a couple of days to draw the toxins out and flavor in. Then they would all get a refreshing shower, a firm truss, and a quick boil, followed by a long, slow roast, like a sauna, to render the yellow fat without cooking it. After the grease was drained off and the birds patted dry, the skin would be basted and glazed with lime and sugar, and a generous dose of Mrs. Suarez's herbal potion. Back into the oven they'd go, stuffed, with the heat on high so the skin would form a shell to hold in the moist goosiness. Vita would then present the members with a bird with meat as tender as baby flesh, skin as crisp as a wafer, exuding a virile essence that would bring gasps of passion from even the most reserved matron of the Club.

She crossed herself and nodded to Mrs. Suarez, who gave a hand signal to a bored Anselmo to gently pull a goose from a cage, swiftly, before it could quite wake up, and put it into one of the killing cones. The underbrush was black in silhouette against the lightening sky, with foliage jutting up in some places, low in others, so that it seemed they were surrounded by a crowd.

"*Tranquilidad,*" Mrs. Suarez whispered to Anselmo. Be calm. Vita had at least been taught this much at the Institute, that livestock could have no fear at death, or else it would release adrenaline and taint the meat. It had not taught her that the only way to be sure was to do it yourself.

Anselmo held up a half-awake goose by its scaly legs and lowered its head down into a killing cone, like a giant metal ice cream cone with the bottom cut off. He put his other hand up the open end to feel for the beak, and pulled it through. The body of the goose stayed confined in the metal, with only two webbed feet and a bit of tail sticking out from the top, the head jutting out from the bottom.

Vita held a flashlight on the animal and bent to peer at his face. They looked each other in the eye. What was he thinking? Did he think?

He blinked. Awake, but not aware. Mrs. Suarez had told her that the blood would rush to the bird's head and make him *sonso,* or slightly sedated. But Vita could feel his eyes upon her, and she prayed. In silence, she apologized and thanked him for his life.

Then she handed the knife to Mrs. Suarez. The older woman would show her how it was done. In the beam of light, Mrs. Suarez's hands were white and disembodied against her black clothes. She pried open the beak quickly so that the goose had no time to react, and then she forced the knife to the back of his throat with a twist. The goose jolted as if given an electric shock, and then relaxed. "*Comprende?*" she asked Vita.

That was it? It wasn't that bad, was it? But then the goose seemed to rise from the dead, trying to push up out of the cone with its wings, shaking and quivering and frantically kicking its feet. The cone shook. Vita shook. "*El morte,*" said Mrs. Suarez, dismissing the commotion with a wave of her hand. "*El solo impulsos.*" But the reactions looked like more than autonomic impulses to Vita. Mrs. Suarez pulled on the head to straighten out the neck and made a small slit at the jugular. Blood poured out black in the dim light, pulsing in rhythm as the heart exhausted itself. Mrs. Suarez looked at the knife in her hand. "*Muy fino.*"

Nice knife. Was that all she had to say? But even as Vita stepped back, Paolo had the next goose prepared in a cone on the other side of the tree. Mrs. Suarez took Vita's arm by her bloody hand and pulled her over. Paolo held the flashlight while Vita reached in and grasped the beak and pried it open with both hands, which took more strength than she had imagined. Concentrating on the physical difficulty of what she was doing allowed her to not think about what she actually *was* doing. Mrs. Suarez put the knife in her hand and then guided it in position for her. "*Pulsar,* Vita," she said, and Vita pushed, giving the knife a quick twist, then pulled it out. In what seemed to Vita to be slow motion, Mrs. Suarez extended the head and laid her hand on the neck to show where to make the cut, even as the goose began to shudder.

Vita cut. The slice bled profusely as the goose kicked, spraying the blood on its executioners. Who knew there was so much blood in a goose? But there was no time to let the enormity of her action sink in, no time for regret or glory. From then on, it was simply a processing line. The caged geese were waking up; time was critical. There could be no honking, which might alert the neighbors that something was afoot. The boys moved quickly, their hoods up so Vita could not see the expressions on their faces, whether they were disgusted or interested in their attendant duties. They were efficient, one holding the flashlight for Vita while the other readied the next goose in the cone. Mrs. Suarez watched with her arms crossed, nodding in satisfaction. The geese were all butchered in under twenty minutes, like a massacre. But it was far from over.

Mrs. Suarez had the boys arrange the piece of plywood on two rocks, making a low table. Anselmo put a dead goose in front of his mother, who motioned for Vita to kneel beside her. Vita knelt. There was a plastic pan between them for the guts, and a white food container for the livers. Paolo stood behind them with the flashlight, chatting with his brother in English about a rap concert downtown. Mrs. Suarez snapped, "*Silencio.*" All was quiet again as she cut a circular opening under the tail and continued up, with the other hand spreading open the stomach cavity, exposing the ropes of blue intestines. Mrs. Suarez tched to herself. Vita knew she disapproved of gutting the geese before hanging because the rotting innards of the carcass would add to the final flavor of the goose. But Vita wanted those livers fresh, and besides, she was not so sure the members really needed that extra bit of decay.

When the cut was done, Mrs. Suarez put the knife down and shoved both hands into the cavity, digging around, loosening things up, and then pulled a mess of stringy offal into the pan. She took Vita's hand and pressed it into the opening. It was like one of those childhood initiations of squeezing "eyeball" Jell-O or tasting "worm egg" tapioca, except this was so very hot and smelled like goose feces, but Vita refused to let herself be sick. She could feel the hardness of the heart under the rib cage. Mrs. Suarez asked her if she could feel the liver on the other side. *"El higado?"* Oh, yes. It was her fat liver as nature intended, a slippery jewel.

She wanted to yank the organ out of the body, but Mrs. Suarez shook her head no, so Vita retreated empty-handed. With the concentration of a midwife, Mrs. Suarez pulled the rest of the guts out and into the pan. She motioned for Paolo to lean in closer with the flashlight so she could point out the small green sac attached to the liver. It was the gall bladder, and if it should break, the liver would be ruined. Vita handed her the knife, and with a flick Mrs. Suarez slashed the sac off in one piece, handing the liver to Vita. It quivered warmly in her hand, dark and intense, and she laid it in her white container and quickly sealed it so not a drop of its essence would be lost to the air. She flushed with the heat of her accomplishment. Dr. Nicastro would be so proud.

After that, they worked in a frenzy of gutting, while the boys dug a ditch for the intestines. Vita reserved the hearts, the rock-hard gizzards, and the sheets of fat that lined the stomach cavity. Everything else was garbage. But would it be garbage to a pig? Or just dinner? If she kept even one pig next summer at the Club, think of the luau she could throw.

Mrs. Suarez acted as line manager, pointing to this goose or that, directing the cages to be folded flat and returned to the skiffs, and sending the boys back and forth with bags as they filled up. Off in the distance, a cock crowed. Phoebe Lambert's roosters were sounding the alarm of sunrise. Phoebe had rescued them from a layer hatchery, where males, useless in the female world of the egg, were destroyed. A few weeks ago, Dr. Nicastro, who'd heard it from Mrs. Lambert, had told Vita that the birds fought each other with spurs all day long and the neighbors were circulating a petition. Vita smiled. She would be happy to take them. Coq au vin?

When the last goose was eviscerated, Vita stood up slowly, drenched with blood. The boys splashed buckets of water on the cones to rinse them and kicked dirt over the congealed blood on the ground. They dumped the last of the guts in the ditch and buried them, then covered them with rocks so animals would not dig them up. Everyone washed their hands the best they could from buckets they brought from the lake, and Vita wiped her knives clean with a cloth and put them away. The boys wrenched the cones from the trees, dismantled the table, and sat down on the rocks to eat croissants and drink orange juice with their mother.

Vita had no appetite, but she laid out four plastic cups and poured a thimbleful of cognac in each. Paolo and Anselmo got back to their feet for this unforeseen bonus. The day, still not quite begun, was already warming up, so they pulled their wet, stained sweatshirts over their heads. Underneath they wore Mr. Clay's shirts, but with the sleeves and collars ripped away, unbuttoned halfway down their handsome chests. Very teenage macho, she thought, with their arms dark and muscled against the fine white cloth. And they knew it, preening loose feathers off their bodies for Vita's benefit. She handed them cognac, and one to Mrs. Suarez, who patted her on the shoulder in return. They raised their cups to the geese and drank. She felt good. She'd done it. To the Great Goose in the Sky. Thank you.

Vita checked her watch. Almost five thirty. "*Vamos,*" she said. They had to hurry. She looked up at the light gray sky for crows, but it was empty. Good. If those scavengers picked up the scent of blood, they would hector them the whole way back to the clubhouse and wake the neighbors. Phoebe would call the police to report that someone was harassing the crows. But they were making good time and would easily beat the crows, the eager-beaver golfers, and Gerard. The cleaning crew would already be at work. Luisa was baking *pasteis de nata,* flaky pastry cups filled with egg custard, a Portuguese goody to lure them down to the kitchen so Vita could sneak the geese in through the front door.

They collected the last few things, but just as they were about to leave, Mrs. Suarez held up a bloodstained hand. *"Espera,"* she commanded. They waited as she pulled a handful of Hershey's Kisses out of her cardigan pocket and left them on the rock. She pointed to the sky, shrugged, and smiled. *"Los dios."*

The boys elbowed each other and shook their heads, but Vita nodded, and they left the clearing. It was too bad she hadn't known that they were expected to leave a small offering. She could have brought Scharffen Berger, a proper chocolate with which to thank the gods.

Chapter Twenty-three

Re-teeing the Shot

EARLY SUNDAY, after feverishly working through the night, Charles wiped his forehead with a rag, then snapped the welder's mask back down over his face. The world turned swampy green, as if he'd been plunged into thick primordial water. As he picked up his torch again, he imagined himself happily bobbing along with the first Precambrian cells, all trying to figure out this warm cocktail called Life. That's what welding felt like, every moment an act of discovery. There was a time—eons ago by his new inner clock, but probably just a matter of weeks by normal reckoning—when the thought of spending a morning not at golf but in the cool darkness of his garage with the smells of solder and oil and metal, the raw materials of creation, would have been alien to him. Now it was his very joy.

The torch trailed a long line down to its power source, the TIG welder, and Charles—in tune now to every change in his environment—took a cautionary glance at the snaking presence of the cord as he climbed the ladder. He had specific gravity now. He knew where his body was in space—knew exactly where to reach for what he needed. Look how tools were designed to the scale of his calloused hand—a world created by humans for humans—for it was tools that made man a formidable animal. Even the humble ladder upon which he stood had rungs spaced to accommodate both the limitations and boundlessness of the human step. Proportion was everything. A simple change could jar the viewer—to make one look, to pay attention.

All this he owed to the goose who had so innocently stood in the path of his Pro V1, forcing him to examine the balance sheet of his soul. Madeline euphemistically called the incident "his accident," but Charles saw it for what it was. His fate. Without transgression there could be no knowledge, and the bird's life had been sacrificed so that he could know his own—and what a sorry sight that had been. Lacking in meaning, tepid in feeling, and misspent at the altar of affluence.

To be fair, how could he have turned out otherwise with all those Calvinist genes coursing through his blood? For generations his family had equated prosperity with virtue, seen material thriving as the path to salvation. But he could have, should have, fought against his natural bent—DNA was not destiny. Twenty-five years toiling in the salt mines of finance was the price he had paid. From now on he must elect a higher path, even though it might not be so generously paved with luxury goods. And what did that matter anyway? Purchases and possessions had lost their power. When he bought that new club last February it had done nothing for him—what he needed was equipment to straighten out his life, not his drive.

He eyed his creation and made a mental note to get more twist in the structure, more flexibility. God knows that's what he'd always needed himself. He could barely even turn his head without turning his entire body, as if his spine, neck, and skull were welded together and not a pliable construction of nature. Steeve had told him as much—that the more he could twist, the more power he would have—but he had taken the advice too literally, spending too much energy trying to contort his body rather than his mind.

But other than that bit of stiffness, he was pleased with how his creation was shaping up. It was invigorating to be actually making something, to be so intimately engaged in the physical world, listening to the music of his own hammering. He flicked on the torch and leaned in, so close to the heat and the white light he felt himself melting into the work itself. From under his mask, he breathed in deeply of the metallic smoke, incorporating it into his body. He began to heat up the iron plate. There was so little room for error—and the price of such an error was so high—that he was soon lost in concentration. It was just him and the light, out in the universe—with the sound of the machine: *Om-m-m-m. Om-m-m.*

When the heat seared off the exact sliver of metal, he was sorry to have it end. When he lifted up his mask, the color of his studio turned natural again, but somehow it seemed less than real. Nod had once told him about *maskenfribeit*—the freedom conferred by masks. Nod loved not only to wear the welding mask, but to use it as his subject matter as well. He welded intricate and moving portrait busts of his friends and family—then fitted the faces with blank sheets of metal so that only the artist knew what was underneath. It was all very "high concept" to Charles. And yet he loved to hear Nod talk about it—he liked to appraise his progress, lend a hand—a son he never had. He flashed on the odd quote pasted up on the wall at school: "'Sooner strangle an infant in its cradle than nurse unacted desires.'—Blake." He wasn't sure exactly what that meant, but it always made him think of Madeline nursing Phoebe, and how happy they had been then. Why had they only had the one? They should have had more, but he had balked. He thought they'd have to divide their love for Phoebe among others, like an inheritance. But maybe love didn't have to be allocated and accounted for. Maybe it grew the more it was spent. He should not have been so afraid of creation.

While he waited for the cut to cool, he ran a leather-gloved hand along the spiraling shafts that served as tendons and decided here was where he could increase fluidity. A few adjustments—here, there. It was a risk to make a change—a positive correction in one place could have a detrimental effect in another. In life as well. An examination of historical data showed a high correlation between material escalation and family dissatisfaction. He, numb; his daughter, rebellious; his wife, depressed. Phoebe was probably just going through a phase—not that it was a phase he ever went through, being an odd conservative duck in his own sixties generation—but Madeline . . . sweet, sad Madeline. He'd fallen in love with her for her happy outlook and wild sense of freedom, but where did it go? What had he done?

He took off his gloves to fondle the cutlery in a box he kept under the workbench. This was the life, to add beauty to the world. He turned the fork over in his bare hand, letting the utensil's essence tell him where it should go. How balanced it was. How ingenious. A financial instrument had nothing on even the simplest physical object. He flipped it over and ran his thumb along the wavy tracings engraved on the handle—Damascene. Great word. People would have to search for the hidden pleasure of it. They would have to look for it.

Could he get Madeline to look? Could he get her to move? There was a time when she would have gone anywhere with him, but she was not quite so game anymore. The fact remained: If he quit his job, they could not afford to stay here, and would they even want to live in a neighborhood where the overriding ambition was to be like everyone else? A place where everyone examined one another's lives so closely that it left no time to look at their own? Maybe they should go back to the beginning, go to California, where they'd met, where Madeline was born. Buy a house among the redwoods, build a studio out back. His sculpture was so large now that he had to take care that it didn't get any taller or he wouldn't be able to get it out of the garage bay. What he needed were ceilings twenty, thirty feet high. Nothing could stop him then.

With a start, he felt the garage shake and creak from the banging of goat horns against the outside wall. He could not see the goats because the garage windows had been boarded up for their protection—and his privacy—but he could hear them. They clacked their heads all day in play. How free and unselfconscious they were. He would have to build a barn as well.

He picked out a few more forks and put them in the back pocket of his mustard Carhartts, suddenly impatient for their new life to begin. He would take the week off from the office to finish his project so that by this very weekend Madeline could gaze upon his monument, and she would rediscover him, and he her. His sculpture would be the key to unlatch their door. Art would redeem them.

He climbed up the ladder and ran his bare hand, too soon, over the spot where he'd just worked, and it was so hot he almost drew back at the touch. But then he remembered what Vincent had said about staying with his pain—so he let his hand rest. It was not long before the burning sensation began to draw something from inside of him—a pulsing wave surging through his whole body. Something less than blood, something more than memory. What was it? When had he felt like this before? This swelling in his chest? This clarity and acceptance? This peace.

He steadied his footing on the stepladder and leaned his head against the warm body of the sculpture. His hand was still on the hot spot, a conduit, waiting, and as the heat moved from metal to flesh, he refelt a moment from many years before—a lifetime, his life—when he had passed a younger hand across the sun-warmed hood of his first BMW, the maroon 1974 Tii that his father, dead now for more than fifteen years, gave him when he graduated from MIT with a major in business—not in aerodynamics, as he had once dreamed of but was too cautious to pursue. But the road noise of his prized BMW turned out to be so loud that he always imagined himself in the cockpit, flying.

The warmth spread through him and made him sleepy. He released his sculpture and sat down on the top step of the ladder, bowing his head in exhaustion, causing the mask to flick back down over his face. And he left it like that, reaching underneath to rub his eyes, releasing tears. How he loved that car, and how soon he had set it aside. After his first promotion, he had bought a newer, more expensive model, which, in its turn, was replaced by another. "Chasing the material dragon," Phoebe had accused him last year when he pulled the new 525i into the driveway—

but he hadn't understood. He hadn't understood so much for so long. In fact, he had told her—with some pride—of his reserve in foregoing the 745i at almost twice the price. She snapped, in that impatient way of hers. "Chasing the dragon is slang, Dad, for trying to recapture your first great high. The thing is, it can't be done, no matter what you shoot up. *No matter what you buy.*"

Where had she picked up such concepts? he had wondered—which only went to show how he was always asking the wrong questions. He sniffed and caught a drip on his flannel sleeve. How could he have been so dense as to not see that he was being given more than keys to a simple car? They were the keys to the world. How eloquent an object can be. He mourned for that car, gone forever, long buried in some wretched landfill with all the other discards. And then he mourned his father for what seemed like the very first time.

He cried easily under the mask. The death of his father had always seemed a distant episode—kept at arm's length. How tremendously long his arm had been. He'd thought he was being so mature, taking it like a man. In truth, he'd been afraid, not wanting to be prey to his own emotions.

But who said pain had to be orderly, or that emotions were a predator to be evaded?

Charles lifted his mask and wiped his nose on his sleeve, then let it drop again. He felt so much better. He stood back up on the top step and faced his art, then switched on the torch, letting it burn. An elegant twist was not enough—his work had to writhe. Beauty was all well and good, but passion, that was the driving force. He bore down on the metal with the flame, and it turned violently white from the heat. It was a risk—but so be it.

All was blackness except for the flame itself. The light, the fork, and a small puddle of melting solder. But from these few inches of vision, anything could happen.

Chapter Twenty-four

The Water Hazard

MADELINE STOOD at the edge of the pool, looking down at the still, green water. The soles of her feet burned from the hot cobbled surface of the deck. She lifted one foot, then another, getting used to the pain. Her sandals were back in the cool darkness of the changing room, but any discomfort was preferable to running into Ellen Bruner again.

"I'm looking forward to meeting with you and Arietta at the end of the week," Ellen had said as she crossed the corridor to go to the sauna, tightening a mocha towel around her body.

"Oh, that's right," said Madeline, pretending the tea had slipped her mind. Earlier in the day, Arietta had told her that Ellen asked to meet again, and they didn't quite know what to make of it. "Friday's okay, then?"

"Perfect," said Ellen. "I'll be in court all week, so it'll be a pleasant start to the Labor Day weekend."

Madeline was about to say something about the sauna, lifting her hand to the red sign at the door that cautioned pregnant women to avoid extreme heat. But then she caught herself. Perhaps there was no more pregnancy. A miscarriage? A change of plans after amnio revealed a fetus not quite altogether? Was this why Ellen wanted to meet?

Madeline felt a rush of compassion. How heartbreaking. At Ellen's age, she wouldn't have too many more chances left to roll the dice. On Friday, Madeline would comfort her and hold her hand. Better than that, she would cry with Ellen as if the loss were her own. Yes, she would start fresh, reaching out to people in a whole new way. Madeline let her hand fall back to her side. "See you then."

"Yes, indeed." Ellen gave her an odd little smile and closed the sauna door behind her.

Now, as she listlessly scanned the pool for Frank, Madeline stood like a crane, with one foot resting on the inside of the other leg. The water seemed murky as it reflected the overcast sky, which had not cooled the late-afternoon air but compressed it. Her foot slid back down her leg from sweat.

A few members were finding relief in the water, partially submerged like hippos. None were Frank, and none returned her gaze. Beryl Hall and Regina Wolfe were at the far end, lolling in the water with Jay Freylinghuysen, happy to have him ramble on about the 1992 Jaguar XJS he'd just gotten at auction and was looking to sell, or "place," like an orphan. The women were deeply absorbed in his words, commenting with exaggeration and laughing with enthusiasm, so as to not have to look in Madeline's direction. The only other person in the pool was Nina Rundlett, sidestroking sadly and slowly. Nature had not, as Arietta promised, come along with another great love.

Only Scott, up on his lifeguard chair, his legs twisted in some unnatural configuration around the armrests, seemed eager to acknowledge her existence. He untangled his limbs and raised his hand in a wave, exposing damp coils of hair under his arm. She wiggled a few fingers at him, then turned her head, feeling flushed.

Where was Frank? He used to always be at the Club on Sunday afternoons, but she hadn't seen him in almost two weeks, not since she had intimated that Vita was stealing. She must have stung him to the core with her dangerous bit of dirt. How could she have done that?

Shock. That's how. Automatic self-preservation. Vita had probably just been shooting the breeze, giving Frank her version of the hunt, and wondering out loud if Charles were a part of it. Look how quickly Madeline had assumed her husband had been rampaging through the thicket with a cocked gun. She had no faith in her family at all. If only Frank hadn't been pushing all her buttons that afternoon, suggesting that she worried more about what people thought about her family than about her family itself. Certainly he knew she was more worried about Charles's sanity than the appearance of sanity, more concerned about Phoebe's rebellion than the manifestation of it at the gates. Or maybe he didn't know. And how would he, when she kept her feelings so guarded? He could only judge by what he could see, and at the moment, what she could see of herself looked pretty pathetic.

The sun beat on her back, pushing her toward the water. She squatted by the edge and dipped her fingers in. Warm, unhealthily warm, ready to culture something lethal. She stood up again and straightened the pleats of her bathing suit. With no energy to pick and choose for the best lounge chair, she sat down on the closest, without leaning back, her bag on her lap, wondering what to do. She missed Frank, the only person who let her talk about the problems in her life. And she had chased him away, for just that very reason.

A phalanx of crows soared overhead. Six, eight, nine. What was that nursery rhyme about crows she used to read to Phoebe? "One is for bad news. Two is for mirth. Three is for . . . ?" She had never been one of those mothers who memorized her child's favorites, who carried the entire Mother Goose oeuvre in her head. Reading at night to her daughter had been just one more chore to cross off the list before running off to some meeting or social event. She certainly hadn't been much of a mother. And what kind of a wife?

Scott stood and stretched on his platform, somewhat elaborately, twisting his torso left, then right, the whistle around his neck swaying with the movement. Madeline realized that he must have interpreted her looking up at the crows as gazing at him. He climbed down from his station like a chimp, using one arm, then another, before dropping to the cobbles. He was barefoot but didn't seem bothered by the hot stones as she was.

"Hey, Mrs. Lambert." He knelt on one knee next to her so that their faces were close. He smelled of coconut oil and sweat, a body exuding warmth from the sun. Her lips cracked as she twisted her mouth into a mechanical smile. "Hi, Scott. How are you?"

"I don't want you to think this is weird or anything," he said in his soft, nasal way. "I've been watching you, and you look like, so bummed. This lady needs cheering up, I said to myself."

If Gerard Wilton knew Scott was talking this way to a member, saying something so personal, Scott would be fired on the spot. And yet, wasn't it Scott's job to save lives?

She opened her mouth to thank him for his concern, but no words came. Tears filled her throat and pressed against her brain. The floodgates of her soul poured out from behind her sunglasses, and she tasted salt on her lips. Ancestors dragged themselves from the briny sea and struggled to be upright and fairly human for what? Here she was, her husband alienated, her daughter an alien, her life a mess.

Scott reached out to steady her. But he must have felt the eyes of the other members upon them, and drew back.

"Mrs. Lambert has had too much sun," he announced to the group in the pool. He turned to Madeline, pulling her up by her hands to a standing position. Her bag fell to the cobblestones. A brush, some lotion, a bottle of Evian, an old *Vanity Fair,* and a few wilted marigolds all fell out and stayed scattered in the sun. "Let's get you where it's cool." He guided her to the safety of the pool house, walking backward as if teaching her to dance. "That's it," he whispered. "You're doing good, Mrs. Lambert. You just have a little heat thing going on." Regina,

Beryl, and Jay, standing chest-deep in the pool, were staring, committing every movement to memory.

Nina, who had never noticed all the commotion in the first place, continued her solitary journey from one end of the green pool to the other. A freshly steamed Ellen Bruner held the door open as Scott helped Madeline into the pool house.

Chapter Twenty-five

Flip Shot

GERARD SAT at his mahogany desk on Tuesday morning, staring out at the lavish landscape through a window free of blinds at last. He had scraped the hawk silhouettes off the glass after the board meeting last week, the House & Grounds Committee be damned. If birds were dimwitted enough to fly into his picture window, then they deserved to be eliminated from the race. That was the natural law. They should in no way be helped by humans to avoid hazards: The stupid must be winnowed out.

Yes, he had a whole new confidence since that fateful meeting, which he had spent under the open window. He had almost cried out in joy when the board, in its own wishy-washy way, had stood up to Clendenning and saved his job.

Of course, he had mortgaged his future for the sake of his present by allowing Vita to proceed with her bloody plans. But in exchange Vita had not just catered to the secret desires of the board but also used her influence with the staff to create an unimpeachable and professional atmosphere at the Club. For the days that led up to the board meeting, the staff, inside and out, upstairs and down, was prompt, polite, organized, and smiling. Oh, those smiles.

He picked up his insulated ERCC mug ($15.99 at the gift shop) and breathed in deeply from the small opening in the lid. Peace and stability now prevailed, in spite of Phoebe Lambert and her freaky friends at the gates. Those kids (and he couldn't help thinking of them as kids, even though they were not much younger than he was) carried on as if a daily vigil would bring the Bellows goose back to life. He took a sip. Aaah. Let them be. They had not an inkling of the more recent, and extreme, decimation of the goose population that had taken place on Friday.

Birdbrains. He snickered at his own little joke, then stopped. It would not be the least bit funny if they got their claws on a Fothergill Cup menu *(Wild goose, Locally raised foie gras)*. But Phoebe wouldn't be there, he prayed as he tapped his buffed nails on polished wood. He picked up the reservation list. Oddly enough, neither would her parents. They, old Club stalwarts, had made no reservations. Gerard shook his head. Charles Lambert. The poor bastard hadn't seemed quite right since he killed the first goose of what was turning out to be a very long goose season. The protest season dragged on as well. Gerard saw Phoebe that morning when he stopped to chat with Aaron Bleane, who breathed unevenly as he leaned out of the guard booth window. Over the sound of the radio behind him, they talked about the Red Sox, but their eyes were on the demonstrators, flapping about with their cardboard wings. Phoebe had the nicest pair. She saw Gerard staring at her and hopped over.

"I've got a riddle for you two," she said, taking off her beak to speak.

"Shoot." Bleane took a loud sip of coffee from his Dunkin' Donuts cup, swishing it around like he was rinsing his mouth. Gerard made a mental memo to ask him to start decanting his coffee into ERCC paper cups.

"What's a common trade name, three syllables, that starts with *B* and ends with *K?*"

Aaron smiled. "Bisquick," he said. "My wife makes pancakes with the stuff. Throws some bananas in them, when we got 'em."

"Wrong," she said, and flapped her wings. "That's only two syllables."

Gerard folded his arms over his steering wheel and closed his eyes, trawling the depths of his mind for an answer. Usually, he guessed jokes incorrectly on purpose to give members the pleasure of "getting" him. But not now. He opened his eyes and gave his best Cheshire cat smile. *"BusinessWeek."*

"I thought so," said Phoebe, her wings drooping. She touched the amber beads at her throat, then turned and flapped away.

Gerard wondered what that was all about. Hadn't he gotten the answer right? Or was *BusinessWeek* technically four syllables? He and Aaron shrugged at each other, and then he headed up the drive, which, because almost all members were using the rear entrance, was practically virginal these days. Paved in peastone and lined with cobble, it was ridiculously expensive to maintain, impossible to plow, and unnavigable by bike or motorcycle, but the members liked a surface that could give under them. The crunch of tires on stone was the sound of money. They had to sacrifice that sensation for the moment, but they would return. Soon, he hoped. There had been no more incidents to beckon the press, and if he could move the Fothergill Cup events smoothly along this week, the board would soon forget there had ever been a problem. Not Clendenning, though. He would not forget. But neither could he live forever.

The phone trilled and the kitchen light blinked. He moaned. "Hi, Vita. Yes, okay . . . okay. If you must." He hung up and put his forehead on the desk. Vita wanted some face time with him because—surprise!—she had a problem. Was he the only one in this place who could solve things?

Yes, he was. He lifted his face to the pink sun pouring through the window and smiled at the rolling, pampered greens, the artfully pruned trees, the perfectly formed lake glinting in the distance. The Club's problems were indeed Gerard's problems. His to solve. He sat up straight and took a comb from his top drawer, swiveling in his chair and checking himself out in the mirror. This was his job, whose roots led back to when the first Eden

Rock managers wore morning coats and white carnations. He could even guess what Vita wanted to talk about. It wasn't the geese, because the worst was over as far as he was concerned. They'd been butchered in secret and brought over to Luisa's mother's house for safekeeping. But over the weekend Vita had mentioned something about changing meat suppliers because she wanted grass-fed beef that had been humanely killed, an oxymoron if he ever heard one. She said it was more expensive, but that she'd serve smaller, intense portions, balancing the plates with heirloom vegetables and Third World grains. But he was not going to roll over on this one. If she wanted to change to an expensive boutique supplier, she was going to have to make the numbers work.

Then, of course, her problem might lie closer to home. On his desk sat the restaurant receipts from the weekend. No Dr. Nicastro. Again. He and Vita must have had some sort of tiff in whatever sick foodie relationship they had, and now look.

In the mirror, he saw Vita appear like an apparition at the open door, with her dark curls piled loosely on the top of her head and held back with a scarf, no toque. She wore a spotless chef's jacket, cinched with a full white apron, but her pants were striped with purple. He wasn't sure he liked this experimenting with tradition. First the white goes, then what? It was just a slippery slope to sweatpants. He was composing a memo about kitchenwear in his head even as he swiveled back around and slipped the comb back in his drawer. Sitting up tall, he folded his hands paternally on his desk, cocking his head in a welcoming and professional manner. Vita held out a plate of cheese blintzes slathered with blue gems of preserves; her lips were stained with them, which brought attention to her toothy smile.

Nervous, he thought to himself. Dear God, the woman was nervous about something. The Vita he knew screamed, slammed cabinets, and waved knives around in a holy terror. But this was something new. New was not good. "What is it, Vita? What's going on?"

"Gerard, I don't want you getting upset," she began, and no

sooner had the words come out of her mouth than he stood up in a panic and knocked his coffee over. A stream of brown liquid trickled across his desk. "You're quitting! I knew it! Six days before the Fothergill Cup and you're going to desert me! How could you do this? After what we've been through!"

"Sit down, Gerard," she said. "And pull yourself together." She put the blintzes on his desk and wiped the spill with the bottom of her apron. "I'm not going anywhere. There's just a small glitch."

He sat again, eyeing her warily. "Well? Spit it out."

"The geese for the dinner."

"Yes?"

"They need to be moved."

"From Luisa's mother's house?"

"They're not there, Gerard. Where would Mrs. Suarez put a stiff gaggle of geese in her crowded apartment? I lied so you wouldn't worry. They're actually . . . ," and she trailed off, looking out the window, where, on the emerald slopes, Canada geese still walked the earth among golfers. Beyond, in the hazy valley, church bells chimed. "Upstairs. Room Thirteen."

Gerard clutched the edge of his desk and looked around his office, wondering where he was. "What?"

Vita twisted her apron in both hands and took a deep breath. "They've been hanging there ever since we butchered them Friday morning. There was no room in the cooler unless we stopped food service for the week, and we couldn't very well do that." She held her arms open in a helpless gesture and let her apron fall before taking another breath. "Besides, word would get out and we might have gotten in trouble because who knows what the law says about keeping dead animals in the kitchen—even though that's all meat is!" She pointed to the ceiling, calling upon the power of heaven. "But now it's an emergency. The AC in Thirteen broke down. We have to move them into the cooler, Gerard. You and me."

"No." He stood up, placing his palms on the desk for support. "No, no, no."

She leaned closer to keep him from bolting, and lowered her

voice. "In this heat, they'll be rotten by noon. Sell 'em or smell 'em, as they say in the business. They'll have to go in the walk-in until Fergus gets the new AC installed and the room cooled down, which probably won't be until the end of the day."

"But that air conditioner was already broken," Gerard said. "Fergus told me not to rent the room out."

"That's Karma for you. I lied through him, and now it's come true. The bottom line is, it's broiling in there and all the other guest rooms are booked. Let the past go, Gerard. I need you now. I can't wait for Luisa or Pedrosa to come in, and I can't trust anyone else. You and I have to move the geese before they go from high to rank." She leaned closer still, right up to his ear. "We're in this together, Gerard."

"No, no, no." Gerard pressed down hard on his desk to constrain it. "Get them out of this building. Now. *Now.* If any of the members find out what you've done, we'll both be fired."

"The emphasis is on the word *both,*" she reminded him. "You agreed I could harvest the geese if I helped save your ass-kissing job. And I did. I can just as easily go back to the board and tell them I've had a change of opinion about our glorious manager."

Gerard released the desk and sank deeply into his chair. It was too much. He'd only just gotten back the reins to his kingdom, and now here was Vita threatening to kick him off the horse again. It was those geese. Those diabolical birds, out to get him. If he could credit them for intelligence, he'd say it was a conspiracy. It was species against species now.

"What are we going to do?" he asked, already knowing his fate.

Vita stood up straight and relaxed, smoothing her apron. "We can have it done in a few trips down the fire escape, each looking out for the other. We'll stack them in Glad bags on the floor of the walk-in for the day, and I'll keep everyone out of there. No one will be the wiser. I'll sneak them back upstairs with Luisa before dinner service."

Gerard shook his head in defeat and whined. "The outside world is sure to find out. I can't afford any more bad press."

"Don't worry about what you can't control. In a few days, the members will have eaten the evidence anyway. Gerard, have you any idea what the profit margin is on these birds?"

He sat up and laid his hand on the restaurant receipts for strength. Yes, he did know. The geese, dead and hanging, were valuable assets to the Club. If anything happened to them now, Vita would have to create a new menu, at great cost. All the goose plates were completely preordered. In fact, the members who had to settle for cod were squawking. Good. Let them beg for it. Next year, he'd have Vita fatten more geese and save more money. The more dinners on the table, the fewer birds on the course. Who knew that the members couldn't eat their way through his problem?

He stood up and took off his red linen jacket. He shook it out carefully, like a matador, then draped it on a silent butler. "Let's get on with it," he said. He tucked in his white button-down shirt and straightened his Club tartan tie. He was the manager of the Eden Rock Country Club, and he must do what had to be done. Vita held the door open for him, and he walked out into the marble hall with the sound of golden trumpets in his ears.

Gerard scaled the front staircase, which ascended in two flights to the right and left, joining at the top in a broad landing. Vita, ever practical, stopped at the broom closet first for Glad bags. As she searched for the hand vac, Vita worried about having Gerard as a partner in subterfuge, but she was a desperate woman. She had no choice. Professionally, she would be devastated if her geese decayed, and personally, she prayed that the geese would heal whatever problem there was between her and Dr. Nicastro. She had paged through the reservation book and cheered when she saw his name listed for the banquet. And he had preordered the goose dinner! Lucky him. Her first taste of Mrs. Suarez's goose was still as vivid to her as her first kiss. After gathering her materials, she joined Gerard on the landing, where he was staring out the Palladian window at the parking lot below. She was glad to see that the Club was quiet. The early golfers were safely on the links. A single tennis ball thumped lethargically at the courts. Best of all, no fanged Grand Cherokee marred the landscape. No Clendenning. Vita and Gerard gave each other a thumbs-up.

Narrow treads as steep as a ladder continued up to the third floor, where the servants once slept. As they ascended the stairs, the heat rose. Twenty years before, the board had resigned itself to the fact that live-in servants were a luxury of the past. The only workers willing to indenture themselves these days didn't even speak English, so how could they be left to fend for themselves in the building at night? The board installed air-conditioning in the rooms to make them rentable to the members and their guests. The long chute of a hall, however, was hopeless and hot. Gerard could smell . . . poultry. They quickened their pace while Vita fished in the pocket of her pants for the key to #13. "This room's getting quite a history," said Gerard. "It's where Eliot Farnsworth was caught canoodling with a call girl at his own engagement party."

"A meathead belongs in a meat locker," said Vita, and she flung open the door. Gerard reeled. More than two dozen fully feathered upside-down geese were tied by their ankles to clothesline, their wings flopped open like falling angels. They filled the room. It was still and earthy. A fly buzzed.

"How long do they have to be like this?" he asked, not following Vita in. She elbowed birds out of her way like swinging doors.

"Mrs. Suarez said they're done when the eyeballs drop out of their heads. Here." Vita flipped out a couple of Glad bags. "Don't just stand there. Bag a bird." She stood up on the bed and untied the first goose from the clothesline. She remembered with what fatigue and satisfaction she had strung the line a few days before, thinking she wouldn't have to deal with the geese again until the plucking. But life was never so simple or straightforward. Nor would she want it to be. If her original trajectory had never changed, she would be a married professional like her mother wanted, instead of preparing the dinner of her life. She would not change a thing. She snorted a laugh. As if she could! You can't retrieve a bunch of grapes from a bottle of wine.

Gerard glanced up at Vita, worried about her mental state, then continued in his struggle to fit the goose cadaver into the black plastic without looking into its eyes, which were very much in its head. "It doesn't fit," he said. Two dark, webbed feet stuck out of the bag's opening, pulled tight with the yellow cinch.

"Put a bag on both ends," said Vita, lowering goose after goose to the beige carpet. Then she untied the last bird and bagged it with amazing efficiency, tucking the neck and wings under the torso and folding up the legs. Hers fit quite tidily in a single bag. "Hurry up."

A little jealous, Gerard devised a two-bag system of his own. It was not as pretty, but it worked. That's what counted. Well, that wasn't true. Looks certainly did count in this world—he'd built his career around that very maxim—but in this case, a little rough edge here and there would have to be borne in the name of expediency. He and Vita labored furiously, and in a few minutes, they made their first of many trips up and down the outside fire escape, slipping unseen in and out the kitchen door. They kept their eyes open. The pile of body bags on the floor of the walk-in was growing, and Vita realized that the birds would soon block off her supplies for the rest of the day. "Gerard, I've got to be able to put my hands on some of this later," she said, holding a tray of marinating halibut in one hand and a bag of kiwis in the other. "I've got to do some rearranging. You go get the last of the birds, and be careful."

"Careful is my middle name." It was almost over now, and Gerard was feeling good, even cocky. He took the front steps two by two, stopping again on the landing to survey the parking lot. Still no Clendenning.

Back in #13, he knelt to attend to the remaining three birds. He pulled out one bag from the box, then the second. Then the last. The box was empty. He dug his hand frantically around inside and felt nothing but panic. What could he cover the feet with? He tried, and failed, to make a more compact package, as Vita had, but there was no way around it. He would have to take them as they were. After all, he'd be able to see everyone coming and going in the parking lot. There would be no surprises. It was better to just get the job done now, rather than wander around looking for more bags, attracting attention.

Before leaving, he coiled up the clothesline and put it in the closet, opened the window to allow the thick air to recede, then vacuumed up a few downy feathers. When he picked up a stray wing feather and stuck it in the pocket of his khakis, he felt like he was cleaning up after a crime scene. Who said being a country club manager was such a bore? Some ex-girlfriend or other, if he remembered correctly, but how wrong she was. A new day, a new challenge.

He grabbed the heavy bird bags and ran, letting the door shut and lock behind him. The fire escape was at the end of the hall. In all the many decades when staff lived on the third floor, the fire department never noticed that there was no escape, but when the fire chief found out the Club was renting rooms, he ordered one built. The House & Grounds Committee at the time, not wanting the place to look like a tenement, had held firmly against iron grid. The chief, after a round of golf and cocktails on the terrace, jovially agreed to the wooden stairs. They switchbacked down the gabled end of the building, fitted handsomely with solid landings, steps, and an elegant rail supported by widely spaced posts. Gerard peeked out the window.

And there it was, Clendenning's SUV, heaving into view like some predatory animal, the teeth of the grille bared. The vehicle seemed to sink into the hot black macadam as Clendenning, hunched over the steering wheel, paused to choose a parking spot.

Gerard scrunched down, shoving the scaly feet of the geese deeper into the bags, but one began to rip, so he decided to leave well enough alone. He watched and waited, taking no rash action. Evaluate the situation carefully. Prepare to move with decision. Clendenning maneuvered himself almost directly beneath the escape and got out of the car. His granddaughter jumped down from the passenger side, tugging at her golf skirt. Her presence did not augur well. She had been there on that horrific day when goose guts dropped from the sky. It had almost been the end of his job.

But he didn't lose it then, and he wasn't about to lose it now.

Gerard watched the two Clendennings unload their golf clubs. Good. They would go directly to the locker rooms and onto the course, and he would be golden. He knew how to handle these things. It was all well under his control.

He heard footsteps and laughing on the hall stairs. Do not panic! Breathe in. Breathe in again. Just one more challenge to overcome. Moving as slowly as a snake swallowing a rat, he lifted the bags through the window and out onto the wide landing of the escape. Then he threw one leg, then the other, over the windowsill, keeping his back low and humped. He peeked back into the hall. It was the irritable Mr. Stillington, of all people, shutting the door of Room #9 behind him, shushing the laughter of a man already inside, a friend of his who had rented it out for the week.

Gerard turtled his head to make himself even smaller. As much as he liked to keep his fingers on the pulse of what was going on at the Club, there were some places he'd just as soon not touch, and Mr. Stillington's private life was one of them. He looked back at the ground. The Clendennings were gone. Leaving the birds on the landing, he leaned over to make sure, too late realizing that a yellow pull-string was caught on the heel of his loafer. The bagged weight of the goose teetered on the edge of the landing, and Gerard felt the blood leave his brain and pour into his liver. He lunged at the bag, causing its weight to shift in favor of the greater gravity. Catching the bag by the yellow cinch was no problem, but that was all he had—the bag. The goose had sprung through the torn opening, free at last, obliquely grazing the next step before tumbling sideways under the railing and out into the atmosphere. It hurtled through the air, down, and down some more, spiraling with wings akimbo in an air ballet before thumping down in a grotesque sprawl on the hood of the golden SUV.

Gerard was never able to fully separate what he saw from what he thought he saw. The granddaughter had come running from Barry's office, summoned by the sound of bird hitting metal, but had she screamed? Or—and this was not easy to admit—did he scream? Was she alone? Did she look up? And could she have spotted him on the landing even if she had? All of these things were seen as if submerged in water. He knew this much, though: Forbes followed at her heels and stood beside her in horror. One screamed and the other honked. The crows swept in from the skies in battalions, cawing with delight, knowing that the cry of any species hinted at the possibility of fresh flesh. Humans screaming, geese honking, crows cawing. Screaming, honking, cawing, until the air filled with one single syllable of hysterical alarm. The noise they made. It would be years before Gerard would be able to get the sound out of his head.

Chapter Twenty-six

The Fairway

"OUCH." Phoebe's feet were raw as she pumped and pedaled her mountain bike through the dark, shortcutting from the frontage road to her back gate, with her rubber sandal straps eating at her instep. She'd made that vow about not wearing the skin of other species, and besides, she couldn't have gone to an ALF meeting with leather on her feet, no matter what. But her blisters, *ouch.* The meeting had been downtown, over Tom's Smoking Supplies Shop, and when she'd gotten there, she'd dropped to the floor all sweated out and Denise asked her why she hadn't just taken the T.

"You know," Phoebe had panted, *"exercise?"* Though, truthfully? She didn't take public transportation because it smelled funny. Next time she'd drive her VW bug and hide it so ALF dudes wouldn't find out she was consuming the earth's resources to go to meetings, and that was that. Sometimes the end justified the means. Didn't it? Could it ever justify a gun? She hadn't taken it on the turkey mission because she'd chickened out. Then she laughed at her silly joke but shut up because she didn't want that manager dude, Gerard, to come running out in some sort of *frenzy,* even if he was kinda hot. Sometimes she looked at him in his uptight clothes and wondered why some people were the way they were when they didn't have to be. Him and his stupid *BusinessWeek.* But why did he seem so familiar?

Whatever. As far as the gun was concerned, it was just as well she hadn't brought it with her to the turkey job. That would have messed things up even more, what with the dogs barking and the turkeys gobbling. Denise had said the birds would be sleeping, but she was so wrong. Lights were kept on 24/7 to trick them into eating to get bigger quicker and murdered sooner. What humans did to animals was a crime. But for some reason the big birds put up a fight when she and Denise tried to lead them to freedom, and that's when the dudes in the farmhouse woke up. She'd grabbed one bird and Denise another, and they ran, and the guys at ALF were not especially impressed. Now, tonight, trying to make nice, she had offered up the gun for the next rescue mission, liberating experimental pigs from an MIT lab.

"Excellent," Lionel had said, their sort-of leader, there being no official dude because they did not hold to social or political hierarchy. That's what had attracted her to this particular group. If there were no leaders there could not be someone like Eric ruining her life—but even so, it seemed as if they all marched to Lionel's drum, and she was getting a little *prickly* about that. He was always saying how he once worked at Out of the Fog, the teahouse in Eugene where all the tree-spikers hung out, like that was enough to make him boss. And what was up with the facial hair? Pointy sideburn things and some crazy smudge of fuzz under his lower lip. When he talked, the smudge moved up and down, up and down, like it had a life of its own. "Speak power to power," he'd said, leaning back in his folding chair. "It's the only thing they understand."

"Well, I don't have bullets, you know," Phoebe had said from her spot on the floor, fiddling with the amber at her neck. "It'll just be for, I don't know, *emphasis,* right?"

"I don't think bringing a gun along, loaded or unloaded, is a good idea," said Grace, sitting comfortably cross-legged on the bare floor next to Phoebe, who was a little stiff in the hips herself. "The violence has to stop with us."

"We should get bullets, man," said Adrian, who paced the edge of the room. "We should fucking blow a few holes in the roof to let them know we're serious. This insanity of eating other species is never going to stop without a show of force."

"Can't Phoebe, uh, get in trouble?" asked Denise, Phoebe's old partner in turkey crime and Lionel's current squeeze. "I mean, if she goes to jail, who'll take care of the animals?"

"It's more of an issue of whether it's right, rather than legal." Lionel let his chair smack upright again. He planted both palms on the board resting on file cabinets that served as his desk, which, other than his chair, was the only furniture in the room. "It's about drawing the line. Either this is worth going to jail for, or we're just sitting around playing games."

"Where a man draws a line in the sand, there he'll be found dead," said Grace as she offered a plate of pale vegan oat bars to Phoebe, who passed.

"Why don't you hold the gun, Lionel?" asked Denise. "You'd be really good at it."

Phoebe knew Denise had fantasies of going underground with Lionel, baking bread and stirring soup in some abandoned farmhouse while he saved the world. It wasn't a bad fantasy as far as it went, the bread and soup part, but it seemed a lonely way to live in the long run. Wasn't it possible to be in the world and save it at the same time?

"Me? Who'll run everything here?" Lionel spread his hands out at the room, stacked with pamphlets, picket signs, bumper stickers, buckets of red paint, and cardboard wings folded up in the corner. Not to mention the giant collapsible cage they used when the circus came to town. Sharon had painted her naked body in black and orange tiger stripes and sat scrunched up in the cage, crying to passersby that the circus was killing her. Phoebe had wanted to be the tiger, but Lionel said she could never look that wild, and maybe he was right, but she wished she could have had a turn anyway. Sometimes she really just wanted to be an animal.

Christine, sitting way in the corner, holding her knees against her chest, started to cry. "We can't imitate the worst behavior of our own oppressor."

"It takes all the tools in the toolbox to dismantle the master's machine," Adrian shouted, punching a fist into his palm. "I say we bring the gun *and* bullets."

Christine cried even louder, and Grace, straining her overall clips, climbed over Phoebe to comfort her. Phoebe stared straight ahead, like nothing was going on, then closed her eyes to meditate, but the more Christine cried, the harder it was to concentrate on infinity, or whatever, and the next thing she knew she was just sort of inching to the door, moving along the floor like a crab. Let them sort out their shit without her. Right? She'd bring the gun, not bring the gun, have bullets, not have bullets, whatever they wanted as long as she didn't have to sit in that room listening to Christine cry.

She continued pedaling in the dark over the golf course. There was no moon to light her way, but she knew each curve and bump and tweak of the course, so when she hit the boggy part she didn't freak, but she was sure getting nowhere fast. Then she heard one of her roosters, and it gave her strength. Poor confused thing, cock-a-doodling in the dark. It would be his undoing. The neighbors had registered a complaint with Animal Control, and if she couldn't shut the birds up they would be impounded. She and Denise planned to crate the boys up the next day and bring them to the country to free them, where she hoped they would settle in with their wilder relatives and not get eaten by them. What else was there to do? If she got rid of the roosters, maybe the neighbors would let her keep the goats. And the rabbits. And the turkeys. She'd gotten really attached to the big one, Olson, and he was so funny, the way he wandered out to the golf course last week and scared the golfers. That Gerard dude, he was so *pissed.*

She changed gears and changed gears, finally got some traction, and whizzed by those gross new houses along the course, and as she did she could smell malathion. Yes, maybe the goat pen could use a cleaning—as Grace said, just because it was natural didn't mean it didn't smell—but it was nothing compared to this chemical assault. These dudes, they panicked after every West Nile alert and bombed every living thing around them to crush the enemy. They lived in constant fear of everything except for what they *should* be terrified of, complete environmental annihilation. If they hadn't killed all the birds and bats and frogs with their lawn chemicals, maybe they wouldn't have to be bombing the mosquitoes now. Tomorrow she'd call the Conservation Commission and make them come and see for themselves that this soggy turf was wetlands and the houses were too close for spraying. She was on a roll, after all; hadn't her persistence won the poison battle at the Club? Her moment of glory had come the week before, when she saw Barry ordering his dudes around, spraying this and spraying that, and she marched out there to stop them and, whoa! He was obliterating the aphids with a little soapy water. She wondered if she shouldn't have argued in defense of the bugs because they totally deserved to live too, but you know what? She liked roses. Roses or aphids, roses or aphids? That sort of thing drove her cross-eyed sometimes.

Barry had told her to come over to the utility shed because he wanted to show her something, and she'd thought, This dude had better not try anything or he's going to go the way of the aphids, *obliterated.* But he had Forbes under his arm, and well, this guy, if he's so attached to this other species, he can't be an ogre. Right? So she went in, and he showed her all sorts of sprays, from hot peppers and seaweed to the whirled bodies of the bugs themselves, because he said they were their own worst enemies. Before she left, he gave her a handful of biodegradable golf tees made from soy protein.

Way to go, Barry. A greens crew that was finally green. All that nagging had finally paid off, and it gave her strength to get serious and carry the gun around. She stopped to catch her breath. Didn't it?

She bent to adjust her sandal straps because her insteps were chopped meat and decided it would be more comfortable to walk the rest of the way, but just as she dismounted, she saw this whopping big rat and she got back on the bike. Her mom, who must be going through the change or something, told her that the rats were all her fault because the members didn't want to drive by her anarchist friends, so they had to use the employee lot. The Dumpster got moved closer to the homes, and now they all had vermin.

"*Good,*" Phoebe had said. "Let them see their own waste for once and suffer from the consequences of excess." But it was like her mom never heard a thing and just went on about the Dumpster and the rats and the crows and the neighbors, who blamed it all on the Lamberts.

"It's too much," her mom had said, and collapsed at the kitchen table and put her head down, and Phoebe thought for a moment she might even cry. She felt bad, but here *she* was, ready to sacrifice her freedom in the name of animal dignity and her mom couldn't even handle a few icy stares?

She started to pedal again, and she thought, wow, was she really ready to sacrifice her freedom? What had Denise said? *Jail.* She could be locked up even if she never fired the gun, even if it wasn't loaded, and how unfair was *that?* But what was her freedom compared to the senseless slaughter of animals in the world? Like Lionel said, only outrageous actions could bring attention to that level of carnage, and if the group decided she should carry a gun, so be it. They were always teasing her, saying her family was a safety net, giving her money and a car and stuff. But she knew better. A safety net was nothing more than a spiderweb, and she was going to show them all she could do it on her own.

She stopped. Right over there by the Dumpster, lit by the distant glow of a security light, was a *bear.* No—not a bear, but something, something really big. Wait, it was wearing pants. Was it a bum? The neighborhood didn't used to have bums, but she'd been away for a while and what with the economy, who knew?

But no, it was just one of the kitchen workers standing on a cement block and digging around in the garbage looking for something or other. Phoebe inched closer with her bike and saw what that something was when he lifted it up with both hands. A box of soggy hamburger patties.

"Oh, gross," she said.

Pedrosa froze, trying to hide the box behind his back. Phoebe held her handlebars with one hand, and with the other, pointed at him. "Don't eat that. A car can drive *twenty* miles on the fossil fuels it takes to create a *single* patty."

"Lo siento, lo siento." He apologized, his eyes wide with fear, and stepped down off the block, pressing his body against the red metal Dumpster. *"Me los hallar. Hallar."* He held out the burgers, then pointed to the Dumpster.

She knew he'd gotten them from the Dumpster! That wasn't the problem, even though it was *disgusting.* She stamped her foot. "You shouldn't be eating meat."

Just then, Vita walked out of the unlit path from the clubhouse, glowing in her kitchen whites, her toque seeming to float above her head. She carried an armful of crumpled, empty Glad bags.

"*Que tal?*" she asked, looking at Pedrosa.

"He's going to eat those things," said Phoebe. "Make him stop."

Vita groaned. Would nothing go right today? First the AC breaks and she almost loses her birds; then that idiot Gerard drops a goose right on Clendenning's car. He deserved to be fired on the grounds of stupidity alone, but she was pretty sure there'd be no repercussions. In the middle of all the commotion, she'd run out and grabbed the bird, and said to the granddaughter, "This must be my goose delivery." Then she was gone, and that was the last she heard of that. After all, the girl and Forbes had been the only witnesses. Clendenning had run out of the locker room too late to see the evidence. If Clendenning was smart, and he was, he'd encourage the girl to keep her mouth shut. He was no fool. He knew where the banquet geese were coming from. When she'd showed him the menu, he had raised a single silver eyebrow, which read, "Don't get caught." And then Gerard starts flinging geese all over the place! If she'd seen him, she might have strangled him, but when she sneaked back up to the fire escape for the other geese, he was gone. Barry told her later he was waiting in his office to be fired, in case anyone wanted to know. He was still there as far as she knew, waiting for the gallows, and she had done nothing to reassure him, just to teach him a lesson. She had not even sent him something to eat.

Now this. And all because she was not paying more attention to the eating habits of her staff. A delivery of organic beef had arrived at noon and she'd had to make space in the goose-filled walk-in. So she moved a pot of stock to the freezer and put the frozen burgers in the snack bar refrigerator. She told Ping to push the burgers because they could not be refrozen. What Vita did not know was that Ping had recently fallen prey to the vegetarians and was evangelical in her new religion. She would not touch meat. At the end of the day the box was still full, and defrosted, because Ping had substituted Boca burgers for every hamburger plate. Vita shook her head. What was all this about food these days, kids deciding to not eat meat or eggs or anything at all? Now good food was wasted.

Or was it? She stuffed the Glad bags into the Dumpster, plucked a feather off her sleeve, then held her hands out to Pedrosa. He gave her the box, and she opened it. No sign of rat damage. She gave it a good sniff and touched the meat. Still cold. According to Health Department standards, they were no longer fit for food service but they were still safe and edible. She had regretted tossing them, what with all the hunger in the world. Once again, she thought how efficient it would be to have a few pigs.

"Translate for me," said Phoebe. "Tell him it's unhealthy to eat ground-up dead cows."

Vita looked at her without speaking, then turned to Pedrosa, giving him the box and waving him off. "*Vamos,*" she said.

So he left, keeping his eyes on Phoebe before disappearing into the darkness.

"Hey," said Phoebe. "He's got to put them back or I'll call the police and tell them he's stealing."

"You would do that?" asked Vita, keeping her voice neutral and low. "Get him in trouble with the law when the man doesn't even speak English?"

Phoebe flushed and fiddled with her handlebars. "Someone's got to save him from himself. Besides, I was only making a point. I don't tell the police everything I see around here, after all."

Vita put a fractured smile on her face and folded her arms to keep her hands from shaking. Did Phoebe know about her geese? "Oh?"

"I've seen you at the Club pretty early." Phoebe narrowed her eyes meaningfully, but she couldn't match Vita's gaze. "You know, like that time you were hanging out on the course when Mr. Bellows shot the goose? Maybe good food gets thrown away all the time. You know. *Accidentally*."

"Stealing?" Vita was so shocked she laughed. Then she sobered up and lied. "Please. My day is very long, so if I want to gather wild greens, I have to wake up early. And you should be thankful I've been playing with foraged food. Barry's switched to integrated pest management because of it. And, of course, for Forbes."

Phoebe slumped down, leaning on her handlebars, totally dejected. "Really? Not because of *me?*"

"In spite of you." Vita moved a step closer. It was dangerous to talk to a member, even a junior member, in anything other than placating tones, but at this point, if Phoebe were out to get her, it didn't matter what Vita said, so she might as well just say what needed to be heard. "Besides that, you're the one who called the police that morning to tell them hunters were on the course, then you tell them it must have been a backfire. What happened in between? Recognize one of them as your father?"

Phoebe laughed, then rolled her bike a few inches closer to Vita. "Don't be crazy. If it weren't for my mom, Dad would've joined me at the gates."

Vita smirked. "Why do I find that hard to believe?"

"It's not your job to believe." A shiver ran down Phoebe's spine because for one gross moment she sounded just like one of the members. She smiled to undo the horror of it. "Anyway, you shouldn't let your staff eat from a Dumpster."

Vita tightened. "The burgers were fine, and Pedrosa's family doesn't have the luxury of deciding what they will and won't eat."

Phoebe lifted the front of her bike up by the handlebars and slammed it down. "It's *wrong* to kill animals. Don't you get it?"

"It's wrong for people to go hungry," said Vita, with a patience that drained her. She took another step. She and Phoebe were now an arm's length from each other, and they could see each other quite clearly.

Phoebe slumped on her bike seat. "There'd be plenty for everybody if we all ate grain instead of feeding it to cows."

Vita shrugged in concession. "But we can't eat grass, and they can." She held her hand out to the darkened landscape. "All this is useless except as a carpet for a small white ball. But if poultry were allowed to forage, and then we ate the poultry . . ."

Phoebe leaned forward, putting her weight on her handlebars. "That doesn't even make sense. Eating meat is only a *preference*."

"So are a lot of things." Vita leaned forward herself until they were almost nose to nose. "Sex is unnecessary these days too, but that doesn't mean people will stop doing it."

"*What?*" Phoebe tugged at her amber. "You are just so . . . *unreasonable.* Food and sex are not the same thing at all!"

Vita smiled for the first time, flushing lightly from some pleasant memory. "I beg to differ." Then she realized Phoebe had tears on her cheeks, and she softened. "Phoebe, food doesn't have to be your only moral concern. Put your energies into social programs so that people like Pedrosa don't have to Dumpster-dive to get by." She clicked the light on her wristwatch, then clicked it off. "I've got to go help close up the kitchen. Everyone wants to go home. It's been a long day. As usual."

And then she left. Phoebe sniffed and watched her disappear through the woods, heading back to the clubhouse. She dried her eyes with the back of her hand. She wasn't very effective in changing the world, was she? She could hear car doors slam and engines start, and see beams of light flash across the course as cars turned around in the lot. Another day was over. Had she helped to make it a better one? Not really. Offering up a gun to scare some security dude to death was not good, and neither was yelling at some hungry kitchen worker. She wiped her face with the bottom of her peasant shirt and heard a nocturnal bird trill up in a tree, like it was asking for help or something, and she took it as a sign. She wouldn't give up. She could change *something,* after all. Like her Karma. She'd put that gun back where she found it; then she'd figure out some other way to bring attention to her mission. Some nonviolent demonstration. Something that would make the people at the Club—and Vita—come to their senses.

The bird called again. Earlier in the summer, she was thinking about doing a tree sit-in to make the course go organic. Maybe this was her chance to go for total victory, inside the clubhouse as well as out. She'd already won over Ping and the snack bar—now it was time to confront the food at its source. Vita and the restaurant. She started peddling again, getting all excited. She would start right now, tonight. She'd return the gun, then bring out the chain and tie herself to a tree, maybe that oak near where the hunters were, somewhere symbolic like that.

Ouch. She stopped to look at her feet, made a mess from rubber, a stupid petroleum product. First things first. She was going to have to change her shoes before she changed the world.

Chapter Twenty-seven

Par for the Course

GERARD STUMBLED out onto the course. It was late. His exquisitely trained eye could tell that his beloved clubhouse was empty, even of Pedrosa. Poor guy, always the last to leave. It was enough to make a grown man puddle up. And so he did, catching his tears with the sleeve of his red linen jacket, whose satin lining now blistered out at the wrist. He hadn't put his coat on the wrong way since he was a toddler. Look what degradation Clendenning had reduced him to! He uncapped the flask of cognac he carried in his jacket pocket (sterling silver, monogrammed, available at the gift shop for $89.99, a present from the board at Christmas) and took a swig to calm the wounded beast inside. Then he swung in the direction of the lake to congratulate the geese on their victory, letting their rank odor lead him to them.

He wandered blindly in the moonless night, stumbling up sand bunkers, sliding down knolls, tripping on cups. All without injury. The landscape was more familiar to him than his childhood home, a place he worked hard to expunge from his memory. But here, not even the night's shadows could hide the Club's beauty from him. His domain. His world. Gone, gone, gone. He hadn't been fired, but it was coming as surely as Armageddon. Clendenning had not been kind with a quick hatchet job, the humane thing to do. No, no. That was not Clendenning's way. Even a public horsewhipping was better than this. Let him get on with it, for mercy's sake!

He took another sip of cognac from his flask to fortify himself, then removed his tartan tie before it choked him, and put it in his jacket pocket. All that long day Gerard had sat perfectly dressed and composed behind his desk, waiting. He waited for the kids at the gate to storm the premises looking for the dead geese. He waited for the *Boston Globe* to document them for posterity and stir the public's wrath. He waited for the police, for Fish & Game, for the ASPCA. How long could mere brick and iron hold them back? They hadn't come today, but they would surely come tomorrow. It was just a matter of time. And then some inferior person with low standards would get his job and sit at his desk, looking out at his perfect view. All because he had tried to make the Club a better place.

Then he saw them. *The geese.* He took a thoughtful swallow of the cognac, then leaned his palms on a ball washer and looked around, a preacher at his pulpit contemplating his flock. Most were in the safety of the water, but others had spilled over onto land, up the sloping embankment. This hill was once some landscape architect's pride, but now it was spoiled with dark humps of sleeping meat. He hated the birds for their peaceful slumber while he had to stay awake, fully conscious to await his end. He hated them for having no knowledge of their mortality. He released the pulpit to reach for his flask and lost his balance on the slick grass. He recovered in time to keep from sliding facefirst in an ocean of goose shit, the very thought of which steeled his spine against his fate. What kind of a man was he that he was standing around waiting to be terminated? If he was going to be axed anyway, then he would die like a pit bull, with his prey between his teeth.

The geese rustled. A few muttered, their beaks tucked demurely under their wings. Look how passive they were. He could kill them in their sleep right now. Even the score. Think of the trouble Clendenning would be in if he arrived at the Club in the morning, dragging his hairy tail in the grass behind him, to fire his innocent, well-meaning manager and found instead the golf course littered with dozens of geese carcasses!

Hee, hee, hee. He took a very long pull of his cognac. Stuck to the flask was one of the wing feathers he'd stuffed in his pocket earlier in the day. Another lifetime ago. He peeled off the feather and whipped it through the air, like a rapier. Even if he could no longer have his job, he could still have control. After he killed the geese, he would tell the kids at the gate that there had been a slaughter and let them have a go at Clendenning. Then he would call the press and invite the outside world in.

How to do the job right? Unlike Vita, he could not just open a vein and let the earth turn red. Rat poison? There was plenty of that around, but how to make them eat when they were asleep? Plus, it might take too long. As much as he loathed the birds, he didn't want to see them suffer the way Clendenning was making him suffer. Never mind what humans did to animals, it was what humans did to humans that was the real atrocity. Were we supposed to treat animals with more mercy than we treat one another? He thought not. He had tried to bring civility to these people, but no. Still, he was going to be kinder than his own tormentor. A club? He could whack the birds sharply in the back of the head with a heavy stick and be done with it.

Gerard stuck his feather behind his ear and began to kick around in the rough for a big stick, but Barry and his crew had done too good a job of cleaning up the course for the Fothergill Cup. He would miss Barry. He would miss a great deal. As he looked around for the proper tool for the job, he wondered what would become of him now. He'd lived and breathed the Club for three years, and without it he would have no purpose. Even if he stayed in the business, he would have to move elsewhere, where no one would know that he'd been fired from one of the country's great exclusive clubs. He might even have to return to the

Midwest, back to a city with so little ambition it was like a pumpkin pie: no upper crust. To think he had once dreamed of his own chapter in some future edition of the *History,* with a snapshot or two of an impeccably turned-out, self-assured manager seeing to everyone's needs—by the pool, in the dining room, on the terrace—amiably and attentively wandering among the rich. "Good old Gerard," the members would be quoted as saying. "Like a faithful dog, he was."

Where, oh where, was a stick? Never mind. Just another challenge to overcome. He would make his own. Feeling very elemental, he grabbed hold of a low maple branch and swung on it like an arboreal ape until it snapped off at the trunk. Maybe in his next job he could do something with his hands. Get closer to nature. He could join the migrant farmworkers who came to the Club every spring and fall to pick up the acorns by hand, finding every seed, every nut. Those were standards. He stepped on the branch and broke off the end piece, then peeled the leaves to fashion his club. They might not be able to call him Good Old Gerard anymore, but from now on, he would be remembered as One Blow Gerard.

A twig snapped. He looked around. The darkness was ripe with menace. All around him it seemed as though something waited. He didn't move. A goose honked softly, as if nudged. He felt the landscape press upon him; the vines and vegetation were closing in, growing with a savage violence. Strange things happened on golf courses after dark. Teenagers turfed around the local munis at night in their rusty Camaros, drinking and drugging. And Eden Rock had its recent history of hunters. What if Bellows was coming back for a second go at the birds? He could be shot by mistake! Should he make himself known? But what if it wasn't Bellows?

What then?

He couldn't think, what with his heart pounding in his eardrums. Not to mention all that fine cognac flowing through his veins. Then it became deadly silent, the pack pausing before the kill. The twist in his stomach made him wish he'd had something more to eat that day than cold, congealed blintz. Another twig snapped. Was it? Yes, it was. Footsteps. *Clendenning.* Was this his idea of getting rid of a valued employee? Hunting him down like some beast?

Gerard backed up slowly. The stone bench was not far. If he could find it, he could hide under it, or tip it up to use as a shield. He held on to his stick and moved with infinitesimal steps, right up to the moment he saw the figure. A shapely figure. *Phoebe Lambert?* Carrying a gun? Clendenning was unconscionable! How diabolical to send her to do his dirty work. But One Blow Gerard would show them both. The girl hadn't seen him yet. He would hide behind the tree and ambush her. He would get the upper hand after all.

He turned quickly. His foot skidded out from under him, and for a nanosecond he felt himself weightless in the dark. Then his head cracked sharply against the stone bench, and for the first time in many hours he was finally out of pain.

Chapter Twenty-eight

The Gear

BY FOUR THIRTY Wednesday morning, Phoebe had set up her campsite under the spreading arms of the oak by Trough, Hole #11. She checked things off in her head: a sleeping bag, a cooler with food, a cooler with water, a tarp in case it rained, and a bucket of clumping kitty litter, with tp. She still wasn't sure how *that* was supposed to work. Then again, she didn't expect to be here all that long. Maybe she could just hold it.

Her sit-in was just about ready to begin. Yes! She felt a little bad about changing into her old leather sandals, but she couldn't get anything done with bad feet. She stood on one of her coolers and tacked her sign—ERCC! SAVE THE WORLD! GO VEGAN!—high up on the tree trunk. Gerard groaned but did not wake. She wondered for the umpteenth time what he'd been doing here so late at night, wandering around in the dark like that. Maybe he'd been stalking her. She got down from the cooler, careful not to step on his face, and looked at him. So peaceful. And familiar in a way too. Whatever, she didn't get any "uh-oh" feeling about him. This guy might be *weird,* but he wasn't a pervert. He was probably just out marking his territory. She tried to wake him up again and send him home, but he was still too drunk, and so she decided it was meant to be. In fact, maybe it would be cool to have him be the first to witness her sit-in. It would move things along, and she wouldn't have to wait to be discovered by golfers. She'd ask for vegan but settle for vegetarian. The Club could still have eggs and dairy, she supposed, because she knew what it was like to need a fix of ice cream. She put her hand in one of the many pockets of her cargo shorts and crumpled the wrapper of a Dove Bar. Why did her mom have to keep that stuff in the house?

She looked around one more time. She should get some sleep for her big day. In just a few hours, Gerard would wake up, or come to, and the Club, begrudgingly for sure, would announce they were going meat-free and declare the Club a sanctuary for the geese (yes, she would include that too!) and everybody would be happy.

Of course, Mr. Clendenning might be a little pissy throughout the whole thing, but in the end, even he would have to agree that it had all been done for the higher good. Her mom might not be too thrilled either, and as for Dad . . . he was too gone to care. The light in the garage had still been burning when she'd gone poking around for a chain sometime after midnight. The windows were all boarded up, but she could see light flashing blue around the edges, like in Frankenstein's castle. It was pretty wild.

She found one end of her chain and wrapped it around the tree trunk, clamping it shut, then wrapped the other end around her ankle and held the padlock in her hand. There would be no going back once she snapped this sucker on. The key was back in her room, hidden away so her mom wouldn't be able to find it if the cops hassled her. Not that her mom would try to sabotage her efforts, only that she always seemed to do what she was told.

Now it was time. This was it. Everything she'd ever worked for was riding on this little padlock. Dare she?

Yes, she dared. The world was more than just a place for humans to trample about for a while in ignorance, then die. There was meaning to be had here, somewhere, and maybe even an awesome future, if they could only get it together to make it happen. The world and its wars and cruelties, it was all so screwed up, but here was something she could do to make it just a little bit better. Ideas were one thing, but action was something else altogether. She clicked on the padlock and smiled.

Chapter Twenty-nine

The Shanks

THE EXCITABLE BIRDS and hacking crows woke Gerard up at what seemed the very depth of night, announcing a dawn invisible to the human eye. He sat up and looked around, tenderly touching the swelling on the back of his head, which triggered a recall of the night's events. Yes, he'd fallen, and fallen hard. Damn geese. And Phoebe! He looked around in fright, and there she was, sleeping. There was no gun. Could he have imagined that? One of her bare legs peeked out from her sleeping bag, and in the dark he thought he saw a creepy bug on her calf. He was going to shoo it away, but then he remembered it was her little Earth tattoo.

He leaned back against the tree and contemplated his head. The chattering of birds got suddenly louder, increasing in decibels as the sky lightened in increments. But instead of becoming annoyed, he became entranced. His skin tingled, and he sat straight up. Light flickered on the horizon, a thin line, a golden thread. So tenuous. So brittle. The birds held their breath as the line shimmered to life. A solar breeze picked up, and he heard the lake lap softly against the shore. The light, tinged with green, began to expand, and along with it, so did he. The earth's inner core seemed to pulsate, filling both the sky and his body with an intense glow. The sun continued to rise, pulling him up, up into the great canopy of the sky, which luxuriously unfolded in turquoise and gold, salmon and magenta, violet and teal. And he was there, a part of it. He was It.

When the sun completed its transformation and sat fully whole and glowing on the horizon, still wet from its dawning, he was back under the tree. By the time the church bells in town chimed a short while later, he was empty of all rage against the geese and filled with grace. Everything around him sparkled with a new clarity. He was not just a new man, but as newly hatched as the original man, in a world so fresh the animals had yet to be named. Here he was, on the morning of Creation, and there, a woman by his side, the miracle of Eve. And Clendenning? Where was that snake?

Forget Clendenning! He was a crusty relic of the old world. Gerard looked over at Phoebe, with the dawn's light washing over her. So sweet. Her yellow tangle of hair seemed utterly pastoral, and the gold links on her ear sparkled. That mouth, with the teeniest protrusion of her upper lip, perfection itself.

No, no carnal thoughts. If he were to be truly free of the material world and all its petty considerations, if he were to maintain this calm and dissociative state, he had to not think of her body. Not think, not think, not think . . .

Phoebe opened her eyes, then sat upright with excitement. It was time! Things were really going to start happening now. She smoothed out her T-shirt with both hands. "Hey, dude, you're up. *Cool.*"

"I'm not just up," he said. "I'm up and open, for the very first time."

Phoebe frowned, grabbing hold of the amber beads around her neck so she could think. That fall on the bench must've crossed his wires. "So," she said, pronouncing her words carefully, "aren't you going to ask what I'm doing here?"

He rolled onto his stomach and tilted his head. "What are *any* of us doing here?"

"I don't know about you, but I'm all about this nonviolent sit-in." She pointed to her poster, then picked up her chain. "I'm going to hang out here until my demands are met. I want the food service to go vegan, no meat, no dairy, *no eggs*."

"Excellent idea!" Gerard stood up and felt around in his jacket. "This is going to be fun!"

"This is serious. Don't you think you should, you know, go to Mr. Clendenning and tell him what's going down?"

Gerard pulled his Club tie out of his pocket. "Let him come to us when he sees us on the news."

"No," said Phoebe. "You can't join me. You're on the other side."

He strung the end of his tie through a link in her chain, then tied the other end to his ankle. "I'll be your hostage. It will make your case that much stronger. After all, you might do me some harm if you don't get your way."

She tried pulling her chain to her. "No! Kidnappers go to prison."

He kept his hand over the knot to keep her from undoing his work. "I thought you had conviction," he said. "I thought you believed in your cause."

He leaned back against the tree in satisfaction. This was so much better than killing the geese. That would have been wrong, and he was glad fate had intervened. His future was tied to Phoebe's now. And what was so bad about that?

"I *do* believe," she said, tugging at the chain. "But I could get into deep shit if I have a hostage. I promised myself a nonviolent demonstration, that's why. . . ." She thought of the gun, only a few yards away, almost exactly where she had found it weeks before, except it was tucked under a bush so it would seem like it had just been overlooked. But now, Gerard might have seen her with it last night. If he told the police she used it to take him hostage, she would go to jail. Her fingerprints were on that gun. She was such an idiot!

Gerard regarded Phoebe and nodded to himself. She hadn't been stalking him last night—that was the imagining of a crazy drunk.

She had the gun Bellows claimed was stolen, and she must have been returning it to where she'd found it. God knows what her plans had been before that, but she must have finally come to her senses. Just like him.

"Get out of here!" she screamed. "Go report me to the police. Go! You're not my hostage."

A cell phone sang from Gerard's pocket, and he held a finger up to Phoebe.

"Barry," said Gerard. "Good to hear from you. What a day." He breathed in deeply, then pushed Phoebe's hand away from his tie.

"Vita told me about yesterday, boss," said Barry. "The goose and all. She said she hadn't seen or heard from you since." In the background, Vita was telling Barry to tell Gerard that she thought his job was safe, to come out of hiding.

"Tell Vita, thank you for her concern," said Gerard. "But things have a way of working out for the best."

"Your car's here in the lot," said Barry. "Where are you?"

"Trough, under the oak." He pulled his jacket over his head and whispered, "Phoebe Lambert has taken me hostage."

Silence.

"Be right there," said Barry, and before he hung up, Gerard could hear Forbes utter a worried, questioning *beep.*

Chapter Thirty

Topspin

AT NOON, Humphrey Clendenning called Vita into Gerard's office. He stood at the picture window and shut the blinds with a single yank on the cord, not so much against the view as to protect himself from being viewed.

"Sorry I'm late, Mr. Clendenning," Vita said, panting slightly. "My mother called as I was leaving the kitchen." She shrugged to indicate, What are you going to do about mothers? but he looked at her as if he didn't know what one was, and that might very well have been the case. She looked around the office and her stomach sank. Still no Gerard. What was taking so long? With the banquet just days away, there was no time for such foolishness. She should be downstairs soaking the giant fava beans, which, when perfumed with garlic and epazote, were to go under all the entrées—be it goose, cod, or organic filet mignon. There was no time for a kidnapping. Or whatever it was. When Barry had returned from seeing Gerard that morning, he was baffled. "Gerard says he's a hostage, but that Lambert girl says he's not. He wants me to bring him a chain of his own, and she keeps yelling at him to leave."

"Hmm." This was all very worrisome, but Vita had her dinner to fret over, and even as she talked to Barry, she kept glancing down at her clipboard, checking to make sure everything was on hand for the first course of stewed corn, red beans, chickpeas, and goose jus to be served with the grilled foie gras, which remained frozen, suspended in time.

"Vita," said Barry. "What should we do?"

Vita bit her pencil. "How does he look?"

Barry stared at his cracked hands and whistled softly for the right word. "Calm."

"Calm?" Vita was concerned but still distracted. Her mind had moved on to the soup course, a Latinized bouillabaisse doused with sofrito, lime, and cilantro that would train the tongue for what was to come. "Hmm."

"I asked him if I should bring him some clean clothes, or a toothbrush or something, and he said no."

Vita put her clipboard down. "Maybe it will all just go away if we do nothing," she said, hoping against hope it would, and soon too.

Forbes pecked on the windowsill, and Barry motioned that he'd be right out. "Vita, Phoebe has demands."

"Oh?" On hearing the word *demands,* Vita remembered that Mrs. Wingate was having one of her library teas on Friday. That meant that Jordan—who was already baking from midnight to six all week to free up kitchen space—would have to make lemon squares for the tea tray in addition to her demanding roster of desserts for the weekend.

"Before she'll let herself go, the Club has got to become a goose sanctuary. Gerard seemed to agree." He looked up at the windowsill to check on Forbes, who had his beak pressed against the glass.

Vita rummaged through a shelf, looking for a jar of lemon curd. "It's been a goose haven for years."

"Another thing." Barry lowered his voice. "The restaurant has to turn vegan."

Vita put one hand on the counter and the other to her heart. *"No."* Who would have thought Phoebe could be so vindictive?

This wasn't about some lofty principles, it was about punishing Vita after their squabble last night. No doubt about it, Phoebe was a Club member, born and bred, and she could stay tied to that tree 'til she rotted. Maybe it would make her more tender, like hanging did for the geese. She looked at Barry, who chewed on his lower lip. "And Gerard is going along with this?"

"Can't tell. Maybe he just wants to be with her."

"Oh, no," said Vita. "Don't tell me he's in this for the nooky."

She tapped the counter with her fingers. She should have gone to see Gerard in his office yesterday afternoon and told him that dropping the bird was not the end of the world. Now he'd gotten himself in love, which she could have prevented with a little kindness.

"There's no way we can keep this from Clendenning," she said, with reluctance. "You'd better call him."

"He's going to be as explosive as a golf ball in a microwave." Barry turned and headed back up the steps, where Forbes waited for his return.

As for Vita, she didn't have to wait long for Clendenning to call her into Gerard's office.

"Vita, Gerard Wilton will be tied up for an unspecified time, and I'll need your help to make things go smoothly in his absence."

"Unspecified?" Vita looked around uneasily. Gerard's absence, or *aub-sunce,* as Clendenning pronounced it, was taking on a rather sinister flavor. "What's going to happen? Are we just going to leave him out there?"

"Barry reports that he can leave any time he chooses, so he is either working on this situation from the inside, or he has snapped. We'll find out soon enough, and since he is still, technically, an employee, he may stay where he is. And Miss Lambert is a member in good standing, as her parents continue to pay her junior dues, so if she wants to camp out there, so be it. But as far as her demands go, the Eden Rock Country Club does not negotiate with terrorists." He'd been looking at the corner of the room while he spoke, but now he smiled and looked right at Vita. "Unless, of course, you've been making plans to give up serving meat anyway, which would be a monumental insult to the culinary world. The steak you prepared last weekend was truly magnificent. I'm looking forward to it again on Saturday."

Vita was pleased. At his request, she had added beef to the banquet menu for those, like him, who needed to see bull blood on the plate to feel that they had eaten well. For vegetarians, she had nothing but sympathy. To make up for that, she'd promised her staff, and Barry, that starting next week, she would include a veggie dish at every meal, but she would never let Phoebe think it was a result of her coercion.

"So, we're not going to rescue Gerard?"

"What shall we rescue him from?" asked Clendenning. "A pretty, unarmed woman? The rest will do him good. As far as logistics, we are making him as comfortable as we can. Barry is moving a Porta John within reach, for when nature calls, and some waterproof tarps, for when nature threatens." Clendenning turned and peeked out of the blinds. "Bleane's brought on extra security to watch for accomplices breaching the walls, but I don't think that will happen. Miss Lambert's friends at the gate have gone away for a few days. I'd arranged for some very desirable concert tickets in Maine even before this situation developed, to get them all out of the way for the tournament. Bleane handled it. He told them he won the tickets from a local radio station and handed them out. Phoebe's been left behind. When she sees that she is alone and that no one is paying attention to her, she'll get tired of her game and go home. For the moment, it seems wise to let sleeping dogs lie."

"But what about the members? Aren't they going to see them and call the police?"

"I've contacted the Rules Committee, sub-rosa, and they authorized the hole to be moved. I'm going to tell a few select members that it's been moved because of a septic problem, which, because of the delicate nature of repair permits and the Health Department, we want to keep a secret. Everyone will know by sunset, and no one will go near the area."

"We've got a possible hostage situation on the golf course and we're going to keep it a secret?"

He addressed the corner of the room again. "People see what they expect to see. I'll let Mrs. Wingate in on the truth, since it's safer than leaving her to her own devices. And I'll call Madeline Lambert to see if she can't exert some influence on her daughter. In the meantime, if I could ask you not to let Gerard starve at the hands of Phoebe. Barry says she seems to have stockpiled only water and oats."

Vita put her hand to her mouth. Wasn't that a violation of the Geneva convention? "Of course."

"Things could be worse." Clendenning leaned on the mahogany desk with both hands and studied his knuckles. "When Barry went to collect the pin and cup from Trough, he found a shotgun in the bushes. Ralph Bellows must have left it there weeks ago, which doesn't say much about standards here lately." He looked up. "Can you imagine if the Lambert girl had gotten her hands on that?"

Vita tucked a curl under her toque. Hmm. Gerard, Phoebe, and the gun all in the same place? Maybe Phoebe had used the gun to kidnap Gerard, in which case she would be up for a felony—if someone ratted on her. Vita could pick up the phone right now and get the girl behind bars, which was nothing less than what she deserved.

But no. Revenge was a dish best served cold, and it was not for her. Right now she had to keep her thoughts pure for the banquet.

"And, Vita, please, it's critical that the outside world not get a whiff of Miss Lambert's exhibition. We don't want reporters sniffing around, do we?" He lifted one of his eyebrows, indicating that she would be left holding the bag if they found . . . anything.

Point well taken. She would call Mrs. Suarez to do the plucking tonight, rather than wait until tomorrow. The sooner they got those birds in marinade, the sooner they'd look more store-bought than caught. Stripped and singed, washed and dried, rubbed inside and out with salt, lime, and herbs, the birds would soon be lined up on the metal shelves of the walk-in like a colony of sunbathing nudists. She shivered with anticipation. On Friday she would combine the wing tips and necks with aromatic vegetables to create a culinary potion that, when reduced, would be the fount from which all the sauces and soups would flow, emitting the earthy essence of goose—indeed, of nature itself. She intended to flavor each morsel of food with the stock, for when would she have such splendid excess at her disposal again?

Next year, God willing, as there seemed to be no foreseeable shortage of geese.

Chapter Thirty-one

On the Short Grass

MADELINE STOPPED to pick a daisy for her hair, in case she decided to go to Labor Day cocktails after the tea. It was Friday afternoon, and she was heading out to the clubhouse to meet with Ellen Bruner, but instead of taking her car, she walked through the golf course to check in on Phoebe. Poor thing. Her demonstration just wasn't panning out. She'd been there since early Wednesday. It had rained all day Thursday, but she refused Madeline's offer of a tent and just wrapped herself in the tarp she'd brought for that purpose. Gerard Wilton had his own green plastic sheet, and together, they looked like two faceless lumps, insignificant disturbances on the earth's smooth crust. There was not much to do except offer thermoses of hot twig tea and miso soup. Today, though, now that it was nice out again, she brought her a goody: ice cream. It must be a trial for her to sit next to Gerard while he ate. Vita sent him bulging hampers of food and wine, complete with linen and crystal, which he offered to share, but Phoebe would have none of it. She didn't want a hostage either, but the man continued to press himself on her cause. Humpy had told Madeline that he didn't quite know why Gerard had tied himself to the tree; maybe it was part of a bigger plan to undermine Phoebe's plan. Maybe not.

As she walked toward old Hole #11, she waved at a foursome trudging across the fairway looking for the new hole. They were passing Phoebe's demonstration, but because she was in a low spot, protected by a steep rise on one side and the island on the other, she was effectively erased from the collective consciousness of the Club. And even if any member did, by chance, notice her down there, why would it ever occur to anyone that she'd been left by Humpy for the crows to peck at her entrails? The golfers would wave, as they waved now, ignoring any difficulties, and keep moving. Even if Phoebe were to shout for help, the members would never, ever call the police. If they thought to tell anyone at all, they would report the mess to Humpy, and he already knew.

Madeline sighed. She could have told someone on the outside—she could still—but she just couldn't bring herself to rally the general public and bring attention to her daughter's wacky crusade. Even as a child, Phoebe had pursued her goals with a passion, first collecting stones, then feathers, and later, silly rubber toys for Ben, their old dog. But those obsessions were condoned by society, so it wasn't until her attention turned to saving the world that her persistence smacked of the mentally unbalanced. She cared too much about what she cared about, and that was a dangerous thing. A person could get hurt that way. When Madeline ran over to the encampment after Humpy called on Wednesday, Phoebe had sent her to tell her buddies at the gate the exciting news. But they were all gone, off to Maine for a concert according to the security guard. Madeline had wished there were some way to absorb the blow herself. All that enthusiasm, all those good intentions. Squashed.

She came to the edge of Trough and waved at her daughter. The geese opened a path, shuffling out of the way without looking at her, and she stepped down the incline with difficulty in her sandals and short sundress. With nothing much else to do lately, and no one to do it with, she'd been shopping, restlessly picking things up and putting them back down again. She craved the order of the small shops, the attentiveness of the saleswomen, the newness of the clothes. The solitude of the dressing rooms. And when she looked in the mirror, all she had to do was examine the merchandise, not herself. She could choose, and she could discard. And no matter what she did, the saleswomen loved her for it and encouraged her in her whims. Which is how she ended up wearing this retro-pop daisies-on-turquoise minidress, bought that morning to make herself feel young and carefree. But now that she wore it out in the world, it was having the opposite effect. She felt exposed and vulnerable.

"Whoa, Mom." Phoebe stood up. "You look . . . *different*."

"It looks terrible, doesn't it? I'll go home and change."

"Mom, chill. You look fine. Has anyone called from the media yet?"

Madeline sighed with exaggeration. "Not a word. How are you doing?" Her baby looked somewhat grubby, still in the same shorts and T-shirt she started out in. And that hair. One good thing about the dreads, there was never any way of knowing if they were dirty. She looked around. "Any progress?"

Gerard Wilton stood up, careful not to disengage himself. Barry had brought him his own chain, as requested, but had refused to bring a padlock, so Gerard was only loosely tied to both tree and ankle and could walk away at any time with a good shake of his foot. He held his hand out to her as if he were greeting a guest in the dining room. "Mrs. Lambert," he said. "You look beautiful today. The apple doesn't fall far from the tree in your family, does it?"

Madeline smiled uneasily. Phoebe glared at him.

"No progress," she said to her mother. "All because Mr. Clendenning moved the hole. These people, they sure know how to step over shit. I'll show him, though. I'll stay here forever if I have to."

"Right on," said Gerard, raising his fist.

"I wish you'd just *go!*" Phoebe shouted at him. "This is *my* scene! You want to be a help? Go get a news team."

"No," he said. "I can't be free while you're in chains."

Phoebe made fists with her hands and turned to her mother to make it stop. Madeline wondered where Phoebe found the energy for so much indignation. "Honey," she said, "you've got to understand. No one wants to make any trouble. Just come home and we'll figure out some other way of bringing attention to your cause."

"No, you've *got* to call the TV station again and tell them what's going down, okay?"

"Going down?"

"Tell them I'm *here!* Tell them it's a story!"

Madeline nodded to avoid an argument but knew she wouldn't call. That would only encourage Phoebe and maybe excite Charles. He still didn't know she'd taken siege of Trough, since he hadn't come out of the garage all week. The last time she saw him, opening and closing kitchen cabinets past midnight, she'd asked is this what he wanted, to be living in the garage, foraging for food? And he'd said that a man was not what he wanted to be, but what he had to be. Then he'd grabbed some bananas and retreated to his smoky lair.

There seemed, now, no chance of him getting better. She could only learn to be less afraid of his madness, and with this grim thought, she burrowed through her bag and pulled out a pint of Cherry Garcia. "Here, Phoebe," she said. "Your favorite."

Phoebe cocked her head toward Gerard. "Mom, you *know* I eat lower on the food chain than dairy."

Madeline stared at her. It was such an innocent food. No cow ever died giving milk, but from the guilty look on Phoebe's face, ice cream still must be against the rules. Which meant, from the empty containers she found in the trash over the summer, that she'd struggled with her principles and sometimes failed.

Madeline felt a surge of relief. Phoebe wasn't perfect, and what a comfort that was. She might be extreme in her actions, but she was going to be okay. Madeline wished she had some smattering of maternal wisdom she could pass on to her daughter to keep her going, but what? Her own mother was always sending her self-help books, all about running with wolves or dancing with anger, but she'd never read them. Oddly enough, she'd never thought she needed the help. And from Arietta, she'd learned the power of good posture and fresh lipstick, but that seemed irrelevant here under the tree. What had she ever learned on her own worth passing on?

She put her arms around Phoebe and kissed her on the forehead. "I love you," she said. "I'll come check on you later."

As Phoebe hugged her mother's neck, Gerard gently lifted the container from Madeline's hand. "I'll take that. Vita only included one dessert at lunch today." He held up his palm to Phoebe, who had released her mother to turn on him. "I know, I know," he said. "Your pamphlet says that dairy consumption is linked to impotence, but I can assure you, I have no worries in that area." He opened the pint and took a nibble from the edge of the container, sighing with pleasure. "I am just loving this radical lifestyle."

Madeline looked at her watch and threw a kiss to her daughter, who didn't catch it, too completely engaged in glaring at Gerard as he chewed. The geese grudgingly moved out of Madeline's path as she picked her way up the incline.

Phoebe leaned against the tree and sunk to the ground. Her mom was right, she really could use a treat right now, even if it wasn't totally vegan. But maybe it was for the best. Cheating made her feel so guilty, and besides, whenever she gave in, she heard Eric's voice harping about the connection between dairy products and phlegm. That might have been his last word to her. *Phlegm.* A crow squawked, then another. She looked up and counted. Eleven of them, heads bobbing, clawed feet shifting impatiently along the branches, all staring at Gerard to see if he really meant to finish the job.

Chapter Thirty-two

Tee Time

ARIETTA WAS in the library idly turning the antique globe. The varnish on the planet had bubbled and a crack ran down Antarctica, but all in all, how much had changed over the years? A few names? A handful of national boundaries, always arbitrary at best? Continents had not budged, nor mountains shifted; neither had the oceans dried to deserts. The world was as recognizable today as it was a century ago, as it would be a century hence. She wiped her hands on her handkerchief, then, on a rare virtuous impulse, used it to dust the world clean. If Gerard Wilton insisted on devoting all his energies to overseeing Phoebe's rather pathetic demonstration, then it was every member's duty to pick up the slack.

Madeline coughed at the open door and waved away a dark cloud of backdraft. "Do we really need a fire, Arietta? It's ninety degrees out there."

"Don't question me." Arietta deported herself over to the fireplace and, with the brass tip of her cane, poked at the damp logs and brought them to life. "If it weren't for a little heat in this room now and then, these books—our book—would have rotted from mildew long ago."

"Maybe that would have been for the best," Madeline mumbled. She placed her bag on the faded window cushion and stared out at the lengthening shadows of the course. Golfers were still on their journeys, but everyone always returned, for better or worse—everyone but Charles. She cranked the casement window open, and the handle came off in her hand.

"Enunciate." Arietta straightened herself and ran both hands down her summer-weight gray crepe skirt. She touched her hair to check that all was in order as she peered at Madeline. "You look positively peaked. If you're going to wear such a skimpy outfit, you should have the tan to go with it."

Madeline tugged at the hem of her sundress and studied her bare arm. Where was that bronzing gel she used to keep for emergencies? "Not everyone can stay covered up like some British missionary in this tropical weather."

"You needn't be snippy," said Arietta. "I'm concerned about your welfare. Go out on the courts and play a few sets. Get some color." She inched closer and lowered her voice. "Just because Charles has been holed up in his dark cave all summer doesn't mean you have to stay home. You'd think women's lib never happened, the way some of you behave."

Madeline screwed the window hardware back on. "I don't have anyone to play with. Just right now, as I was walking up the driveway, Holly Quilpe slowed down in her BMW X5 and looked like she was going to say hello, but she must have reconsidered. She sped off so fast her tires spun pebbles." Madeline rubbed her shoulder. "One hit me. I don't know what hurt more."

Arietta took her hand and patted it. "I'm sorry, Madeline. This will pass. Everyone will come around when Charles gets back into the swing of things. You shouldn't take it so personally."

"I am a person. How else am I supposed to take it?"

Arietta raised both hands in defeat and turned away, checking the door to make sure it was locked. "Can you blame anyone for steering clear of you with that haunted expression on your face?" She stopped and rested her hands on the back of a pierced chair. "If things are so bad you can't put up a good front anymore, then you will just have to make some changes. I told you earlier this summer you should get away. Have you thought of going to a spa? Ariel Weber retreated to Canyon Ranch when Peter was going through a rough patch last year, and she came back fresh as a lemon. She was able to move forward, and the problems worked themselves out on their own. They always do."

"Do they?" Madeline looked at her watch. She remembered Peter Weber's "rough patch," as Arietta called her. His office manager. "I'll call for the tea tray."

"You're too late. I had to do it myself." Arietta grabbed the chair by its peak and dragged it closer to the hearth, refusing Madeline's offer of help. "After the weekend, you and I will have a talk about all this, but for now, we've got to make haste." Arietta arranged the chair just so in front of the fire, sat, and reached for her cane against the fireplace. She unscrewed its handle and pulled out the brass key, letting it sway by its silky cord.

Madeline looked away. The fire seemed to be casting more shadow than light, and she rubbed her eyes. "We don't know that we'll need the book. Maybe Ellen just wants to socialize."

"Unlikely. She has her friends, and we have ours, and we are all quite content with that situation."

Yes, they ran in totally different sets. Or had, until Madeline was reduced to a set of one. But today, no matter what the reason for the visit, she would make up for any former aloofness to Ellen and reach out to her. She would start over.

"Go on." Arietta pressed the key on her.

Madeline took it by the cord and held it from her as if it were a dead mouse, then trudged to the cabinet to retrieve a book that recorded and protected the most dire secrets of women who no longer even looked her way. Her dress bunched up when she knelt, her bare knees hard on the wooden floor as she opened the cabinet. The yellow barrier of ancient *National Geographic*s faced her, helping to conceal the true nature of the Club.

"My guess is Bruner lied the first time around." Arietta came up behind Madeline, directing the action with a small flashlight as Madeline emptied the shelf of magazines, letting them drop heavily to the floor before removing the false back. "Now she wants to set things straight. It can take a while for these newer members to come around and realize the importance of the truth."

"If that's the case, the book is meaningless." Madeline had trouble making the key fit. "We can keep it from thieves, but we have no protection against liars. For all we know, we have the truth now, and she wants to change it."

"She's a lawyer; she knows you only get one good chance to get a lie right. The truth you can squeeze in later, if necessary. The door doesn't swing both ways."

Madeline couldn't argue. She never could.

"Hurry up." Arietta poked at Madeline's back with her cane, leaving a dark circle of ash among the daisies.

Madeline finally got the compartment open and wondered how long the lock would last, and who could they get to repair it when it finally broke? Who could be let in? "What with Charles the way he is, and Phoebe where she is, it seems silly that I should be doing this at all. I'm hardly here these days, and who knows what the future will bring?"

"Have faith. Phoebe and Charles are at awkward ages. I remember my Binkie at fifty. He got it into his head that what he needed was to sail around the world. Have you ever heard of such a thing? I just said no. Stay firm. That's what they really want."

Madeline lifted the crumbly book with both hands. What exactly was there to say no to? Tell Charles not to go crazy? Should she have made a fuss when he began the sculpture class? And what if she had? Old Binkie Wingate, sour and dissipated to his miserable end—if that's what happened when wives made them stay, then maybe she should let Charles go. Let him drift off into the hazy distance. A quick laugh escaped from her throat. *Let him.* As if she had any say in the matter. "We have to start thinking of what will happen if I'm no longer here."

"Has it come to that then?" When she took the book from Madeline, a fleck of leather binding fell to the rug. "If there is to be a divorce, you must petition for the Club membership."

Madeline rearranged the magazines and forced the swollen door shut. It was a shock, and a relief, to have the word out on the table at last. *Divorce.* "It's Charles's family that's connected to the Club. I only married into it."

"Yes, but you are the mother of his daughter. The Queen Mother, so to speak. And this"—Arietta held up the book—"is Phoebe's inheritance."

Madeline stood up and adjusted her dress before taking the book from her. "We've been through this before, Arietta. Haven't you noticed Phoebe's trying to bring down the Club, not carry it on?"

"Then she's putting an awful lot of effort into something she professes to hate." Arietta pulled her handkerchief out of her sleeve, wet it with her tongue, and rubbed at a spot on her palm. "Time will prove me right. Now, hide the book until we need it."

"*If* we need it."

There was a knock. "Tea, Mrs. Wingate."

Madeline hurried to the window and lifted the seat, hiding the book in the empty space before unlocking the door. Luisa wheeled a cart in ahead of her. "Afternoon, ladies."

"Busy in the kitchen today, Luisa?" said Arietta, warming her narrow behind at the sputtering fire.

Luisa arranged the tea items and uncovered the lemon squares. "Banquet tomorrow night, then over. Whew." She crossed herself. "I get some sleep then, I tell you."

"Vita does such a lovely job. We are all atingle with anticipation." Arietta bent to inspect the tray. "Very nice." She lifted a lemon square, thick with confectioners' sugar, from its doily.

"You ring, ladies, you need me."

Arietta opened her eyes wide at the first bite of pastry, holding one hand under to catch the falling crumbs. Madeline prepared herself a cup of tea, selecting one with the strongest kick, Constant Comment. "Thank you, Luisa. You can leave the door open."

As Arietta mumbled a good-bye, a morsel fell from her mouth, and she quickly brushed it into the fire with her foot. They heard

Luisa say something in the hall, and then Ellen Bruner appeared, framed in the open door.

Madeline stopped pouring. Ellen must have come directly from court. She had on a short skirt and long jacket in brown tailored linen, edged in black, with the obvious severity of an expensive garment. Her heels were high, and her hair was low and slicked back, like some amphibious animal, which brought attention to what appeared to be gold Phillips head screws in her ears. Under one arm she carried a briefcase of ostrich skin. She smiled as if she'd learned how from a textbook.

"Hello, Ellen." Madeline walked over, intending to kiss her on the cheek, but Attorney Bruner held out a hand instead, her nails the color of blood. When they shook, a sense of foreboding passed to Madeline. Something was wrong. Ellen didn't appear at all pregnant, and yet she didn't seem quite ripe for sympathy either.

Arietta finished her lemon square in one bite, then patted her lips with her handkerchief. "Madeline, finish pouring the tea. Ellen, sit down over here."

"No. I need the table. But please, you two sit." Ellen established her territory firmly in the middle of the room and turned her back to them. She laid her briefcase on the table and unzipped it slowly, even liturgically.

Arietta and Madeline glanced at each other. Madeline put their cups and saucers on the tea-scalded table in front of the hearth and stood uncertainly as orange spice filled the dank room. Arietta spoke as she carefully lowered herself into her chair. "Well, Ellen, have you come to make a change in the book then?" There was a wisp of confectioners' sugar on her upper lip.

Ellen turned to face them. In the warmth of the room, old acne scars seemed to melt through her coverup. "A couple of changes."

Arietta smiled, not looking at Ellen but at the fire next to her. "Conscience got the better of you then?"

"Conscience?" Ellen squinted, deepening her crow's feet, then turned to Madeline. "Is the door locked?"

Madeline moved slowly across the room and secured the bolt, performing the duties of her own jailer. When she turned and leaned against the carved door, a heraldic shield, part of the intricate design, dug between her shoulder blades.

"Could you get the book, please?" Ellen continued to take papers out of her briefcase and lay them out on the dark, fumed oak.

Madeline looked at Arietta, who nodded. There was still sugar around her mouth, and Madeline licked her lips to indicate to Arietta to clean herself up. Then she went to retrieve the book, with Ellen's emotionless eyes on her, the determined blankness that in predators conceals their next move. When Madeline turned, clutching the frail ledger, Ellen patted the table in front of her.

"No," said Arietta. "Madeline, just open it to the last entry, which is Mrs. Bruner's. She may make any changes and addenda to it as she wishes before the baby arrives." Arietta's eyes rested on Ellen's narrow waist. "And when is that happy date, dear?"

Ellen pulled a Montblanc out of her inner jacket pocket, ignoring the ERCC promotional pen that Madeline held out for her. She looked briefly at her entry, dated July 13, 2003: "Ellen Gibowsky Bruner, of Watertown. Husband: Alexander Bruner. Biological father: Alexander Bruner." For a moment, one so fleeting that Madeline was not sure it had ever been there, Ellen looked sad and a little human. But then, just as quickly, it was gone. The lawyer clicked her pen and crossed out the entry.

"Oh," said Madeline, making a consoling move toward her. "I'm so sorry."

Ellen tapped her pen on her palm, and it clinked on her wedding ring. "For what?"

Madeline put her hand on her own stomach and was surprised at the ache she felt. "Your loss."

"There was nothing to lose."

Arietta, who had been taking a sip of tea, spritzed a bit from her mouth and onto the fire, making the hot embers hiss. "Nothing?"

"I am here to represent Roger Rundlett in a matter that concerns the book."

"This is nonsense." Arietta stood without the aid of her cane and placed her cup and saucer on the tea table. "Are you saying you falsified your pregnancy? You lied?"

Ellen held up a legal document. "I am going to make an adjustment to the book, with or without your cooperation. We can do it quietly, here today, or I can get a court order. My client has ascertained that he is the biological father of Nina Rundlett. The only one. Out of respect for tradition, and for you, Mrs. Wingate, he is not seeking damages for spreading misinformation. My job is only to see that the record be set straight. Why don't you sit down and I'll go over the details."

With that, Ellen looked at Madeline, who did not sit. She had wanted to regain some small connection with another human being, and instead, here was Ellen Bruner. How could she ever trust her judgment of people again? Was everyone a liar, all putting up false fronts?

Arietta would not sit down either. Her veins thickened with the pulsing blood of generations of Club members, every corpuscle reacting against the intrusion of this legal interloper. She reached for her cane and tapped it against the fireplace, hitting one of the Roman divinities in the face. "Go on."

Ellen tightened the buttons on her jacket and looked down at her notes for a moment before speaking. "In late June, I was engaged by Roger Rundlett to investigate the events surrounding the termination of his daughter's engagement. He had been informed by his wife that Nina, his daughter by his first wife, might have been sired by Mr. Willard Farnsworth." Ellen looked up. "Gwen Rundlett claims she got this information from you, Mrs. Wingate."

"Has Nina found out?" asked Madeline. It seemed too much that the poor girl would have to cope with the memory of an unfaithful deceased mother as well as an unfaithful departed fiancé.

"No. The first part of my job was to confirm the inscription in the book. And I did that, on July thirteenth, distracting your attention long enough to find Karen Rundlett's entry of March twenty-second, 1980, where she indicated that the biological father might be either her husband or Farnsworth."

"That is very low." Arietta closed in on Ellen.

Madeline thought back. It was all there. What an idiot she'd been. First of all, Ellen had asked for regular tea, not herbal, the beverage of choice for preggies. Then she'd promptly spilled some of it on Arietta's skirt, insisting Arietta go rinse it off right away. The moment she was out of the way, Ellen tearily claimed to have lost a contact lens. Madeline had attributed the events to new-mother nerves and got down on her own hands and knees to look so that Ellen would not get dizzy. And all the while, Bruner must have been quietly paging through the book.

"You had no right," said Arietta, her white head lowered like a butting animal.

"Neither did you," said Ellen. "Your enterprise terminated the engagement without first undertaking a complete investigation of the facts."

"We had enough facts to know the risks. If Karen Rundlett was uncertain as to who the father was, then how could we be sure? We prefer to err on the side of caution."

"I have advised my client that he could bring suit for your failure to take advantage of any and all avenues for uncovering the truth." Ellen pulled out two medical forms from one of her piles and held them out for inspection. "DNA testing. It takes a bit of time—six weeks or more—but these Club marriages seem arranged from birth, so that shouldn't have been a problem. The lab reports might be too technical for you, but let me read Dr. Coull's statement."

Madeline sat down. Why hadn't *they* thought of genetic testing? But under what guise could they have gotten samples? Through her confusion, she heard a few words about this and that chromosome—but they were enough. Ellen finished with ". . . therefore, Willard Farnsworth cannot be the father of Nina Rundlett."

"Don't you need blood or something?" asked Madeline.

"Easy enough for Nina. Mr. Rundlett sent her to Dr. Coull to have her throat swabbed for SARS after her trip to Europe. If she noticed she was in the office of a certified genetics counselor, she didn't question it."

Madeline groaned audibly as she remembered Frank telling her how he'd seen Nina at the professional building.

"Getting a cell sample from Mr. Farnsworth was trickier," continued Ellen, "but manageable. Mr. Rundlett did not want the mess of legal maneuvers, which would have resulted in unpleasant publicity, and so he collected his own blood sample by forking Mr. Farnsworth. I'm sure you remember that evening. I'm afraid my client was more enthusiastic in his task than I advised. It was supposed to be more accident than attack." She put her papers in a pile, then leaned back on the table, resting on her palms. "The results are conclusive. Mr. Farnsworth is not the father of Nina, and she is free to marry Eliot. Of course, that is hardly a possibility anymore, seeing as how their affections have been so brutally alienated. Not to mention the open hostilities between the families. But the important matter at hand, and for which I have been retained, is clearing up the misinformation in the book."

"What are you saying?" asked Arietta.

"My client wants the record set straight and for me to notarize the change. The test results and a copy of Dr. Coull's assessment are to be annexed to the book. Mr. Rundlett will not reveal the book's existence to other male members; right now the book lives only in their minds as a colorful myth, if at all. Even my law partner—my husband, Alex—has been kept in the dark about the specifics of this case. In exchange, you must whisper the news of Nina's true paternity among the female members who might have been privy to the breakup of the engagement."

Arietta was silent as she turned the situation over in her mind. Now that daggers were drawn, her first impulse was to send this woman out of the room, then ruin her with gossip until she resigned from the Club. But there was the greater obligation to the book to consider. Perhaps it was time to make an ally of this insufferable woman. "Then your client recognizes the complete and total authority of the book?" she said at last.

"He does." Ellen reached into her briefcase and pulled out her notary stamp.

"Let's get on with it then," said Arietta.

"Wait." Madeline had difficulty composing her thoughts after such a stunning piece of information. "What are we doing? DNA testing makes the book outdated. From now on, paternity can be proven by a prick of a fork."

"It seems a most helpful tool," said Arietta as she picked up one of the silver dessert forks fanned out on the tea tray. She lovingly ran her thumb over the elaborately engraved Eden Rock insignia on the handle. "I wish we could have everyone tested."

Madeline was aghast. "Why not exhume the dead while we're at it?" In all the years she had helped Arietta with the book, it had seemed more ritualistic than anything, a quaint tradition that occasionally deterred accidental incest. But now, with medical opinions and legal documents, it was turning into something else altogether, something closely resembling a police state.

"Let's not forget to test the staff as well," Ellen said, looking pointedly at Madeline, who cringed. When Ellen had held the pool house door open for her and Scott earlier that week, she had been both solicitous and smarmy.

"The book causes more pain than prevents problems," said Madeline, slightly flushed. "I think it's time to end it."

Both Arietta and Ellen made a protective motion over the book. "Never let it be said that we are behind the times," said Arietta. "We shall embrace modern technology. I must have this Dr. Coull over for cocktails."

"It's too invasive," said Madeline. "We should just let nature take its course from now on, and if the families have any uneasiness, let them deal with testing."

"Horsefeathers," said Arietta. "Are prospective mothers-in-law to compare notes on whom they've slept with and when? And in this case, Karen's secret went with her to her grave."

"The thing to do is put Coull up for membership," said Ellen, thoughtfully twisting the screw in her ear.

Arietta nodded. "Yes, make him one of our own." She reached up to the mantel for her glasses and caught the eyes of Henry Fothergill above. Apart from his many amorous interests, he also found time to change the main sport of the Club from horse racing to golf, a bold but widely successful action, and he seemed to smile approvingly on her own next move. She put on her glasses, blinked, and made a small correction on the page next to Karen Rundlett's entry of 1980. Ellen clamped down hard with her stamp.

"Now," said Ellen, "I'd like to make another entry."

Madeline thought maybe this meant that Ellen was pregnant after all, and she reached out a hand to touch her arm. Ellen backed away. "Not for me." A pained look passed across her face. "For another client. Could you open to the year 1999?"

Madeline and Arietta looked at each other. Madeline shrugged and opened to a listing of five Club pregnancies that year. Arietta pulled her handkerchief from her sleeve and shook it out, using it to cover up the entries, leaving Ellen a blank space.

"Don't trust me?" Ellen asked.

"It's not your business."

"You'd be surprised what is my business." Ellen pulled another sheet of paper from her pile. "Will you examine this statement carefully?"

After Arietta read, she lowered her glasses. "The woman who wrote this was the manager before Gerard Wilton?"

"Yes," said Ellen. "I wasn't joking about culturing the help. The poor woman didn't discover her predicament until after she was fired, and had some romantic notions of single motherhood. She wanted to go it alone, but now I think she'd like some cash. She'd gotten a separation package from the Club, of course, most of it taken from the president's discretionary fund, but the cost of raising a child can put a damper on the most independent of spirits."

"Well, he certainly wasn't very discreet, was he?" said Arietta.

Ellen folded her arms. "I have an appointment to see him now, here at the Club, before I call it quits for the long weekend. We're looking at sexual harassment and paternity."

"I don't understand," said Madeline.

"You are slow on the uptake sometimes." Arietta watched as Ellen filled in the space provided on the page with information: "Rowan Whiting, manager of the Eden Rock from 11/1/99 to 5/1/00, delivered of a male child on 12/22/00. Husband: None. Biological father: Humphrey Clendenning."

Then Arietta signed underneath, the common procedure for third-party registries. "I was always a little suspicious when Humpy hustled Rowan out of here so fast. The hateful things he said about her, you just knew she'd been screwed, one way or another."

Madeline picked up the paper Arietta had put down. "But you don't have proof. It's just Ms. Whiting's word that he's the father."

"We will have the truth soon enough." Ellen clamped down on Rowan Whiting's entry with her notary stamp, then put it in her briefcase, along with the papers, removing the one from Madeline's hands. "The state has an abiding interest in identifying paternity so that it doesn't get stuck with child-raising costs. But we can bypass court-ordered testing if this problem can be settled sooner. If Clendenning makes it worth our while."

But he was so old, Madeline wanted to say, only not in front of Arietta. And in spite of what he'd done, she felt a stab of pity for him, knowing that Ellen would soon be at him like a dog on a bone. "How could he have done this to Brenda? Five beautiful grandchildren. To put everything at risk for sex."

"A powerful force, is it not?" Arietta picked at a corner of a lemon square with her fork.

"You don't have to yield to it," said Madeline, blushing uncontrollably. "Not everyone has the sexual mores of a monkey."

"No," said Arietta, without looking up. "Not everyone, by any means."

Madeline felt the sting of insult on her cheek and could not even say why.

"My bet is there'll be an open space on the board soon," Ellen mused, tucking her briefcase under her arm. "I think Alex might run for it. Being on a prestigious board is good for business. Look how much interesting work we've gotten just by being members."

"Oh, yes." Arietta rubbed the sugary fingertips of one hand together. "Sharks need a good quantity of meat, don't they?"

Ellen and Arietta laughed together like two old cons and exchanged air kisses good bye. Ellen held out her hand to Madeline. "Please call me if you need any legal help. Any at all."

Madeline could barely bring herself to take the hand. Ellen kept her colorless eyes steady on hers as they shook, and Madeline felt the words *divorce case* hanging in the air between them.

After the door shut, Madeline stood in a catatonic posture until Arietta began to rearrange the furniture as if nothing untoward had happened.

"That went well, don't you think?"

"No, Arietta, I don't think." Madeline's voice quavered. "Don't you realize what happened? We killed love over nothing. If it weren't for the book, Eliot and Nina would be getting married this fall. Don't you see what unhappiness we've caused?"

"We cannot blame ourselves. Karen and Willard are responsible for this mess. We were only doing our duty. Put the book away."

Madeline picked it up, the legal and medical slips sticking out like a bad haircut.

"This could be a very good thing," Arietta said, more to herself than to Madeline. "We won't have to worry about mistakes in the future. All we'll have to do is figure out how to collect samples."

Madeline's sandals slapped the bottom of her heels as she walked. "Any system that after a hundred years suddenly needs lawyers and doctors is hardly worth keeping." She bent over to struggle with the cabinet door. "Besides, even a normal pregnancy goes through the wringer now, with ultrasounds and amnio. Any genetic problem that might have come from close breeding will get caught."

"Caught, yes. But not prevented." Arietta paused, her papery hands clutching the back of a chair, and she looked up at the coffered ceiling, thinking how a simple swab might have prevented her marriage to Binkie and spared her a lifetime of disappointment. For certainly her mother, if she had known they had genetic similarities, would have tried to protect her, as Arietta had, in turn, protected her own daughters. It was all done for love. Even the way she kept track of Binkie's illegitimate spawn, celebrating the births of grandchildren and great-grandchildren as if they were her own. A dry sob escaped her throat, which she muffled with a hacking cough.

"Oh, Arietta." Madeline reached out, but Arietta had already turned away, busying herself with the chairs.

Madeline did not want to intrude on Arietta's private grief, whatever that might be. She went back to the cabinet door, which was firmly stuck shut with all the humidity, but when she gave it a yank, it popped open so suddenly she almost lost her balance. Arietta continued to straighten chairs in silence, until she got to the far end of the table, where she stopped to give the globe a gentle spin, continuing their discussion. "The book serves an important bonding service, besides. Remember when McWhorter and Swanson went at each other with putters, all because Emma jumped the fence to McWhorter's pasture? I had a talk with both men and explained that they had more in common than not. Oh, they got my meaning. They understood I was saying there was blood between them. That knowledge kept them civil in the face of the divorce proceedings, and they never missed a beat when it came to Club events. Unlike some people."

Madeline heard laughter rise up from the lounge down the hall. The weekend festivities were beginning. Away from the Club social scene for so long, she thought the shrieks and howls sounded more threatening than inviting. She finished secreting away the book and forced the cabinet door closed. "I should get home," she said, standing with effort. "Maybe I can talk Phoebe into coming back to the house with me."

"Forget her." Arietta held up her hand when Madeline began to argue. "You're coming with me for a drink, and that's that. We both need it. And deserve it."

Madeline considered. She didn't really want to go home, what with Charles in the garage and Phoebe under a tree. Maybe it was time to get another dog so there would always be at least one household member who wanted to see her. "All right, a quick one."

"I'm going to the powder room to freshen up. I'll meet you inside."

Madeline listened as the cane tapping faded away down the marble hall. Then she looked at the key in her hand. Arietta must have been more flustered than she let on, not to snatch it from her. Madeline stood on tiptoes and put the key on a high shelf, behind an aged collection of Thomas Mann. Let Arietta panic when she realized she forgot it. Let her be the one to suffer for a while.

Chapter Thirty-three

Lucky Putts

GERARD, sitting against the tree, had his shirt unbuttoned to allow for a more intimate contact with the sun-filled universe, and as he crumpled the empty Cherry Garcia container a drop of ice cream fell onto his bare chest. He rubbed it into the hair until it disappeared. Phoebe continued to pace back and forth like a tethered animal, dragging her chain behind her, then stopped to examine the bottom of her foot. She wrinkled her nose. "Next time Barry comes," she said as she wiped her heel vigorously on the grass, "tell him to keep his little friend from pooping in my area, okay?"

Gerard smiled. It was funny, how the very sight of Forbes used to drive him into a rage, and now he didn't even notice him. Didn't care where he pooped. Forbes was just another part of the natural landscape, like Phoebe. Like himself. All oddly shaped pieces of a giant puzzle whose grand design remained a mystery. He balled up his jacket for a pillow, then nuzzled closer to the earth, folding his hands neatly on top of his chest and gazing at the branches above. He'd given up cigarettes for Phoebe's sake, but it would be nice to blow some smoke rings right now and watch a part of himself dissolve into the atmosphere.

"Hey, dude, did you hear me?" Phoebe stood over Gerard, scratching her arm. She was getting worried about this guy, with his hair sticking out all over and that stubble scene on his face. The weird thing was, the mangier he got, the more familiar he became. But who did he remind her of? "You seem, you know, a little *out* there."

"It's a peaceful place out here. You should join me."

She raised her arms to beseech the leaves, then, with a rattle of chains, collapsed in frustration, landing butt-first on an acorn. *Ouch.* She couldn't even pick the right species of tree to tie herself to. She punched her damp sleeping bag into a chair of sorts and folded her arms. Where was all the good Karma that was supposed to rain down on her for putting the gun back where she'd found it? What had gone wrong? This whole tree-sit thing got buzz in other places. Here, nothing. She thought maybe when the rain stopped everyone would show up, but *no.*

Gerard giggled to himself, and she gave him a sidelong glance. This dude was *gone,* so why wouldn't he just *go?*

A single crow soared in a circle before coming to land on the highest branch of the tree, looking down at them. "Why, hello bird," Gerard called out, causing Phoebe to groan.

Gerard smiled at her. He remembered being wound up as tightly as that once. He pulled out the goose feather he kept behind his ear and gazed up at the crow through finely constructed wisps. A quill. He could strip some bark for paper, make ink from his urine and vegetable matter—weren't prisoners always doing clever things with their urine?—and write a book about his experience. His father, that old college professor who never quite understood Gerard's chosen path, would understand a book.

Unfortunately, a couple of days in the shade with a Porta John and food service was not going to cut it as a narrative. He'd have to suffer more. He could only do so much with a day of drizzle. With some fiddling, he stuck the feather back behind his ear and looked at Phoebe. He would need more material. More conflict.

He rolled over on his stomach and propped himself up on his elbows, so that his white shirt spread across his back like rumpled wings. He flicked an acorn at her, and her upper lip curled in warning.

"Did you know that the first golf balls were made of cowhide stuffed with goose down?" he asked. "In fact, regulations stated that the volume of feathers be not less than a beaver-hatful."

"Isn't anyone going to start *looking* for you? Don't you have any friends or family on the outside getting worried? Isn't *any*one ever going to call the police and the press?"

"That's three species." He held up his fingers. "A cow, a goose, and a beaver."

Phoebe brought her knees to her chest, dragging the chain. Her stomach rumbled. She should have taken the ice cream from her mom. Who cared what Gerard thought? Who cared what anyone thought? She looked at the cooler but decided against any more trail mix. The raisins only got stuck in her molars and tasted like dried turnips. She wanted to brush her teeth.

"Next time Barry checks in on you," she said, "let's ask him for a toothbrush and some magazines, okay?"

"Yes, he could bring *BusinessWeek*. A trademarked three-syllable word that starts with *B* and ends with *K*."

"That's *four* syllables, doofus."

She called him doofus. They were getting more intimate by the day. "Okay, if you don't think the *i* is silent, what is the answer then?"

She opened her mouth, but closed it at the cracking sound of a club against a ball, then a swell of voices. Then nothing. She tightened her mouth. Not so far away, golfers were slashing and hacking across the fairway, but they were too focused on their stupid game to wonder what had happened to old Hole #11. It was just poof! Gone! No curiosity at all. They were off, following a new course laid down by a higher power.

"It still all just goes on, doesn't it?" Gerard said. "With us or without us."

Phoebe was surprised that their minds were so in sync, another depressing thought. She stared up at the ridge lined with pudding stone, like teeth along a jawline. It would be dark in a few hours. Another day gone with nothing to show for it. "My friends will be back soon," she said in a sickly voice.

"No one's going to rescue us," said Gerard. "You must learn to live without hope, as I have." (Was that too dour a thought to use in his book?)

She snatched at a clump of turf and pulled at it, like hair. "This demonstration is going to work. Chaining yourself to a tree always works. It gets in the paper. *TV.* We're *going* to save animals."

"I like animals. Maybe I could raise mink, for coats. Your mother has a real beauty, if memory serves. Of course, the little critters would have to die, eventually. But so don't we all? I think I could handle that part with a clear conscience."

"A clear conscience is *no* conscience," she hissed.

Wasn't she darling? It was amazing how everything in the world seemed so beautiful when there was nothing, except this chain, to tie him to it. (That was very profound. He would have to remember to put that in the book.) "Or I could raise laboratory rabbits. I like rabbit. Have you ever had one grilled under a brick, the way Vita prepares it?"

Phoebe could almost taste it, and she'd never even had it. The first thing she would do when this was resolved—and with a shudder she wondered just how and if *that* would happen—was head to Falafel Queen for a double order, extra tahini.

"If you think there's nothing wrong with testing lethal products," she said, "why don't *you* volunteer for the job?"

Gerard ran his hand over the mat of dark hair on his chest, then smelled his palm. "I wouldn't mind testing out a little soap right now."

Phoebe took her eyes from his body. "Well, if your stupid boss would just pony up to my demands, we could be in the shower right now."

Gerard propped himself up. "Could we?"

"*Stop* that."

"I'm not doing anything."

"You're, you *know,* thinking."

"You might have control of my body, but not my mind." (That sentence was very good. Maybe the time had come to make ink.)

"I *don't* have control of your body! I don't have control of a thing around here. Untie yourself and *go.*" Phoebe put her forehead to her knees, her dirty, bug-bitten, green-stained, scratched knees. Everything was just so messed up.

Gerard picked at the tree bark. How did people write on this stuff? It was an inch thick and came off in chunks, not sheets. Yet another obstacle to overcome in his journey!

Phoebe opened her fist and contemplated the hard green ball of grass in her palm. She threw it at the plastic water bottle on the cooler and knocked it over.

"Nice shot," a voice called from the top of the incline. It was Dr. Nicastro, silhouetted against the sun and swathed in wisps of steam that rose from the turf.

The sight of a Club member set off Gerard's professional reflexes, and as if jolted by a cattle prod, he got to his feet. "Welcome!"

With some clicking of metal, Phoebe stood up too. "*Sweet.*"

"What in blazes is going on here?" Nicastro took off his Red Sox cap, moved his damp hair off his forehead, then put it back on. He picked his way past the grazing geese, stepping gingerly through the grass, down the slippery slope toward the chained couple. One large gander made a feeble attempt to rear up and flap his wings at the doctor, but it was too hot, and the flock soon settled down again to the business of eating.

Gerard tucked in his open shirt, giving him a piratey sort of air, what with the feather behind his ear. "Dr. Nicastro, how nice of you to stop by." He held out his sticky hand.

Nicastro, breathing hard from his walk, shook it with hesitation. "I hope I'm not disturbing anything." He examined the shambles around him. Unrolled sleeping bags, nylon tarps, coolers, paper cups, bug repellent, scattered shoes. Just like any other poorly organized campsite except for the chains connecting the campers to the tree and the hand-lettered sign tacked to the tree trunk, whose red ink ran like blood: ERCC! SAVE THE WORLD! GO VEGAN! He smiled broadly as the situation dawned on him.

"It's a demonstration," said Phoebe. "You know, a tree-sit thing."

His eyes were drawn to her chest, and he examined the logo on her shirt. "I've got a PETA T-shirt too," he said. "Except it stands for People Eating Tasty Animals." He put a hand on his ribs while he laughed.

Phoebe stiffened. "That's not funny."

Nicastro wiped his eyes. "By God, you sound just like your mother. Does she know you're here?"

Phoebe's right eye twitched. Her *mother?* "She just left. She's supposed to be calling the TV stations." She lowered her voice. "Maybe you can call them."

"Why don't you?"

"I can't report myself." She picked up her chain and shook it. "Can't you see I'm tied up? Aren't you going to help?"

Nicastro looked Gerard over. "Everything okay here?"

"Fine, super." Gerard rubbed his hands together.

Nicastro massaged his stomach, which bulged out from between the top of his green Bermuda shorts and the bottom of his yellow Hawaiian shirt. "Didn't there used to be a golf green nearby?"

"Mr. Clendenning decided the hole was better off elsewhere. He didn't want to disturb Ms. Lambert's demonstration. Please, Doctor, have a seat." Gerard held his hand out to one of the coolers. Barry had taken the bench away to repair the crack.

Nicastro opened the lid of the cooler, drained the contents of a bottle of Evian, then closed it up again. He sat down with a loud grunt and a slosh, then splayed his legs, balancing his paunch between his spread knees. Phoebe and Gerard sat back down against the tree trunk, and he took the two of them in. "How long has this been going on?"

Gerard wiped the mud off his watch. "Three days."

"He's not with me." Phoebe edged away from Gerard. "I don't know what he's doing here."

"I'm here for her," said Gerard.

Nicastro pulled a Mars Bar from his shirt pocket, then peeled a narrow strip of wrapping off one end while he eyed their chains. Yes, indeed. Phoebe was locked tight, but Gerard had to keep fussing with the chain to keep it tied to his ankle. "I think you should both call it a day."

Phoebe banged the back of her dreaded head against the oak. "It's not like I'm asking for the world. What's so hard about going vegan? What's so difficult about a goose sanctuary?"

"The geese need to be culled, not given a sanctuary," said Nicastro, taking a bite. "Three pounds of manure from each one, every day, is a health hazard."

Phoebe took in breath to respond, but Nicastro put up his hand as he swallowed. "And if the Club went vegan, you'd lose my favorite cook. Then you'd lose me." Then again, he thought wearily, the way things were with him and Vita right now, maybe he was already lost. As it was, he'd had to leave the clubhouse because it smelled of Vita's stock, a scent so tantalizingly feral it made him restless, propelling him outside to work off his arousal with a brisk walk. Anything to keep himself from going downstairs to the kitchen and throwing himself into her pot to poach in her juices. "And never mind giving up meat, how could I live without the egg?"

Phoebe squeezed her body. "But people *die* of salmonella from eating eggs."

"Not nearly as many as will die at this Club Vegan of yours because they can't get inoculated with serums and vaccines made from eggs." He adjusted his elastic waistband. "Phoebe, I know you don't think it's fair that humans have power over animals, but believe me, microbes and bacteria have a great deal more power over us. We've no defense against them. No defense against fear and paranoia either." He took a bite to even the edge of the bar. "Besides, if God didn't intend for us to eat animals, why did he make them out of meat?"

Phoebe looked away while Nicastro and Gerard chuckled.

"Look, Phoebe." Nicastro rolled the soft nougat around in his mouth. "You have power over this defenseless man. Does he have less rights than a chicken?"

"I'm not doing anything to him!" said Phoebe. "He did this to himself! Besides, *I'm* not going to eat him when this is over. He gets to go free and live a happy life. I'll probably just go to jail. And for nothing. I won't even get publicity out of it."

Nicastro suppressed a smile and turned to behold Gerard. "Is that true? Will you leave here uneaten and go on to live a happy life?"

Gerard held his wrists together as if shackled. He looked at Phoebe with a wistful expression. "I am already happy."

Phoebe edged farther away, but Nicastro registered Gerard's look. Biology was so blissfully blind to politics and personality. But then, how else could nature ensure a good mix of genes, individuals being as difficult as they were?

"How is Vita?" he asked, the teeniest bit of warbling in his voice.

"Busy," said Gerard. "You know how insane a kitchen gets right before a big event. Not that I've seen her lately. I've been pretty tied up." He held up his chain and grinned.

Nicastro rubbed his gallbladder under his right ribs. His diet had been terrible since he stopped letting Vita feed him, worried as he was about thievery in the kitchen. But was it worth forgoing the pleasures of Vita's talents? He didn't know. He took a deep bite from the top of the soft bar, leaving tooth imprints in the nougat. He would be at the banquet, though—how could he possibly resist? He pushed up another inch of candy bar and severed it at the wrapper. "Phoebe, if you tied yourself up, you can untie yourself as well. That's how I remember it being done."

Gerard rearranged his jacket pillow. "Man is born free, and yet we're all in chains, aren't we?" (That was a good line. He could not wait to get started on his book!)

Phoebe touched the padlock near her dirty ankle. "*No.* I hid the key at home."

"Tell me where it is. I'll go get it. I haven't seen your mom in a dog's age." He wiped the corner of his mouth with his finger, then licked it. Maybe it was time to make nice.

Phoebe made a low animal noise. Gerard wondered how to spell the sound: *Arrrr-ggg-hhh*.

"You can't just unlock me!" Phoebe pulled at her dreads. "I'll have suffered for *nothing.* Animals are being killed and tortured every minute. Corporations are destroying the foundations of life with gene-splitting. But we don't have to wait until there's no life left at all. We can *do* something. There has to be some justice."

"There's a difference between vengeance and justice." Nicastro picked at some nougat in a back molar. "Watch you don't become what you hate."

"That's right," said Gerard, holding up a finger. "Love what you might be." The other two stared at him with concern, then ignored him.

"Besides which," Nicastro continued, "institutions don't change. That's what makes them institutions. In fact, people don't change either. I guess that's what makes them people."

"What it makes them is beasts," said Phoebe.

"Grrr," said Gerard.

Nicastro squeezed up the last bit of nougat from the wrapper. "Have pity, Phoebe. In order to live as you suggest we'd have to rise above our nature. It's not impossible. But the problem is, it's just so much work. And if life is happy and privileged, why bother?"

"Our nature *sucks.*" She let herself flop hard against the tree trunk.

Gerard shook his head peacefully. "It's not true that the members don't care about anything. They love their museums and charities. Especially animal charities."

"True that. They love their dogs more than they love people." Phoebe's voice caught in her throat. Where'd *that* come from? Is that what she believed? Is that how she felt about her parents, who liked animals well enough but hadn't even gotten another dog when Ben died? Phoebe held herself very still and listened to a silence inside her so profound it was like being in the hollow of a tree. The crow in the branch above cawed. Who was more concerned about animals than humans around here?

She guessed she was. Or that's how she'd been acting anyway. Like that dishwasher dude. She'd threatened to call the police on him, and for what? He was only trying to stay alive. If she got any hungrier, *she'd* be going through that Dumpster.

Maybe she was doing the right thing the wrong way. If nothing else, once she got out of this mess, *if* she got out, she'd move. Living with the weird parents had screwed up her judgment. She should go visit her grandmother in Sedona and see if she could find her energy there. There were probably some pretty cool enviro-dudes in Arizona to hook up with.

But how long would it take her to find the right group? She didn't want to be alone, but she didn't want to be messing around with a bunch of crackpots either, who cared more about their cause than about her. Who believed in violence to end violence. Where did that leave her?

The echoing silence within her expanded. It was hopeless. She rubbed her cheek, releasing tears from her eyes. Even her nose ran. "*Oh,*" she said, looking at the dampness on her hand.

Gerard sat up. Tears? That was in his thesis manual too. *Place a light hand on the member's elbow and lead her or him (yes, there will be an occasional him) to the privacy of your office, where a tissue box awaits. A leather-covered box will be most soothing and in keeping with the professional atmosphere of your office [see ch. 5, sec. 3—Office Decor]. Your demeanor at this juncure is crucial.* You must pretend nothing is happening. *Close the door behind you and go back to your business, leaving the member in distress to pull him- or herself together.*

The member in distress. He shook his head. So much unhappiness, so many good fronts. And he, with his misplaced but impeccable standards, had put his faith in the integrity of the fronts, helping to reinforce them instead of tending to the human beneath. He laid his hand on Phoebe's bare arm, not with any aim to hide her tears or stop them. No agenda. No professional courtesy. Just him.

Phoebe remained still and watchful. To her surprise, his hand spread warmth and contentment through her body. Why was his touch so familiar? Who *was* it? After three days of sleeping under a tree, he even smelled like someone she knew, not unpleasant either, just sort of a woodsy funk. Gerard's scruffy head was cocked in anticipation as he stared at her, and when she looked into his brown eyes she felt intense adoration, and then she knew.

Ben! Her old dog, the best friend of her life, her companion, her chum and confessor, her ally in difficult times, her coreveler in happy ones. She felt his loss all over again, and then she felt his presence.

Gerard. She wanted to bury her face in his hair and rub his belly, take him for a run and give him a good brushing. She wanted to feed him and tell him her troubles. She wanted him to follow her home.

Nicastro sat respectfully silent while Phoebe and Gerard had their little moment together, lost in some deep communion of thought. He split the side of the Mars wrapper lengthwise and ran his tongue along the insides. A paper bag picked up in the wind and rolled to his feet. He looked in it, then deposited his wrapper. With an old tissue, he wiped away the drop of chocolate that had oozed from his mouth and put it in the bag as well. Standing up, he brushed down his shirt and shorts. He'd better tidy up the site as well before he left, or social services would come to take the two of them into protective custody. He gathered the garbage and folded the tarps, then found both of Gerard's Cole Haan loafers, but just one of Phoebe's Birkenstock sandals. He caught Gerard's eye and held up the shoe, as in, did he know where the other one was? Gerard gave him an inane grin in return, so Nicastro called it quits and nodded good-bye. He tripped on a clublike branch on the ground and used it as a cane to get up the slope.

When Nicastro was out of earshot, Gerard leaned in close to Phoebe and whispered, "Birkenstock. The answer is Birkenstock, not *BusinessWeek*."

She took in a breath, as if she'd just witnessed some clever animal trick. Who would have expected it? She wiped her eyes with both hands, thinking that if she could turn Gerard around, she could change anything. And not just here either, but in the real world, where it mattered. She wished she had some treat for him. Then she smiled and touched her chain. "Gerard, want to go fetch the key?"

When Nicastro reached the top of the incline, he looked back down at the couple, locked in a scene of enormous peace. He checked his pocket for another candy bar, but no, all gone. A crow, oily blue against the softening pink of the sky, swept over his head and landed in the tree to join his two cronies. What was that old nursery rhyme about crows? "One is for bad news, two is for mirth." What was three? Or was he thinking of four and twenty blackbirds baked in a pie?

He walked away, one hand on his stick, the other on his gall-bladder. He would not take any action on this right now. Not quite yet. What was needed here was time. Well, didn't they all need just a little more of that? He chuckled to himself, then rubbed the persistent ache under his ribs.

Chapter Thirty-four

Membership Dues

THE CLUB'S lounge resembled the inside of Madeline's head. Crowded, confused, and pulsating with competing voices, all a bit much to take. She stood at the threshold of the high-ceilinged room and hesitated, but habit got the best of her. She entered and got sucked right in, easily absorbed into the pack. The members were arrayed in canary yellows and Kelly greens, as colorful as jungle parrots, flush with drink or sport, eyes puffy from a day of squinting in the sun. Madeline was feeling overheated and unsure, already too deep in the throng to see where she stood in it. She twisted around and recognized Jay Freylinghuysen's back, with his pink neck protruding over the collar of his blue blazer. She'd overheard at the pool that he was in some sort of trouble having to do with a car, but here he was, so it couldn't be all that serious.

"Howard goddamn Amory," he said, joyfully relating the day's news to someone just out of view. "Can you believe it? Sneaky little underdog made it into the finals tomorrow. Goes to show you. Nothing fancy, just goddamn determination. A solid six-wood into the wind, right to the pin. There's performance under pressure for you."

She heard garbled words and knew Jay could only be talking to Eugene Hollowell. She got on her toes and glimpsed Gene's tufted scalp. If Humpy had to step down, this incomprehensible man would be in charge. "Yes, uh um, it's, well. I've, where? Oh."

Gene was trying to escape, but Jay was too quick and put a used-car-salesman hold on his elbow. "I'll tell you what performs under pressure. This 'ninety-three Beamer I've got right outside. Have a look. Your boy is going to be driving before you know it. They grow up quick, don't they? Breaks my goddamn heart."

Then they were gone, leaving Madeline in a clearing. She tried not to catch anyone's eyes as she looked around for Arietta, but she was not so lucky. Beryl Hall, with a peevish smile of cunning on her deeply tanned face, approached her.

"Madeline," she rasped. "Where have you been hiding yourself?" In her left hand she held aloft an elephantine martini glass of ice-blue liquid, with a tiny blue ice pop as a stirrer. With her other hand, she touched her hip, as if she carried a knife in her support hose. She leaned in to peck Madeline's cheek, almost spilling the drink, then stepped back to admire the dress. "Look at you. Aren't you the fashionable one? Here, take this. Enrico is making another batch." She looked over her shoulder, ready to impart some intimate secret. "It's called Smurf Pee! I won't tell you what's in it. You'll have to guess."

Madeline tried to refuse, but Beryl had already spun away, off to the bar to arm herself for her next mark. Madeline was left holding the sticky glass in two trembling hands. She shouldn't have come. The encounter in the library had been not just disturbing but ominous. What would the future be like with Arietta going around poking members with forks, compiling her incriminating data? Who was to benefit? She felt she'd been drawn into something illicit and intrusive, something just plain wrong, despite Arietta's "boys will be boys, and girls, girls" argument. Despite Ellen's cold legalities.

She took a sip of the blue drink, which, oddly enough, tasted orange, reminding her of the tea left untouched in the library and making her a little sick. But her thirst overrode the nausea, and she swallowed more than she intended. Best exchange it for ice water. As she turned to the bar, the sun dipped below the protection of the awning and flooded the lounge with a pink light, making her feel like she'd been thrown onstage. Forget the water. Where was Arietta? She parked her mouth on the rim of her glass as she looked around at the golfers, both men and women, sparkling with sweat as they mimed key swings of the day. Arms were flexed and hips canted, with hands clasped in the air like a disorganized rite of pagan worship. Through this forest of limbs, she saw Arnold Quilpe goose Linzee Gibbons, who jumped, then laughed a bit too lewdly. Holly Quilpe, who'd been standing next to her husband, found something fascinating to look at on the other side of the room, but everyone else was laughing and touching one another, very much alive and in their element. Would she and Charles still be a happy couple if they had something, or someone, to keep their hormones pumping?

Behind her she heard two voices whisper to each other about "*the septic problem*" over at Trough, and how that was the reason for moving the hole.

"Such a health hazard."

"Can you imagine if the authorities find out!"

Poor Phoebe, thought Madeline, she never had a chance. The Club had successfully covered her up with a lie. She wished now that she hadn't been so chicken-livered; she should have rallied the media and helped her daughter achieve her goals. What kind of a mother wouldn't even do that?

Madeline needed air, but standing between her and freedom was Ralph Bellows, lumbering in her direction, still clutching a bullhorn from some minor official post he'd held at the tournament. He'd been away in Maine for weeks, so he would certainly ask her how their summer had been. She didn't have the strength to turn the conversation, and she definitely didn't have the stomach for the blue tartan tam-o'-shanter he wore on his head. She slowly wormed her way to the back wall, where she could feign interest in the trophies while she watched for Arietta. Behind the locked doors of the glass case stood an army of urns crowned with miniature golfers commemorating glories long past. Little silver people, slightly tarnished, on display for all eternity. Her focus changed, and she saw her own reflection in the glass.

"Madeline Lambert? Is that you?"

Madeline turned with a smile, ready to run. It took a moment to disengage her words from her thoughts. "Oh, Isobel. How go the wedding plans? I saw Duncan and Bonnie at the Copley."

Isobel Crane was a wiry, weathered blonde, with white linen sleeves pushed halfway up her forearms. Her hair was teased in a botanical sort of way, but the warmth of the room was making it wilt. "Yes, they went to Cartier to choose barrettes for the bridesmaids. It never ends."

"Busy, then?"

"Them, not me. I'm the mother of the groom. I don't do anything but buy myself a plain blue dress."

Madeline tried to join in on her laugh and failed. "They make such a lovely couple," she said instead. But for some reason, she choked on her last two words, and returned the unnatural drink to her lips.

Isobel smiled openly, which made Madeline shudder. Isobel wouldn't be so happy if her Duncan had fallen in love with Bonnie's cousin Courtney, a marriage Arietta hinted could not be. Madeline felt like a tyrant even knowing so much.

Isobel held up her own blue drink, and they clinked glasses. "I see Beryl caught you too. They're actually not too bad." They both took long sips. "We'll be sorry tomorrow, though."

Madeline smiled weakly. "Have you seen Arietta?"

"She's out on the terrace with Anne. I'm so glad to see you. Is Charles here?" She looked around, expecting he might be standing just a few inches away, then reddened to her diamond studs.

"He's . . ." Madeline trailed off. "He's been tied up on a project . . ."

The silence lay awkwardly between them, until Isobel leaned in and put her hand on Madeline's arm with great tenderness. "I'm sure he's fine," she whispered.

Madeline stared at the hand. Don't do that, she thought, don't touch me, don't say one kind thing or I'll fall apart. Isobel backed right off, and in that instant Madeline felt untethered from the world, floating in a cold, empty space. A tiny lump, the size of a pearl, lodged in her throat, and she tried to wash it away with the rest of her drink.

"I've got to talk to Arietta," Madeline murmured, glancing up with a painful smile as she stepped away.

"Call me," Isobel said. Madeline nodded as she walked away, as if she would.

Whatever was in that drink was positively toxic. As she ducked and angled herself between rigid bodies, she struggled to keep her balance. Her dress stuck to her body from the heat, the fabric refusing to adjust itself to her movement. It was strangling her. Old friends looked like they might brave a word, but she pointed to the terrace as she walked, to spare them.

An arm reached out from the crowd. Peter Weber grabbed her elbow and pulled her in for a jovial kiss. She was too weak to escape. Besides, he was so boring as to be actually soothing. So she said hello, which was enough to get him going on his game that day, a conversation that allowed her to ruminate peacefully on her own thoughts. Peter, whose face was crisscrossed with a network of broken blood vessels, began to complain at length that moving Trough was throwing the entire tournament off. "What was Humpy thinking? How could he do such a thing?" he asked loudly, looking around for approval from passersby.

"How *could* he?" Madeline said, with such depth of feeling that Peter shut up and stared at her. He opened his mouth, then closed it.

"I've got to go," she said in the ensuing silence, and they both moved on.

Food. Food was what she needed. The kitchen always put munchies out for cocktails, so Madeline turned in the direction of the sideboard, then stopped. There was no getting near it, what with bodies three-deep grabbing for cheese straws and tuna tartare, swallowing and chewing, everyone talking in cocktail Esperanto, with their mouths full. She'd always depended on Charles to get her plates of things. But there was no Charles now.

She was starving, but the blue ice pop would have to satisfy her hunger for the moment. She stood there sucking on it, immobile, blocked on one side by a waiter taking an order from a large group, and the backup from the bar on the other. They were all absorbed in getting Enrico's attention, so she went unnoticed, contentedly so. The thought of making an effort to be agreeable exhausted her. Today's weather, tomorrow's weather, yellow Labs. She had no interest in any of the acceptable subjects.

She spotted Arietta weaseling her way to food, right to the choice bits, the caviar. Two kinds. She scooped both on a mini-blini, one on top of the other, then smothered it in sour cream. Frank would be appalled. It was like mixing two fine wines together, then adding seltzer. Arietta folded the blini in half and ate it in two bites, smearing cream on both sides of her mouth. Madeline was about to wave her down, when her empty glass was suddenly wrenched from her hand and another Smurf Pee put in its place. Beryl pecked her on the cheek, winked, and was gone again to swoop down on some other pigeon before Madeline could force it back on her. But why should she want to? Why shouldn't she have a good time too, like everyone else? She peeled the paper napkin off the foot of her cocktail glass like dead skin and placed it on a passing waiter's tray. By the time she remembered about Arietta, she was gone. She must have slipped back out to the terrace.

Madeline took a sip to fortify herself to follow, poking her eye with the ice pop. Then she began to squeeze through a weak spot in the crowd, pausing to rest at the table whereupon stood the Fothergill Cup. She put the brimming glass to her lips and, to her horror, slurped. She looked around to see if anyone heard, but the airwaves were dominated by Neddy Fenwick, braying to an indifferent audience how he had finally mastered the dogleg at #9 and come in at par for the hole. He'd made a poor showing in the championship but found joy in that one hole. He tapped his forehead, which in spite of being out under the sun all day, remained as white and unblemished as an egg. "It's all in here. It's not a matter of how well you play, but how well you handle how you play."

How true, Madeline thought as she delicately slurped again. How very true. She ran a finger along the Fothergill Cup, pausing on Charles's name, engraved in brass, from fourteen years back. She remembered that day. He'd been so happy. They'd been so happy. Hadn't they?

Maybe not. Maybe they were one of those couples who only operated well within the confines of a larger group, depending on it to fill in the silences between them. They were always safe here, within the social proprieties. Maybe what they'd been happy with all this time was not each other but the Club.

There seemed to be no going back for Charles, but she didn't have to be alone. She stroked the stem of her empty glass, thinking, then put it down next to the trophy, almost missing the table. She would jump back in. Hilary Fisher was over by the door, talking to a new member—something Galton—with waxy blond hair and oversized jewelry. The Galtons were incredibly rich, so the rumor went. New people always were. Madeline made a move toward them but stopped when she realized Hilary had her on her hook.

"I hear you have the most beautiful home west of Boston," said Hilary, standing too close and eyeing the Galton woman over her wineglass.

"Oh," said the woman, blushing. She flapped a hand, glinting with stones, warding off the compliment. "We like it. You'll have to come see it for yourself some day."

"I'd love to," Hilary said, barely moving her lips but rotating her hips in pleasure. There was a pause, and the Galton woman's mouth opened slightly as she understood she was now expected to be more specific.

"Let's see," she said. "When the festivities are over this weekend?"

"Perfect," said Hilary. "We're free next Friday. In a week, I'm sure we'll all be bored again." Then she screeched like a howler monkey and leaned in even closer, until the Galton woman was forced to join in on the laugh. The volume of the whole room intensified, a group guffaw confirming that all was right with the world, creating a trumpet of sound that finally propelled Madeline to one of the French doors. Andrew Sortwell and Gregg Thayer, Charles's old golfing buddies, stood on either side of the doorway, sucking in their stomachs to let her out.

Andrew laughed hello with a second-drink enthusiasm, a handkerchief tucked smartly in his breast pocket pointing up to his slightly simian features. As usual, his back was too stiff to bend for a kiss, but Gregg leaned to her as she passed, and breathed, "Hope to see more of you, Madeline."

She turned, deeply offended. He raised his glass of yellow wine, hardly keeping his grin concealed. Was she considered fair game now? "Give my love to Ella," she said, and kept moving.

The humid air outside was not as reviving as she'd hoped, but she took in a deep breath anyway, gulping it like food. Set up on the old croquet lawn, the tent for tomorrow's banquet was vast and empty. She looked around for a canapé table and spotted Arietta sitting on the low stone wall with Gwen. Madeline took a step toward them, but her brain and legs seemed not to be in communication with one another, and she tripped on a mislaid flagstone. At that moment, Ellen Bruner rushed out of the lounge behind her, rosy and triumphant, and almost bumped into her. The two women, who now knew each other for enemies, were startled to see each other again so soon. Ellen ground out a greeting through her teeth.

"How did it go?" Madeline whispered. "With Humpy."

Ellen looked around and lowered her voice. "Humpy?" She undid the top button of her silk shirt with extreme self-satisfaction. "It's very warm, isn't it? I might have to change."

"I don't think that's possible," Madeline said.

Ellen looked like she might just rise to the bait, but Alex Bruner interrupted them, his face wrinkled up like a Pekingese. Ellen excused herself with a curt nod and walked away with her husband, their heads bent together.

So that was that. Madeline hiccuped. It was time to leave.

Before she could escape, a blast came from beyond the terrace. She almost dropped to the ground before realizing it was just the Club's cannon, announcing sunset and the lowering of the flag. She was never prepared for the explosion, even though they'd been doing it for more than a year now. She reached for her heart like everyone else and could still feel it racing. No one talked. No one took pleasure in the ceremony. The only time the silence had ever been broken was by Phoebe. Of course. It was the summer before, the last time her daughter had come to the Club as a member and not a tormentor. She'd left in disgust after the jolt of the cannon, announcing that pompous nationalism was the forerunner to fascism, and that it wouldn't be long before they'd all be goose-stepping around the course.

Madeline loved her country; she considered herself patriotic and had never failed to vote, even in the primaries, but at the moment, standing so unnaturally straight with all the others, so uniformly solemn, she wondered if Phoebe was onto something. She had never felt the yoke of group pressure weigh so heavily upon her.

The flag creaked and flapped noisily down, attended to by Pole, with what Madeline felt was practiced irony. As her mind wandered, her fingers absently went searching for the raised biopsy scar near her underarm. A small, meaningless fibroid, but big enough, apparently, to alienate Charles from her body. Now he was gone. Everyone was gone. She tried to feel her heart, but it was too well defended behind its cage of bone. She knew it was there by its pounding, but even that became distant and muffled.

A few tears began to slide down her face, and she didn't wipe them away. She let them fall, landing on her dress, creating small dark spots among the daisies. She stood like that long after the flag had been folded into a pastry and put away, long after the others had wandered off in their relentless pursuit of happiness.

Chapter Thirty-five

Sinking the Putt

BREATHING IN THE WARM, moist air, Charles raised his bare arms over his head in a stretch and felt a deep animal satisfaction. Tomorrow was the day. All he had left was some polishing and he'd be done. The two goats pressed their noses against the wire to watch him, their leader, and a young rooster stood on a rock and flapped his wings, interpreting Charles's stretch as an open invitation to battle. Charles could set the bird crowing by making a few challenging snorts, but the neighbors were getting very testy about those sorts of things. He bent to touch his work boots, loosening up all over, and while he was down there, he plucked some grass for the goats. Leaning against the fence, he opened his hand and let Randolph—Randy for short—the tweedy billy with the full, handsome beard, snatch the grass away with yellow teeth. Charles wished there did not have to be a wire barrier between him and the animals—but what was the alternative? There was no natural habitat for domestic livestock—they'd evolved, for better or worse, with humans, and there was no going back to the savanna for any of them. Randy continued to probe his palm with a leathery nose even as his cheeks bulged with what he already had. From the back pocket of his Lees, Charles pulled out a piece of rumpled paper—Randy's favorite treat—and the goat tilted his head to better maneuver it down his throat. Madeline had left it pinned to the garage door that afternoon, saying she was going to the Club, "as if anyone cares."

"She doesn't mean that," he told the goat, who cocked his head as he munched. "I don't think." How could she not know how much he cared? She was all he cared about—the reason he labored to get his sculpture done, so they could begin again. Renewed and reloved. Was that a word? He would make it one. He would make it theirs, even though, at the moment, they didn't even have a bed in common. Lately he'd been camping out in the garage, only letting in Vincent and Nod to confirm he was still on track. They talked about the most amazing things—pain, passion, despair, divinity. It made him wonder whether he'd always confused socializing with friendship. He hoped he'd not also been confusing marriage with something else. When he'd proposed, he'd told Madeline that they'd make a great partnership, when what they needed was another kind of merger altogether.

But tomorrow night he would tow the sculpture to the Club, a memorial to commemorate the end of one life—the goose's—and the beginning of another—his own. The more he worked, the more he desired Madeline, and yet he couldn't seem to tear himself away from his sculpture.

How to get Madeline there? A love letter? He could leave it on her pillow tomorrow morning, while she slept. "Meet me at Plateau, at ten tonight." Pretty romantic, he had to admit.

He pressed his forehead against Randy's skull, not in aggression but in affection, like rubbing noses. But Randy took it as a challenge and pushed back hard until Charles gave up. He was not so thickheaded. He brushed fur from his scratchy cheek with the back of his hand. When had he shaved last?

Who cared? His whole life he'd kept himself clipped and pressed, trying to control one thing or another, even his facial hair. He should just let it go altogether—why hold growth back? But first, as Steeve said, he had to make room for abundance in his life, and to do that, he would have to toss a few things on the pyre. His job, for instance. Bond trader. He would turn bond traitor.

He smiled at his play on words. Trader, traitor. That sort of thing never happened before—how truly dull he must have been. No wonder Madeline had grown distant. But now, words and images flooded through his brain, latching on to one another to forge new life-forms, like exuberant molecular strands. He had always been a careful gatekeeper of his thoughts and emotions, only letting in so much at a time. But excess of the mind was good. Excess created. During the bull market, he'd thought of the world as a place that would keep on expanding, like the universe—but the only true expansion was in the human brain. He did not want to be one of those men, living without sense and dying without desire, sitting on the edge of the grave, still calculating yield. His father was dead at sixty from a stroke. What time was left to him?

Irving, the other goat—spotted and dainty-bearded—bleated meekly for a bit of grass, and Charles had to hold Randy back by his curved horns to keep him from Irving's share. When the chewing died down, Charles scratched both their bony heads, and they arched their necks in heathen pleasure. He remembered taking Phoebe to a petting zoo when she was a little girl and telling her not to touch the goats—or anything, for that matter. "Dirty creatures," he had called them. How silly. Nothing was wrong with them—there had been something wrong with him. They made him uneasy with his own animality, and in the process, he had probably warped Phoebe's notion of farms, livestock, and life. The goats thrust their heads under his hands to redirect the scratching between their horns. Their desires were so wonderfully unmediated by conscious thought—if they felt physical delight, they showed it. When they were hungry, they ate. And if they were horny, they mounted each other—the fact that they were castrated males notwithstanding. It was not possible for humans to be as spontaneous as all that without being locked up; in fact, it was horrific to think of people going around letting instinct lead them—what with fear, aggression, and sexual impulse taking up so much real estate in the gray matter. Instinct was best left to art—the stylized expression of the full range of arousal, good and bad. When he and Madeline first met, she used to lead him into discussions like that, and he would encourage her, just happy to hear the sound of her voice even though he understood nothing. But then the first time he heard her talk like that at a cocktail party, he'd stepped in and deflected the conversation to golf, and she got the point. From then on, she never said another word that she hadn't already heard from someone else at the Club, and he praised her for fitting in so well. What a jerk he was. But why hadn't she pushed back?

Music drifted down from Phoebe's open window on the third floor, along with a sound he hadn't heard in the house all summer: laughter. She had a visitor, a man by the sound of it. A romantic interest? Maybe, but more likely just one of her ALF compatriots, gleefully helping to plot a meatless humanity. He hadn't seen her in days, and he hoped she'd been staying out of trouble. He should go up and say hello, reconnect. They had drifted apart after he told her he couldn't join her in the demonstration—she refused to understand it would have killed her mother.

Phoebe would have to wait—she had company now anyway, and he had things to do. He had to find his chain. He thought he'd left it coiled up by the door, but it wasn't there, and he'd need it tomorrow night to pull his work over to the site with his John Deere lawn tractor. The goats put their cloven hooves up on the fence, absorbed in his every move as he burrowed through piles of material lying around the yard, bits of interesting iron and brass he'd rescued from Dumpsters and charity shops. It was too bad the neighbors didn't find this collection as fascinating as he did. A designated representative had called Madeline, accusing the Lamberts of running a junkyard. Why that sort of thing should bring her to tears he did not know—it was more of a reflection of the neighbors' insecurities than anything else.

Charles scratched his hair with both hands and was entranced by the heady bouquet of goat musk on his skin. It made him want to roll in the grass and scratch in the dirt. The sky was turning in streaks from blue to apricot as the low sun settled behind the maples. How fast the summer goes. Crickets in the lawn warmed up for the evening recital, and families of crows gathered in the treetops. A clamor rose at the golf course, the harsh honking of geese as they clustered to the safety of water hazards. Close by, he heard a satisfied warble.

Olson. He was one of Phoebe's two Bronze Beauty turkeys that she had, as she put it, liberated from its animal prison this summer. In spite of Olson's size—more than forty pounds, and barely able to carry his breast about—he was a real escape artist, quite nimble when it came to slipping through weaknesses in the fence. Charles followed the warbling to the back porch, where Olson liked to roost, waiting for the milk delivery in the morning. But he'd grown too big for the railing and could only perch on the top step, a sitting duck for any predator. Until they kept livestock, he had no idea how hard wildlife was pressing against the suburbs—he'd seen a coyote sniff around the animal pen one night, and soon afterward he found an eviscerated goose on the course. Nature had her own ways of controlling an explosive population, and she was none too subtle. It would be a shame to have Phoebe rescue the turkey from the knife only to have him done in by the claw.

"Here, Olson," Charles whispered. The turkey gobbled softly and let himself be picked up. Charles groaned under the weight. "Let's get back home, big boy." He buried his head in the feathery folds of Olson's broad back, which made the wattles on the bird's head and under his beak turn electric blue and erect. He was a magnificent specimen, so very male, so exceedingly virile. Charles understood how his own vulnerable species might wish to borrow some of this vitality by eating its flesh and wearing its skins.

It took some adjusting to get Olson comfortably cradled in his arms before heading back to the pen. The other turkey, Tribble, stood forlornly at the fence, waiting for her husband's return. As they brushed up against some foundation plantings, Charles heard the clinking of chain.

"Can it be?" It *was*—all forty feet of his chain, lying on top of the rhododendron. He looked up. It was directly below Phoebe's open window, three flights up—she must have borrowed it for one of her protests.

Kids. But she wasn't a kid anymore, was she? Where had the time gone? What had he done with it?

He shook his head, and the turkey warbled in sympathy. Considering Phoebe's communal attitudes about property, he was probably lucky to get the chain back at all—but he would have to have a talk with her. She had to ask permission to borrow other people's things, and then she had to put them back where they belonged. Toss his chain out her window! He nuzzled his nose into the bird's back again. It could have landed on Olson.

Chapter Thirty-six

The Gimme

THE SUN cast no afterglow. It had turned dark abruptly, and no moon was rising. Madeline brushed mosquitoes from her leg as she walked, and realized she'd forgotten her bag in the library. But she wasn't going back. She couldn't. Last week she had collapsed at the pool; now she had cried on the terrace. There was no hope. Arietta had tried to help, grasping her by the arm to drag her to the safety of the shadows, but she shook her off. She was not so sure she wanted to be saved.

In her rush to escape, she'd run down the fieldstone steps and turned into unfamiliar territory around the side of the Club, hoping to shortcut to the golf-cart path that would lead her home. She could not have made a worse move. A delivery door opened and out stepped Humpy, like some unearthly specter. A yellow bulb lit his face in profile; it sagged in pain. They stood facing each other for a moment. He seemed to be waiting for a word from her, but what could she say that he didn't, by now, already know? The word was *guilty*. He turned away without speaking, in the direction of the employee parking lot. He moved with extreme care, as if he'd suddenly, and atrociously, aged.

She waited for him to get a head start, but she was fidgety. This was not a part of the Club she was familiar with. From what she could tell, it was more of a service area, with some overgrown courtyard farther on. At her feet, piles of cigarette butts lay like animal droppings on the ground, which meant that this was where workers came to smoke. The last thing she wanted was to be caught by any of them, but neither did she want to follow closely on Humpy's heels. The thing to do was forget the cart path and cut across the turf, taking the long way home.

On an impulse, she removed her sandals to feel the grass wet and alive between her toes as she put distance between herself and the clubhouse, with the tent butted up against it, unlit from within, a dead space. The terrace, however, was bathed in a golden circle of light, highlighting the few stragglers who had not yet gone in or out to dinner. Not many on this holiday weekend would be going home so early, like her.

Home to what? As she walked, she contemplated life as a divorced woman. It might not be so bad. She'd seen with what enthusiasm women arranged dates for the newly single, quickly getting them coupled again, like they all lived on the Ark. She wondered what it would be like to be with another man after all these years, and thought of Charles's indifference to her. Was the unexamined wife not worth living? She laughed out loud at her little joke, which made her realize she was more than just tipsy. She closed her eyes for the drunk test and the world spun around her. Good thing she had walked to the Club that afternoon, because she couldn't possibly drive home in this condition. She breathed in through her nose, but there was no fragrance in the air. It was not that time of year. The heavy foliage all around her had no blooms, and even the leaves had stopped growing, just gathering dust, waiting for the season's end.

She looked longingly at the pool across the fairway. She could go for a quick dip, couldn't she? She wasn't ready to go home. She didn't know if she'd ever be ready. She turned so sharply she almost fell, but quickly uprighted herself with what she considered to be grace. As Neddy said back at the lounge, it didn't matter what happened out on the course, it was how you handled it that counted. Or something like that. The point was, she had to handle her life better. There was no reason to be so unhappy. Or hot. She listened to the birds whistling to sleep in the trees and the crickets making music in the grass. A firefly blinked brightly. She might have lost her old life, such as it was, but the future could be sweet, really, if only she would let it.

The pool house had a security light on but was otherwise deserted. She unlatched the wooden gate to the pool area with great care, so as not to make a noise, and hung her sandals on the picket fence so she could find them later. In the shadows, she struggled with her dress as she struggled with her conscience. What about the bra and underpants? The throbbing of the water pump seemed to get louder. Dare she? She remembered skinny-dipping here long ago, with Charles, before they were married. They had snuck away from their engagement party and swum together like two happy sea mammals, one with the water and each other. The moon had been out then, casting a silver glow on the scene, and afterward Charles had carried her home piggyback.

She groaned. What made them think they were ready for marriage? She'd been younger than Phoebe was now; Phoebe, who for all her outrageous behavior was more sensible in many ways. Marriage was still a long way off for her, while she and Charles had been mere children. She shook the memory from her head, then shook her panties down to the cobblestones. With a single flourish she removed her Maidenform.

At the sharp sound of laughter from up the hill, she instinctively covered her crotch with her hands, but the Club was very far away. And those members weren't going anywhere. She turned to the water, clear as vodka and glimmering with underwater lights. With no more self-consciousness than an otter, she walked to the deep end and dove in.

The water, warm from the day's heat, enveloped her. She held her breath and moved effortlessly through this other reality, a refuge where change could begin. Even love. How easily that had happened with Charles. Perhaps Arietta was right, maybe it was biology, but it was magic too. She came up for air, then went back under, all the way to the bottom, feeling her way with her fingers. When she finally let herself float to the surface, she rolled on her back in a dreamy trance. She wanted more of this. She wanted more, period.

Distant hoots and guffaws echoed from the Club. It was time to get out. One never knew, after all, who might have the same unlikely idea, although drunken leaps into the pool were generally unknown before midnight. She stroked gracefully to the ladder. Climbing up the metal steps, with her hair clinging to her shoulders and water dripping off her naked body, she felt refreshed, renewed, and ritually cleansed.

But then her throat tightened when she heard a quiet cough by the pool house door. A male figure. She slipped back into the water, terrified.

"It's okay, Mrs. Lambert. It's just me, um, Scott."

A woozy wave of anger rushed over her. "You might have said something sooner," she said, trying to keep her voice flatly matter-of-fact and sober. "I thought I was alone." She peered through the dark, trying to determine how far away her clothes were.

"I'm sorry, Mrs. Lambert." Scott was still in his bathing trunks, over which he wore a long-sleeved shirt, open in the front. He moved forward slowly, tentatively holding out a *Lion King* towel in front of him. "You looked so peaceful, I didn't, like, want to disturb you."

Or disturb his free peep show, she wanted to add, but that would be acknowledging that there was something to peep at. She backed down the ladder a step to hide her breasts under the surface, but they bobbed up, glowing white in the watery dark. "That's okay, Scott. I shouldn't be out here. I'm making your job harder."

There was a brief pause as she choked down a laugh.

Scott smiled. "I brought you a towel. I thought, maybe, you hadn't thought ahead."

He draped it on the railing, then politely looked up at the sky as she climbed out and grabbed for her cover. She was, thankfully, too drunk to die of embarrassment. A sober Madeline would have drowned rather than come out. She sometimes felt she had no survival skills whatsoever. She wrapped the warm towel around her and relaxed into it. When Scott turned, she studied the sweetness and newness of his mouth, his face so smoothly symmetrical and unlined by anguish. All summer, her eyes had been drawn to the boyishness of him, his perfect legs, his muscular arms. But that had been from an indifferent perspective, sizing him up only as a specimen, not as a partner. Or had she known all along this moment was at hand? Was he to be the instrument of her transformation?

"I was getting ready to split when I heard you dive in," he said. "I stayed around to make sure you were okay. You know, after last week."

Yes. He'd been so kind, helping her to the pool house without a scene, caring without prying. Leading her by the hand.

She reined in her thoughts and opened her mouth to say she was fine now, then decided against it. She was going to tell the truth. After all, here he was again, appearing like an angel so soon after her scene on the terrace. If that wasn't fate, what was it? "I wish I could say I was better," she said, tightening the plush fabric under her arms. "But things are a little uncertain for me right now." Her voice weakened.

He reached out his hand and brushed a fingertip against her bare arm, fleetingly, like a moth. "Is it, um, Mr. Lambert?"

Madeline nodded, barely moving her head. A trickle of water ran from her hair down her nose. "I'm not sure what's going to happen." No, that wasn't true. She did know. "I expect we'll divorce."

His hand reached out to brush her arm again, resting longer this time, long enough for her skin to heat up beneath his fingers. "That just blows," he said. "He's a pretty dumb dude to leave a beautiful woman like you, Mrs. Lambert."

Huh. She was not mistaken about his intentions, then. "It could be for the best," she mused. Another trickle of water ran from her hair and down her cheek, and Scott wiped it away with the palm of his hand. He stood very close to her now, his breath smelling faintly of butterscotch.

"Mrs. Lambert," he said slowly, drawing her name out. "Want to, you know, come with me to the Lost and Found and get a towel for your hair?"

Her eyes darted to the pool house. If she went with him through those doors, she would come out a different person. That's what she wanted, wasn't it? She stared at Scott's face, lit only by the reflection of the water. He had a sweet mole by his lips, and his lids draped heavily over dark blue eyes, looking not quite awake. He had the long lashes of a calf, and he looked at her with nothing less than adoration.

This was it, she thought. Here was someone who admired her and desired her. She was wanted, here and now.

A breeze picked up, chilling her wet skin.

"Let's go, Scotty," she whispered, her voice watery. She touched his mouth with her finger. Let's get on with it.

The dressing room was dark and cool. It was spacious enough for the pampered horse for whom it was built so long ago, and more than enough for a half dozen women, but of course, it was meant for just one at a time. The original oak paneling had been carefully restored and maintained over the years, but the thick varnish failed to hide the ancient hoof marks of horses fighting captivity. The room had been lavishly fitted out with a bench, brass hooks, and indoor-outdoor Oriental carpeting. Cream curtains hung on the inside of the barred windows of the doors, which opened and closed on oiled rollers. As many as twenty horses in as many stalls once poked their noses out between the bars, watching for the stable boys.

Madeline reached for the chain, turning on the overhead light, and for a moment she felt herself fully in the role of the Older Woman, initiating a young man into the pleasures of the flesh. It made her feel slightly eroticized, until she turned and saw the drenched stranger in the full-length mirror. She yanked the chain again, returning to darkness. She pushed apart the curtains a crack to let some light in from the hall and to hear if the outer door opened. Scott hurried from the office with an armful of towels from the Lost & Found. He kissed her on the neck, letting his tongue stud flicker against her skin, before spreading the towels on the wide wooden bench.

"So many towels," said Madeline, clutching her own tightly with one hand. She slid the heavy door closed with her bare foot, and the metal latch fell into place. "Doesn't anyone even *try* to find what they've lost?"

Scott sat down, hesitated, then took her by the hands and pulled her to the bench. She went slowly, but with no resistance. Did she go along because of desire, or because she just always went along? She sat on a pile of towels, like a princess. He brushed her wet hair from her face with both hands and kissed her on the mouth, and she promptly forgot how to breathe through her nose. When they separated, she was gasping.

"You're so hot, Mrs. Lambert." He loosened the tight tuck at her sternum, looking at her to make sure it was okay, and, when she didn't say anything, helped the towel drop to her waist. She was afraid, but only for a moment. She was tired of being ruled by caution. She wanted to be her free, youthful self again, who didn't think twice about having a little fun with men.

The light through the parted curtains landed on her breasts like a beacon, and Scott leaned back to admire them. With a soft purr, he bent down and gently kissed each one.

"If you had a ring right here," he said, putting his finger on her nipple, "it would give us something to play with."

She laughed uncomfortably. Wasn't there too much to play with as it was? She cautiously slipped her hand into his open shirt and felt his heart pumping under his hairless chest. Tentatively, she felt for his nipple ring, but he'd not put it back in yet. She wondered if he was still on duty.

He put his hand over hers and tried to guide it lower, but she pulled back. Things were progressing too rapidly. She moved the action farther up, caressing his face, so untouched by life, then mussed his hair. It felt like straw from a summer under the sun. "You used to have long hair when you worked at the snack bar, didn't you? You kept it pinned up on top of your head."

He pulled her close and nestled his chin on her shoulder. "Gerard made me cut it all off to become a lifeguard. I missed it at first, but I don't know. Now that the season's over, I might even keep it like this. Sarah says she likes it short."

Madeline stiffened. "You're still dating Sarah Quilpe?"

Scott looked unperturbed. "You know her mom, I bet, but don't tell her or anything. Gerard will have my head." He took one of her breasts in his hand. "You and me, though, it's cool. Sarah and I have this understanding."

Understanding? What kind of relationship was that? "*I* like it longer," she said, with some petulance, even though she didn't.

Scott wrapped his arms around her. Her lips were still pursed from pouting, so he kissed them, and she warmed toward him against her will. "I'm so psyched, Mrs. Lambert. I just knew you and me were meant to hook up."

"You don't have to call me Mrs. Lambert," she whispered.

"What do I call you?" He smiled and ran both hands down her ribs, all the way to the towel bunched up around her bottom. "What Dr. Nicastro calls you? Pet?"

He said the word in his slow way, making every letter a syllable, and she got a bad conscience thinking of how she'd driven Frank away. This uneasy feeling grew, and she considered leaving while she still had her virtue, more or less, but when Scott bent down to kiss a breast, she decided to think about it a little more.

"What's this?" he asked. He ran a finger along the raised scar on her left breast.

"It was a false alarm," she said. "It's over now."

"Lucky. Here," he whispered, "I'll make it better." He kissed the scar with great care. Charles had avoided even talking about the whole thing, and here was this stranger putting his mouth right on it. Scott was right. She was lucky. Of all the outcomes that might have resulted from that procedure, it had been nothing more than a scare. She was so easily frightened. Well, no more of that.

She reached down in the darkness and awkwardly, with only a thin layer of fabric between her hand and his body, caressed the swelling between his legs. He arched against her with a certain, persistent rhythm that alarmed her. She pulled away, and he laughed. "Don't be afraid, Mrs. Lambert. I won't bite." He leaned toward her and rubbed her nose with his. "I've got to turn on the light for a minute," he said quietly, and pulled the chain over their heads. She shielded her eyes, but when she got used to the glare, she peeped to see what he was doing. When he reached for his shirt pocket, she steeled herself for the sight of a condom, but instead he pulled out a gold loop and clipped it to his earlobe. He saw her looking at him and smiled. "Help me," he said.

He took another loop out of his pocket, then removed the shirt, letting it fall on the floor. He put a loop in her hand and touched his left nipple. "Put it on for me."

With great difficulty and much giggling, she maneuvered the gold through the holes. She thought of his tongue stud, sitting quietly in the warm wetness of his mouth, and she leaned up to kiss him and felt like she was back at the pool, under water, swimming in the dark. His mouth gave her breath, pulling her back to the surface. "Want to see the other one?" he whispered.

She opened her eyes to the sight of him running his hand over his bathing trunks, under which an erection pressed. He rested his other hand on the back of her damp neck.

They were both very quiet. "Before we go any farther," she said, not quite believing the words were coming out of her mouth, "shouldn't we talk about what we're going to use?"

"Use?"

"Condom?" She felt very liberated saying the word. It was what they all used now, wasn't it? To protect not so much against fertility as disease.

"Pet." He nuzzled her cheek with his nose. "I didn't think we'd be doing, um, all that."

"All that? All that what?"

"I mean, you could play the snake charmer with your mouth, and I could do something for you." He nuzzled her neck and stuck his tongue in her ear. She pulled back.

"But, what about . . . sex?"

He put his hand to her cheek. "I couldn't do that to Sarah."

Madeline was stunned, humiliated, and immediately sober. She tasted Smurf bile in her throat and pushed herself away to the corner of the bench, hating him. He held his hands out for an explanation. But what was there to explain to this boy? He, at least, was being loyal, in his own perverse way, to his girlfriend. Yet she, legally married, had been willing, more than willing, to go the whole hog. It was herself she hated.

"I've got to go," she said, pulling the towel up around her.

He looked at her with a mixture of longing and confusion. "Don't, Mrs. Lambert. I mean, let's talk about it, okay?" He knelt on one knee in front of her and rested his chin on her thigh like a puppy.

Madeline leaped up and froze. A face was looking at them through the open curtain and bars. She grasped for the chain and snapped off the light, shielding herself from Ellen Bruner, who was out in the hall.

In the sudden darkness, she scrambled for more towels, practically kicking Scott away. It took him a second to realize what was happening, and then he looked up. "Oh, Mrs. Bruner," he said, with a certain practiced calm. "We're looking for Mrs. Lambert's contact lens."

Madeline winced, and Ellen softly snorted. Scott grabbed his shirt off the floor and, in the same motion, slid open the door. Ellen stepped back to let him through, then stood at the opening, holding a bundle of clothes in front of her.

"I came down to take a shower before dinner, rather than go home," Ellen said, with unrestrained glee in her voice. She held out Madeline's clothes. "I thought I was doing you a favor."

Madeline gathered a towel around her with great primness and murmured, "Thank you."

Ellen turned to go to the showers, then spoke, somewhat gently.

"Remember to call me if you need any help, Madeline. Legal or otherwise. I'm in the book."

As Madeline listened to Ellen's heels tap and echo down the hall, she realized with relief that her life at the Club was over. Everything was over. Her marriage. Her reputation. The person she used to be. She wanted change, she got it.

Chapter Thirty-seven

The Yips

VITA OPENED and closed more drawers than necessary as she charged around the crowded kitchen looking for something she could not name. Her head throbbed with the hum of hood fans; her nerves recoiled at the clatter of dishes being stacked and loaded. Filthy plates, sparkling plates, plates licked clean, plates hot and steamy in the dishwasher—which among them was Dr. Nicastro's? She stared intently into a utensil drawer, hoping basters and skewers would point the way.

When she shut it, the drawer screeched painfully on its rollers. Out of habit, she flipped two latex gloves from the box on the counter, then struggled to put them on. Gerard—the old Gerard, the one whose bedtime reading included the *Department of Health Code Book*—would have curdled if he'd known she'd been barehanded all night. She had wanted nothing to stand between her and the geese, but now, what did it matter? The entrées were served, and she was as unnecessary as tits on a bull. It was Jordan's time to shine. The pastry chef was already beginning to glow as she carefully, oh so carefully, removed trays from the walk-in. She'd created little beehives of meringue, with honeycombs of dark chocolate. Studded with nougat "bees," they were going to be served on an ethereal landscape of whipped cream. Dr. Nicastro would die at the very sight, and it would serve him right.

Vita adjusted one of her gloves with a sharp snap. The saturated fat in the goose was lethal enough for one meal. She would save Dr. Nicastro's life and make faux cream from egg whites, just for him. But it was too early yet; he hadn't even finished his entrée—if he was eating it at all. Wasn't he going to send down a verdict? She stood uncertainly, staring at the back steps, which tonight led up to a protected corridor that ultimately connected to the tent, to him. Him and her offering of goose.

She found a quiet place next to Sloane to help with the fruit and cheese plates. From a colander of glassy strawberries, she chose one shaped like a plump heart. She sliced it, keeping it connected at the stem, and tenderly spread it out. The deep, wet red against the starkness of the plate stirred some bleak emotion within her, and she had to rest both hands on the counter to pull herself together. She had wanted to give Dr. Nicastro a perfect evening and, in doing so, had given him a piece of herself. Was he really going to reject it?

She pushed a sodden strand of hair back under her toque and lifted a green Maradol papaya from its wooden box.

Conner, one of the tuxedoed waitstaff, appeared at the door clutching a giant pepper mill under each arm while maneuvering an overburdened tray of dishes to the sink, where Pedrosa helped him set it on the counter. The workers were beyond exhaustion. "So, where did Gerard *go?*" Conner hadn't been on duty since the weekend before, so in between the relentless action of the banquet, the kitchen staff tried to fill him in on the week's strange events: that Phoebe Lambert had staged a sit-in at Trough in exchange for vegetarian concessions, and Gerard, seemingly just to annoy her—or maybe he had just gone mad—chained himself to the tree too, but Mr. Clendenning refused to cough up so much as a carrot stick for either of them. They camped out under the tree for a few nights, and then yesterday, sometime after lunch and before dinner, they disappeared. Not only hadn't Gerard come back to the clubhouse, but Barry couldn't find him at his apartment either.

Conner removed the pepper mills from under his arms and held them out like a pair of pistols. "Does anyone suspect foul play?"

"Barry thinks we should call the police," said Merle, who was helping Pedrosa with the dishes, scraping up a few extra dollars to pay for the semester's textbooks. He hadn't caddied in days because fate had paired him with early losers in the tournament. Success could make the members insufferable, but failure always made them terrible tippers.

"Good idea," said Conner. "I think the big cop is sweet on Vita."

"Will you people please stop your yammering and get to work," snapped Vita. Everyone paused to look at her, and she bit her lip. Her temper was something she usually exercised only on Gerard. But there was no Gerard. "We have two more courses to serve, and we haven't even cleared all the entrées. Don't worry about him." She debated whether to let them in on the secret. If dish of this magnitude leaked out to the members right now it would distract them from her food, but maybe her staff could use a high-energy goody right about now. She motioned them all in closer and whispered, "He's flown off with Phoebe Lambert."

"Ewww!" The staff stepped back and gasped in unison, slightly revulsed, partially disbelieving. Vita glanced at Pedrosa, who had looked up in terror at the mention of Phoebe Lambert, quite possibly the first English words he'd learned to recognize. Vita had a surprise for him, though. It had certainly been a surprise for her: an envelope of supermarket gift certificates from Phoebe. A regular supermarket too; she hadn't even tried to control his purchases by steering him toward some organic emporium far from where he lived. It made her feel better not just about Phoebe but, after the initial shock of seeing her and Gerard hand in hand, about the two of them. Maybe they were so different they canceled out the worst in each other. Maybe they would even go on to bring out the best.

"Not that chick with the messy dreads?" Merle's voice echoed from inside the giant stockpot he was scrubbing, his upper torso almost entirely enveloped in stainless steel. "What's Gerard thinking?"

"Never mind him." Sloane went back to slicing fruit and did not look up. "What does a vibrant girl like Phoebe want with a stiff like him?"

Vita shrugged and contemplated her papaya. "Love happens."

Gerard and Phoebe, wet from showers, had shown up in the kitchen that afternoon while the rest of the staff was setting tables in the tent. Vita was so engrossed in her first pan of hot, gorgeous geese that when she saw the couple at the door she almost dropped them, her beauties. As Mrs. Suarez had promised, the slow heat had drained the birds of fat, and their dark, mysterious flesh was sealed in a mahogany armor. Deep within lay the grain stuffing of barley cooked in the stock, with morels and hazelnuts. She quickly shoved the birds into a warming oven, away from Phoebe's eyes. Gerard gave Vita a congratulatory wink before the birds disappeared, but Phoebe saw nothing but Gerard. The two of them looked so happy, so normal.

"Good-bye, Vita." Gerard gave her a hug, and she smelled patchouli on him. "We're off to Arizona for a Southwestern adventure. Good luck tonight. I'll be thinking of you." He stepped back, looking so happy that Vita decided he was either truly in love or completely deranged. "Do you know where Barry is?" he asked. "I want to pass the crown to him."

"*And* Forbes," said Phoebe. "The Club can be, you know, ruled by a partnership of man and bird."

Gerard took both of Phoebe's hands and beamed. He'd bonded to her, as surely as that baby goose had bonded to Barry.

"Barry's setting out parking cones," Vita said. She was getting nervous about the next batch of geese, which she could not take out of the oven until Phoebe was gone. "Why don't you two go find him?"

Phoebe threw her arms around Vita, who thought for a moment she was being attacked. "I'm sorry about the other night,

Vita. Here." She pulled out an envelope from the front of her bib overalls. "For Pedrosa." As she handed it over, she abruptly lifted her nose and smelled the air around her. She stood very still, thinking.

Vita gave Gerard a desperate look, which he registered. "We've got to go, Phoebe," said Gerard, pulling her toward the door. "We still have to stop at my apartment to pack."

Phoebe paused at the bottom of the stone steps, and Vita thought this was it, she's just identified the scent of roast fairway goose. Well, go ahead, prove it!

"Vita," said Phoebe. "Gerard and I, we're going to start a therapeutic spa with my grandma. It'll be all about massage and hot stones, and we'll be in the desert, where people are really into environmental walks and stuff. Gerard said he'd run the inn, and grandma will do the spa stuff, and they want me to do the cooking. Can I e-mail you for some recipes?"

Vita did not have time to roll on the floor and laugh. She would have to save that pleasure for later. Right now, her geese had to be taken out of the oven, and this girl had to go. She gave them both a little nudge up the steps. "I don't have any vegan recipes except for those cookies I brought to the gate."

Phoebe made a face. "Not those. I'm thinking of your food, how it seems to make people happy even if it is full of meat and dairy. So you send me the recipes, and I'll convert them to vegan."

"We could do a cookbook!" said Gerard.

"Convert?" Vita prodded the two of them farther up the stone stairs. "Could you replace Gerard with someone else and still be the same couple?"

"I guess not," Phoebe said, sighing. "But send them anyway. I need all the help I can get."

"So long, Vita." Gerard waved, backing up. "We're off to explore the beauty of the soul and the joys of ecotourism. Call me on my cell if you or Barry have any questions."

"I will," said Vita. "Safe trip. Both of you."

Vita watched them go. An odd match but a handsome couple. They would produce beautiful kids, if it came to that. No matter what, it was good to see Gerard finally get a life outside of the Club. Maybe a day would come when she would too.

After they left, the afternoon became a single blur as preparations shifted into high gear. In no time, service officially began with cocktails on the terrace and moved along with great success, as the Romans would say, *ab ovo usque ad mala*, from eggs to apples. The members were on their best behavior, since Gerard wasn't there to raise their threshold of self-indulgence. Clendenning's absence had helped in that respect too, since there was no big cheese in the center of the room for all the other men to pose for.

It was odd, the president not coming. Clendenning had called Vita early that morning, canceling his dinner reservation, saying that he and his wife had been unexpectedly called away on family business. He put Vita in charge, unless of course Gerard happened to show up.

"Vita," said Conner, going back up the stairs with a tray of fruit and cheese plates. "The Wiggleworths said to tell you that the goose was the best thing they've ever eaten."

Vita just nodded, cutting the papaya into translucent slivers, which she would then roll into delicate flutes. The compliments had poured in from the start, as had a couple of hesitant requests for the beef instead. That was fine. She had never expected everyone who tried goose to love goose, and she did not take those exemptions personally. One man's meat is another man's poison, after all, and such a robust flavor was not an experience for the weak of heart. But Dr. Nicastro had the heart of a lion. There was no flavor too strong for him, no aroma too earthy. She refused to believe he had not prostrated himself before the plate, offering himself up to the meal and to her.

She was arranging her papaya around the splayed strawberry, deciding what next, when Luisa ran into the room.

"Table six, ready," she panted. Sloane lined up four finished plates, dipped a ladle into a pan of wine sauce, and dribbled a fine, ruby-colored spiderweb over the fruit and cheese.

"How's it going up there?" Vita asked, with what she hoped

was a casual tone. She picked up her knife, wiping the blade on her apron.

"Mrs. Fenwick say to tell you that the goose was 'sup-perb.' She wants recipe."

This put a smile to Vita's lips, the first all night. She pictured a dead goose hanging to age in Mrs. Fenwick's pseudo-chateau down the street.

Luisa laughed. "I tell her, secret recipe." She arranged three plates up her arm and held the fourth in her hand. "Guess who sitting with who outside?"

Vita twitched and cut herself, drawing blood. She peeled off the latex glove and put her finger in her mouth. "Who?" she mumbled.

"Nina and Eliot."

Vita, and the entire kitchen staff, expelled a satisfied "Awww."

Except for Sloane. "I guess there's forgiveness for just about anything," she said, then slammed down a fresh row of plates with equal, measured thunks.

Luisa adjusted her grip on her plates. "He make a little mistake, but he love her."

Sloane laughed, a sound so unfamiliar that everyone stared. "You're so young. Don't confuse lust with love."

Luisa stuck her tongue out and hurried back up the stairs, with the sound of Sloane's bitter snicker behind her.

Vita refused to sound needy by calling after Luisa to ask how Dr. Nicastro was faring. It was bad enough being the one in the basement, with her sensible work shoes and her chef whites, while there he was, upstairs under the stars with the upper crust, *le gratin*. She felt like a high school dietitian in comparison.

Her dinner had failed to reconcile them, but at least the geese had worked their magic on Nina and Eliot—although she hated to think of the young couple out on the terrace, so exposed to the Club's judgmental eyes. Atmosphere was everything, with love as well as with food. The enclosed garden was the place to be, even in its moldering state. Maybe she would free herself between cheese and dessert to contemplate its prospects. With Gerard gone, and before the next manager was hired, maybe she could sneak some restoration funding past the board.

"We'll need more sauce." Sloane made a feathery movement with her gloved hand over the plates. "I've got all these to dribble yet." She did not include in her gesture the single plate that Vita had been fussing over for twenty minutes.

"I'll do it," said Vita, adjusting a bandage on her finger. "I don't trust myself with a knife right now."

Merle and Pedrosa whispered to each other in pidgin English as they emptied the racks of dishes. Pedrosa had picked up enough words over the summer to gossip, which had warmed him to the other employees.

"Vita, why don't you go take a break," said Sloane. "It's been a long day." Sloane then reached out and quickly grazed Vita's shoulder with the tips of her fingers. It was the first physical contact they'd had since Vita hired her two years before, when they had shook on the deal. How bad must she look?

But Vita still shook her head. She was not ready to leave her post yet. She arranged her ingredients, taking a good Burgundy out from under the counter. The wines had been matched by the distributor weeks before, and he had paired the cheese course with an ancient sherry, but it was so refined it tasted of nothing at all, and was therefore useless for cooking. She poured a splash of the Burgundy into a pan with some brown sugar and took a swig, *à la chef,* softening her anguish with a warm glow. She put the bottle away, for now.

The phone rang, and Vita ignored it, even though she was standing right there. Sloane reached behind her and got it. "Hello, Mrs. Pasto." She eyed Vita, who shook her head.

After a few "uh-huhs," Sloane hung up the phone. "Your mom just wanted to know how everyone liked the goose."

Vita knew that "everyone" meant Dr. Nicastro. Her mother had gotten it into her head that he had potential to be more than just a stomach for her daughter's cooking, that he might appreciate her other charms as well. There was a time when Vita entertained some notions along those lines too, confusing, as always, feeding with loving, but that was over and done with. As she stirred, she rested her hips against the counter, exhausted. Luisa came running down the stairs with a single dinner plate and began to scrape its graveyard of bones into the trash.

"Wait." Vita grabbed Luisa by the wrist. "Whose was that?"

"Dr. Nicastro's," Luisa said, backing away.

Vita retrieved a bare bone from the pile, its marrow sucked dry. "Did he say anything?"

Luisa moved her head slowly from side to side. "He very quiet, Vita, all night."

"Oh." Vita laid the bone back in the trash. It was over. He had eaten her food for pure animal survival, not desire. She could have fed him garbage, just like *el puerco* Mrs. Suarez wanted the Club to raise, and it would have all been the same to him. Fine then. She would fall on her cleaver and prepare his cheese plate herself. She knew just what he liked, and she wanted him to never forget it.

"Luisa, don't go back up yet. I want you to bring this one to him."

With her hands bare, she centered a cluster of glaucous ruby grapes alongside the strawberry and papaya, and on top of a few arugula leaves, she arranged a lump of mild local chèvre at twelve on the plate. At four, she placed a Pecorino Toscano that smelled of the Italian hills where the sheep had grazed; then she closed the circle with a wedge of Persillé du Beaujolais, a blue cheese made with raw cow's milk. Almost losing the bandage on her finger, she pawed through the red Bartlett pears and chose one so ripe it could be drunk rather than eaten, and felt the pressure of tears behind her eyes. She cut the fruit lengthwise, placing one half cut-side down on the plate, rosy bottom up. After a moment's consideration, she split open an intensely fragrant fig with her thumbs and pressed an almond into the flesh. To finish, she drizzled the bloodred sauce, signing her name.

She handed the plate off to Luisa, who was staring at her. "You'd better hurry," said Vita. "Helga said the society band wants to start setting up for the dance."

Before Luisa could comfort her, Vita wiped her eyes with the sleeve of her chef's jacket, readjusted her toque, and turned away.

Chapter Thirty-eight

Small Ball

FRANK NICASTRO stood up from his solitary table, his cummerbund creaking like the girth on a horse, and hit the back of his head on one of the tent brackets. He rubbed his skull with one hand while extending the other to Howard Amory, the winner of the Fothergill Cup.

"Congratulations, Howie, quite a coup."

Howard, a thin, quiet man in his early sixties, smelling of soap, with red freckles across his nose, raised his pilsner glass of beer. "Thank you, Doctor."

Frank tried to move closer, but his feet got caught in tenting that draped on the lawn, so he stayed where he was and reached for his goblet instead, clinking Howard's glass. After drinking loudly, he smacked his wine-dark lips. "I guess they never even saw you coming. What's the secret?"

Howard examined the foamy contents of his glass, looking into other worlds, and Frank, familiar with his conversational lag time, patiently waited and gazed around the tent, filled with rustling silk and piped-in Bach. A warm breeze wafted through the open sections, bringing with it the first tang of autumn, making the crowd restless. They looked as if they might start flapping south for the winter any minute now. The red-faced men, flaunting new heart valves and hips, strained against their monkey suits. The women, severely pruned and carefully gowned, swiveled their necks, keeping everyone under surveillance. Beverly Freylinghuysen, the winner of the Nine Hole Ladies Challenge, glowed, having played cheerfully through her husband's arrest and arraignment that day. Jay, on bail, sat by her side, basking in her glory.

Just when Frank thought Howard had gone to sleep, he spoke ever so slowly. "Flexibility is the trick. When they moved that hole, I was able to change my game faster than the others." He rested his glass against his pleated shirt. "Not only that, I changed my attitude. This summer I decided to accept my game as it was, no matter what, to know what the end would be and go on anyway." He looked up at Frank and smiled. "It's been a great season, while it lasted."

Frank stared. He had never heard so many words from this man before, who even in the liveliest of social situations, always seemed to be somewhere else. Frank always assumed that "somewhere" was the golf course, but now he was not so sure. "It's hard to accept loss," he said.

Howard nodded somberly, and the two men stood for a moment, observing a silence. Frank breathed in as deeply as his engorged stomach would allow, hoping to catch the last whiff of goose in the air, but it seemed all the plates were gone now. The tent was no longer filled with the essence of old-growth forests and glacial streams. Instead, cut flowers released their fragrance as they died, and stale perfume rose from wrinkled décolletage. The candles in their crystal holders grew low and sent up thin pillars of black smoke. Such was his loss. Would he be able to accept it?

The harsh crack of Palmer Stillington's voice broke their reverie, and everyone in the room, from members to busboys, rolled a collective eye. At the other end of the cavern of white canvas, Helga, the stout maître d', took Stillington's abuse without expression. There would be no fluffing up of members on her watch. Her smile still had to do duty for three more hours, and she was not going to have it ruined by the likes of Stillington. Whatever his problem was, it went away when she did, turning on her efficient heels with a polite nod. His tantrum withered on the vine.

"Talk about your turd in the punch bowl," said Frank.

"He drinks too much," said Howard. "That's his problem."

"We all drink too much," said Nicastro, raising his crystal chalice and taking a deep swallow of his Clos Puy Arnaud 2000 Bordeaux. Dark and lively, the wine had held its own with the intensity of the goose. "But we don't end every conversation in a pool of blood."

Howard laughed as slowly as he talked, and his freckles bunched up on the bridge of his nose. "No, but at least you know where you stand with him. The others plot dark revenges, all the while smiling in your face. Now that I've won the Cup, I'll have to start watching my back."

Frank was shocked. Not that Howard would have to now watch his back, which was all too true, but that he referred to the members as "the others." Howard was a second-generation Club member, and even though his family owned strip malls, Frank thought them quite established. But then again, so few at the Club were real Wasps. It was a dying breed, yet they all aspired to it, himself included, all trying to conform to the standards of a nearly extinct species.

"I'm off," said Amory. "They're expecting me at the dais to collect my tribute."

After a warm good-bye, Frank stood a moment longer to watch the man work the tent. He was heartily congratulated, but as soon as Howie moved on, Frank could sense the members eating him alive, their heads closing in to the middle of the tables like carnivorous plants. But being cannibals did not make them complete monsters. By and large, they were kind to one another when they chose, attentive to their children, and loving to their pets. His meal had made him generous, and he blessed his fellow members with goodwill, that they might find what they sought in status, money, beauty, and love.

He should be so content. He sat back down with a grunt and looked at the empty space where his plate once sat. The goose had made him want to tear hunks from a spit-roasted boar with his teeth, wipe grease from a hedge-sized beard with the back of his hand, and clink a mammoth tankard with his brothers, the bowmen. He'd growled at Luisa whenever she came near to take his plate, but finally he had to let it go back from whence it came. Vita.

Vita. He touched the tablecloth and wondered what to do. He should run down the stairs, lift her over his head, and march her around the dining room to further her glory. But he still couldn't shake his suspicion that the kitchen was a front for hot goods. Why this need to have his chef be pure of heart? Was he so perfect? He could think of plenty of things in his life he was not so proud of. Wasn't sauce for the goose also sauce for the gander? Or was there no such thing as gander sauce?

He cursed Madeline for ever suggesting something fishy was going on in the kitchen. He looked around the tent but did not expect to see her, although he heard that she'd gone to cocktails the night before in a scandalously short dress. Good for her. A scandal was a service to the community. Gave them something to chew on for the rest of the weekend. Although God knows she and her family had given them their meat and drink all summer, with Phoebe at the gates and Charles in the garage. Madeline's problem was that she was such a poor liar. If she had only gone on in a chirpy manner, pretending that her family's problems were no affair of hers, like Beverly Freylinghuysen over there, nothing would have changed. But she wore her unhappy heart on her sleeve, which meant that the other members could not pretend everything was fine in their little world. And that was unforgivable.

He leaned over and touched his nose to the tablecloth, to see if any goose lingered in the fibers. Where could Vita have gotten her hands on so many wild geese, and where, in this day and age, did she learn what to do with them? He spotted a smidgen of sauce on the tablecloth and stuck his tongue out to lick it, but caught himself. Instead, he rubbed his finger on the spot and put it in his mouth. Oh, Vita! He wanted to massage the precious ointment on his arms, over his thighs, and across his chest. He wanted to feel it between his toes. *Mi fa libidine.* It gave him a hard-on.

He sat up. People were staring. He was eating like a pig, and he didn't even have any food in front of him. He looked over at the open flap that served as a door to see if Luisa was coming with his next course, and he caught the eye of that little leapfrog Hilary Fisher. She was dining with some fresh kill. New members. Both the Fishers waved furiously at him from across the room, as if they were still friends.

He lifted his glass to them and took a sip. It might sound harsh to say that when Hilary had got all she could out of people she discarded them, but there it was. In the end, though, he forgave her everything when he heard her laugh and saw how she was enjoying herself. Her new friends laughed along, all without spitting out any food, as he'd been known to do. He would dump him too, if he could.

He saw Luisa, the perfect handmaiden to the meal. Other waiters were more polite but less sincere, fussing over the members like decorators, and he had not wanted that sort of intrusion. Luisa just let him eat, allowing him to be lifted by the wings of the goose itself. She placed the fruit and cheese in front of him. A poem on a plate.

"Vita, she make this one herself," said Luisa.

"Of course." As the museum curator can tell whether a paint stroke is the master's or the apprentice's, so Frank could tell by the very arrangement on the plate that this was the work of Vita's own hand. That and the fact that she had signed her name in sauce. As Luisa brushed a single surviving crumb off the white tablecloth, he heard the pear whisper, "Me first, eat me." The fruit barely held its shape as he assisted it down his throat. He closed his eyes, feeling fructose rush through his veins, raising him from lethargic digestion.

He reached for Luisa's wrist and smiled conspiratorially. "Luisa, where did the geese for the dinner come from?"

She looked over her shoulder and whispered, "You keep secret?"

The doctor raised his hand to God.

Luisa bent. "It is geese here at the Club."

"Impossible. Those stringy things would taste of lawn chemicals and Aquashade."

Luisa shook her head. "Barry don't spray poison all summer, and Vita, she tend the island birds like babies. Up at five to feed, so no others have her goodies. She spoil them with food. What you taste when you eat, that is her love for them."

Nicastro's face went cold. "Water," he croaked.

Luisa looked around the tent with her hands on her hips. "Where useless water boy go? I never get to tell him what to do." She tapped the table with her knuckles. "I will bring it myself."

He nodded. What had he done? The geese were why Vita was at the Club at all sorts of shifty hours this summer. She had been hiding something, all right, but she hid it in the name of her art and for the good of the community. She hid it for him, who did not deserve such devotion. He'd listened to gossip that turned him against this woman, this alchemist who could turn golf course pests into gustatory splendor. He stared with desolation at the shuddering candle.

Luisa returned with a silver water pitcher. Frank leaned close, for he had to know the truth. "Luisa, tell me. I went down to the kitchen a few weeks ago and the staff was tossing around some expensive shirts. Why?"

"Stupid shirts." Luisa looked like she might spit. "The Clays give them for us before they go out of country. Tips!" She snorted as she poured. "My cousin make them into smocks for the daycare kids." She placed the glass down. "Something wrong, Dr. Nicastro?"

Chapter Thirty-nine

Ball in Play

MADELINE ENTERED the clubhouse from a side door, wearing the plain black shirt, pants, and sneakers of a cat burglar. Hugging the walls, she maneuvered the maze of corridors to the library door, then paused. Sounds of the banquet drifted in from a window at the other end of the hall—the clinking of knives on crystal, the clearing of throats—as one member after another stood to toast the winner. Beneath the applause, beneath the goodwill, she heard a rumble of forced heartiness that made her sad beyond all words.

Someone tested the microphone with a cough and a gurgle. Eugene Hollowell must have stepped up to the podium to give the president's after-dinner speech in Humpy's place. Perfect. Gene not only couldn't separate his vowels from his consonants, but also couldn't recognize when a thought had reached its natural end. The members would be held captive for a half hour or more, logy from dinner and drained from trying to decipher his muddy words. She closed the library door behind her, noiselessly, and shoved the forged latch into place.

She reached for the table lamp, with its spiderweb of lead on glass, then decided against it. Instead she opened the heavy drapes, letting the security light shine in at an angle through the diamond panes, landing on the Oriental carpet in slashes. As she cranked the window open wide to let in the night air, insects began to settle on the screen. Below, on the window seat, was her bag, exactly where she'd left it the day before. She bemoaned the deteriorating standards of the Club, that the room had not been swept clean overnight, then laughed at herself for sounding just like Arietta. She was getting out none too soon.

She had to keep moving. She did, after all, have a date to keep that evening: Charles had left a note on the bed while she was still unconscious that morning, asking to meet her at Plateau at ten. She could guess what he wanted. A divorce. Or perhaps something more sinister, like drowning her in the lake. It was uncanny that he—who had not left his garage in weeks—had obviously already heard about her and Scott, the memory of which made her wince to her bones.

What had she been thinking? Was she that drunk? That unhappy? It was as if she'd set herself up to be caught in the act, in the same way she had once helped to set up Eliot and the hooker. There's Karma for you, as Phoebe would say.

Madeline panicked when she saw one of the cabinets ajar, thinking that someone had come looking for the book, but she realized, no, it must have been Gene, sifting through the books of golf jokes to prepare for his speech. She reached up and felt behind the undisturbed Thomas Mann collection for the key, then knelt down and took out, for the last time, the moldy stacks of *National Geographics*. She removed the false back and set it aside. It was difficult finding the keyhole without a flashlight, but she'd gone through the motion so often she could do it in her sleep. How many relationships had she brought to ruin with the turn of this key? How much heartbreak had she caused? The inner mechanism released and she lifted out the tattered leather book with great care.

At the fireplace, she checked to make sure the damper was open. There would be no second chances. For all she knew, Gerard Wilton was lurking in the shadows, since he was no longer under the tree with Phoebe. She wasn't sure where either of them was right now, so he might very well be back on the job. As for Phoebe, two empty Ben & Jerry's containers in the trash meant she'd been home at some point, which was a huge relief in itself. Maybe Humpy, a lame-duck president with nothing to lose now, had freed her with some vegan concessions. But whether Phoebe's sit-in worked as planned or not, Madeline was proud of her for putting her beliefs on the line. The fact that the Land Rover was gone meant that she'd probably already embarked on some new animal rescue mission, which was the only time she'd stoop to drive the gas-guzzler. Oddly enough, a little black Mercedes was parked in its place. It was vaguely familiar, yet none of Phoebe's friends would have a car like that. Had she seen it at the Club? Did Charles have a lover in the garage with him? Or a lawyer?

The trouble was, if Phoebe didn't return tonight, Madeline would have to leave home in the acid-green VW, which meant, among other things, she'd have to be very careful about what she took with her. Which was just as well. How much of her present life was worth lugging all the way to Arizona? The less she brought to her mother's home, already full of chimes, cats, and massage tables, the better. She needed to simplify while she figured out her next step. She pulled Ellen's various legal forms from the book and crumpled them in balls on the grate, arranging pieces of kindling on top.

She sat back on her heels and listened to the electronic squawk of feedback as Gene continued to sputter away at the podium. She lit a match, and when she held the small flame to the crumpled paper, Ellen Bruner's name jumped off the page at her. Madeline somberly reflected on the lawyer's stupefied, and faintly amused, face as it had appeared behind the bars the night before. She wondered what would have happened if Ellen hadn't showed up when she did. Would Madeline and Scott have worked out some sexual arrangement that would have kept him chaste for his girlfriend while still having his sport with her?

She shook her head. It was already over by the time Ellen appeared. Never mind sex without love, what Scott wanted was sex without sex. She couldn't even have a proper affair. She couldn't do anything right. Until now.

Ellen's papers flared up along with Madeline's heart. She needed more. She could rip a few pages from the book, but that didn't seem right. The historic tome must be disposed of properly, set upon a pyre in its entirety.

She retrieved her bag and rummaged through it. A credit card holder. Some mints. A wilted daisy. That was another thing she finally got right. She'd slept most of the day, too hungover and grief-stricken to get out of bed, but when she did, with her note from Charles in her grasp, she decided to leave the house better than when she found it. She went out to the roadsides and the golf course (where she cleaned up the best she could her daughter's abandoned campsite) and gathered armfuls of wildflowers, ferns, ivies, branches, and vines. A bird's nest. Some feathers. She filled the rooms with arrangements, for once not caring about using just the right vase for the material or the perfect blooms or even the correct combinations. She put the flowers together in abundance, mixing forms and colors in the largest containers she could get her hands on, her stockpots. The result was magnificent, and she wondered why she hadn't been able to accomplish such beauty before.

At the bottom of her bag she found her spiral-bound book on flower arranging, filled with her own cramped notes. She tore out the pages, filling the hearth with a bright heat, lighting up the impassive deities on the marble columns, making them look alive. She reached into her pocket and took out Charles's note and added that to the fire as well. The paper caught easily, and it rose up the flue as it burned. She waited for the kindling to fully engage, then lifted the book with both hands. If she wanted to know anything about the past, including Charles's, now was the time.

But that would be giving the book too much credence. There was no way of knowing if the entries were true, and even if they were, what did it matter? Whatever generations of Club women had or had not done, she was worse. They might have lied, cheated, fornicated, and committed bestiality for all she knew, but she was the one who had kept their secrets. She had not just gone along with the game—she had enforced the rules.

From down the hall, she heard heels on marble, then the sound of Beryl Hall's raspy voice followed by Linzee Gibbons's manly guffaw. Madeline tensed, but the women kept on going, past the library door to the powder room. The members were beginning to sneak away from the oppression of Gene's words, and soon they'd be galloping from the tent in a thundering of hooves. She dropped the book gently on the fire and blew it a kiss.

The draft was strong; the wind was picking up. The edges of the pages began to brown and curl as the book turned in on itself; then the binding began to smolder, the leather reeking like scorched skin. The book slowly opened from the heat, and Madeline caught glimpses of names and dates as the pages flipped through the years, going backward in time, roasting with shame. She had redeemed herself and freed all the women of the Club, even if they never knew how weighted with shackles they were. Even if those shackles were made of gold.

There was a sharp knock on the door, but she didn't even flinch. Not yet. There was something else. She walked to the broken grandfather clock, both hands covering the VI, as in an act of modesty. She opened the clock's face, checked her watch, and set the brass hands to IX, an expansive gesture, with one hand pointing ahead and the other in the air—*Olé*—forever fixing this moment in time. The Club, sentimental about things that no longer even worked, would never get the clock repaired. Whatever pain or happiness the next few years would bring, she wanted to be able to think back to this room and this hour, when she had moved the Club just a little bit forward.

The knocking became frantic, and a familiar, imperious voice shouted her demands. "Who's in there? Open this door."

Arietta. Madeline had known that when smoke rose from the chimney, Arietta would smell it from the tent and come hobbling. No one but she had ever lit a fire in the summer. No one but she and Madeline.

She let the knocking escalate to cane-rapping before unlatching the door and opening it wide. She stepped back so the first thing Arietta would see was the burning book, and its flames lit her up like an ancestral portrait. She was dressed in a dark blue satin gown such as Mamie Eisenhower might have worn, so thickly taffetaed it could have stood on its own. Strapless, it revealed a wide expanse of translucent skin stretched over her collarbone. Black opera gloves bagged at her elbows, and the tiara in her hair had fallen slightly askew. She slammed her hand on the wall switch, washing the room in a sick amber light. It was then that Arietta saw Madeline behind the door, and a terrible look of understanding swept across her powdered face. Raising her cane, she rustled to the fireplace, stopping short of the flames. But it was too late. Too, too late. She had to pull her dress away from the falling cinders of the book.

Clutching at her satin, she spoke in a dead, even tone. "Madeline Lambert. What have you done?"

Madeline closed the door and leaned against it, scratching her back on the heraldic carving. "I've saved us from ourselves."

Arietta struggled to speak, but her red lipstick had turned black and pasty on her lips, sealing her mouth shut.

"Cat got your tongue?" Madeline asked.

Arietta swirled on her. *"You should be ashamed."*

"*Me?* What about *you?*" Madeline pointed her finger, but withdrew it, afraid Arietta might snap it off. "Controlling and intimidating the women just so the men can screw around without worrying about the consequences."

"It takes two to screw, as you so crudely put it." Arietta gave her a penetrating stare. "And as you well know."

Madeline looked away. Damn that Ellen Bruner. She softened her voice. "The book might have served some purpose once, Arietta, but no more. It's time to let the chips of love fall where they may."

Arietta wrinkled her face. "This is no romance novel, Madeline. This is life, and there is nothing wrong with tidying it up a bit."

"Tidying is different from cleansing."

Arietta turned her head without moving her neck, like a parrot. "Maybe there is some reason why you have such a craving for a clean slate."

Madeline blushed but would not defend herself. Besides, any defense of her virtue would be a mere technicality. She pulled a stiff chair over from the table and set it near the hearth, in Arietta's spot. "Sit down. You don't look well."

Arietta took the seat with an elderly sigh, her spine leaning heavily against the back of the chair. She looked like she could crumple with a touch, and Madeline felt wholly responsible. She hadn't realized how connected she was to her, how they had shared a bond that was now nothing but ashes in the grate.

"We had such order," Arietta said at last. "Everyone could sleep at night knowing that someone was keeping an eye on the big picture."

"Who could sleep?" Madeline inched closer. "The women had to cough up their sex lives every time they got pregnant. Let's let the Ellen Bruners of the world keep track of paternity from now on. Let them unearth the truth with legal argument and science, let them make it a product of the law. I don't want any part of it, this . . . institutionalized lying."

Arietta smiled wryly. "Sometimes only a lie can protect the truth." She gurgled a laugh and squinted at Madeline. "And don't make that face. You'll look your age. Remind me, how old is that?"

"Forty-four."

"Yes, still within the range of childbearing. Is that why the sudden need to dispose of the book? Worried you might have to cough something up yourself? A hairball?"

"If you must know, I'm leaving Charles and I'm leaving the Club." Madeline pointed to the smoking hearth. "I just wanted to do one decent thing before I left, something to make up for all the pain I've caused."

Arietta pulled herself to a standing position and raised her cane. Madeline backed up, but Arietta only used it to point at the globe. "Go then, Madeline. And I hope you will discover the dark truth: The world is a chaotic and violent place, and you will have no control over it. *It* will have control over you. The Club is a defense against that world, and once you find yourself outside its walls, cold, hungry, and alone, you will understand what I mean. But it will be too late. There is no coming back for people like you, who have no respect for the past. Who do not understand its meaning."

"I understand all too well." Madeline knew that much of the color would drain from her world once she no longer had a group around her to uphold the illusion that life was sweet, and they were its cherished guests. But that was the price she had to pay for freedom.

Arietta shrugged, and her skin, thin and yellow as parchment, looked like it might tear with the effort. She probed among the scorched fragments with her cane. "It was only ink and paper, after all." She turned to Madeline and tapped her white-haired temple with her finger, making the tiara slip a bit more. "It's still here. The women of the Club will carry on. They always have and they always will."

Arietta grabbed her gown by its neckline and yanked it up, then turned to leave in a crinkling of fabric and tapping of cane. Madeline walked her to the door, where Arietta held out her hand. "Since we cannot have agreement, then let us at least have good manners."

"Wait." Madeline reached in her pocket. "Here, take this." She pressed the brass key into Arietta's lined palm and closed her fingers over it. She pointed to the open cabinet. "Lock up before you go."

Arietta parted her lips, but Madeline put her finger to her mouth at the sound of foot traffic in the hall. All normal exits were closed to Madeline now, so she headed for the casement window. When she opened the screen, moths that had been clinging to the rusty mesh, yearning for the light, rushed past her toward the Tiffany fixture over the table, beating their wings against the hot bulb before falling to their deaths. Madeline tried not to project. She threw one leg over the sill and then the other, but before lowering herself to the ground, she looked up at Arietta still standing at the door, a single tear carving a path through her face powder. Madeline threw her a kiss, then lowered herself to the ground, landing with a thump on her own two sneakered feet. It was time to go see Charles, for what would certainly be their last meeting outside of a lawyer's office.

Chapter Forty

Making the Cup

GRIPPING A WHISK, Vita wandered out to the garden with a copper bowl cradled in one arm and sat defeated upon the stone bench. If nothing else, it was cool outside, and dark, so the staff couldn't see her bitter tears. Leaves rustled in the trees, but here, behind the brick walls, it was calm and quiet, so unlike the stainless-steel dungeon where she had slaved all night, ignored by the big man upstairs to whom, in her heart, she had dedicated her efforts. Even now she continued to labor for him, making a whipped cream substitute from egg whites, sugar, cream of tartar, and vanilla. Tears fell into the cream, and she beat them in with a vengeance.

It was not long before the egg whites frothed and gained volume, and she tipped the bowl to see if the cream was peaking. The light was indirect, coming from the clubhouse windows behind her. She turned to see members wandering the halls, cast in single dimensions, like shadow puppets. Where was the beautifully upholstered silhouette of Dr. Nicastro?

The iron gate creaked on its hinges, and she sighed and went back to her cream. She'd hoped all the employees would be too busy right now to take a cigarette break, that she might have a moment alone with her grief. But there was no privacy for anyone at the Club, and besides, as her mother so often pointed out to her, she had plenty of opportunity for solitude in her empty bed. As a dedicated servant in the temple of art, she had no life.

"Vita?"

She stopped whisking.

"Dr. Nicastro?" In this light she could only make out his teeth, glowing in the dark, and his dimpled chin, glistening with goose. She hesitantly raised her hand so he could see where she was, then used it to wipe her eyes. A thin mist crept along the ground as the cool night air met the warm grass, and Dr. Nicastro stepped out of it like some massive ancestral primate standing erect for the very first time, heading toward civilization, toward her. Even though his bow tie hung at loose ends and his pleated shirt was unbuttoned to the top of his hairy chest, he cut a magnificent figure in his dinner jacket.

Frank, even before he called Vita's name, had seen her from across the neglected garden, shimmering in her kitchen whites. *Angelita della cucina.* But he could have found this angel of the kitchen by following his nose, tracking her fragrance, like a truffle: earthy, exotic, complex, and complete. He approached the stone bench as solemnly as an altar. "Vita." Nicastro knelt down on one knee before her. "I am undone by dinner."

She turned her head to hide her raspberry eyes. Not to mention her look of triumph! She did not want him to think her smug. "All in a day's work," she said, giving the cream a petulant turn of the whisk.

His generous mound of a nose trembled, and he pointed to the bowl. "What is that?"

"A special order for dessert. Jordan is sending the plates up now. You'd better go back to your table."

He adjusted his weight on his knee. "No, this is the perfect ending to such a meal. To be here with its creator."

Blood rose to her cheeks, and she looked down at her bowl. "You've missed a lot of meals."

He put his hand on her thigh. "I'll never miss another."

Vita, shocked and pleased, looked directly at him. "Don't kneel there," she said irritably. She moved over a few inches. "Here. Sit."

Frank smiled and stood with a groan, holding his stomach, against which his cummerbund was sorely tested. When he arranged his buttocks snugly next to Vita's, the stone bench sank an inch into the earth.

"It was all a terrible misunderstanding, Vita."

"Was it something I cooked?" She turned her attention back to the cream, pretending indifference.

He turned to look at the windows behind them. "It was this place. I was fed gossip, and it almost killed me. It almost killed us."

She stopped stirring. "Are we an us?"

"We could be an us, if you can forgive me." He leaned closer, and she could feel the animal heat of his body. "It's not just your food I hunger for."

Before Vita could control herself to speak, she saw his nostrils widen, then quiver.

"Do I smell smoke?" he asked.

"Smoke!" Vita stood in a panic, holding the bowl under her arm like a football, ready to run. Fat fires often erupted in the kitchen ventilation ducts on busy nights, easily controlled, but only if she was there to keep order.

"It's not a kitchen fire." Frank pulled her down next to him again. "Look. It's coming from one of the chimneys."

Vita waved at the air. "It's putrid."

Frank breathed in deeply, increasing the pressure on the few mother-of-pearl buttons still attached to his tuxedo shirt. "Strange," he said. "It smells like burning leather. Or skin. It's a little early in the night for human sacrifice, even for the Club."

Vita laughed against her will. "Dr. Nicastro, that's terrible."

"Call me Frank." He nestled closer to her, and she did not object. "What's terrible is that I believed the most horrible things about you." He shook his head at his own foolishness. "Phoebe Lambert had told her mother . . ."

Vita stood up again, this time not so careful of the whipped egg whites. Frank reached up to keep the bowl from spilling, but Vita snatched it from him. "Phoebe told her what?"

Dr. Nicastro rested his head in his two large hands. "She thought you were fencing stolen goods."

Vita put her hand to her mouth. It was bad enough Phoebe had accused her of stealing to her face, but it never occurred to her that she was spreading it around. Vita could have lost her job. She'd almost lost Frank. "And you believed her? After all the food I've served you?"

He looked up at her, his black eyes damp. "What reasonable man would have thought you'd be raising a flock of geese for the banquet?"

Vita smiled. "Who told you that? I'll go to jail if Fish and Game finds out."

"The evidence is gone now." He belched like a bullfrog. "But look, you *were* hiding something and acting suspiciously because of it. You should have just told me what you were up to. Didn't you trust me?" He beseeched her with his hands, and after a moment's consideration, she sat down, letting one of his arms, a bulwark of flesh packed in black twill, surround her shoulders.

"I only wanted to surprise you," she said. "Who knew you'd believe anything that came from someone who lives on soy wastes."

"I was weak. You had me on that low-fat diet." He pulled her closer to him. "My mind wasn't working right."

She wanted to melt into his body, to be folded into his flesh, to live on his bones with him and share his expansive stomach. Unfortunately, much of that stomach would have to go. He'd gained back all the weight she'd lost for him earlier in the summer and then some. She could not continue to feed him if she could not keep him alive.

"If you only knew what Phoebe did this week, you wouldn't be so tolerant," she said. "She could have ruined my dinner with her theatrics."

"I do know." He rested his head against her toque, like a pillow.

"I saw her and Gerard partaking of a fruitless demonstration out on the course yesterday. They're not still there, are they?"

Vita hugged her copper bowl to her body. "You'll never guess." She looked up. "The two of them have run off to Arizona to open a New Agey spa with grand-mama. And Phoebe is threatening to cook."

Dr. Nicastro sat up and shuddered. "That's horrible." They were both silent for a moment, contemplating the dry, totalitarian menu that Phoebe would produce. "It'll be grim pickings, but maybe the clients will think it's part of the treatment. And as for Gerard and Phoebe, all I can say is, there's a lid for every pot."

Vita stuck her finger in the bowl to test for stiffness. "I have a hard time believing Gerard has changed so much."

"Maybe he's just expanded without changing shape, like a sponge. At any rate, he seemed quite in love. That's transformative enough."

"Here." Vita held her finger up to his lips.

"For me?"

She nodded and placed the dollop elegantly on his tongue. He closed his eyes, rolling the froth around his taste organ. "Egg whites, superfine sugar, a pinch of tartar, vanilla." He opened his eyes and smacked his tongue against the roof of his mouth a couple of times. "A teardrop or two of salt?"

Vita gasped. He had such a sensitive palate!

He took her by the chin, her perfectly formed chin, as smooth as a mango. "You made this for my health, didn't you?"

She waved his question away. "It's good for your heart." She held up the bowl with two hands. "And the copper helps hold the cream's shape."

"Really?" He dipped a finger in and held the dab of white up for inspection, then put it near her mouth. "How does that work?" he whispered. The light from the windows gleamed gold, highlighting his knuckles and creases, reflecting softly off his nails. He might have been the hand model for God in the Sistine Chapel.

"It's chemistry." She clamped her mouth on his finger, then pulled back, smearing her lips. He leaned over and kissed them.

They sat quietly, nose to nose, listening to the rumble of noise and polite applause from the tent. The speeches were finished.

"It's over," she said dreamily after swallowing. "You missed dessert."

He pulled her closer, which made the stone seat sink deeper on one side. "No I didn't."

She sighed. "I can't stay. I've got to oversee the kitchen cleanup."

A saxophone played a few notes and the piano tinkled as the band warmed up. Frank stood and reached for Vita's hand. "Would you care to dance?"

She stared at the window well of the kitchen and thought she saw figures hurry away. Her staff could see to their own mopping and scrubbing. "I would." She placed the bowl on the bench, reached one hand up to his shoulder, and with the other took his hand. He bent to smell her fingers and moaned at all the food she'd touched that day, the geese, the livers, the onions and mushrooms, the lemons and stock. The cream. "Darling," he whispered, "you didn't wear latex tonight."

She put her finger to his mouth. "Sssh. The Department of Health has ears everywhere."

He kissed her fingers and tasted . . . blood.

"I forgot!" He released her, patted the pockets of his tuxedo, and pulled out a bandage, still in the shape of a ring. He took her hand and slipped it back onto her injured finger. "I believe this is yours."

Vita turned red. "Oh, no, where did you find this?"

He took her in his arms for dancing again. "In the fig."

"Sorry." When she pressed herself against the great slab of his stomach, he belched. "I hope you didn't do that at the dinner table," she said.

"Not only that, but I licked the table," he said with great pride. He kissed her on the forehead, pushing her toque back on her head with his nose.

She laughed. "Your nose is cold."

"A sign of a healthy animal, and that's all I am, Vita. You could scoop up a better man than me in a place like this. I've got as much breeding as a housefly, and I've been known to eat peas with my knife."

"That's okay." She pressed her head against him. "A good wine will hold its flavor no matter how crude the cup."

They slowly fox-trotted along the cracked brick paths to a melody popular when the garden was young. Frank's heart was inches from Vita's ear, and she thought of the geese, and their insides, and all the vital organs protected under the ribs. She remembered the layers of fat she had to tear off the goose hearts, fat formed from the cornmeal. She might have killed them with food as easily as she had done them in with the knife. "We have to get you back in shape," she said.

"I went to my doctor yesterday."

"This sounds like the beginning of a joke."

"It is. After I weighed in, the doctor told me, 'Your body might be a temple, but your congregation is far too large.'"

Vita gave his circumference a squeeze. "You need someone like me to control the crowds."

"Better yet," he said, "be my priestess."

They danced past the fountain. Vita could not wait to get it flowing again. "Tell me, Frank, from the beginning, how much you loved the dinner." They swung around the sundial. "I want to hear everything. I want to live it through you."

He looked at her in the soft light, her pupils black as picholine olives, her cheeks rosy as ham, her lips a mysterious sea creature, whose edibility was waiting to be discovered by some adventurous gourmand, like him. He kissed her lightly. "I could eat you up."

He touched her on the small of her back, and then they kissed again.

Off in the muffled distance, in the basement kitchen of the old building, the phone on the wall rang and rang. The staff giggled, and no one picked up for Vita's mother.

Chapter Forty-one

Ball at Rest

HURRYING TO MEET CHARLES, Madeline stayed in the deep rough so as not to be seen from the terrace. She brushed up against evergreens as she walked, releasing their piney scent. No matter the outcome of their meeting, it was almost over now, whatever *it* was. As she was about to disappear around the bend, she took one last look. The tent glowed, and in the darkness, it hung in the air like a ghostly shadow of the clubhouse. Sparks rose like stars from the chimney, burning brightly against the black sky before disappearing forever.

In spite of herself, she felt a twinge of sadness. So many milestones in her life had taken place in that old ruin, with its timbered facade and cracked stucco. She and Charles had gotten married here, under a five-pole tent such as that one. She remembered the first time she came to the Club, as a nervous bride-to-be with her mother, to discuss the wedding plans. Her mother, dressed in an ankle-length skirt and peasant shirt, lobbied for a ceremony in some daisy field back in California, but what did she know about weddings? She'd never even had one herself. It had seemed to Madeline, back then, that her mother was insufficiently grateful that the Lamberts offered to foot the bill—as long as the wedding was at the Club. "The shakier the institution, the more elaborate the ritual," her mother declared, a comment that thankfully flew right over Charles's parents' heads. At the end of the day, when it was just the two of them, her mother had cried and wondered where she had gone wrong, that her own daughter would want to get married in a place like this, would want this life. Madeline had just laughed. What was there not to like about "this life"? And here she was leaving it, returning to her mother, because as wacky as she was, she would ask no questions and pass no judgment. Something Madeline hadn't experienced in a very long time.

The band was playing an old Dorsey tune, heavy on the horns, light on the melody. The terrace was almost empty. Those with willing partners were on the dance floor in the tent. There were just a few smokers huddled by the door, and a young couple was sitting alone on the fieldstone wall. Madeline smiled. Even at this distance, she could not mistake Nina and Eliot, their heads resting together in great tenderness, looking up at the stars, with all of life and nature on their side. Madeline tilted her neck. It was mystifying. Billions of stars burned through the darkness, waltzing in space, yet with the right tools and knowledge, it was possible to navigate the world with only two.

She turned away and quickened her pace, crushing dry needles beneath her feet. A final, haunting echo of laughter burst from the Club, following her, then died out.

Coming from the other direction, Charles drove the lawn tractor toward Plateau, the small engine straining up the hill with its heavy load. He was so happy with his sculpture. He'd done everything he'd set out to do, even if some patches were a little rough. You have to break some eggs to make an omelet, after all. He envisioned his next project, and the one after that—and with each attempt he believed he would come closer to closing the gap between the image in his head and its physical manifestation. He had limitations—he was born with a silver spoon in his mouth, not a blowtorch in his hand, after all—but even within his wall of skin, he might be able to sometimes soar. This sculpture, coarse as it was, still managed to encompass a great deal of emotion—excitement and heartache, weariness and joy. Who'd have thought it was possible for an object to do all that, when most of the people he knew didn't have that range?

He spotted his dear Madeline at the meeting place, prompt as always, with the distant security light of the pool house casting her in silhouette. Her arms were folded; she was obviously troubled. He giggled to himself—she would be so surprised! She must think him crazy to want to meet out here. He shouted over the sound of the panting four-horse power of the engine. "Madeline, look what I made for you! For us!"

Madeline squinted in the dark. She recognized the voice and the lawn tractor, but what was that . . . thing? She bent, and she ducked, trying to see what it was her husband dragged behind him, not believing her eyes. She reached a hand out, grasping for support, trying to steady herself on air.

Charles had built a giant goose. A big messy thing assembled from old golf clubs and garbage. Forks for feathers. Spoon plumage. Golf balls for . . . balls. The bird tilted forward, stretching its neck toward some unseen finish line. The neck was its most prominent feature, eight feet in length, a double helix of clubs, twisting and narrowing to the head, which—seared on the bottom of an enamel gratin pan—had a human face. A face not unlike Charles's, but with an unearthly serenity.

This is what he'd spent the summer building? This is what he'd given up his family, his job, and his old life for? Their marriage?

Charles killed the engine and jumped off the tractor as excited as a little boy. "Isn't it great? Can you believe it?" He began to unhook the chain, releasing his creation to the world. He kicked two brakes into place and pointed to the wheels behind its webbed feet. "Stability and flexibility. I wanted the Club to be able to move it from one trouble spot to another."

Madeline was dumb with astonishment. The Club would most certainly want to move it around; they'd want to move it right out the front gates. She watched with deep concern as Charles placed the coiled chain on the lawn mower seat and grabbed the searchlight hanging on the back. He lit up the bird from beak to tail, as if better lighting was going to change the way she saw it. The beam glinted off the cutlery, some of it marked with the Club's insignia. Madeline recognized the golf clubs as Charles's own, his precious Callaways, all twisted and warped.

"I made it for you," he said. "But if you don't mind, I'd like it installed here, in memory of the goose I killed."

She tread around the goose-man with great care. "I like the way the forks hang down and create the illusion of feathers," she said, not daring to ask the question that was really on her lips: What were you thinking? Whatever that was, though, it certainly made him happy. His face was radiant in the reflection of the light in his hand. But he was a little seedy, and unbrushed. He'd lost weight too, but he was more muscular and rugged, in a goofy sort of way. He was even untucked. No, it was worse than that. He was half-tucked.

But those eyes, how bright they were. He was animated, truly alive. How long had he been dead before this? And how had she not noticed? If they were as alienated from each other as all that, divorce was going to be a blessing for the both of them. "Very nice," she said.

"Nature doesn't fool around with being nice," said Charles, turning toward her, flashing the beam in her face. "It all serves a purpose."

The light blinded her and made her wonder if perhaps Charles was plotting to kill her after all. And when she was dead, everyone would ask each other how it was she hadn't seen it coming.

Charles clicked the light off. "Sorry."

"If it all serves a purpose," she said, in a somewhat angry tone, which surprised her, "then what is the story with the human mask?"

He put the light down on the grass and stepped up on the back of the lawn tractor to reach the sculpture's face, lovingly cupping the "chin" of the gratin pan with both hands. "It's not a mask," he said. "It's an integral part of the whole organism—beast and god—human and animal. The ancients understood. Their gods were a tangle of limbs from all of creation. The people bowed down to statues and totems with wolf heads and human torsos, elephant trunks and human feet. In our own churches, angels have wings. Priests have to call on the power of other animals because we are just too pathetic on our own."

Madeline tried to wipe the look of utter dismay from her face. "Have you checked with House and Grounds to make sure they want this memorial of yours?"

Charles jumped to the grass and ran his hands down the length of the bird. "It's not just a memorial—it'll help keep the geese off the fairways too, like a scarecrow. More important, it'll be a reminder to the members that art can clarify, that it can be a part of daily living. You tried to tell me all this years ago, and I crushed it. Can you ever forgive me?" He paused and turned to Madeline, waiting.

She nodded vaguely, her mind very far away. It was true. She once thought seriously about all these things, art and life, death and politics, and she once talked about them too. But then one night, after a party, he accused her of sounding just like her mother, and that was the end of that.

"You see how the neck sticks out?" Charles continued. "It's in attack mode. The fairway geese would know the posture and stay away. But the face, see how it's not angry? Just understanding. This is part of life too—accepting the good with the bad, accepting that geese sometimes do the wrong thing—like getting in the way of a ball."

"Humans sometimes do the wrong thing too," Madeline said.

"We're in luck." He began to untie the bits of rope that secured the wings. The hot wind blew a few leaves and trash around his feet, paper cups, a Mars Bar wrapper, all the turbulence that marks the change of season. "It's a good wind. The moment of truth."

The truth. Madeline cringed. Charles apparently knew nothing about her almost-affair. He had not met her to ask for a divorce, but he would before the night was over. It was better this way, for him to hear it from her own lips.

"Charles, we should go back to the house. It's getting late, and we have to talk."

He turned to her, clasping the rope in front of him. "Do you know what I've called it?"

She put her hand to her throat and shook her head.

" 'Winged Defeat.' Get it? It's about how you have to come to an emptiness before you can fly—you can't rise until you understand what falling is all about."

Madeline looked again at the monstrosity. He seemed to be asking an awful lot of his art. "I see," she said, in the same way she used to keep up her end of their conversation when he talked about his job or his game.

But no. The pedestrian lies that maintained a marriage were no longer necessary, because there was no more marriage to maintain. "Actually, Charles, I don't see. I'd like to understand, though; I'd like to know what you were doing and thinking in the last months of our marriage. I think it will help me, later, to figure out what went so wrong."

Charles's mind went blank for a moment—then he felt like the scaffolding was knocked out from under him. The last months of their marriage? She did not mean the previous months, she meant the last. The final. He was too late.

He dropped the rope as he walked to her, to Madeline, his wife, and put his hands on her shoulders—how long had it been since he touched her there? Since he had touched her anywhere? She resisted when he tried to pull her to him.

"You don't understand," he said. "I was in such a strange funk—making this seemed the only way out, the way out of me to you. And here I am. Tell me you're here too." He touched her face. "You, sensitive Madeline, with feelings no thicker than an eggshell."

"Not as sensitive as all that," she said, turning her cheek. She wished now that someone had told him what Ellen saw, to spare herself this reckoning. "I've done something horrible, and now I have to leave."

"Yes! It's time to go, for both of us."

She looked at him so suddenly she got a kink in her neck. "Where are you going?"

"*We're* going." He covered her hand with his and massaged her neck muscles. "The West Coast somewhere. A new habitat, a fresh environment."

"Back where I came from?"

"Yes! Where we met, where we began. Where we can begin again." He pulled her to him, but she kept him at arm's length. She did not want to make her confession into his collarbone. She wanted to look into his eyes and tell him the truth. If only she knew where to start. With the Smurf Pee?

Before she could begin, the breeze whipped up from the lake, and they both stared at the sculpture, which seemed to be straining in place. The night air began to move through its many metal twists and tubes, making a sharp whistling sound. Forks started to vibrate, adding to the noise. Joints loosened up, and the wings raised a few inches with a creak, then fell against its sides with a crash. A dozen crows in a nearby oak were rudely awakened, and they flew off in a flapping, muttering huff, heading toward the relative peace of the Lamberts' yard.

Charles reached for Madeline's hand, and she let him take it. "Not as graceful as I'd have liked," he said. "I should have gone into aerodynamics, way back when. But it's a start."

Madeline looked down at the ground and spoke to her black sneakers. "You might have told me what was going on. If you'd talked to me, we could have prevented a great deal of pain." She felt stinging accusations form on her lips. It would be easy to be angry with him for keeping her in the dark, letting her flail around. But she hadn't the energy for all that. In fact, she was happy for him and wished him well. It was too late for her to go along, though. She'd already gone too far.

"Listen," said Charles, and he tugged at her shirt. "Listen to the music."

The cutlery continued to clink, and the wind whistled through the double-helix neck like a flute, then an oboe. The wings performed their awkward lift and crash again as the wind moaned through the metal. *Oommm.*

Charles and Madeline heard the geese rustling at the lake, waking up. As the whistling and clanking increased, the flock became more uncomfortable. A few started to run on land and water, suddenly and furiously alive, churning powerfully along to make speed. Charles picked up his searchlight and flicked it on in time to see them lift their feather-laden wings in unison, trying to get airborne, until finally one of them lifted its fat carcass off the earth. As if they'd been waiting for an example to be set, the others began to follow, in twos, threes, fives, flying off into the dark heavens.

Madeline shook her head. "How do they reach the sky with those heavy bodies?"

Charles clicked off the light. They watched the gray figures against the black night and heard the mighty chorus of wings beating and voices honking in time, communication that helped them stay together in flight. "Nature," he said. "Instinct. An act of will."

"But where will they go?"

"I don't know," he said, and looked at her. "We've got to trust they'll be all right."

She looked at him. It was impossible for him to have changed so dramatically. More likely, he'd just changed obsessions, from golf to art, from the office to welding. But maybe that was enough.

In a few minutes, only a couple dozen geese remained, completely unperturbed by his metallic goose-man. Were they braver than the others? Or just plain stupid?

"Charles," Madeline said. Unable to complete an adulterous affair, she could at least see the divorce through. He'd hear about what she'd done with Scott sooner or later, and even if he never knew, even if they never saw each other again, she could never live with her conscience unless she came clean. It was better to suffer with the truth than prosper with a lie. He tried to kiss her, but she put her finger to his mouth. "I behaved poorly," she said. "And I got caught. Everyone at the Club knows. . . ." She was not quite brave enough to say what it was she'd actually done. "I was drunk. I went skinny-dipping in the pool. . . ."

He grasped her with both arms. "Remember the night of our engagement party?"

"There's more." She pushed him away. "The lifeguard was there, and things got out of hand."

Charles looked at her carefully. "How out of hand?"

She looked over at Oxbow. "Some touching, that's all. It was ridiculous, and I'm mortified. To make it worse, Ellen Bruner walked in on us." She took a deep breath and looked at him. "I'm sorry. I'm all packed. I'm just waiting for Phoebe to bring back my car."

He kissed her forehead, rubbing his nose through her hair. "That could be a long wait. She left us a note. Besides, I don't care what you did, and I certainly don't care who saw you. From now on, we start every day knowing nothing. Everything we did in the past stays there."

He pulled her toward him, and this time she did not resist.

"I'm the one who should be sorry," he said. "I was idiot enough to leave you alone all summer while I tried to sort it all out." He let his hand run down her spine. "You know what Steeve always said, 'You don't have to follow one bad shot with another.'" He planted a wet kiss on her lips, opening her mouth with his tongue.

Steeve? she wanted to ask, but at that moment, from deep within her, an ancient, dozing creature stirred and looked around, lifting its nose to the air. It tickled the insides of her ribs and gently poked at her interior organs. It touched a hot spot and she jumped.

She pushed Charles away to take a breath. "Do you mean it? You won't get mad later when you hear ugly rumors at the Club?"

"You know what I say? Fuck 'em. We're out of here in a cloud of donkey dust anyway."

He got on his knees and pulled her down on the grass with him, and as he began to unbutton her clothes, she felt her worries fall from her like a molting of feathers. Charles was right. Fuck 'em. She pulled his T-shirt over his head, releasing the familiar scent of his body and sending her trembling. As he grappled with her black pants, she grappled with the memory of the night before, how she had tried to summon desire, throwing herself into the arms of someone who was not prepared to catch her. You couldn't will lust, any more than you could will yourself to fly. It was a gift from nature, whose only interest was in getting the job done.

All the while, the goose-man continued its metallic clamoring and crashing, and it occurred to her that the members would soon wonder about the noise.

"Wait," she said, pulling up her pants. "We'd better go home. Gerard will probably come running down here soon to see what's going on." She touched his nose with the tip of her finger and felt herself blush. "And I have to get my diaphragm."

Charles rolled onto his stomach and looked up the hill, the light from the tent glowing dimly above the majestic oaks. "Gerard isn't here," he said. "The inmates are in charge of the asylum tonight. A few members might get curious, but they won't wander off the golf path to find out." He returned to his back and pulled her on top of him.

Madeline sat up and looked at him. "How do you know Gerard's not here? Where is Phoebe?"

"I'll tell you later." He reached both hands around her. He buried his face in her neck, and she smelled like a wood fire, as if she'd been propitiating a heathen god. How very strange and enormously erotic.

As he pressed his lips on hers, Charles felt like a mighty hunter, returning to his small circle of hide tents, his clan huddled around the protective fire in the center. They rush to the edge of light to welcome him home. He had gone far, for a very long time, his only sustenance the waterskin hanging from his shoulder, but today he drags the arrow-pierced body of a deer behind him, and his people are relieved. They will survive a little longer because he ventured out into the darkness, and back again. Children tug on his ragged vestments for his attention, and old men nod their hoary heads in approval. The women open the flaps of their tents to him.

Such happiness. As Charles arched his back to let Madeline unzip his jeans, he thought back to what Steeve had said about becoming the ball. That was true as far as it went, but it was not nearly enough. It was only the beginning. Be the ball, by all means, but be the club, the tee, and the lowly divot too. Be the deeply rooted oak, the water rushing over stones. Be the lush grass pressing up from the wet earth. Be the goose on the wing, soaring over this tremulous existence. Be the warm, furry vole underfoot. Be aware. And be it all.

Chapter Forty-two

Keeping Score

IN THE DIM LIGHT of dawn, Rosangela Silva vacuumed up the ashes from the marble hearth, then ran a polishing cloth over the andirons. Who keeps making these fires in summer? Were these people so cold? She dragged the vacuum to the door and went to grab her bucket, when she saw a quilted bag on the windowsill. She stuck her head out in the hall and listened. The rest of the crew was still in the lounge. Okay, then, one little look. She held it open and shook it, but there was nothing much to see. All their money and they never seemed to have any. Some lotion for the fair skin, mints for the breath, a wilted flower. Lipstick with no color. She picked up the brush and pulled out hairs and held them to the light. Dark blond. She tucked a few strands in her pocket to show her friend Marianna in beauty school. She would get her to dye her hair that color and be that much closer to rich.

She put the brush back in the bag and slung it over her shoulder. Another thing to lug around, over to Lost & Found in the office, and if that manager was in early he would give her a dirty look like she took something. And she would smile while he muttered English words she did not know, but he would never find anything missing on her watch. You had to be very careful with no green card. Hector had not been careful. She told him not to tell police about them getting hit by the expensive car. Now he was being deported to Brazil. Not her. She would keep her head down if she wanted to rise up.

She was closing the drapes when she paused to watch rays of light fall on the course, just like in church. *Um dia.* One day she would not wake up in the dark to scrub toilets and empty trash, even on Sundays. She would learn the language, organize her own cleaning crew, get her own jobs, make her own money—then she would have a view like this out her own window. And she would have a car as big as a truck, a TV as big as a wall, a house as big as a mountain. A bathroom with gold faucets. Food to waste. Buckets of money. One day she would even belong to a club like this, and if not this club, then another. If not her, then her children. But it would happen, because this was America, where anything was possible.

"Rosangela, vem!" called her boss. *"Nós atrasado."*

"Eu com," she shouted.

Yes, they were running late, but she didn't come right away. She stood another moment to watch the redhead man do the flag. It was so strange to keep a goose instead of a parrot. When she got home tonight, she would look up the words to ask him his pet's name, practice her English on him. He clipped the flag on wires, then pulled as his goose pecked at the rope like it was some snake. The flag slapped and fought its way up to the top where the golden eagle sat; then the cloth shot out and rippled in red bars and white stars against the blue, blue sky. *Um dia.* She adjusted the pretty bag on her shoulder, picked up her bucket of supplies, and went off to the next job.

(Page 136)

The Newly Revised Eden Rock Country Club Book, continued

. . . .

Marriage, Nina Rundlett and Eliot Farnsworth, of Concord, Massachusetts, 12/31/03

. . . .

Marriage, Phoebe Lambert[1] and Gerard Wilton, of Sedona, Arizona, 2/14/04

. . . .

Baby boy, born to Madeline Lambert, of Humboldt, California, 5/31/04

Husband: Charles Lambert

Biological Father: Charles Lambert (?) There was a rumor concerning the Club lifeguard, but I, Arietta Wingate, have had a talk with the young man (M. refused to cooperate), Scott Volpe, of Quincy, Massachusetts, and he insists nothing happened, but best to make note of the possibility.

And so completes the book to this date, as dictated to Ellen Bruner by Arietta Wingate, replacing, by her memory and with new information, the *Original Book,* lost in an unfortunate accident, Labor Day weekend, 2003.

Signed—Arietta Wingate
Witnessed & Notarized by Ellen Bruner, Esq.
Dated—7/4/04

[1] Even though the Lambert family no longer belongs to the Club, it seems prudent to continue following matters, where possible, for the inevitable day when future generations return to the fold.

Acknowledgments

Addled owes much to the Raymond Street Writers Group, whose wise council and encouragement helped me to keep the faith through the book's many crossroads and roadblocks. Thank you to Marcie Hershman, who believed in it from the start and kicked it out of the nest at the PEN New England Discovery Awards, where it was caught by Wendy Strothman. Thank you to Reagan Arthur, who made room for it on the Little, Brown perch. Thank you to Maxine Rodburg, who started me writing; for Bennington Writing Seminars, which kept me writing; and to my family, who cheered me on—as long as it didn't interfere with dinner.

ABOUT THE AUTHOR

JoeAnn Hart has an MFA from Bennington College, where she studied under Lucy Grealy. A regular contributor to the *Boston Globe Sunday Magazine,* she lives with her family in Massachusetts. This is her first novel.